Disinherit

THE

IRS

REVISED EDITION

Disinherit

THE

IRS

REVISED EDITION

E. Michael Kilbourn

CHARTERED FINANCIAL CONSULTANT

CAREER
PRESS

Franklin Lakes, NJ

DISINHERIT THE IRS, REVISED EDITION
EDITED AND TYPESET BY JOHN J. O'SULLIVAN
Cover design by Design Concept
Printed in the U.S.A. by Book-mart Press

To order this title, please call toll-free 1-800-CAREER-1 (NJ and Canada: 201-848-0310) to order using VISA or MasterCard, or for further information on books from Career Press.

The Career Press, Inc., 3 Tice Road, PO Box 687,
Franklin Lakes, NJ 07417
www.careerpress.com

Library of Congress Cataloging-in-Publication Data

Kilbourn, E. Michael.
    Disinherit the IRS, revised edition : stop Uncle Sam from claiming half of your estate …or more / by E. Michael Kilbourne.
        p. cm.
    Includes index.
    ISBN 1-56414-621-9 (paper)
    1. Estate planning—United States—Popular works. 2. Inheritance and transfer tax—Law and legislation—United States—Popular works. I. Title.

KF750.Z9 K498 2003
343.7305'32—dc21   2002073368

To my best friend and wife, Mauri, who has worked by my side for most of our 30 years of marriage. To my father, Austin Peter Kilbourn, a generous and giving person who left this world much too early, and to my sister and friend, Helene, who became the mother I never really had and the one who, in spite of my faults, always believed in me.

Acknowledgments

No one achieves success in life without guidance and help. I am no exception. Craig Hall, president of Hall Financial Group, Dallas, is one of the top private syndicators in the country. Craig's numerous business accomplishments in the area of investment real estate, along with his high standards, were always great examples for me to follow. Craig's faith in me helped me earn honors as a registered representative for the Hall Financial Group and Hall Securities Corporation. Craig's confidence in me led to my being appointed to the board of one of his savings and loan companies, Resource Savings & Loan, where I learned a great deal about the banking industry. Craig has been a true inspiration and a true friend.

Joe Allen, CLU, ChFC, of Kansas City, has been a financial planner and an insurance professional for more than 50 years. His reputation as a top professional in his field is well established. Joe was instrumental in getting me to focus my energies in the financial planning industry with an estate planning specialty. The six months I spent with Joe in 1991 were very rewarding and helped me develop my business plan and career goals to the fullest. I cannot thank Joe enough for his guidance and foresight!

I particularly wish to thank Guy Baker for his kind permission to reproduce his article "The Box," Ken Ziskin for letting me excerpt his article on grantor trusts, and Tom Rogerson for allowing me to use some of the concepts he covers in our joint presentations at our Wealth Protection Network seminars. Special thanks go to Natalie Choate, author of the best-selling book on retirement benefits, *Life and Death Planning for Retirement Benefits* (*www.ataxplan.com*), for allowing me to excerpt material from her many articles on retirement planning and for reviewing my chapters on the subject. I am also indebted to Frank Rainaldi (*www.kuglersystem.com*), CLU, ChFC, and attorney Jonathan Mintz, associate editor for *The Journal,* for reviewing my chapters on retirement plan taxation and distributions.

I also must thank my colleagues and close collaborators. Without them this book would not be possible. My thanks to Mark Merenda, my friend and marketing consultant, for his help in writing, editing, and otherwise making sense of the technical jargon; Renno Peterson and Robert Esperti, for their inspiration and guidance and for allowing me to excerpt material from their 26 books written on the subject of estate planning; Rob O'Dell, my friend and a founding member of the Wealth Protection Network, for his ideas and counsel, especially on charitable estate planning strategies, and for his continued encouragement; attorney Richard Gumm, for his technical edit and his suggestions for improving my descriptions of certain highly technical concepts; and Chet and Sue Gottfried, for their expert editing of my manuscript, including the graphs and charts—without Chet and Sue's assistance, this book could not have been completed.

Jim Sennett of Richmond, Virginia, assisted me with my research on indexed insurance and gives me his continuing support and counsel in the design and implementation of sophisticated insurance plans. Joan Gardner, my very capable assistant, spent many hours organizing and typing my research notes and manuscript. She also deserves credit for keeping me organized and focused on my goals and helping ensure that I have the time to pursue them.

As I noted before, no one reaches lofty goals without a great deal of help. My beautiful, loving wife, Mauri, has worked by my side for most of our 30 years of married life. I'd like to take this opportunity to thank her for her patience and understanding while I've worked on this book and for her counsel and guidance as my business partner and best friend.

To all of these fine professionals, my deepest thanks. And to you, the reader, my sincerest wish for a sound and secure financial future for you and your family. I hope *Disinherit the IRS* helps you in making the important decisions that will allow you to give what you have to whom you want, when you want, and in the way you want and at the same time pay the least amount of court costs, attorney fees, and estate taxes possible.

If you have any questions, you can contact me at Kilbourn Associates, 3033 Riviera Drive, Suite 202, Naples FL 34103. You're welcome to contact me any of the following ways:

- Telephone (800)761-2300 or (239)261-1888.
- Fax (239)643-7017.
- e-mail *mike@kilbournassociates.com*, or visit my Web site *www.kilbournassociates.com*.

—E. Michael Kilbourn
May 2002

Contents

Foreword

by Robert A. Esperti and Renno L. Peterson

E. Michael Kilbourn is an uncommon man and professional: He has earned four master's degrees and been awarded the Bronze Star. He has received 13 professional designations and holds positions of authority in 14 professional organizations. A voracious student of the planning professions, Mike is a master estate and wealth strategies planner.

We are tax attorneys who have been practicing collectively nearly 60 years. In that time, we have had the opportunity to lead workshops for thousands of attorneys, CPAs, registered representatives, and life insurance agents. Experience has taught us that finding uncommonly gifted financial planning and life insurance specialists, as with all other professionals, is a rare experience. Mike is such a professional.

Our first meeting with Mike involved a workshop sponsored by a major life insurance company. We were asked to lecture to advanced agents and the attorneys who had been invited by those agents. The workshop was aimed at practicing state-of-the-art estate planning and building professional teams that had client needs as their primary objective. Mike was in attendance.

Mike took an interest in what we were doing, particularly in light of our book *Loving Trust*. In it, Mike recognized a similarity in our mutual planning approaches and philosophies. He saw that we were kindred souls in our commitment to serve clients for their best interests, always keeping promises made and finishing what was started to the very best of our ability.

After our first experience with Mike, several years passed as he built his practice and we built the National Network of Estate Planning Attorneys and the Esperti Peterson Institute. Mike's life objectives led him to Naples, Florida, where he set up a successful life insurance practice.

In addition to developing our companies, we continued to practice estate planning law on a limited basis, having offices in Sarasota, Florida, and Jackson Hole, Wyoming. Unknown to Mike or us, our practices were taking on similar characteristics. Mike's clientele expanded, and the wealth of his clients increased. Our practice experience mirrored his: After many years of practicing, teaching, and writing a number of books, we decided to limit our practice to high-net-worth clients.

Mike kept track of us and eventually decided that he needed legal and planning expertise commensurate with his clients' needs for significantly greater technical advice. He called upon us, and we reacquainted ourselves with each other. It was then that we learned what a consummate professional Mike Kilbourn really is.

Professionalism encompasses many characteristics. We have found that the word "professional" is often applied to people as a courtesy but is rarely earned. Mike's professionalism is definitely earned, as can be seen by his many accomplishments.

Mike is one of the most highly educated professionals that we have ever met. He holds a bachelor of science degree in mechanical engineering, a master of business administration in management and finance (cum laude), a master of arts in human communications, interpersonal (cum laude), a master of arts in teaching in the community college (cum laude), and a master of science in financial services (MSFS).

These degrees would be enough for almost anyone, but not for Mike, who is committed to being the very best he can be. Over the years, Mike has earned numerous professional designations, each of which requires a high degree of knowledge and expertise. All are impressive, particularly the Certificate of Estate Planning and Taxation from the American College, Chartered Life Underwriter (CLU), Accredited Estate Planner (AEP), Chartered Financial Consultant (ChFC), Certified Commercial Investment Member (the highest designation for commercial real estate given by the National Association of Realtors), Master Real Estate Consultant from the National Association of Real Estate Consultants, and Fellow of the Esperti Peterson Institute.

Of course, being named a Fellow of the Esperti Peterson Institute is the designation most near and dear to our hearts. The Esperti Peterson Institute is the only estate and wealth strategies think tank in the world that is devoted to high-net-worth clients and their families. The standards for being a fellow are very high. Acceptance into the institute is limited to very few and, once admitted, each candidate must complete a rigorous three-year course in sophisticated estate and wealth strategies. When a candidate is designated a fellow of the institute, he or she is without doubt one of the nation's top planners, having demonstrated a wealth of knowledge and expertise in the many planning disciplines.

One of the best results of teaching this course is that we are able to get to know the fellows extremely well. We see them in the classroom interacting with their colleagues. We socialize with them. The three years we spend together allows us to find out about one another's strengths, weaknesses—and even idiosyncrasies.

In our time with Mike, we found him to be extremely caring about serving clients and their needs. His understanding of advanced planning techniques was demonstrated time and again in the dynamics of his collaborative program. His colleagues found him to be highly professional and easy to work with, and he has developed strong relationships with institute fellows nationwide.

It has become apparent to us that Mike has several unique abilities. He is able to connect with people in meaningful ways, instilling confidence in them and helping them achieve their goals. Mike is a very effective communicator; he takes complex material and translates it into creative solutions for difficult planning problems.

Mike also excels as a teacher. We encourage all of our fellows to teach in the institute, in the National Network of Estate Planning Attorneys, in professional associations, and within their communities. Mike taught before his involvement in the institute and continues to serve as a teacher for his clients and as a mentor for his colleagues.

This book is a direct result of Mike's communication ability. For years, Mike has collected articles and data that were relevant to his clients. For each client, he has compiled information pertinent to the client's goals and objectives. *Disinherit the IRS* is the distillation of the stories, experiences, articles, and anecdotes he has shared with his clients, seminar audiences, and professional colleagues.

We are proud of our association with Mike Kilbourn, who is truly a professional's professional. We know you will enjoy this book, and if you get a chance to meet him, we know you will share our high opinion of his character, expertise, and commitment to excellence.

Introduction

The title of this book, *Disinherit the IRS*, is supposed to get your attention. However, you might not even be aware that the IRS is one of the principal beneficiaries of your estate. And perhaps you do not even know that you *need* to disinherit the IRS.

I don't know about you, but I didn't work hard all my life in order to leave the greater part of my wealth to the Internal Revenue Service. It took you a lifetime to accumulate your wealth, yet the government will spend it—all of it—in a matter of seconds. And what it will spend your wealth on might, or might not, meet with your approval. You can be sure the government won't be concerned with your wishes or the wishes of your "other" heirs.

The fact is you are worth only half of what you think you are worth!

That statement may shock you, but it shouldn't. Today, estate taxes range from zero on the transfer of estates worth less than $1 million to 50 percent on estates valued at $2.5 million or more. Few people are aware of the extent of this tax or its consequences. Fewer still have planned for it. The results can range from inconvenient to catastrophic.

Studies estimate that more than $10 trillion will pass from one generation to the next over the next 10 to 20 years. In fact, more wealth will change hands in the next eight years than in the previous 238 years.

In spite of these numbers, many people fail to take steps to plan their estates properly. According to estimates, more than 70 percent of the people who died last year in the United States did so without a will, and more than 60 percent of those were college-educated Americans.

One reason for this lack of planning may be that most people think of estate planning as "death planning," so they procrastinate. Some people even believe everything can be taken care of after they are gone. As one client put it, "It's easier to shoe a dead horse than a live one." That may be true for horses, but not for estate planning. The truth is that estate planning is not an option. Federal and state laws require an accounting of every deceased person's estate and payment of the resulting taxes. If people do not plan their own estates, the government will do it for them, and it will usually not be done in the way they would want.

From reading *Disinherit the IRS*, you will realize that estate planning can and should be *living planning* and that many things can be done during your life that will provide living benefits for yourself and your loved ones while paving the way for a smooth transition at death. In addition, you will learn that, with proper planning, you can minimize or eliminate estate taxes and thus leave more for your heirs and/or the social causes that are important to you.

I explore those issues and more in this book, which is intended for attorneys and financial planning professionals as well as the general public.

Disinherit the IRS is not intended as a definitive encyclopedia on the subject of estate planning. The subject is large, and I'm not sure anyone but estate planning specialists would have any use for, or want to read, such a work. And because economic conditions and the tax codes are constantly changing, new issues crop up regularly. Any attempt at a "definitive" work would soon be out of date.

Rather, this book is a sampling of some issues that are perhaps less well known and more useful than the usual clichés. Because many of these issues have no connection other than coming under the general heading of estate planning, the chapters are not arranged in continuous sequence. You should pick and choose the issues and chapters that interest you and skip others, if you are so inclined. Also, beginning with Chapter 2, each chapter opens with a real-life story (with the names of the participants changed) to give an overview of the discussion that follows. In keeping with the friendly nature of this book, I have also provided more than 30 diagrams to illustrate the dynamics of any particular line of planning. The following list summarizes the main topics of each chapter:

- *Chapter 1:* Estate planning is not optional; many people have misconceptions about who should plan and the "right" steps to take to put an effective plan in place.
- *Chapter 2:* Estate taxes take from 41 to 50 percent of estates (after applying the applicable exemption) and can deplete an estate in only two or three generations. There are four basic ways to cover estate tax costs.

- *Chapter 3:* Trusts are essential tools for developing effective estate plans. There are four important reasons why virtually every estate plan should include a revocable "living" trust as its base.
- *Chapter 4:* With a dynasty trust, you can leave your wealth to more than one generation without the imposition of tax at each generation. At the same time, a properly drafted dynasty trust will protect your heirs from claims of creditors, predators, and divorcing spouses.
- *Chapter 5:* Life insurance can be easily understood when the components are separated and the premium payments are treated as though they are paid into a box. The size of the premiums and the growth of policy cash values in the box will determine how much is needed to fill up the box to provide the contracted benefits. Much depends on the assumptions used in connection with the three basic components of all permanent life insurance policies.
- *Chapter 6:* It is important to understand the differences between the five basic types of insurance—whole life, universal life, variable life, indexed life, and term life. No one type of policy is best: The best policy is the one that fits your personal situation.
- *Chapter 7:* Because of the many benefits, an irrevocable life insurance trust is ideal as the "owner" of a life insurance policy. The benefits include protection of the assets in the trust from the claims of creditors, the ability to leverage your generation-skipping transfer tax exemption, and avoidance of estate taxes on the policy proceeds.
- *Chapter 8:* When purchasing insurance for estate tax purposes, it is best to obtain offers of insurance from various companies and then, depending on the amount of coverage sought, divide the coverage between carriers. Dividing coverage can protect against economic changes that might hurt a single company and potentially affect policy values and death benefits.
- *Chapter 9:* There are some distinct advantages to using borrowed funds to purchase life insurance. For one, resources used to pay off borrowed funds at your death will reduce your taxable estate and the corresponding estate taxes.
- *Chapter 10:* Designing an optimal insurance plan to help offset estate taxes can often be very difficult given the possibility of gift taxes on premium payments above the amount of your available gift tax exemptions. A funding technique known as "split dollar" can help substantially reduce gift tax exposure and can provide many additional benefits.

- *Chapter 11:* Even though gift taxes and estate taxes are computed from the same tax table, the taxes are applied differently for gifts made during life and for amounts bequeathed at death. During life, the tax rate is applied on the amount of the gift, but at death, the tax rate is applied to both the gift and the tax. Thus, it is usually better to give than to bequeath!

- *Chapter 12:* By making a gift to a grantor retained annuity trust (a type of irrevocable trust), you can retain the income from the trust in the form of an annuity for a period of years. At the same time, you can effectively reduce or even eliminate gift taxes due on the remainder interest that will end up in the hands of your heirs.

- *Chapter 13:* An intentionally defective grantor irrevocable trust is a unique tool that allows you, as the grantor, to completely remove assets from your estate for estate tax purposes but not for income tax purposes. This enables you to pay any income taxes due on the trust income directly, without exposure to gift taxes, thereby benefiting the trust beneficiaries. This trust can also be used to avoid capital gain taxes on highly appreciated property sold to the trust and provide substantial benefits for both you and your heirs.

- *Chapter 14:* When estate planning goals call for making sizable gifts that could exceed gift tax exemption amounts and when it is important to maintain control of assets given to family members, a family limited partnership is potentially the best solution. Not only can a family limited partnership provide the opportunity to obtain "discounts" on the value of partnership units transferred (given or sold) to family members (or trusts, for their benefit), but it allows the general partner to retain control of the assets owned by the partnership. This is true no matter how small the general-partner interest retained by you and/or your spouse.

- *Chapter 15:* With a qualified personal residence trust, you can give a residence and/or a vacation home to your beneficiaries at a substantially reduced gift tax cost while retaining the use and control of the home for the lives of you and your spouse.

- *Chapter 16:* Social capital is that part of your estate that goes to social causes upon your death—usually through the tax system. Through proper planning, it is possible to direct your social capital to causes important to you while avoiding estate taxes and providing more for your family.

- *Chapter 17:* A charitable remainder trust is truly synergistic: It can provide more income to you, as the grantor, along with a tax deduction and tax savings, a greater inheritance for family members (through a wealth replacement trust), and a substantial charitable legacy.
- *Chapter 18:* A charitable lead trust can be used during life or at death to help reduce or even eliminate gift or estate taxes on amounts transferred to the trust. This is done by having the income from the trust paid to one or more charities or private foundations for a period of years, with the remainder interest going to your beneficiaries at the end of the trust term.
- *Chapter 19:* Your individual retirement account (IRA) is a "tax time bomb": A number of heavy taxes will be levied on amounts that remain in the IRA at your death. The estate tax laws, which cover qualified retirement plan assets and IRAs, make proper planning a must!
- *Chapter 20:* Planning for qualified retirement plans (QRPs) and IRAs, including their ultimate distribution during life and at death, is complex and requires knowledge of the rules governing IRAs. With this knowledge, you can avoid some of the pitfalls and give your heirs the opportunity to "stretch out" your IRA—an approach that could save a substantial amount of tax and increase the amount that passes to your heirs.
- *Chapter 21:* In our litigious society, lawsuits are a constant threat to wealthy families. Two remarkable tools, offshore trusts and the new Alaskan trust, can help provide a "paper fence" around assets, protecting them from exposure to collection in lawsuits.
- *Chapter 22:* It is one thing to know about the tools of estate planning and quite another to put them into use. Taking the time to get a "diagnosis" and a "prescription" from a team of knowledgeable planning professionals is the only way to achieve an optimal estate plan. The steps involved in the design and implementation of a proper estate plan are relatively simple and straightforward.

Concluding the book are five appendixes: Appendix A summarizes the most common IRA mistakes; Appendix B lists the formal distribution rules; Appendix C includes the minimum required distribution charts; Appendix D contains an analysis of the Economic Growth and Tax Reconciliation Act of 2001, including the federal transfer tax table and various related charts; and Appendix E is a worksheet for your family and finances.

Working on *Disinherit the IRS* has allowed me to expand my own knowledge base and to provide my clients with the most comprehensive information on estate planning available to date. It complements my previous involvement as a contributing author of *Ways and Means: Maximize the Value of Your Retirement Savings* (Esperti Peterson Institute, 1999), *21st Century Wealth* (Quantum Press, 2000), *Philanthropy: Giving for Everyone* (Quantum Press, 2002), as well as my work on my forthcoming book, *Loving Legacy.*

Although I'd much rather talk about estate planning than about myself, I realize you might like to know something of my background. For the last 25 years, I have been involved in the financial services and investment industries in various capacities, including sales, management, teaching, investment counseling, financial consulting, and so on.

In 1992, I moved my firm, Kilbourn Associates, from Michigan, where I had spent much of my life, to Naples, Florida, to specialize in estate planning. In 1995, I founded the Wealth Protection Network, Inc., a national cooperative alliance of attorneys, CPAs, financial planners, money managers, trust officers, charitable development officers, and insurance professionals who specialize in family wealth transfer planning. The Wealth Protection Network is designed to serve the best interests of our clients using the team approach with client-centered, value-based planning. Both Kilbourn Associates and the Wealth Protection Network continue to expand and serve an increasing number of clients in Florida and other states.

I am also affiliated with the Academy of Multidisciplinary Practice as an adjunct professor. The courses I teach (see *mdpacademy.com*) for the multidisciplinary designation program are fully accredited by the Estate and Wealth Strategies Institute at Michigan State University.

Estate planning is like every other field in this sense: It is not enough to know what to do; you also have to choose the right professional guidance. Unfortunately, there are individuals in the financial service field whose advice is determined by which course would bring them the greatest compensation. For me, *personal integrity* is paramount. Only after my clients' goals are firmly established will I make recommendations. In making my recommendations, I endorse only the course of action that I would apply to myself in the same situation.

True service means always doing what I say I'm going to do and always finishing what I start. That said, I am a specialist and I know my limitations. Thus, I believe firmly in working with other professionals in the team approach to financial planning.

Everyone has goals, and one of mine is to be the best in my business. This is the primary reason why I continually pursue more education and certifications. I want to be considered an expert in my field and earn a steady stream of referrals while continuing to meet the needs of my existing clients.

1 Creating an Estate Plan

T
There once was a little boy named Bobby who wanted a hundred dollars and decided to ask God for it. He wrote his request in a letter to God and put it in the mail. The postal service didn't know what to do with the letter but, eventually, decided to send it to the president with the theory that he is the closest person to God in the United States.

The letter made it to the president's desk. Amused, he directed his staff to send a check to Bobby for five dollars. The president felt this would satisfy the boy's desire, keep his faith, and make him a better person.

When he received the check, Bobby was grateful and decided to write a thank-you letter. He wrote, "Dear God, Thank you for responding to my request. I noted, however, that you sent the check to Washington first and, before forwarding the money to me, those bums took 95 percent! Sincerely, Bobby."

🏛 🏛 🏛

Funny joke, right? The problem is that when it comes to estate taxes, it is not far from the truth.

A Little Background

What are estate taxes? In fact, what is an estate? Many people think of an estate as a large mansion on many acres. However, in legal terms, an *estate* is everything that you own at the time of your death.

The idea that things can be owned and further, that property may be passed on to heirs after death, is relatively new in human history. Our earliest ancestors did not own land, as far as we know. Their personal possessions were often buried along with them.

The earliest evidence for the practice of handing down property is found among the ancient Egyptians. The Code of Hammurabi and the laws of Solon in Greece decreed that property would pass, on the death of the owner, to heirs.

This tradition continued under Roman law. And in the time of Caesar Augustus, we find the first estate tax. Augustus levied a 5-percent tax on all estates to help fund his army. (Unfortunately, modern estate taxes have not remained at this reasonable level.)

Roman law, which became codified under Emperor Justin of the Byzantine Empire (also known as the Justinian Code), allowed for formal wills, along with a contract that resembles modern-day trusts. This law spread as the Roman Empire expanded to other corners of the world, including modern-day Britain. Much of modern law find its roots in ancient Roman concepts, just as much modern language is derived from Latin and most of Western religion from the spread of Christianity under the Roman curia.

The idea of property and inheritance, and the roots of our American system, evolved in feudal Great Britain. By the mid-1660s, all property was allowed to pass to heirs by will (the Statute of Wills) and transfers of land were required to be in writing, signed by the owner and witnessed (the Statute of Frauds). *Primogeniture,* the system by which all land descended automatically to the eldest son was replaced by a system of wills, under which a property owner could designate his or her chosen heirs.

These rules were adopted by the British colonies in the New World. We now refer to them as our English common-law heritage.

The idea of the "right" of government to tax property upon the owner's death arises from this tradition. Under colonial law, wills and other official documents had to bear certain stamps in order to be considered valid. These stamps could only be purchased from the government and thus amounted to the first estate tax on our shores.

The new U.S. Government adopted federal estate taxes four times in order to fund wars: The first tax was enacted in 1797 to pay for the naval buildup during tensions with France, and it was repealed in 1802. The next one came in 1864 during the Civil War. This estate tax was deliberately high—15 percent—to help discourage a class of superrich people and to serve as a wealth distribution tool. However, it was eventually repealed in 1870. The pattern was repeated during the Spanish American War in 1898 (the tax was repealed in 1902) and in 1916 during World War I. In each case (except for the last) the tax was repealed as soon as the need for it was gone (see Table 1-1 on pages 26 through 29).

The modern federal estate tax system began in 1916 and was amended in 1917, 1918, 1924, and 1926. The 1924 amendment created the gift tax so that there would be a tax on all property that was transferred from one owner to another without a fair market price being charged.

So, what is the situation today? In brief, you now have a very special beneficiary: the IRS. Would you deliberately designate the IRS as the primary beneficiary of your estate? Of course not! If you are like most people who have worked hard all their lives, you want your family to benefit from your efforts—not the IRS. However, if you haven't developed a proper estate plan, you could lose more than half the value of your life's work to estate taxes. Before I discuss the actual process of preparing an estate plan, let's review some of the more common misconceptions about estate planning.

One misconception is that estate planning is optional. In reality, the only options you have are *when* and *how* you do it. Federal and state laws require an accounting of every deceased person's estate and payment of taxes due. So, you can do your own estate planning or let the government do it for you.

Another misconception is that estate planning is necessary *only* for the wealthy, those people who have large estates. In reality, the smaller your estate, the more you need estate planning to ensure that your family keeps as much of your estate as possible.

The final misconception is that estate planning is an expensive time-consuming process that you can put off indefinitely. The truth is, the better prepared you are before you meet with your attorney, the less time and expense will be required.

Although we all assume we're going to be here tomorrow, someday we won't be. Therefore, you shouldn't delay your estate planning. The biggest villain in estate planning is not the IRS—it is procrastination!

The 4 Steps

Estate planning doesn't have to be complicated; it's simply a matter of taking the right steps to make sure your property passes after your death to your heirs, intact, without jeopardizing your current financial independence and security. After all, you've spent a lifetime accumulating what you have today: a home, real estate, securities, savings, works of art, perhaps a business, and so on.

TABLE 1-1   Estate Tax History

Year	Taxes±	Legislation
1797–1802	↑/↓	Federal stamp tax imposed in 1797 on certain estates. Repealed in 1802.
1815	↔	Congress contemplates the first estate tax to finance the War of 1812.
1864	↑	An estate tax is enacted due to Civil War. Rates run from 0.75%–5%.
1870	↓	Estate tax is repealed due to reduced budget pressure.
1894	↑	An estate tax (designed as an income tax on inheritances) is enacted at a flat 2% rate.
1895	↓	Supreme Court repeals the 1894 estate tax.
1898	↑	Congress enacts what it calls a death tax based on shares passing to heirs. This time it is upheld by the Supreme Court.
1902	↓	Congress repeals death tax because of reduced budget pressure.
1916	↑	Budget pressure forces Congress to enact an estate tax imposed on the value of transferred property. Rates run from 1–10%.
1924	↓	The 1916 tax is in addition to estate and inheritance taxes already imposed by most states. Differences among state rates result in a federal credit (1924) and, ultimately, the development of "sponge taxes" linked to the federal credit which now exists in most states. The original credit was limited to 25% of the federal estate tax. Over the years this credit has increased (up to 80%) and decreased to the current limit of 16%.
1924	↑	Additionally, in 1924, the first federal gift tax is imposed.
1926	↓	Only 2 years later the gift tax is repealed.
1932	↑	Budget pressures and reduced tax yields due to the Depression cause Congress to reinstate a federal gift tax. Unlike the system we use today, this tax is handled as a separate system, distinct from the estate tax system.
1935	↑	Popular pressure for the redistribution of wealth, in part driven by Franklin Roosevelt, raises the maximum estate tax rate to 70%.

TABLE 1-1   Estate Tax History (*cont'd.*)

Year	Taxes±	Legislation
1948–1953	↑/↓	Miscellaneous legislation sees estate tax expand and contract. Rates increase as high as 77%; gift tax rates increase as high as 57.75%. The marital deduction is first introduced.
1954	↓	The Internal Revenue Code of 1954 adopts provisions that exempt most qualified retirement plans from estate taxation.
1960–1969	←→	Increasing interest in reforming wealth transfer taxes develops, in large part driven by efforts to close loopholes. In 1969, Treasury Department and American Law Institute studies call for a unified (gift and estate) transfer tax system, a generation-skipping tax and complete exemptions for transfers between spouses.
1976	↑/↓	The Tax Reform Act of 1976 contained a wide range of reforms, thought by some to fall short of those called for in the 1969 studies. Among the changes: <ul><li>Estate and gift tax rates were combined under a unified transfer tax schedule.</li><li>Top tax rates dropped to 70%.</li><li>The Unified Tax Credit (UTC) is adopted, initially sheltering $175,625 of property.</li><li>The first generation-skipping taxes were imposed with maximum rates linked to the regular transfer tax rates.</li><li>Step-up to date-of-death value was repealed and replaced with a complex set of rules calling for the decedent's income tax basis to "carry over" into the hands of the heirs; certain adjustments could be made under a "fresh-start" rule to December 31, 1976 values.</li></ul>
1978	↓	Carryover basis rules, imposed on individuals dying after the 1976 Tax Reform Act became effective, are postponed until after 1979.
1980	↓	Carryover basis is eliminated by the Crude Oil Windfall Profit Tax Act. It will not surface again until the Death Tax Repeal Act of 2000 calls for its reinstatement.
1981	↓	Additional estate tax reforms are enacted with the Economic Recovery Act of 1981. These include: <ul><li>UTC raised to shelter up to $600,000 of property after a phase-in period.</li><li>Unlimited marital deduction is adopted 11 years after it was proposed in 1969.</li><li>Annual exclusion raised for first time since 1940s to $10,000.</li></ul>

TABLE 1-1   Estate Tax History (cont'd.)

Year	Taxes±	Legislation
1982	↑	Qualified retirement plans lose most of their exemption from estate taxes. The Tax Equity and Fiscal Responsibility Act of 1982 (TEFRA) drops the exemption down to only the first $100,000 of value.
1984	↑	The Tax Reform Act of 1984 defers the scheduled drop in federal estate tax rates until 1987. Qualified retirement plans completely lose their exemption from estate taxes.
1986	↑	The Tax Reform Act of 1986 redesigns generation-skipping taxes. Imposes a flat 55% rate instead of the progressive rate in place for the previous 10 years.
1987	↑	The Omnibus Budget Reconciliation Act of 1987 (OBRA) and Revenue Act of 1987 make changes to earlier reforms. These include: ■ Schedule rate drops are frozen at 55% through 1992. ■ A surcharge on estates over $10,000,000 to eliminate the benefit of the UTC in large estates. Effect is to raise the top rate on estates up to $21,040,000 to 60%. ■ Rules against estate freezing techniques.
1988	↑	Qualified retirement plans, once exempt from estate taxes, face new taxes. The Technical and Miscellaneous Revenue Act of 1988 (TAMRA) provisions include an additional 15% excise tax on "excess" accumulations held in retirement plans at death.
1990	↑	Estate freeze provisions enacted in 1987 are repealed and replaced with gift tax valuation rules that were modified periodically throughout the 1990s.
1992	↑/↓	The Revenue Act of 1992 is vetoed. It would have extended the 55% top tax rate and 5% surcharge to 1998. Proposals surface to drop the UTC sheltered amount from $600,000 to $200,000.
1993	↑	The Revenue Reconciliation Act of 1993 makes the 55% rate permanent, ending an anticipated drop to 50%.
1995	↓	The Contract with America Tax Relief Act of 1995 is vetoed. It would have raised the UTC sheltered amount to $750,000, with indexing after 2001.

TABLE 1-1   Estate Tax History (*cont'd.*)

Year	Taxes±	Legislation
1997	↓	The Taxpayer Relief Act raises the UTC for the first time since 1981. The fully phased exemption equivalent increases from $600,000 to $1,000,000 (scheduled for 2006). Act also repeals the 15% excise tax imposed on estates with large retirement accumulations. Various items are targeted for indexing with inflation. These include the annual exclusion amounts and the generation-skipping transfer tax exemption.
1999	↑/↓	Federal budget proposal calls for gradual elimination of estate taxes through 2008. Because of technicalities in the balanced budget rules, estate taxes would be revived in October 2009, resulting in just a 10-month elimination.
2000	↑/↓	Both Houses of Congress pass the Death Tax Elimination Act, which is then vetoed. It would have phased out all transfer taxes and reinstated carryover basis rules similar to those repealed in 1980.
2001	↑/↓	The Economic Growth and Tax Relief Reconciliation Act of 2001 introduces new reforms and a temporary suspension of estate taxes. These include: ■ Top tax rate gradually reduced to 45% in 2009. ■ Elimination of the 10% surtax on estates of $10 million +. ■ Gradually increases the UTC exemption equivalent to $3.5 million in 2009. ■ Eliminates estate and generation skipping taxes in the year 2010 but not beyond. ■ The gift tax exemption is fixed at $1 million and is not eliminated in 2010. ■ The step-up in basis on assets transferred at death is replaced with a carryover basis for 2010 but includes an exemption of $1.3 million, plus $3 million for spouses, on the amount of capital gains transferred. ■ Various other provisions.
2011	?	On December 31, 2010, the law sunsets, and on January 1, 2011, it reverts back to the tax law in place in 2001.

Source: Reprinted with permission from "Phoenix Wealth Management Report," first quarter 2001.

If you want to pass on your accumulated assets to your family, you have two options. First, you could give them everything right now while you're still alive. However, in addition to paying a substantial gift tax, you might also sacrifice your financial independence and security. A second more practical alternative is to transfer your assets to your heirs *after* your death. To accomplish this, you must establish the goals of your estate plan, determine the size of your total estate, and designate in legal documents who is to receive the assets. You must also estimate and provide for estate settlement expenses and choose appropriate strategies for minimizing your estate taxes. In short, you need to prepare an estate plan.

Step 1

The first step is to write down a list of specific objectives for your estate plan. The general goal is to maximize what is retained by your heirs while maintaining your financial independence and security. You still have to decide which of your heirs get what and when they should receive it.

Step 2

Once you've decided on your objectives, the next step is to determine the exact value and composition of your estate. This isn't as hard as it sounds; It's simply a matter of adding up what you have and subtracting what you owe.

Step 3

For the third step, consult a qualified estate planner or Wealth Protection Network specialist to help you design your estate plan on the basis of your specific objectives and the makeup of your property. A qualified planner can show you options and help you choose the best alternatives to satisfy your objectives. With a proper design, you can leverage some of your assets in a way that will not only cover estate taxes at your death, but will also keep your assets free from taxation in your children's and grandchildren's estates.

Step 4

Once you and your estate planning professional have designed your estate plan, you'll need a document that conveys your wishes and implements the plan. That is, you'll need a will or a living trust (or both) which directs the distribution and transfer of your assets after your death. If you die without a will or living trust, you are "intestate" and the state will control the distribution of your property.

Note: Estate planning is an ongoing process—it is not something you do once and then forget. You will need to adapt and update your estate plan as you experience changes in your family life, business, or financial position. It is important to consult with an expert who specializes in family wealth transfer planning and who has, as part of his or her practice, a system that calls for annual reviews of your plan.

2 Understanding Estate Taxes

T
Tom Rogy, an investment banker, was only 42 when he came to my office to discuss estate planning. He wasn't concerned about his own estate but wanted to learn about what he and his sister, Barbara, could expect upon the death of their parents, whose estate was rather extensive. Tom was disturbed when he learned the size of the tax bite that would be due on his parents' estate at their death. Although it probably wouldn't affect his lifestyle, the thought of losing more than half his inheritance to the IRS upset Tom greatly. Because his parents' estate was made up of nonliquid assets, such as real estate, a business, and various partnerships, Tom was even more disturbed to find out the taxes would be due within nine months after the second death.

We went over the various options for paying estate taxes, and Tom was grateful to learn that there was an option that would effectively discount those taxes substantially. In addition, Tom learned that his parents could take steps, by using trusts and something known as an "ascertainable standard," that would protect his and his sister's future inheritance from the claims of creditors in a lawsuit, divorce, or from predators. Tom was especially happy to find out how, with proper planning, the inherited assets that remained at the time of his death would pass to his children without another layer of estate taxes!

The Estate Tax

The crucial issue in the estate planning process is implementing your plan while overcoming specific obstacles. The biggest obstacle in most cases will be the estate settlement costs. These normally include funeral expenses, attorney's fees, executor's fees, probate court costs, appraiser's fees, state death taxes, and federal estate tax. The biggest expense of all will usually be the federal estate tax, which may represent the largest tax you will *ever* have to face. After applying the applicable exemption, federal estate tax currently takes from 41 to 50 percent of your total estate. To add insult to injury, the taxes are due within *nine months* after death.

The high level of taxes that will be levied on your assets at your death has been somewhat modified by the Economic Growth and Tax Relief Reconciliation Act (EGTRRA) of 2001, which calls for a gradual reduction in the top rate and an increase in the applicable credit until 2010 when, for that year, estate taxes (but not gift taxes) are eliminated. (Additional details of the 2001 act are covered in Appendix D.) As you can easily see, federal estate taxes pose the greatest single threat to your estate and can quickly deplete the wealth you have spent a lifetime accumulating. No one will argue with the fact that this tax is confiscatory!

Before the enactment of the Tax Act of 2001, the tax table was known as the *unified gift and estate tax schedule* because it applied to gifts made during life as well as to the net estate at death (above the annual $11,000 exemption). As a result of the Tax Act of 2001, there is a limit of $1 million on the credit exemption equivalent for gifts made *during life*. Thus, while the tax rates apply universally, the credit exemption equivalents in Table 2-2 are not applied to lifetime gifts beyond $1 million.

On gifts made during one's life, the tax applies only to the gift amount. At death, the tax applies both to the gift *and* to the tax itself. For example, ignoring exemptions and exclusions, the tax on the gift of $1 million at 50 percent is $500,000, resulting in a true cost of $1.5 million. At death, the tax on $1.5 million is 50 percent of the total or $750,000, leaving $750,000 for your heirs. Thus, even though both taxes are computed from the same table, it is often better to make gifts during one's life than to wait to pass those gifts at death.

The estate tax code provides a break for small estates. This break is usually referred to as the *exclusion* or *exemption*, but a more accurate term is *applicable credit exemption equivalent* because it is really a credit, not an exemption. The distinction is important because of the way

TABLE 2-1 Estate Tax Schedule

Taxable estate		Tax before applicable credit			Year of death
Over	But not over	Pay	Plus	On excess over	
$ 0	$ 10,000	$ 0	18%	$ 0	
10,000	20,000	1,800	20%	10,000	
20,000	40,000	3,800	22%	20,000	
40,000	60,000	8,200	24%	40,000	
60,000	80,000	13,000	26%	60,000	
80,000	100,000	18,200	28%	80,000	
100,000	150,000	23,800	30%	100,000	
150,000	250,000	38,800	32%	150,000	
250,000	500,000	70,800	34%	250,000	
500,000	750,000	155,800	37%	500,000	
750,000	1,000,000	248,300	39%	750,000	
1,000,000	1,250,000	345,800	41%	1,000,000	
1,250,000	1,500,000	448,300	43%	1,250,000	
1,500,000	2,000,000	555,800	45%	1,500,000	
2,000,000	2,500,000	780,800	49%	2,000,000	
2,500,000	–	1,025,800	50%	2,500,000	
Maximum tax rates, 2003–2010					
2,000,000	–	780,800	49%	2,000,000	2003
2,000,000	–	780,800	48%	2,000,000	2004
2,000,000	–	780,800	47%	2,000,000	2005
2,000,000	–	780,800	46%	2,000,000	2006
1,500,000	–	555,800	45%	1,500,000	2007
1,500,000	–	555,800	45%	1,500,000	2008
1,500,000	–	555,800	45%	1,500,000	2009
0	–	0	0%	0	2010
Maximum tax rates, 2011–					
2,500,000	3,000,000	1,025,800	53%	2,500,000	
3,000,000	10,000,000	1,290,800	55%	3,000,000	
10,000,000	17,184,000	5,140,800	60%	10,000,000	
–	17,184,000	9,451,200	55%	17,184,000	

TABLE 2-2   Applicable Credit and Equivalent Exclusion Amounts

Year	Applicable credit	Equivalent exemption
2002–2003	$ 345,800	$1,000,000
2004–2005	555,800	1,500,000
2006–2008	780,800	2,000,000
2009	1,455,800	3,500,000
2010	N/A	N/A
2011 and later	345,800	1,000,000

Note: For gifts made during life, the applicable credit is limited to $345,800 ($1,000,000 exemption) and is not scheduled to increase.

taxes are calculated from the estate tax schedule. Table 2-2 shows the applicable credit as well as the equivalent applicable exclusion amount.

In calculating your taxes, it is important to compute the tax on the full value of your estate (which consists of all your assets, including joint property, qualified retirement plans, IRAs, annuities, and so forth). Then, subtract the applicable credit amount for the corresponding year to get the correct amount of tax (see Table 2-2). Most people start by subtracting the applicable exclusion amount ($1 million for 2002, for example) and then computing the taxes on the balance. This is wrong and will likely yield an inaccurate tax. Even though the credit of $345,800 equals the tax of $345,800 on $1 million, it would yield an incorrect tax on a larger estate to subtract the exemption equivalent of $1 million and compute the tax on the balance of the estate. If we subtract the $1 million credit exemption equivalent from a $2.5 million estate, and then calculate the tax on $1.5 million (or $555,800), we wind up with a major tax error—the real tax is much higher than $555,800. The correct tax is found by first calculating the tax on the $2.5 million estate (or $1,025,800) and only then subtracting the credit of $345,800 from $1,025,800 (or $680,000).

The Erosion of Your Estate

If your estate is worth $20 million and we assume Congress decides to keep the top estate tax rate at 50 percent rather than letting it return to 55 percent (which is scheduled to occur in 2011 under EGTRRA) and you take no action, your children will inherit $10 million upon your passing. Your grandchildren will receive $5 million. In only two generations, what you have worked so hard to earn and protect will be depleted by 75 percent!

Presumably, your children could use the inherited money to make more money through their own investments and accomplishments, but that wealth will be subject to the same estate tax table. On the other hand, there is always the possibility that your children may not be terrific moneymakers. They might even *lose* a substantial part of what you leave them through poor investments, emergencies, national economic downswings, or an exorbitant lifestyle. It is often very difficult for heirs to hold on to wealth they did not create.

Whether your estate gets bigger or smaller over the next generations, the biggest damage to it will come from estate taxes as it passes between generations. If your estate is worth $20 million and is earning a 10 percent rate of return, you are grossing $2 million in income a year. After state and federal income taxes of approximately 40 percent, you have a net annual income of $1.2 million.

When you die and your estate passes to your children, and assuming the earning power of your money remains constant at 10 percent, they will earn $1 million in annual interest income on the $10 million they inherit. After they pay income taxes, they will be left with $600,000 in yearly income. By the time your estate passes to your grandchildren, their net inheritance of approximately $5 million will produce $500,000 before taxes and only $300,000 after—a far cry from the $2 million yearly income with which you started. When you consider that these funds probably will be further diluted when spread between children and grandchildren and affected by inflation, you can see that even your $20 million is not enough to provide a financially secure future for your descendants if it is left unprotected from the confiscatory estate tax.

Clearly, if $20 million is not sufficient to ensure financial security for future generations, $10 million will provide even less security after it suffers similar depletion. An estate of $10 million currently produces $1 million *before* income taxes and $600,000 *after* income taxes. This will decrease to about half, or $5 million, after estate taxes. In turn, that $5 million will produce $500,000 before income taxes and $300,000 after income taxes to be shared by *all your children*. Your grandchildren will share an inheritance of only $3 million from your original estate (utilizing the rates and applicable exemption after 2010—see Table 2-2). This will generate approximately $300,000 before income taxes and $180,000 after income taxes, based on current tax rates. The security you thought you had provided quickly dissipates as your grandchildren are left with only 30 percent of your original estate. The missing 70 percent has been taken by the government in just two generations.

If this scares you, wait—it gets worse.

Basic Alternatives to Estate Taxes

Even if your estate is worth $10 million, it is probably not all liquid. Chances are you have a portion of your assets in property and investments. Nonetheless, estate taxes are due on the *total* value of your entire estate within nine months of your death. Thus, you may realize additional shrinkage in your estate if your heirs are forced to liquidate your property at discount rates in order to pay estate taxes.

If your estate is large enough to exceed the 2002 and 2003 applicable exclusion amount of $1 million (which is scheduled to increase—see Table 2-2), there are a number of perfectly legal, commonly used methods for reducing—or even eliminating—estate taxes. Two of these are listed here:

Marital Deduction

The *marital deduction* allows you to pass on your entire estate to your spouse free of estate tax. (It might be the only tax reduction strategy you need.) If you don't care what happens to your estate after your spouse's death, the marital deduction will be the answer to your estate-tax problem. Of course, in relying solely on the marital deduction, all you have done is defer the estate tax payments to the settlement of your *spouse's* estate. If your spouse doesn't remarry, there will be no additional marital deduction and your heirs will bear the full impact of estate taxes on the combined estate of you and your spouse.

Annual Gift Program

An *annual gift program* is also an effective way to reduce estate taxes. An outright gift to your children (or anyone else you choose) is the one way to achieve an immediate reduction in the size of your estate and your estate tax. Tax laws permit you to give up to $11,000 a year tax-free to as many people as you choose (in 2002, subject to annual cost-of-living adjustments rounded down to the nearest multiple of $1,000). Such gifts are free of all taxes for you *and* for the recipient. This means you and your spouse (if you are married) could transfer $22,000 worth of assets tax-free to each of your children every year to reduce your taxable estate. In theory, if your estate did not grow and you lived long enough, you could transfer your *entire* estate to your heirs without paying any estate tax.

Traditional Ways to Pay Estate Taxes

If you are worth $10 million when you die, and the taxes on your estate are $5 million, how will those taxes be paid? There are five traditional methods for covering your estate taxes: paying cash, selling assets, borrowing, making installment payments, and using life insurance. Let's look at the advantages and disadvantages of each:

Cash

Cash is the simplest and most direct means of paying your estate taxes. However, using $5 million to cover the taxes will leave only a $5 million inheritance for your heirs. However, you probably don't have that much cash in your estate (nor should you).

Sale of Assets

To raise the additional cash, your heirs may be forced to sell some of your assets. Because of the limited time for liquidation, the assets might have to be sold for less than fair market value. As a result, your $10 million estate could shrink in value to $7 or $8 million, while remaining liable for a full measure of tax (which is approximately 50 percent), leaving only $3.5 million or $4 million for your heirs. In addition, your heirs will have to forgo the assets' potential appreciation and pay commission and other sales costs. These disadvantages are magnified 10-fold if the asset in question is your family business.

Borrowing

Your heirs could always *borrow* some or all of the $5 million to settle your estate, using estate assets as collateral for the loan. Allowing for interest payments over time, this might actually cost $10 million (including interest and principal), effectively leaving your children a legacy of debt.

Installment Plan

Your heirs could pay in *installments.* Your estate might qualify for Section 6166 of the IRS Code, which provides a 14-year period for the payment of estate tax resulting from the estate's interest in a farm or other closely held business. If you qualify, your estate can pay interest at only 2 percent (nondeductible) for four years and then pay the balance in equal installments (with the nondeductible interest at 45 percent of the penalty rate charged by the IRS) over the next nine years. But the program has several drawbacks. First, very few estates qualify. Second, the deferment is not available for nonbusiness or nonfarm assets, and it is available at the lower 2 percent rate only for business and farm assets for the first $1.1 million (in 2002) in excess of the value sheltered by the estate tax credit amount. And third, if you miss a payment, the total amount of the unpaid tax becomes due. Effectively, your heirs will have the IRS as their partner in the family farm or business for 14 years or until the balance of the installments is paid.

Life Insurance

The final way to pay estate taxes is with *life insurance.* By purchasing enough insurance to cover estate settlement costs, your estate can avoid forced liquidation of assets and inopportune borrowing. However, the proceeds from your life insurance are also included in your estate for purposes of calculating your federal estate tax. In other words, your life insurance proceeds could also be reduced by 41 to 50 percent before they reach your beneficiaries. (Later in this book, you will see how life insurance proceeds can be removed from your taxable estate and be used to discount your estate tax cost up to 90 percent or more.)

W W W

All this sounds very unsatisfactory, doesn't it? However, through proper planning, utilizing the various strategies discussed in this book, you will be able to pass on your estate without losing your current financial independence and security. You will be able to effectively *disinherit the IRS!*

Generation Skipping

The federal gift and estate tax system is structured so that property will be taxed at each generation of a family as that property is handed down from generation to generation. Gifts made by an individual to children during life, and bequests after death, are normally subject to tax before receipt by the children. Similarly, property received by children from their parents, which they do not consume during their lifetimes, will again be subject to taxation when it is transmitted to their own children. Thus, in the normal course of events and ignoring certain exemptions under the gift and estate tax laws, property will be taxed *twice* on its way down from an individual to his or her grandchildren, and again repeatedly as it is passed down to each subsequent generation. In a 50-percent estate tax bracket, a dollar would be worth only 12.5 cents after only three generations of taxation.

In the past, wealthy people could avoid paying more than one gift or estate tax by placing property in a trust for the benefit of their children, grandchildren, great-grandchildren, and even later generations. To eliminate this planning loophole, Congress in 1986 passed a new federal *generation-skipping transfer (GST) tax*. The GST tax imposes an additional tax to match the highest estate tax rate (50 percent in 2002 and 2003) on transfers to beneficiaries who are more than one generation younger than the person making the transfer. In its simplest form, the GST tax is imposed on a "direct skip" from a grandparent to a grandchild during the lifetime of the grandchild's parent. The GST tax is also imposed on a "taxable termination" (a skip person has an interest in the property on the termination of a trust) and a "taxable distribution" (a distribution to a skip person that is not a taxable termination). Without any exemptions, the combined effect of the gift/estate tax and the GST tax is a total transfer tax of 75 percent.

Fortunately, there is an important exception to the GST tax called the *GST exemption.* This exemption allows every individual to shelter up to $1.1 million (to be adjusted for inflation in 2003) of gift property from the GST tax. Beginning in 2004, the GST exemption is to parallel the proposed estate tax exemption (see Table 2-2 and Appendix D). The exemption means that the first $2.2 million of transfers by a married couple to grandchildren, who are skip persons, is exempt from the GST tax (for 2002, adjusted to a total of $3 million for 2004–2006).

In most of the revocable and irrevocable trusts discussed in this book, you can include provisions that allow the trusts to continue for the benefit of later generations by taking advantage of generation-skipping transfer planning that utilizes the $1 million GST exemption.

A typical GST plan allows your children and/or other heirs to enjoy full benefits from the trust (or trusts) set up by you. Each child can receive income and principal distributions from his or her individual separate share trust at the discretion of the trustee and each can serve as trustee of his or her share. Trust wording can even provide that the children are free to designate in their own wills who is to receive the property upon their deaths, with some unimposing limitations.

The benefit of all this is that the children have full use and enjoyment of the funds during their lives, but the funds are not taxed in their estates at their deaths. Instead, regardless of its value at the time of their deaths, the property will pass to their children—your grandchildren—free of any estate tax. The trust document can even accomplish multiple generation skipping, in which the property would remain in trust and pass *without gift or estate tax* for the benefit of your great-grandchildren and later generations.

Thus, GST planning (sometime referred to as "IRS skipping" planning) has the effect of disinheriting the IRS in regard to assets you leave to benefit your children, your grandchildren, and their descendants—as long as the assets are in the trust. It also has ancillary benefits, such as protecting the assets held in trust for multiple generations of heirs from any claims of creditors or of a spouse in a divorce.

Although a GST plan is structured so that the intervening generations have full use and benefit of the property during their lives, current tax law limits the amount that you and your spouse can leave in such a "tax-skipping" scenario to $1.1 million each. However, there is a way to leverage your $1.1 million exemption and create a *dynasty trust* with tens of millions of dollars or more (see Chapter 4).

3 Trusts: The First Step

C Cleves and Kathy Lewiston have a son-in-law, Brad, who is an attorney. They were convinced that even though their estate was large, probating the estate would not be a problem for their son-in-law. They felt they could get by with a simple will. They maintained their belief in spite of these facts: probate is public, the cost of probate in most states ranges from 3 to 15 percent of the estate, and the process often takes a year or longer.

Cleves said that Brad told him he would probate his estate for only "a few thousand dollars" and get the whole job done "in a few short months." Although I did not dispute the good intent of Brad's offer, I was skeptical. I didn't ask the obvious question: "What if Brad is no longer married to your daughter?" However, I did ask Cleves how long he expects to live. After an interesting conversation about life-expectancy tables, we agreed that it was reasonable to expect that Cleves will live another 15 years and Kathy at least 20 (her mother lived to age 94). With tongue firmly in cheek, I pointed out that in 15 years Brad will be 68 and in 20 years he will be 73. Not only is it likely that Brad will be retired from his law firm by then, but he may even be living in a different state than Cleves and Kathy.

At that point, Cleves mentioned that he was about to change his declared domicile from Ohio to Florida. This change would make it difficult for Brad to probate his estate even if Cleves died sooner than expected.

When Cleves and Kathy learned about the many benefits a revocable living trust offers (such as eliminating the probate

*process completely and providing for them in the event that either or both
become incapacitated) they decided to use revocable living trusts as the
base of their estate plan.*

Trusts have come down to us from medieval England, a time of kings and
queens, knights and ladies, bishops and monks, and yes, judges and lawyers.

The king imposed heavy taxes on the disposition of land. In fact, everything that could possibly be taxed was taxed (including, at one time, the win-
dows in a subject's home). Furthermore, custom decreed that only the eldest
son could inherit land, whether or not he deserved it.

Between the increasingly onerous taxes owed to the king and the tradition
limiting land bequests to first sons, there was growing unrest. Now, enter the
attorneys. Their ingenious solution was a transaction in which a landowner
gave title to his land to persons he could trust. These "trustees" administered
the land for him and, upon his death, disposed of it according to his wishes. The
beneficiary escaped paying inheritance taxes because he did not have title to
the land. The trustees, because they did not receive earnings or other benefits
from the land, could claim they were not liable for taxes.

As England moved from an agrarian to a mercantile society, trusts began
to hold other types of property in addition to land. With this change, the modern
trust was well under way, accommodating the many forms of wealth and the
varied needs of property owners that would arise in the following centuries.

Trust Basics

A *trust* is nothing more than a legal document that creates a holding place
for property. A trust holds temporary title to assets, which are ultimately distributed to heirs. Placing assets in trusts legally separates some or all of the
property rights inherent in personal ownership. These include legal title, control, and economic benefit. Under personal ownership, all property rights, taxes,
and other obligations are vested in a single person—the owner. Under trust
ownership, those rights and obligations are vested in two or more persons.
Although trusts may vary according to their goals, they all have some features
in common. To begin with, all trusts have four parties:

1. *The grantor, trust maker, or donor:* the person who establishes the
   trust and puts assets in the trust.
2. *The trustee*: the person or institution appointed by the grantor to
   manage the trust.

3. *The interim beneficiary:* the person (or persons) who benefits from the trust during the life of the trust.
4. *The ultimate beneficiary:* the person (or persons) who receives the assets at the termination of the trust.

Trusts enable people to pass the title to their property to others either during lifetime or at death. When a person creates a trust and places assets in it, the trust maker is making a gift. Thus, trusts allow their makers to make gifts to their beneficiaries and to exercise significant control over trust property before, and even after, death. In effect, trusts allow people to transfer property to others with "strings attached."

Trusts can be classified by the manner in which they are created. If a trust is created by a will and activated at the time of death, it is called a *testamentary trust*. Such trusts are set up by a couple to preserve the estate tax exemption of the first to die, but they are also used to handle such things as life insurance proceeds and uncollected retirement benefits that do not come into existence until after the first death. A trust that is created and activated during the grantor's life is called a *living trust*. A living trust is frequently used as an alternative to a will.

There are only two basic types of trusts: revocable (living) trusts and irrevocable trusts. With a *revocable trust,* the grantor can change or eliminate any of the terms at any time before death as he or she chooses. Because the grantor has so much control over the trust's assets, the property held in a revocable trust is subject to estate tax when the grantor dies. An *irrevocable trust,* in contrast, cannot be altered in any way after being established. And if it is properly structured, its assets are not subject to estate tax when the grantor dies.

Trusts have evolved into highly sophisticated instruments used by people today for the prudent and flexible management of their assets. The various kinds of trusts provide a wide range of benefits for single individuals and married couples. Advantages can include higher income, income-tax savings, control of distributions to ultimate beneficiaries, gift and estate tax savings, avoidance of the generation-skipping transfer (GST) tax, cost-effective philanthropic distributions, and wealth replacement to heirs for amounts directed to charitable organizations.

Revocable Living Trusts

Last year, approximately 70 percent of Americans who died did so without a will. If you think that figure primarily represents uneducated Americans, you will be surprised to learn that 60 percent of that figure consists of college-educated Americans.

You may already have a will in place or you may be contemplating signing one soon. Although a will is not a bad first step, there is a much better one—a revocable living trust. This effectively replaces the basic will and contains all your instructions on the management and distribution of your assets.

Advantages of a Living Trust

A properly drafted revocable living trust has numerous advantages. One of the most significant is that it leaves you in control of your assets. In most revocable living trusts, you, as the trust maker, are the trustee of your trust during your lifetime. As trustee, you continue to manage your assets and file your tax returns as you always have. In addition, you may transfer assets to and from the trust as well. When transferring assets in and out of your trust, you simply add the word "trustee" after your name, where appropriate.

A revocable living trust offers four additional major benefits to you and your family: avoidance of probate, protection for you and your family in the event of your incapacitation, estate tax planning, and protection for your heirs.

Avoiding Probate

The most talked-about advantage of a revocable living trust is avoiding probate. Many people mistakenly think that by having a will they avoid probate—the opposite is true. A will guarantees probate because the purpose of probate is to prove the validity of the will. A properly funded trust, on the other hand, completely avoids probate.

There are many reasons why it is best to avoid probate, even in states such as Florida or Nevada where the probate process is considered to be fairly simple. Some of those reasons follow:

Cost

The cost associated with probating your estate, including attorney fees, court costs, appraisals, and so on, ranges from 3 to 15 percent of the estate, depending on the state in which you live. Most of these costs are virtually eliminated through the use of a revocable living trust because if a trust is fully funded with your assets, there is no probate! The cost of preparing a typical revocable living trust is usually very small in comparison.

Time

Probate takes time, and in many states it can easily take a year or more before the process is completed. Heirs can suffer financial hardship during this needless waiting period. With a revocable living trust, there is virtually no waiting because the trust doesn't die; only the grantor does.

State lines

Wills do not cross state lines very well. If you have real estate in more than one state, for example, your heirs will likely face probate in every state the properties are located. This can add to the cost and time delay. With a properly funded revocable living trust, probate is unnecessary, regardless of where the properties are located.

Contests

Wills are easier than trusts to contest. You may believe that your heirs will not challenge your will, but when a person dies, people change. You cannot be sure that no one will contest your wishes. As a client once remarked, "If you really want to get to know someone, share an inheritance with that person." A revocable living trust is harder to dispute because it is in place before you die and it has withstood the test of time. If an heir believes he or she has a basis for a lawsuit, the heir would have to sue the trustee and all beneficiaries, which is a difficult and costly process.

Public

Wills are public. Some salespeople make it a practice to read probate proceedings, including wills, and prey on decedents' families. A revocable living trust is private: Virtually nothing is known by the public about your estate and the details of the inheritance your heirs receive.

Providing for Disability

Another major reason for having a revocable living trust (and one that many experts consider more important than avoiding probate) is the possibility of becoming incapacitated. The fact is, you are four to six times more likely to become disabled than to die in the next year. Therefore, it is important to be prepared so that you and your loved ones can be cared for in the manner you desire during your incapacitation.

Many people feel safe because they have set up a durable power of attorney. A *durable power of attorney* is a legal document that gives the person of your choice the right to act in your place regarding all financial matters. Unfortunately, some financial institutions won't recognize a durable power of attorney, especially if the document is old and does not contain certain language dictated by state law. A revocable living trust, on the other hand, allows you to choose, how you want your affairs handled and lets you set the priority of your wishes, in detail. And financial institutions are more likely to recognize and follow revocable living trust instructions when the grantor of the trust is disabled.

Without a durable power of attorney or revocable living trust, you and your spouse would have to go through the legal process of *conservatorship*. And although the probate court would most likely appoint your spouse to manage your affairs, he or she would have to report annually to the court. Your affairs would be subject to legal costs and the red tape of the court system. In some jurisdictions, this can be a nightmare. Fortunately, with a revocable living trust this can all be easily avoided; your alternate trustee (typically your spouse) manages your affairs beginning the moment you become disabled without any legal proceedings or court intervention.

Planning for Estate Taxes

A third major reason for utilizing a revocable living trust relates to estate taxes. In a typical will arrangement, everything passes from one spouse to the other. This is known as an "I love you will," and it avoids any estate tax at the death of the first spouse because of the unlimited marital deduction (no tax on assets left to your U.S. citizen spouse). At the surviving spouse's death, the property owned by that spouse (including the property inherited from the first spouse to die) is taxed after the applicable credit is applied. The problem with this arrangement is that it wastes the applicable credit (the equivalent exemption amount—see Table 2-2) of the first spouse to die. That is, property that could have passed to someone other than the surviving spouse (including a trust for his or her benefit) free from estate tax at the first death and instead passed to the surviving spouse, will be subject to estate tax when he or she dies.

A better plan involves the use of a revocable living trust that splits into two trusts on the first death: a *qualified terminable interest property (QTIP) trust* (often referred to as a "marital trust" or "A trust") and a *credit shelter trust* (often referred to as a "bypass trust," "family trust," or "B trust"). The credit shelter trust preserves the tax credit of the first spouse to die while providing for the needs of the remaining spouse, while the QTIP trust preserves the unlimited marital deduction for the balance of the estate. These trusts are further discussed later in this chapter.

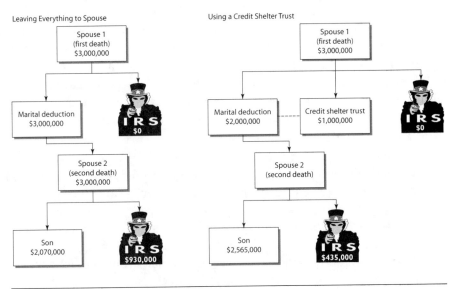

Figure 3-1. Tax advantage of credit shelter trust.

Figure 3-1 shows the tax results of leaving everything directly to a surviving spouse (in 2002–2003) versus utilizing a credit shelter trust, in this case for a couple with an estate of $3 million.

Protecting Heirs

The fourth reason for creating a revocable living trust is that it offers flexibility in regard to how you leave your assets. You may, for example, pass assets to your heirs with "strings attached." That is, you can control how your assets are to be distributed, and when, even after death.

One client had a son who was a "deadhead" (a follower of the Grateful Dead). Their son would follow the group from concert to concert and sell tie-dyed T-shirts to make enough money to eat and to travel. His parents were quite wealthy, but they were worried about their son's lifestyle and propensity for spending money. So, in their revocable living trust, they arranged for their son to receive one dollar of their estate (which was to remain in trust) for every dollar he legitimately earned, with certain tests installed to prove this. In this example, our clients found a unique way to provide their son with some incentive (and perhaps motivation) rather than just their wealth.

No one should leave anything of any consequence to anyone *outright*. Instead, everything should be left to heirs *in trust*. By leaving assets in trust for children, you can *protect them* in a way they cannot do themselves. Your revocable living trust could provide for each child to serve as his or her own trustee. As trustees, the children can manage the funds however they desire. In addition, by retaining everything in trust, you are preventing an unwanted creditor from a failed business venture, an overzealous litigator, or even a child's ex-spouse from ever reaching the assets. In essence, you have accomplished two very important goals: you have set the assets aside, allowing each child to manage and benefit from his or her own share and preserved the assets so a third party cannot grab them.

You may be concerned that by leaving assets in trust you are overcontrolling your children. To me, keeping assets in trust for children is never a question as long as the children can serve as trustees. This gives them all the flexibility they need to do whatever they deem appropriate. The only issue you face is whether to allow your children to leave the assets in their respective trusts to anyone they desire at their deaths, for example, to their spouses (who might remarry and choose to disinherit your grandchildren), or whether to restrict them to leaving these assets to your descendants.

By including generation-skipping language in your revocable living trust, you can also protect your grandchildren from another layer of taxation on the assets that remain in trust for their benefit at the deaths of your children. There is a limit on how much you can leave in trust that "skips the IRS." This limit is $1.1 million (in 2002) per grantor ($2.2 million for couples), but with proper planning, there is a way to leverage this limitation dramatically. (See Chapter 4 for more details.)

For example, if you and your spouse left $2 million (utilizing your estate exemption of $1 million each plus a portion of your GST exemption of $1.1 million each in 2002) to your children in a trust with generation-skipping (IRS-skipping) provisions, there would be no estate tax due on the value of the assets remaining in trust at the death of your children. If the entire principal remains intact, your grandchildren will have the benefit of the whole $2 million (or possibly more) with investment growth. Alternatively, if you left the $2 million directly to your children and the money was still in their estates at their deaths, it would again be subject to estate taxes and, at 50 percent (2002-2003), would reduce your grandchildren's inheritance to $1 million.

In summary, the revocable living trust can be a very flexible tool that will allow you to remain in control of your estate. At the same time, it will provide a way to avoid probate, follow your wishes in the event of your disability, help save estate taxes, and provide a way to protect your heirs while avoiding additional estate taxes at your children's deaths.

Irrevocable Life Insurance Trust

Life insurance is a critical tool in estate tax planning. Life insurance proceeds create needed liquidity for paying taxes and expenses. It also provides cash for beneficiaries. Yet, if life insurance is not owned correctly and the premiums are not paid in the proper manner, its benefits can be greatly reduced. An *irrevocable life insurance trust (ILIT)* is designed to own a policy of insurance while protecting the cash value from creditors and the proceeds from the IRS. The insurance is the "fuel" that can power an ILIT and provide a way to "discount" estate tax costs. Because ILITs play such a key part in sophisticated estate planning, they are covered in detail in Chapter 7. (Life insurance is discussed more fully in Chapters 5 and 6.)

Credit Shelter Trust

The unlimited marital deduction for gifts and bequests can give married couples a false sense of security because they anticipate that when one of them dies, his or her assets will pass tax-free to the surviving spouse. This ignores the fact that the same assets in the survivor's estate will be subject to tax on everything over the value of his or her (single) applicable estate-tax credit. In other words, the marital deduction merely *delays* the estate tax; it does not avoid it permanently. A credit shelter trust can eliminate or minimize federal estate taxes on a couple's combined assets by protecting the applicable estate tax credit of the first spouse to die.

One of the most fundamental purposes of trusts in estate planning for married couples is to ensure the use of both the husband's and the wife's individual federal estate tax credits. This is important whenever the combined assets of a couple exceed (or can be expected to exceed) the amount that can be passed to other heirs sheltered from tax by the applicable exclusion amount available to each spouse (see Table 2-2).

The credit shelter trust is created at death with property owned by the first spouse to die that has a value equal to the decedent's applicable unused estate tax-exemption equivalent. This trust can provide for the surviving spouse through distributions of trust property as needed. The surviving spouse can be the trustee of the credit shelter trust. When both spouses are deceased, the assets in the credit shelter trust pass to the heirs with no further gift or estate tax (see Figure 3-1).

To take maximum advantage of the applicable credit of both spouses, it is often advisable to balance the ownership of assets between spouses so that, no matter which spouse dies first, he or she will have enough assets to at least fund the credit shelter trust. When asset ownership is concentrated in the name of one spouse, putting a credit shelter trust only in that spouse's estate plan is not so much a plan as a wager on the order of death. If the nonowner spouse dies first, his or her credit is wasted, and at the second death only one credit will be available. Therefore, it is important that assets be spread between spouses and that each spouse have a revocable living trust that creates a credit shelter trust upon death.

Qualified Terminable Interest Property Trust

Tax legislation in 1981 created a new form of trust, the *qualified terminable interest property (QTIP) trust*. The purpose of this trust is to solve the dilemma of a spouse with children from a previous marriage. Under former laws, it was necessary to give the surviving spouse the full power to decide who would receive the property at his or her death to enjoy the unlimited estate tax marital deduction. If the owner spouse wanted to ensure that assets eventually went to the children of the first marriage, it was necessary to give up the estate tax marital deduction.

Under current law, it is possible to provide maximum financial support for a surviving spouse who is a U.S. citizen through a QTIP trust, while ensuring that the trust assets pass at that spouse's death to recipients named by the grantor (such as children of the first marriage). All income of the QTIP trust must be paid to the surviving spouse and the trust agreement can also provide for other distributions to the surviving spouse as needed. All assets remaining in the trust will be included in the estate of the surviving spouse for estate-tax purposes but will pass to heirs chosen by the grantor spouse. For flexibility under changed circumstances (such as the death of an intended beneficiary) the surviving spouse can be given certain limited power to alter the distributions.

The QTIP trust can also be useful when each spouse has differing family or charitable distribution wishes, and it can also protect the surviving spouse from any pressure to change the eventual distributions.

Note that the use of a QTIP trust is not available if your spouse is *not* a U.S. citizen. U.S. tax laws have eliminated the estate tax marital deduction on property passing to a spouse who isn't a U.S. citizen. Apparently, Congress felt that numerous foreign spouses returned to their homelands following the death of their spouses, taking the marital property with them without paying any U.S. estate tax. It is, however, possible to obtain the marital deduction

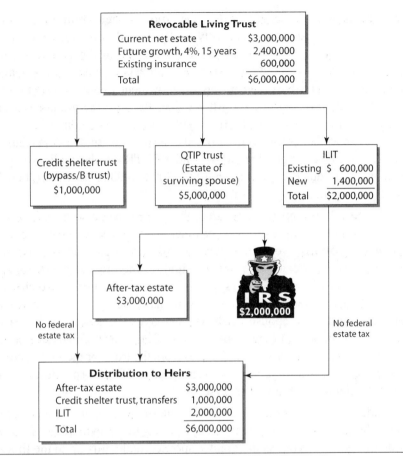

Figure 3-2. Sample plan showing estate conservation with multiple trusts and a $1 million exemption. (Note: Taxes are rounded.)

with a noncitizen spouse by using a special form of QTIP trust known as a *qualified domestic trust (QDOT)*. If you or your spouse is not a U.S. citizen, be sure to inform your estate planning attorney of this fact so that your revocable living trust can include a QDOT.

Figure 3-2 shows how using several trusts can conserve your estate.

Spousal Estate Reduction Trust

An alternative to creating the credit shelter trust at death is to create an irrevocable trust during life and shelter the growth on assets transferred to the trust. A *spousal estate reduction trust (SERT)* is an irrevocable trust created by one spouse for the benefit of the other spouse, their children, and other descendants. The grantor's spouse is typically named as trustee of the SERT. All assets the grantor transfers to the SERT are out of the grantor's estate, free from the claims of creditors and free of all estate taxes. And by making gifts within the applicable credit exemption equivalent amount limit ($1 million for 2002–2003) there will be no gift tax due. Because the grantor typically uses up all or most of his or her lifetime applicable gift tax credit in funding the SERT, the credit shelter trust is not funded at death or is funded with whatever amount of unused exemption remains. (Under EGTRRA, the credit exemption equivalent is scheduled to increase above the 2002–2003 limit of $1 million, but *lifetime* gifts are limited to $1 million.)

If the SERT is properly structured, the grantor can also transfer annual gifts of up to $11,000 of cash, stock, or other assets per beneficiary (including children and grandchildren) without paying gift tax. This is accomplished by giving the trust beneficiaries the right to withdraw their respective shares up to $11,000 each in value for 30 days. After 30 days have passed, the children, grandchildren, or other descendants no longer have the right to withdraw those assets, and the trustee-spouse holds and manages the assets for his or her benefit and the benefit of other beneficiaries of the SERT. The trustee-spouse also has the authority to make distributions from the trust for the health, education, maintenance, and support of the beneficiaries of the trust, without incurring gift tax (including himself or herself).

Besides the obvious estate reduction, one of the primary benefits of the SERT is the estate tax savings realized by keeping the growth of the gift assets outside the estate. If you, as the grantor spouse, made gifts up to the lifetime applicable gift tax exclusion amount of $1 million and lived another 18 years without your spouse taking any withdrawals, at an 8 percent per year growth rate the money would quadruple to $4 million during that time—outside your estate. If you wait until death, only $1 million would escape taxation. Another potential benefit is the opportunity to leverage the generation-skipping transfer tax exemption of approximately $1.1 million (2002), which each person can leave in a trust without additional tax. If proper GST tax elections are made with respect to the assets contributed (up to $1.1 million) to the SERT and the spouse is not given a temporary withdrawal right as to a portion of the annual gifts to the trust, all future growth of those assets will avoid the additional 50 percent tax that would otherwise be due on a SERT designed to serve more than one generation.

Figure 3-3 shows a SERT in action, and Table 3-1 on page 56 summarizes the various trusts discussed.

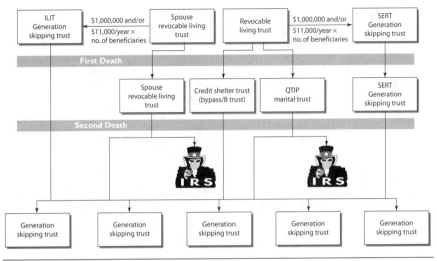

Figure 3-3. Spousal estate reduction trust (SERT) plan.

Total-Return Unitrust

In a typical trust, the trustee, who may be a spouse, sometimes finds himself or herself in a conflict of interest with various classes of beneficiaries. The *total-return unitrust (TRUT)* is designed to eliminate such surprises and provide for the best interest of all beneficiaries. The TRUT came about as the result of legislation that was passed in more than three-fourths of the states and is currently being considered in several more.

Investment Guidelines

Generally, trusts have two types of beneficiaries:

1. Present-interest or income beneficiaries, who receive current distributions of income (and possibly principal), and
2. Remainder persons, who receive distributions from the trust only after the income beneficiary's interest terminates.

Trusts usually include language that is similar to the following:

I hereby give, devise, and bequeath my estate to my trustee, Mr. Goodman, in trust for the following uses and purposes: To collect and receive rents, income, dividends, and profits thereof and to pay the same to my wife, Julie White, as long as she shall live. The remainder interest I leave to the children from my first marriage.

TABLE 3-1 Types of Trusts

Trust	Primary features
Revocable living trust	Avoids probate (costs, time delays, publicity, etc.); helps during incapacitation; offers potential tax benefits via credit shelter trust; protects heirs; enables maker to retain control of assets while alive. Useful for individuals whose goals include estate tax reduction, avoidance of probate and/or public scrutiny, and protection in event of incapacitation.
Credit shelter trust (bypass trust, B trust)	Created at first death for family, including surviving spouse; allows married couples to transfer all assets to surviving spouse and take advantage of applicable credit in each estate. Useful for couples who want to pass entire estate to spouse while preserving applicable tax credit of first spouse to die.
Qualified terminable interest property (QTIP) trust	Provides for spouse in event of grantor's death; surviving spouse entitled to income, may or may not have access to principal; grantor's wishes control disposition of property after spouse's death; assets in trust qualify for marital deduction but are subject to estate tax in spouse's estate. Useful for grantors who want to provide for spouse during spouse's lifetime, before distributing assets to children, especially useful if there are children from a previous marriage (grantor decides on the ultimate distribution).
Spousal estate reduction trust	Provides a way to remove assets from estate but retain indirect access to income and principal via spouse; protects trust assets from creditor claims; appreciation in value is outside estate. Useful for couples who want to reduce taxable estate without losing control of assets.
Dynasty trust	Avoids estate taxes as assets pass from generation to generation; grantor's wishes built into trust distribution arrangements; allows leveraging of lifetime and annual gift tax exemptions if set up during life. Useful for grantors who want to protect their children and avoid gift and estate taxes in estates of their children and later generations.
Irrevocable life insurance trust (ILIT)	Provides liquidity which can be used to help cover estate tax costs; pays tax-free benefits to surviving spouse and/or other beneficiaries. Useful for grantors who want to fund estate tax liability or provide additional funds for heirs free of income and estate taxes.

This type of arrangement frequently creates tension between the income beneficiary and the remainder persons (the ultimate beneficiaries) because of their opposing interests in the trust assets. The income beneficiary, who generally has a right to dividends and interest only, is happiest when trust assets are invested in investments that produce a steady, high rate of income, even though the investments may subject the principal to some risk. On the other hand, the remainder persons are happiest when the trustee selects investments that preserve the trust's principal, which thereby grows in value but produces little or no income.

Until recently, in most states, the trustee had the task of satisfying both sets of beneficiaries within the confines of the "prudent man rule." Under this rule, trustees were required to manage trust assets in a way that ensured preservation of the trust principal through the selection of investments that minimized risk and losses and maximized current income (such as conservative, dividend-paying stocks, bonds, and treasury notes). In addition, many traditional trusts provide that any capital gains that are generated in the trust are to be added to the trust principal. Under this conservative rule, trusts were likely to generate poor investment returns (2 to 4 percent, after taxes), have little growth potential, and erode from inflation, because the investment income is not usually reinvested.

The prudent investor rule

To respond to this problem, many states have adopted or are in the process of adopting the *Uniform Prudent Investor Act* or some variation of it. This legislation gives all fiduciaries—including persons acting as agents for individuals or estates, conservators, custodians, and persons acting through powers of attorney—the same fiduciary duty as a *prudent investor*. In some states, the act applies to all existing and new trusts, except revocable trusts.

Under the prudent investor rule, trustees have a duty to consider more than the remainder beneficiaries' interests. Their investment and management decisions will be evaluated in the context of the entire trust portfolio and as a part of an overall investment strategy with risk and return objectives that are reasonably suited to the trust provisions. The prudent investor rule emphasizes diversification and asset allocation. It is no longer considered prudent to invest all the trust assets in bank accounts and treasury bills. In fact, in some states, the act permits the trustee to delegate the responsibility for managing the investments of the trust to an agent, although the trustee must exercise care in selecting the agent and must periodically review the agent's performance.

TRUT Features

The total-return unitrust concept combines an established investment philosophy with an established planning technique.

The trustee invests trust assets according to *modern portfolio theory,* which emphasizes diversification and asset allocation. Thus, the trust is designed to maximize its total return over the long term. There is no pressure to produce income only.

Instead of having a right to all income, the income beneficiary is given the right to receive a fixed percentage of the trust assets each year. (Payouts generally range from 3 to 5 percent. However, payouts up to 7 percent are reasonable.) When the income beneficiary's interest terminates, the remaining trust assets vest with the remainder persons. For a total-return trust, a bequest could look like this:

> ...pay to my wife, Martha Wintergreen, an amount equal to 6 percent of the fair market value of the trust assets or $60,000 annually, whichever is greater, valued as of the first day of the year.

Thus, with a total-return trust, the income beneficiary's only concerns are that the trust grows at a reasonable rate (as the trust grows, so does his or her percentage) and that the investments are not too risky. Likewise, the remainder beneficiaries favor steady growth without undue risk. And by promoting family harmony, there is a better probability that the grantor's objectives regarding trust distributions will be achieved.

The provisions of a total-return trust can be refined in many ways, including the following:

- The payout percentage may be applied to a rolling average of the previous three years' market values, rather than the value at the beginning of each year. This approach helps smooth out fluctuations in value that may result from wide market swings from year to year.
- The trustee or a third party may be given the power to modify the percentage used in calculating the payout. This allows for consideration of unforeseeable future circumstances.
- The *payout floor* can be indexed for inflation.
- The trust may permit distributions of trust assets in addition to the percentage amounts if the beneficiary needs funds for living costs or extraordinary expenses.

Advantages of TRUTs

A total-return unitrust offers a number of advantages:

- *Predictability:* The trust produces a more predictable flow of cash than an "income-only trust." Thus, income beneficiaries can estimate annual distributions and plan accordingly.
- *Control:* Grantors can generally control the amount of income the income beneficiary is to receive.
- *Professional investment management:* In some states where the Uniform Prudent Investor Act has been enacted, trustees are allowed to delegate investment decisions to skilled investment professionals. Thus, trustees who are not comfortable making investment decisions can shift liability away from themselves.
- *Optimized trust values:* Use of the modern portfolio theory may generate higher returns and increase the trust's growth. Thus, income beneficiaries and remainder persons should receive larger distributions than they would if the trust were administered under the conservative prudent man rule.

Example

In 1960, Mr. Clark died. A $1 million death benefit was paid to his irrevocable life insurance trust. The trust provided that his wife, Mindy, was to receive income for life. His children from a previous marriage were to receive the remainder at Mindy's death. Mr. Raffe, the trustee, bound by the prudent man standard, invested the money the way he always had: 50 percent of the proceeds in stock that mirrored the S&P 500 index, and 50 percent in long-term U.S. bonds.

At the end of 1998, Mr. Raffe determined that after deducting typical trading costs and a 1 percent annual trustee fee, Mindy had received a total income stream of $2.7 million. Her income stream had increased from $41,250 in 1960 to $108,620 in 1998. The trust principal was $3 million.

If Mr. Raffe had been able to administer the trust under the prudent investor standard inside a TRUT, he could have invested the death proceeds in, for example, 80 percent stocks and 20 percent bonds. And if the trust had provided a fixed 4 percent annual payout to Mindy, she would have received $3.1 million by the end of 1998. (Although the income stream would have fluctuated from year to year, it would have grown to $221,000 by 1998.) In addition, income received from the stock sales would have been taxed at capital gain rates, and this would have increased Mindy's after-tax income even more. Finally, the principal would have grown to more than $8 million.

Appropriate Use

The total-return concept is not appropriate for all trusts. For example, a trust intended to qualify for the federal estate tax marital deduction must provide for the distribution of all income to the surviving spouse. For such trusts, the total-return concept can be modified to require the distribution, at a minimum, of all income. In trusts that are designed to provide for the care of young children, or in special-needs trusts for disabled beneficiaries, payments based on a percentage of assets would run counter to the trusts' purposes.

In most cases, however, a TRUT can protect the interests of all parties to a trust and create a synergistic approach to trust administration. A knowledgeable estate planning professional can show you how to incorporate the total-return concept into your plan.

4 Dynasty Trusts

W

With five children and 10 grandchildren, Ed Newman thinks of himself as a patriarch. Like many of my clients, Ed and his wife, Pat, were interested in an estate plan that provided for more than one generation of their heirs. At our initial meeting, much of our discussion centered on how to provide for their 10 grandchildren. The Newmans were disturbed to learn that not one but two taxes would apply to any sizable gifts (above their gift tax exemptions) made directly to their grandchildren.

We estimated that at the second of Ed's and Pat's deaths, more than 50 percent of their estate would be lost to estate taxes. They were outraged when they realized that the IRS would confiscate another 50 percent when the remainder of their estate passes from their children to their grandchildren. Without a plan, the Newmans' estate will be worth less than 13 percent of its value today after only three generations of taxation.

The Newmans were pleased to learn that by setting up a dynasty trust and funding it while they are alive, the trust would enable them to leverage their various exemptions and avoid the estate taxes that would be due at each generation. Through dynasty trust planning their estate will remain intact for the benefit of their children, grandchildren, great-grandchildren, and even later generations. In addition, Ed and Pat learned that the dynasty trust can also protect the assets they leave in the trust for their heirs from the claims of creditors, predators, and divorcing spouses.

61

If your years of hard work and diligent savings have yielded some wealth, the thought of having the IRS take a large bite (up to 50 percent) of these assets may be very painful. Unfortunately, as the wealth passes down the family tree, successive application of estate taxes may significantly erode the amount that later generations will inherit.

If you want to leave tax-free wealth to your children, grandchildren, and future generations, consider using a generation-skipping trust. The name belies the true value of the trust because the only one that is "skipped" is the IRS. Therefore, a more appropriate name is the *dynasty trust* (also referred to as the *D trust* or *descendant's trust*). Coupled with life insurance, the dynasty trust becomes a powerful tool for maximizing wealth for generations to come.

Consider the radically different results for the grandchildren in the following two examples, in which a grandfather wants to transfer $10 million:

- *No planning:* At the grandfather's death, federal and state death taxes reduce the $10 million by approximately $5 million. If the after-tax wealth passes to his daughter and remains intact during her lifetime, at her death the $5 million will be further eroded by approximately $2 million in estate taxes, leaving a balance of $3 million for her children. Thus, the $10 million that the grandfather had at his death has been reduced to $3 million by the time it reaches his grandchildren. Because of the generation-skipping transfer (GST) tax, even if the grandfather left his entire estate directly to his grandchildren, they would receive less than $3 million. This is true even if the grandfather took advantage of his GST tax exemption of $1.1 million.

- *Comprehensive planning with a dynasty trust:* To avoid the large estate tax bite for two successive generations, the grandfather leverages his GST tax exemption of $1.1 million (this amount adjusts annually for cost of living in 2003 and then parallels the increasing estate tax exemption in 2004 and beyond) through a dynasty trust. The terms of the trust allow the trustee to distribute trust property to his daughter, as needed, but the trust is not subject to estate tax when his daughter dies. After the daughter's death, the property remains in trust for the benefit of her children and their descendants. With this planning, the grandfather is able to pass more than $10 million to his daughter, grandchildren, and great-grandchildren.

Table 4-1 illustrates the dramatic difference a dynasty trust can make.

Under federal and most states' laws, all assets are subject to estate taxes when they pass from generation to generation. A dynasty trust, however, is

TABLE 4-1   Effect of Dynasty Trust (figures in millions)

	No planning	Dynasty trust planning
Estate	$10	$10
Transfer to dynasty trust	0	$1
Insurance purchased in trust	0	$10
Taxable estate	$10	$9
Estate tax	$5	$4.5
Net estate to daughter	$5	$14.5
Amount free from taxation	0	$10
Estate tax at daughter's death	$2	$1.75
Net estate to descendants	$3	$12.75
Growth in trust at 3% over 80 years	0	$106.4

designed to maximize your available estate and GST tax exemptions and keep assets from ever being subject to gift, estate, or generation-skipping tax.

Dynasty Trust Basics

A dynasty trust is an irrevocable trust created for the benefit of the grantor's descendants (children, grandchildren, and so on) to which the grantor allocates all or a portion of his or her GST exemption. If the grantor is married and his or her spouse participates in making transfers to the trust, a total GST exemption of approximately $2.2 million (subject to previously noted increases) is available.

Once exempt from GST tax, the trust property, and all appreciation in value and income, remains free from further federal transfer taxes. It is also free from the claims of creditors. Given the effects of compounding, a successfully invested trust can accumulate to a value of tens of millions of dollars, available to future generations of beneficiaries undiminished by estate or generation-skipping tax costs.

Objectives

The primary objectives of a dynasty trust are:

- To receive cash or other assets as gifts that can be invested and/or used to pay the premiums of life insurance on the grantor and/or the grantor's spouse.

- To escape gift, estate, and generation-skipping taxes on the assets and any growth therein (such as insurance proceeds) in perpetuity.
- To maximize and leverage the available GST exemption amount, without paying gift tax, by investing in growth stocks and the like and/or by purchasing life insurance on the life of the maker or the lives of the maker and his or her spouse.

A dynasty trust permits wealthy individuals to preserve and create wealth to provide a lasting legacy for future generations. This is accomplished by transferring property to a trust for the longest possible period of time and structuring the trust so that no part of the principal that remains in trust will be included in the estate of any descendant.

Example

To see how a dynasty trust meets these objectives, let's look at the example illustrated in Figure 4-1: the estate plan of a Massachusetts couple who met with a Wealth Protection Network affiliate in Boston. When they met the advisor, the couple, both age 65, had a combined estate of $12 million and virtually no estate plan. After a lengthy fact-finding session and thorough analysis of the couple's goals and objectives, the advisor recommended immediately funding two dynasty trusts to take advantage of and leverage each of their $1 million lifetime gift tax exemptions and most of their GST tax exemptions for the benefit of their children and future descendants. Both trusts were set up and funded with $1 million.

To achieve the optimum result, the advisor recommended funding the father's dynasty trust with stocks and bonds and the mother's dynasty trust with a survivor life insurance policy. The total amount that will eventually pass to their descendants from the two trusts depends mainly on the performance of the investments in the father's dynasty trust. Because the mother's dynasty trust is funded with insurance, the proceeds in her trust are available if death occurred immediately.

To provide maximum flexibility, the father's dynasty trust was set up so that the mother was trustee and a beneficiary. The trust wording allowed the mother to take income from the father's dynasty trust, as well as principal as needed for health, education, maintenance, and support. At life expectancy, and on the basis of conservative growth, the combined assets in the two dynasty trusts could easily exceed $17.5 million at the death of the father and mother, $35 million at the death of the children, and more than $70 million at the death of the grandchildren. The plan removes approximately 17 percent of the couple's estate from taxation and leverages that amount

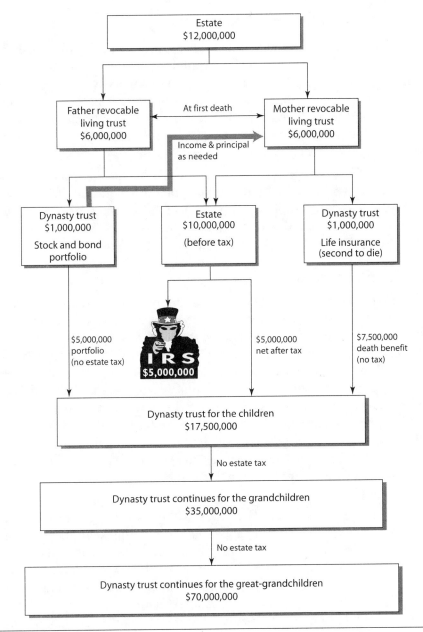

Figure 4-1. Sample plan for a dynasty trust.

substantially for the benefit of three or more generations. The only one that is disinherited in this plan is the IRS!

Leveraging Your Exemption

A dynasty trust may be created during the grantor's lifetime or at death. The advantage of the GST exemption is magnified if it is used *during life,* because once property is transferred to a dynasty trust within the exemption, all appreciation and accumulated income generated by the property is exempt as well. As a result, in most cases the trust holds more property when the grantor dies than could be placed into the trust exempt from GST and estate taxes at the grantor's death.

By transferring property to a dynasty trust during life, the grantor makes a taxable gift which may require that the grantor pay gift tax. In order to avoid gift taxes, many individuals prefer to fund a dynasty trust with annual exclusion gifts and/or gifts shielded from gift tax by the amount of the available applicable lifetime credit exemption equivalent.

Annual gift considerations

If annual gifts are used, there are limitations that should be considered. One involves the question of how to make an annual exclusion gift qualify as a "present gift" (one that the recipient has the right to enjoy in the present) rather than a "future gift" (such as trust proceeds held for the benefit of trust beneficiaries). Thanks to a famous 1968 court case, *Crummey v. Commissioner,* there is a solution. If the trust beneficiaries are given a temporary (15- to 30-day) right to withdraw their share of amounts given to an irrevocable trust *(demand right)*, the gifts are considered present-interest gifts and qualify for the annual gift-tax exclusion. Once the temporary term expires, the "Crummey" right lapses and the trustee can invest the gift funds for the future benefit of the trust beneficiaries.

The benefit of using the Crummey withdrawal notice to convert a future gift (such as life-insurance proceeds) into a present gift requires very careful drafting by an attorney who specializes in estate planning, because the law governing trusts includes a rule that may limit the amount of gift to $5,000 or 5 percent of the trust principal each year (otherwise known as the *five-and-five rule*). In many situations, you will want the gift to exceed this amount, typically up to the limit of the annual gift tax exclusion ($11,000 per beneficiary or $22,000 on "split gifts" in 2003). Proper drafting and structuring of the trust by a qualified attorney can overcome the five-and-five rule limitation and also make sure the gifts to the trust fit within the grantor's GST tax exemption, allowing the trust proceeds to benefit more than one generation without tax.

Leveraging strategies

There are several ways to leverage the gifts made to the dynasty trust. Often, the trust invests in life insurance on the grantor's life to increase the trust's value on a guaranteed basis from the first day of the investment in the policy. Probably the greatest effect may be achieved by having the dynasty trust invest in second-to-die or survivorship life insurance on the lives of the grantor and his or her spouse. With this insurance only one benefit is paid even though two lives are insured, at the time of the second death. Survivorship is less expensive than other types of insurance, so more insurance may be purchased with the same amount of money. It is not unusual for a dynasty trust to own very large policies ($20 million, $50 million, or more on the lives of the parents). Additionally, because two lives are insured but the only benefit paid is at the second death, it is possible to insure a person who is "rated," not in good health, or even uninsurable if the other party is insurable.

Other forms of leverage relate to the type of asset transferred to the trust and the type of investments made by the trust. Although cash and marketable securities may be transferred, interests in closely held businesses, real estate, and family limited partnerships (FLPs) are better because they are potentially subject to substantial valuation discounts. For example, if a marketable security has a fair market value of $2 million, the same security in an FLP will usually be entitled to marketability and minority discounts. These discounts may reduce the value for gift-tax purposes by 20 to 50 percent. For example, with a discount of 50 percent, the parents may transfer stocks worth $4 million at a gift tax value of $2 million. (Valuation discounts and FLPs are discussed in greater detail later in this book.)

Benefits of a Dynasty Trust

Continuity of Exemptions

In addition to avoiding gift or estate taxes on the appreciation and accumulated income, lifetime funding of a dynasty trust offers other benefits. Because a dynasty trust is irrevocable, future changes in the transfer tax laws should not affect it. Thus, the grantor is assured of receiving the benefits of the GST exemption and any applicable credit equivalent exemption amounts used in funding the trust, and those benefits cannot be eliminated if the exemption or applicable exemption amount is reduced in the future. As the GST exemption is adjusted, as noted earlier, it should be possible to add to the trust beyond the initial $1.1 million per-donor GST tax exemption. Of course, the income taxation of the trust will be subject to the income tax laws and any changes to those laws.

Taxation

To avoid the higher income tax rates that apply to trust income, the grantor can arrange to have any trust income taxed to him or her while alive by designing the trust to intentionally violate tax rules known as the *grantor trust rules* (see Chapter 13). This provides an added benefit for the beneficiaries, as the trust can retain and invest funds that would have otherwise been paid out for income taxes.

Planning Flexibility

A dynasty trust may take any number of forms, depending on the desires of the grantor. All the property of a grantor can be held as a single fund for all descendants, or it can be split into separate trusts, one for each child of the grantor and his or her family line. In a typical trust, the trustee can distribute trust property to one or more beneficiaries according to whatever standards of distribution the grantor includes in the trust, so the trust assets should be viewed as readily available to the family. It is even possible to name the beneficiary (or beneficiaries) as trustee or co-trustee of a dynasty trust, thereby providing maximum flexibility. For example, a grantor spouse may act as trustee as well as an income beneficiary (see "Spousal Estate Reduction Trust" in Chapter 3). When the spouse dies, the trust assets can be split into separate trusts with each child acting as trustee of his or her own dynasty trust.

Personalized Provisions

Another benefit of a dynasty trust is the ability to include provisions for the specific needs of children or other heirs. In essence, a grantor can include virtually anything in a dynasty trust, as long as it is not illegal or against public policy. For example, a wealthy couple desired to set up a dynasty trust but were concerned about a daughter who dropped out of school at an early age, divorced, and was out of work. Concerned about their daughter's lifestyle and spending habits, the couple included a provision in their dynasty trust which required that the daughter finish school (which the dynasty trust would pay for) and obtain a degree before receiving any substantial wealth from the trust. In addition, they tied the amount of future distributions from the trust to the amount of earnings from her future employment. This plan allowed the parents to pass on more than just their wealth: It was a way to pass on some incentive.

Creditor Protection

Neither the income nor the principal of a dynasty trust is subject to the claims of the maker's creditors or attachment resulting from a lawsuit or divorce unless the transfer into the trust was made to avoid creditors (such as a fraudulent transfer). Because the assets and their income have irrevocably been given away, creditors have no rights to them.

The same is true for the beneficiaries of the dynasty trust. Creditors and divorcing spouses of the beneficiaries have no right to the trust's assets even if the trustee of the trust is the beneficiary. However, any assets and/or income paid out to beneficiaries may be subject to the claims of creditors.

Disadvantages of the Dynasty Trust

As with all planning strategies, there are a few drawbacks associated with using a dynasty trust. Because the dynasty trust is irrevocable, it is essential that both the maker and his or her advisors have a clear understanding of its operation in light of the objectives involved before a dynasty trust is implemented.

One problem with a dynasty trust is the grantor's loss of income and net worth when he or she funds the trust. Once gifts are made to a dynasty trust by the grantor, the assets and the future income from them are *irrevocably gone*. However, a married grantor may name a spouse as a beneficiary of his or her dynasty trust, thereby benefiting indirectly from the trust as long as that spouse is alive. Thus, even though the dynasty trust is often referred to as a generation-skipping trust, it doesn't have to skip or disinherit anyone.

Another drawback is the administration required with a dynasty trust. Choosing the right trustees and ensuring compliance with the rules regarding demand-right, "Crummey" beneficiaries is critical. In addition, the monitoring of life insurance and/or other financial products that are owned by the trust is important to ensure that the goals of the dynasty trust are met.

The Rule Against Perpetuities

A dynasty trust is typically structured to continue in existence for the maximum period of time permitted under applicable state law. In most states, this legal maximum is limited by a doctrine known as the *rule against perpetuities*. Under this rule, the typical trust must come to an end after about 80 to 120 years. Thus, state law effectively limits the estate tax, creditor, and spousal protection benefits of the trust vehicle to this period of time. At the end of the period, trust assets must be distributed and eventually subject to estate or gift taxes—which often causes family holdings to be sold. For example, the recent sale of the *Boston Globe,* was prompted by the expiration of family trusts that had owned the newspaper since 1872.

Some states such as Michigan have adopted a statute that allows for a flat period of 90 years before a trust must terminate. Although it is not necessary for a dynasty trust to continue for the full 90 years, by doing so the trust property can be sheltered from transfer taxes for the longest possible time.

Several other states either have abolished the rule against perpetuities or permit the trust maker to opt out of the rule by specifying an express term of the trust. Trusts may continue for as long as the grantor desires in these states: Alaska, Arizona, Delaware, Idaho, Illinois, Maine, Maryland, New Jersey, Ohio, Rhode Island, South Dakota, and Wisconsin. Therefore, trusts that have a trustee or co-trustee in one of these states may continue forever and grow without the threat of the federal transfer tax system consuming a huge portion of trust assets. Several additional states are contemplating changes in their state laws that would eliminate or substantially modify the rule against perpetuities. For example, Florida has not repealed the rule, but it permits trusts to last for 360 years. The dynasty trust uses funds that otherwise would have been paid to the IRS to invest for the benefit of future generations of trust beneficiaries.

Of the states that have eliminated the rule against perpetuities, South Dakota and Alaska give a dynasty trust the best edge because they have no state income tax. In addition, Florida also does not have a state income tax. If the trust is set up in one of these states, more of its income can stay in the trust so the trust will grow even faster. To establish a trust in Florida, South Dakota, or Alaska, it is only necessary to have a trustee or co-trustee, such as a trust company, in that state.

An irrevocable Alaskan trust may even allow the grantor to be a trust beneficiary (under certain conditions) and still make a completed gift that removes the asset from his or her estate. (See Chapter 21.) As you can see, the state where the trust is set up can make a *big* difference.

Summary

Here is a summary of how the typical dynasty trust operates:

- The grantor gives property to the trustee of the dynasty trust, which is controlled by the laws of the state in which the trust is formed.
- There can be one or more grantors and one or more trustees of a dynasty trust.
- The trustee generally cannot be the grantor but can be another individual (including a beneficiary or a professional advisor), a bank trust department, or a trust company. The trustee administers the trust and

invests the trust assets. To allow the trust to last more than 90 years, at least one trustee must reside in a state that does not have the rule against perpetuities.

- The descendants are usually the beneficiaries of a dynasty trust.
- The dynasty trust may have *demand-right powers.* If it does, the trustee notifies the *demand-right beneficiaries,* who have a limited period of time to withdraw the grantor's gift. The demand right allows gifts to the trust to qualify for the $11,000 annual gift exclusion. If the beneficiaries do not exercise their demand right, the funds stay in trust and are frequently used to leverage the gift assets via life insurance on the grantor and his or her spouse.
- At the death of the grantor, the trust principal, including any life insurance proceeds, is *not* subject to gift, estate, or income taxes. At the death of each generation of trust beneficiaries, the trust continues to shelter trust assets from all gift and estate taxes.
- The trustee of the dynasty trust administers the trust as provided in the trust agreement. Generally, trust income and principal are used for the health, education, maintenance, and support of descendants on the basis of needs.
- A beneficiary may be a trustee or co-trustee of his or her separate share trust.
- A dynasty trust ends *only* when it runs out of assets or no more descendants are living. In the latter case, the trust usually pays the funds to a charity or charities that the grantor has named in the trust instrument.

🛡 🛡 🛡

Several aspects of the dynasty trust are beyond the scope of this book and should be discussed in detail with your advisors. As with all estate planning, it is important to work with estate planning attorneys and financial advisors to review your personal situation and create an overall estate planning strategy based on your specific goals and objectives.

5 The Box

(The author is indebted to Guy E. Baker and Jeff Oberholtzer for the material in this chapter, which is adapted from their publication, "The Box.")

W*hen Hal and Helen Bernstein first came to my office after attending a seminar on estate planning, they were distrustful of new advisors, especially if the topic of insurance was involved in the discussion. Their anger stemmed from an experience with one particular insurance agent whose advice they had followed years earlier. Because of his bad advice they felt that their estate plan was "full of errors" and their life insurance was "all screwed up."*

One of their biggest problems was a $1.5 million insurance policy that was about to lapse for lack of cash value. The insurance carrier had financial problems and had been in receivership for the previous five years. The Bernsteins were paying the minimum premium, which equaled the cost of the insurance. Although this amount was less than their original premium, they had no cash value and none was building up to help keep the premium "level" in the face of increasing mortality charges. In effect, their policy had turned from a "permanent" policy to an annually increasing term insurance policy. Helen was angry and often referred to the fact that the agent had promised them the premium would "never go up," so they had never contemplated that they might have to pay higher and/or more premiums than planned or face losing their insurance.

The Bernsteins did not understand the purpose of cash value in their policy. To make matters worse, they couldn't get the answers to many of their questions from the insurance company because, being in receivership, it was very hesitant to give out information. Perhaps the company feared losing too many policyholders once they realized how little interest was being paid on policy cash values.

In the 16 months I spent helping the Bernsteins revise their estate plan, I was able to earn their trust and confidence. Part of this was accomplished by teaching them how to understand their insurance by means of the "box concept," which is a no-nonsense description of how life insurance works.

🛡 🛡 🛡

To understand the value of life insurance in estate planning, you first should understand life insurance, and that's not as easy as it sounds. Most people—even financial professionals—are confused by life insurance. Buyers are often mystified by its complexity, structure, and pricing. In fact, most people don't feel very comfortable with the entire subject of life insurance. But it's too important to the financial fabric of the family and business to be ignored. And it is a vitally important strategy in sound estate planning.

Many financial writers and commentators have made their living trying to explain how insurance actually works. The jargon and vocabulary often stop people cold. What most buyers want to know is quite simple: What is the best policy for me? How much insurance should I buy? What will it cost?

When these questions go unanswered or confusion clouds the real value of insurance, and buyers often make a purchase that ends up not providing the expected benefit, or they make no purchase at all. This chapter is designed to clear up some basic confusions and provide a simple vocabulary to let you communicate your questions.

Definition of Life Insurance

Before explaining the key to understanding life insurance, let's define "insurance" along with a few fundamental terms.

Insurance is a legal contract referred to as a "policy." It guarantees to pay a certain sum of money (death proceeds) to a specified person or entity (the beneficiary) when the insured dies. The policy remains in effect as long as the cost for it (the premium) has been paid according to contractual provisions.

You can own the policy personally or have someone else own it instead. The owner has the legal right to name the beneficiary and may change the beneficiary at any time. The owner is responsible for the tax-consequences of the premium and the death benefits.

Most people don't think of it this way, but life insurance is risk-sharing between a group of people with the common goal of providing money for beneficiaries when a policy owner dies. It is most often purchased because a purchaser loves someone or something. It can be used to:

- Pay a debt.
- Finance a tax obligation.
- Purchase an interest in a business.
- Buy a piece of property.
- Provide guaranteed income and financial security for loved ones.
- Pay estate taxes.

Life insurance can also be used by a corporation to recover the cost of an obligation (or a promise) made by the employer to an employee. For example, an employer may want to recover costs for an advance of insurance payments or promised retirement benefits. Life insurance is often the *only* way that the owner of the policy can provide money to meet these needs. And in most cases, it is the least expensive solution to these problems.

Life insurance is based on the mathematical principle of probability. People die according to a predictable pattern. This pattern is reflected in a mortality table that is based on accumulated historical data. Insurance companies don't know who in a group will die in a given year—they just know how many. This predictable pattern and the amount of coverage, is then mathematically converted into a lump-sum amount. The company needs this amount in order to make the contractual payment at death.

The lump sum is usually financed with annual payments based on a specified rate of interest. By providing coverage to hundreds of thousands of people, insurance companies can offer coverage to each insured for a small amount of money each year. Because each insured pays a proportionate share, a large lump sum is available when an insured dies. Life insurance is *not* a gamble. It is a proven mathematical principle based on probability and it is available to anyone who can qualify.

With this background, let's look at how insurance works.

Understanding Life Insurance

Life insurance is based on the statistical odds of one person among a group of insureds dying. Life insurance is simply a group sharing the same risk who fund the dollars needed when a member of the group dies. The first to die are paid by the last to die. So, let's consider a group of 1,000 men who are 45-years-old. Insurance company mortality tables assume that they are all in good health today but project that none will be alive by age 100. The mortality chart shown in Table 5-1 predicts the chances of a person's death in any given year between ages 45 and 100.

Let's assume the money earns no interest. If all participants die according to statistical probability, there will be enough funds to pay each participant his or her share of the account. Those who die early will benefit most on the basis of the ratio of their contribution to the proceeds. Those who die later will still receive proceeds, but they will have paid more compared to those who died early.

When interest earnings are factored in, the last to die will still have to pay more into the fund than the first. However the compound interest earnings will offset the need for them to place the full value of their expected benefits into the pot.

Staying with the group of 1,000 healthy 45-year-old males, let's follow what is likely to occur if they want $1 million of insurance.

Determining the Cost

The cost of their insurance is determined by the relative probability of death at various ages. If the people in this group die as predicted by the mortality table, one of them will die in the first year. The cost of this death to the group is $1 million. Spreading this cost over the group of 1,000 people ($1 million/1,000) results in a cost of $1,000 per person.

However, at 50 years of age, two of the original 1,000 will die each year. This equates to a cost of two deaths times $1 million of insurance divided by approximately 1,000 people, or $2,000 per person. At age 60, the cost is $4,145 per person, at age 70 the cost is $16,949 per person, and so on.

When you graph the outcome of this analysis, you get the curve pictured in Figure 5-1 on page 77. Notice the flat part of the curve in the beginning. Obviously, the coverage is very inexpensive to own during the early years. The real increases in the cost of coverage come in the later years.

So, how does an insurance company develop information about a group of people to build a mortality table? Each insurance company has created its own

TABLE 5-1 Age-45 Mortality Table

Age	Chance death, %	No. living	No. deaths	Age	Chance death, %	No. living	No. deaths
45	0.11	1000	1	73	3.59	810	30
46	0.12	999	1	74	4.26	776	35
47	0.13	997	1	75	5.01	737	39
48	0.14	996	1	76	5.89	693	43
49	0.15	995	1	77	6.93	645	48
50	0.16	993	2	78	7.81	595	50
51	0.17	991	2	79	10.22	534	61
52	0.19	990	2	80	11.10	475	59
53	0.21	987	2	81	12.36	416	59
54	0.23	985	2	82	13.41	360	56
55	0.25	983	3	83	14.55	308	52
56	0.28	980	3	84	15.78	259	49
57	0.32	977	3	85	17.09	215	44
58	0.35	973	3	86	18.51	175	40
59	0.39	970	4	87	20.03	140	35
60	0.44	965	4	88	21.66	110	30
61	0.49	961	5	89	23.40	84	26
62	0.54	955	5	90	25.26	63	21
63	0.60	950	6	91	27.24	46	17
64	0.66	943	6	92	29.34	32	13
65	0.73	937	7	93	31.57	22	10
66	0.82	929	8	94	33.92	15	7
67	0.94	920	9	95	36.40	9	5
68	1.03	911	9	96	39.00	6	4
69	1.14	900	10	97	41.72	3	2
70	1.68	885	15	98	44.55	2	1
71	2.25	865	20	99	49.00	1	1
72	2.88	840	25	100	56.00	0	1

Source: Adapted with permission from "The Box," by G. Baker and J. Oberholtzer.

data bank of experience based on its own book of insurance in force. In addition, the industry has calculated nationwide statistical measurements of mortality probabilities.

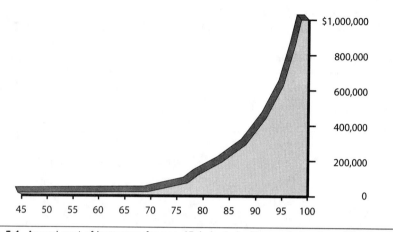

Figure 5-1. Annual cost of insurance for age 45 (adapted with permission from "The Box," by G. Baker and J. Oberholtzer).

Each company's table is based on death claims over an extended period of time. The national statistics are developed without the benefit of any physical determinations, but all the company tables assume quality underwriting and good health. This means that company underwriters have received full disclosure of any medical history so that they can make an accurate assessment of the insured's health. If, from the outset, a company can eliminate people who are in poor health from its table of experience, it stands to reason that the table will be more reflective of the actual statistical probability of death for the company's insureds.

Now ask yourself which would you rather buy: Insurance based on statistics developed from the population at large, or insurance based on a select group of people who are all in excellent health and have a lifestyle that suggests they will maintain their health over time?

To determine pricing, insurance companies select the mortality table most appropriate to the risk they are willing to insure. If medical information is not readily available, the company uses the mortality table that best reflects that higher risk.

Without dwelling on the relative merits of these tables, it is important to understand that each table measures the cost of dying for different groups of people. Figure 5-2 on the next page shows the difference between five commonly used methods for determining premiums.

Life expectancy and cost

When is the best time to measure the cost of insurance: Age 50? 60? 90? Any specific age would be arbitrary. We think life expectancy is the most

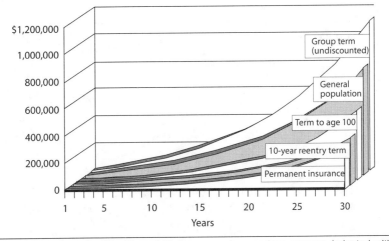

Figure 5-2. Premiums for $1 million of life insurance from various sources (adapted with permission from "The Box," by G. Baker and J. Oberholtzer).

meaningful calculation, but most people don't understand the *true* meaning of life expectancy.

When the newspapers announce that the life expectancy of a male in the United States is 71.2 years, the figure sends shivers down most spines. Fortunately, life expectancy is not the age at which a person is *expected* to die. Instead, *life expectancy* (LE) is the predicted age at which half of the people in the measured group will be dead. It is the median age of death for the group. But LE is different for each given age group at a point in time.

So, when the papers say that LE is 71.2 for males and 75.4 for females, they mean for people being *born* at the time of the statistic. The LE for a 45-year-old, as shown in Table 5-2 on page 80, is 80.58. That means that 50 percent of all 45-year-olds in the group will be dead by age 80.58. But it also means that 50 percent of the group will still be alive. In other words, you have a 50 percent chance of living longer than the LE. An 80-year-old male has an LE of 85. Even a 95-year-old has an LE. Table 5-2 shows life expectancies for various ages of males and females in the general population.

The Cumulative Cost

Many people don't count the cost of insurance over an extended period of time—they only focus on the cost today! However, what happens when you add up the total cost of insurance (the mortality costs) from today until life expectancy? Figure 5-3 on page 81 shows these results.

TABLE 5-2 Life Expectancy

Age	Age at life expectancy	Age	Age at life expectancy	Age	Age at life expectancy
45	80.58	64	81.05	83	87.60
46	80.59	65	81.11	84	88.34
47	80.60	66	81.18	85	89.09
48	80.61	67	81.25	86	89.86
49	80.62	68	81.33	87	90.66
50	80.63	69	81.42	88	91.47
51	80.65	70	81.55	89	92.28
52	80.67	71	81.72	90	93.09
53	80.60	72	81.93	91	93.93
54	80.70	73	82.20	92	94.79
55	80.72	74	82.51	93	95.67
56	80.75	75	82.86	94	96.56
57	80.77	76	83.26	95	97.44
58	80.80	77	83.72	96	98.30
59	80.83	78	84.21	97	99.17
60	80.87	79	84.84	98	100.00
61	80.91	80	85.49	99	100.90
62	80.95	81	86.17	100	
63	81.00	82	86.87		

Source: Adapted with permission from "The Box," by G. Baker and J. Oberholtzer.

Assume you are part of our example group of 45-year-old males. The sum of the mortality costs to life expectancy is 74.7 percent of the face amount for a 45-year-old male. So, if you wanted to own $1 million of insurance starting today and you paid the annual mortality costs every year until your life expectancy, you would pay $747,000.

This cost has been measured for more than 20 major insurance companies and the cumulative rates all come out within dollars of each other. Actuaries (the mathematicians trained to calculate the cost of insurance) all work from the same base of statistics. Every insurance carrier must mathematically be near the same target; a carrier that isn't has violated the fundamental theory of risk sharing.

But let's look at what happens if you are "unfortunate" enough to live until two-thirds of the initial group is dead. This is called the *first standard deviation from the mean*. The standard deviation is the next statistical breaking

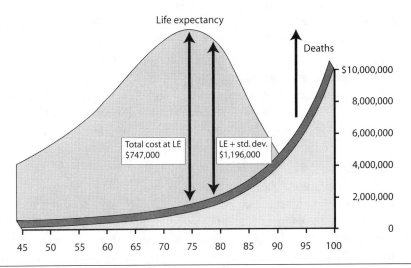

Figure 5-3. Cost at life expectancy (adapted with permission from "The Box," by G. Baker and J. Oberholtzer).

point from the average age of death (usually 6 to 8 years later). Let's add up all the mortality costs for $1 million of insurance at one standard deviation. The total equals 119 percent of the face amount. That's right—you would have to pay $1,196,000 for $1 million of coverage if you died at the two-thirds point.

It gets worse. What if you should live two standard deviations (when 95 percent of the group is dead) beyond the mean? The ratio of mortality costs to benefits increases to 240 percent. That means you have paid $2.4 million for $1 million of insurance. It's "expensive" to live a long time if you want to retain your insurance.

Consequences of Aging

Okay, here's a test: What would you do if you were 80 years old and your insurance premium notice came in the mail telling you to pay $150,000 this year for your $1 million policy? Most people would say they wouldn't pay it and throw the notice away. They would let the policy lapse and laugh at the absurdity of paying $150,000 that year. However let's change the scenario. Suppose you just came back from your physician and knew you had only six months to live. Now what would you do?

Most of us have had enough experience with people dying to know it is only the "fortunate" who die quickly. There are those who linger for months—sometimes years. Terminally ill people still get mail, and their mail may include a bill for life insurance premiums. If you were terminally ill, would you laugh and throw the premium notice away as well? Of course not.

The ability to choose to keep your policy on the basis of health conditions creates *adverse selection* against the insurance company. Deciding whether to keep the insurance solely on the basis of probability of death ruins the mathematical principle. Insurance must have statistical randomness to protect the integrity of the product. There must be an incentive for healthy insureds to stay in the pool.

It has been said that the actuaries calculate insurance premiums so that the policy will lapse the day before the insured dies. But statistically, very few (less than 1 percent) pure insurance policies (term) ever pay a claim. People can't afford to pay the term insurance premiums when they are most likely to die. As the price rises, if the only insureds who retain their policies are those who know their chances of claim are certain, the insurance carrier faces financial crisis.

In the early 1800s, only people who were "near dying" retained insurance. And because there were no healthy insureds left to pay premiums, what happened? If you guessed bankruptcy, you are correct. Virtually all insurance companies now in business started after 1820. That's because so many of the older companies went out of business due to this adverse-selection problem.

So the insurance companies called in the actuaries and told them to solve the problem. The actuaries sat with their abacuses and determined there was only one solution—*the box.*

The Box

The actuaries developed a solution that made retaining lifelong insurance possible: Insurance companies had to help insureds "prefund" their insurance premiums so that they could afford to retain their coverage throughout their lives. As you have seen, if they only offered insurance premium plans on a "pay-as-you-go" basis, no one would ever be able to keep his or her insurance in old age.

That's where the box comes in. The *box* is an individual account in an insurance policy. It holds all the premium payments the insured makes (see Figure 5-4). From the box, the insurance company pays the annual cost of insurance (mortality costs) and policy expenses.

Unfortunately, the cost of funding the box without interest was still too expensive. So the actuaries had to add an interest element to the box. The insurance company invests the premiums it receives (net of expenses) and

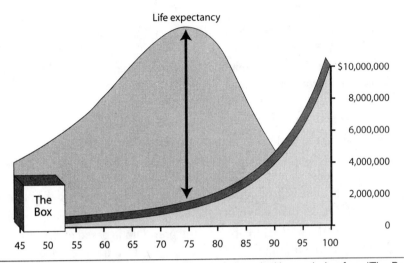

Figure 5-4. Cost of coverage deposited in the box (adapted with permission from "The Box," by G. Baker and J. Oberholtzer).

then allocates the net earnings to the box after management fees. The amount allocated varies according to the insurance contract.

In 1913, Congress passed the Sixteenth Amendment, authorizing the collection of income taxes. The insurance industry successfully sought regulatory relief to allow the money in the box to grow without tax. Thus, the government actually subsidizes the cost of insurance as a contribution to the welfare of society.

Box Designs

Once the concept of the box was developed, insurance carriers began to design different configurations. A policyholder could purchase an insurance contract which required premiums for specific periods, say, 20 years or until age 65. As the market developed different needs, the carriers responded with appropriate policy designs. One type is called *whole life*. The premiums are fixed on the basis of a guaranteed interest rate the carrier is offering in the box.

Any excess interest earnings, adjustments to mortality experience, and expense loads are credited and debited to the box through dividends. These dividends combine the earnings and costs together in one amount. This is often referred to as the *bundled approach*.

In recent years, some insurance carriers have expanded their portfolio to include a product which allows the policyholder to determine the amount of premium and frequency of payment. This policy is called *universal life*. Although universal life can be mathematically designed to look more favorable than whole life (you pay a lower premium for the same coverage, for example), remember that the box still needs the same amount of money to accomplish the same objective over the same period of time.

It is important to understand that if all the assumptions for whole life and universal life are the same (same mortality table, expense loads, and interest credit rate), the cost should be the same and the outcome should be the same. With whole life, there is little control over these assumptions, and the premium is fixed according to the guaranteed interest rate in the contract.

With a typical universal life policy, the premium is based on the projected interest rate over the lifetime of the policy contract. If the guaranteed rate is 4 percent for a whole life contract and the projected rate is 6 percent for the universal life contract, then the annual premium you would pay will be lower for the universal life policy. Why? It is assumed that the higher interest earned in the box will make up the difference in premium deposits. However, when you factor in the dividend credit for the whole life policy, which will match the 6 percent performance of the universal life policy, both approaches should end up economically the same.

The main difference between whole life and universal life is the flexibility the policyholder has to skip premiums if he or she can't afford to pay them in one or more years. However, this freedom may ultimately jeopardize the goal of lifetime coverage if insufficient premiums have been deposited—this would defeat the entire purpose of using the box in the first place.

If the projected lump-sum value of the box falls below the target, the insurance carrier is unable to fulfill the terms of the contract. Either the policy will be discontinued or the annual funding amounts will be increased. This is true for both universal and whole life policies, although individual companies deal with the problem differently.

If you have a whole life policy, you can be underfunded if you borrow too much from the box, fail to pay the interest on the policy loans, or fail to pay your scheduled premiums. With universal life, you become underfunded by failing to have enough in the box to pay the annual mortality costs. Ultimately, the result is the same. The policy will be canceled for insufficient funds.

There are many reasons why advisors favor one type of insurance over the other. However, in the end, the box must have enough money to pay the mortality costs or you will be faced with paying them yourself. (Whole life,

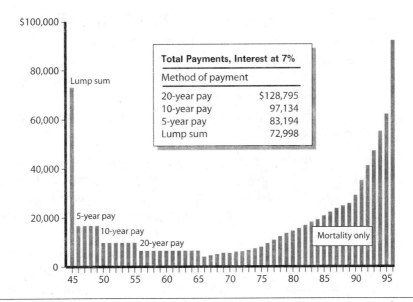

Total Payments, Interest at 7%	
Method of payment	
20-year pay	$128,795
10-year pay	97,134
5-year pay	83,194
Lump sum	72,998

Figure 5-5. Different ways to fill the box (adapted with permission from "The Box," by G. Baker and J. Oberholtzer).

universal life, and other types of life insurance policies are discussed in greater detail in the next chapter.)

Insurance Pricing

Before looking at pricing in detail, let's recap some earlier points: Probability is the key to determining insurance premiums. People die according to a predictable pattern of death depicted in a mortality table. The predictable pattern and the face amount of the policy are mathematically converted into a lump-sum target that must be in the box in order to fund the contractual promise made by the policy. This amount can be financed by estimating the annual premium needed by the box in order to stay on target for the lump sum.

As mentioned earlier, total mortality costs at life expectancy for a 45-year-old male are 74.7 percent of the projected death benefit. Figure 5-5 shows the total amount of payments required to fund this 74.7 percent for a $1 million policy, assuming 7 percent interest. Notice the different amounts required at various funding periods. The single-payment lump sum required in the box is only $72,998. However, if the insured elects to fund the box over five years, the total payment increases to $83,194 ($16,639 annually), and over a 20-year period, to $128,795 ($6,440 annually). But how do insurance companies determine these prices?

Four specific factors affect the amount you have to put into the box:

1. The predictable pattern of death (mortality costs).
2. The cost of doing business (expenses).
3. The amount of interest credited to the box each year (interest credits, which are sometimes called *dividends*).
4. The number of people who actually keep their insurance policies ("persistency").

Your individual account (the box) holds your annual payments or your lump-sum deposit as long as you retain the insurance contract. As long as all the original assumptions are achieved, the value of the box will increase to meet the projected lump-sum target according to the illustration provided by the insurance company.

Each year, the box must pay the annual cost of insurance (mortality costs) and the policy expenses. The box also receives the interest credited each year by the insurance company. The box provides a way to prefund the cost of insurance so that compound interest can actually pay the insurance costs at older ages.

What happens if someone wants to cancel his or her insurance early? In the first year or two there may be a significant difference between premiums paid and the surrender value of the policy. This is primarily due to expenses and surrender charges for early withdrawal. The box must be assessed a surrender charge if the insurance company hasn't recovered all its start-up expenses. It usually takes between five and 15 years for a company to recover its costs.

Assumptions Versus Results

Insurance company projections are based on assumptions. So, the actual results may vary from the original illustration depending on the actual performance of the four pricing factors. The box will adjust in size to accommodate the performance of these factors. It will get bigger, smaller, or possibly, stay the same size.

What if interest rates fall, expenses rise, or people die faster than expected? The box will need more money than originally illustrated to subsidize the changes in the assumption. To increase the size of the box, you will either have to pay premiums longer (for both whole life and universal life) or have to increase your annual payments (universal life only) in order to reach your targeted lump sum. Remember, you have to fund 74.7 percent of the mortality costs by life expectancy.

But the opposite is true if interest rates rise, expenses fall, or people live longer. The box will not need as much money from you as originally illustrated. The box can become smaller to reflect the improved performance. As a result, you might pay premiums for fewer years, or you could reduce your annual payments.

In the final analysis, the box must have enough money to equal the mathematical lump sum targeted by the insurance company for your age. Otherwise, the company will be unable to stay in business. If it has underfunded all its contracts, the company won't have enough assets to meet its obligations.

The Pricing Factors in Detail

Let's examine the four pricing factors to see how much impact future economic conditions can have on the box. Illustrations of the box will vary from company to company according to how each firm handles these factors. If a carrier uses assumptions that are too aggressive, the box may not achieve the performance illustrated.

It is virtually impossible for most insurance buyers to know for certain how the four factors will affect the specific product they purchased. But the surest way to protect yourself is by asking for a copy of the company "IQ," or *illustration questionnaire.* All insurance companies have been asked to voluntarily provide their respective IQ. In it, questions about pricing assumptions for the four factors are clearly stated, and the answers should be easy to understand. If they are not, or if the carrier does not have an IQ, perhaps you should look elsewhere for your coverage.

Many insurance buyers believe that an illustration comparison between companies is a valid method for determining the best product to purchase. However, purchasing a policy because one illustration shows better results than another may be the wrong approach. The "best" illustration might be based on very aggressive assumptions that make a direct comparison with an illustration from a company with more conservative assumptions impossible.

Let's look at some of the specific issues that affect the pricing structure of the box.

Mortality costs

As medical technology improves, people have been living longer. So, what happens to the box if the mortality experience for the insurance company is different from that projected in your illustration? The company's actual mortality experience results from how long the people it insures actually live. If its underwriting assessment was shoddy and inaccurate, the pool of the insured may die too soon. The company's financial reserves will be impaired and this will affect all the other policies. The company will need to raise mortality costs, and doing so will drain money from your box faster than expected. This could cause you to pay more in premiums.

Unforeseen negative events can also cause problems for an insurance company. For instance, the AIDS epidemic could affect the overall mortality experience of the industry or of a particular company. An outbreak of an unknown virus or other illness might adversely affect the statistics. Any such occurrences could cause the box to be underfunded and unable to generate enough compound interest to pay the increased mortality costs in future years.

On the other hand, breakthroughs in medical care could reduce the company's mortality costs. The box would grow faster because lower costs are being deducted. Some insurance companies are very aggressive and anticipated improvements in mortality costs when they designed their illustrations. Check to make sure the carrier's IQ clearly discloses how such assumptions are made and how much the savings are projected to improve the firm's product. If it doesn't, stay away from the company's box.

Expenses

Expenses associated with an insurance policy include administration, premium taxes, federal DAC taxes (deferred acquisition costs levied on insurance company profits), and sales commissions. Another cost factor is risk capital. Companies also have to measure the cost impact that poor investment results might have on their products. A conservative company will project expenses in its illustration, including a factor for inflation. A more aggressive company will often hold expenses steady, assuming there will be no increases for the maintenance of its contracts over the next 20 or 30 years. Again, the IQ should disclose how the carrier has priced its product to reflect its projected expense loads.

Interest credits

Interest credits are the third factor in the pricing equation. Premiums (net of expenses) are invested by the company in a variety of bonds, stocks, and mortgages. The returns credited to the box are based on the investment's performance.

In recent years, some insurance companies credited interest in anticipation of earnings they had not yet achieved. The company illustrations showed the box growing much faster than current performance could support. Carriers justified this, as interest rates were rising and their investment portfolios were benefiting from the higher investment yields. But when interest rates declined, the

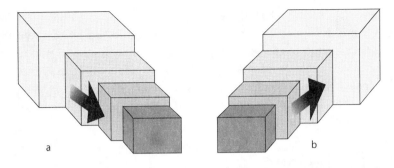

Figure 5-6. Dynamics of the box: a. When interest rates rise, the box becomes smaller. b. With falling interest rates, the box must become larger. (Adapted with permission from "The Box," by G. Baker and J. Oberholtzer.)

same illustrations, which were originally based on higher rates, look substantially worse since they never achieved the original level of anticipated returns.

Persistency

Persistency refers to the number of policies that stay in force from inception to death. Adverse selection can negatively affect the financial stability of a company, and persistency is directly tied to the same problem.

An important aspect of persistency is the acquisition cost for each policy. It takes several years (usually five to 15) before an insurance company can recover its costs. If a policy terminates before the company has recovered all its costs, this could adversely affect other policyholders and the profitability of the company.

Persistency can also affect your policy through *lapse-supported pricing*. Some companies assume that an inordinate number of policies will terminate before the death of the insured. (By assuming lower death benefits will be paid, they can project higher insurance benefits for a lower premium cost.) But if the policies do not lapse, the higher benefit payments will hurt the company's financial performance and affect your box.

Box Dynamics

The size of the box will expand or contract depending on how the four factors perform. If mortality costs or expenses go up or interest goes down, the box must get larger (more premiums required). The insured must either pay the premiums for a longer period of time or pay higher premiums to reach the projected target. Likewise, if mortality costs improve, expenses stabilize or decline, and/or interest rates increase, the box can become smaller; fewer premiums are required to reach the projected target (see Figure 5-6).

The box isn't static. The long-term nature of the insurance obligation makes the box quite dynamic. The size of your box is affected by the investment performance of the insurance company. It is also affected by the ultimate results achieved in the company's underwriting (mortality costs), expense control, and business retention (persistency). A conservative company is more likely to attain its original assumptions than an aggressive company that uses illustrations to attract new business.

Funding the Box

It would be wise for the fiscally prudent insurance buyer to consider overfunding the box to minimize the possible consequences of poor investment performance or overstatement of pricing assumptions.

Consider this question: If you are purchasing life insurance for your *entire* life, do you want to pay the mortality costs on a pay-as-you-go basis each year with your money or would you rather have the box pay them for you from the compound interest and tax benefits?

Before answering this question, let's review: The box is very flexible. When you start your box, you can select *how* you want to fund it. You can put premiums in the box as one lump sum, or you can fund it over five or 10 years (until age 65) or for life. In most cases, you can change your mind and raise or lower your contributions at any time. It is important to remember that the sooner you fill the box, the less you actually pay out of your own pocket.

When you select your box, the target is calculated on certain interest assumptions, mortality costs, and expense assumptions. If interest rates decline or mortality costs rise, the box will need more money. Likewise, if interest rates rise and/or mortality costs drop, the box needs less money. The box should be evaluated every year to determine whether it is on target.

Interest earned by the box is tax-deferred and potentially tax-free if the policy is held until death. Tax is owed on withdrawals in excess of the amount you have deposited into the box. This can be a real economic advantage—so much so that in 1984 Congress instituted Section 7702 of the Internal Revenue Code (IRC). Section 7702 defines life insurance and limits the amount of money you can put into the box. If you exceed that limit, all the earnings in the box become taxable. Your insurance carrier monitors this for you each year to make certain your plan does not exceed these guidelines:

- The amount of contribution you can put into the box ranges between the pure cost of insurance and the maximum amount allowed under Section 7702.

- The minimum amount needed to fund the box is just enough to pay a level contribution to fund the mortality costs until age 95. At this point, the policy would be canceled and you would receive nothing back. However, you can elect to fund for amounts greater than the minimum. But whatever your targeted premium, it is an individual choice based on your individual needs.

Let's assume for the sake of example that you are 45 years old. Let's say you want to have your insurance fully paid by the time you retire. You would design the premium to fill the box during the next 20 years. At the end of that time, if the assumptions are accurate, the policy should stay fully funded for life.

Another option might be to fully pay the box in 10 years. In this instance, the premium would be calculated to fill the box in 10 equal installments. At the end of 10 years if the assumptions are accurate, the box would need no further payments. However, if the performance of the box declines, you would have to deposit some additional premiums even though the 10-year period had been attained. It is better to be conservative and overfund the box than to play it too close and be surprised in your old age. You need a margin to protect yourself against economic change.

There is one final consideration in determining the amount you can put into the box, and it is discussed next.

Modified Endowment Contract

In 1989, Congress placed another limitation on the tax advantages of life insurance. IRC Section 7702 already limited the size of the box, but Congress was concerned that life insurance taxation still offered too many income tax benefits when compared to other investments, especially annuities. So Congress enacted the *modified endowment contract (MEC)* limitation to minimize the tax benefits. This limitation is sometimes referred to as the "seven-pay test" because the limit on how much you can pay into the box is based on the first seven years of the insurance contract.

If the box becomes overfunded (less than the Section 7702 limits but more than the MEC limits), any distributions from the box will be taxed like an annuity. Annuity distributions are taxed on the ratio of the premiums paid to the gain from interest earned. If the box is not a MEC, all premiums come out tax-free before any of the gain is taxed.

Look at Figure 5-7 on page 92, which depicts a range of premiums you can put into the box. Notice that the range starts at the low end, with the pure mortality costs. At the high end, the maximum you can put into the box is

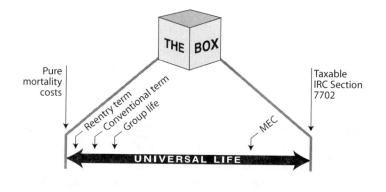

Figure 5-7. Premium cost range to answer the question: "How much can I put into the box?" (Adapted with permission from "The Box," by G. Baker and J. Oberholtzer.)

limited by Section 7702. The MEC limit reduces even further the amount you can put into the box if you want the most advantageous tax treatment on withdrawals. If you are willing to keep the premiums in the box until death, the insurance benefits increase untaxed for your beneficiaries. This could be a significant advantage.

Retail Insurance Pricing

Carriers increase insurance premiums according to the amount of risk they feel they are going to assume in each specific situation. This risk is usually determined by asking the potential insured to provide evidence of health. However, some policies are issued with no evidence of health being required by the carrier. In this situation, the company usually adds a mortality surcharge to offset the possible risk it is accepting. Such loads can increase the cost of insurance as much as 30 to 50 percent or more.

Figure 5-2 illustrates the premiums carriers charge on the basis of the amount of risk they feel they are being asked to accept. The base rate for *group life insurance* products is referred to as "New York Table Y." Depending on competitive pressures and the size of the group, carriers will often discount these costs to obtain new business. Sometimes the discounts are as much as 50 to 70 percent. *Annual renewable term to age 100 (ART-100)* has a premium based on the risk associated with only one physical, conducted when the policy is first issued. After the beginning of the policy, the insurance company must continue to provide insurance coverage as long as the premiums are paid each year.

Reentry term requires that the insured submit new evidence of insurability before the policy will be renewed. The frequency of requalification depends on the contract. It can be every five, 10, 15, or 20 years. If you cannot requalify, you may still keep the policy, but at a significantly higher rate that will increase each year.

It is apparent that carriers set the premiums for their products on the basis of the amount of risk they are contractually assuming and their ability to cancel the policy. If the company has a reasonable expectation of retaining the policy for the lifetime of the insured, it will set the mortality costs at or near its actual experience. The box is the only way the insured can benefit from such savings. In fact, most carriers offer mortality rates as low as or lower than the least expensive term rates to the policyholder who purchases the box.

Investing Money

Once you start putting money into the box, insurance companies will credit interest earnings to your box. There are two different ways they do this:

- *Declared credit rate:* Most policy owners are content to accept the carrier's stated interest rate. This rate changes on the basis of the overall performance of the underlying company assets. Two types of underlying assets (investments) may be offered by carriers: A rate credited to a policy based on the overall assets of the carrier is called *portfolio yield.* A rate based on the return attributed to new money received by the company each year is called *new-money yield.* Over time, the two rates blend together and achieve a similar rate of return. In these types of policies, the insurance carrier will provide a guarantee of the principal in the box.

- *Market rate:* The policyholder may want to assume the investment risk by selecting a variable life product. Such products offer a variety of investment options, which can be diversified according to the risk tolerance of the policyholder. The selections range from cash equivalents (money market, guaranteed government securities) to fixed returns (bonds, high-risk bonds) to equity (balance, index, international, growth). Funds may be shifted by telephone transfer as often as the policyholder desires.

Typically, each fund is managed by experienced, professional investment managers who specialize in particular fields. All funds increase tax-free during the accumulation period. When the policyholder assumes the risk of investment by selecting a particular combination of funds, there is some risk of losing principal. This risk is offset, however, by the potential for gains over a more conservative declared rate. If the plan fails to meet the basic growth assumptions of the funds, the values in the box could be much lower than projected. In this case, the death benefit might decrease, or the policyholder might need to put more premiums into the box to maintain the planned death benefits.

Conclusion

- The application and selection of life insurance products for sophisticated tax, retirement, and estate planning solutions requires more than just a computer illustration.
- "Mortality-only" products offer a temporarily inexpensive solution to the cost of life insurance. However, not everyone wants his or her insurance coverage to disappear (or become too expensive) when it is needed most—near life expectancy.
- The box is a unique means of taking advantage of compound interest in a tax-advantaged way, ultimately paying significantly less for the mortality charges.

🛡 🛡 🛡

Either way, insurance provides a unique product which delivers large amounts of capital for a nominal cost. Over time, the cost of coverage must reflect your older age. If coverage is still desired, the box provides the best, economically acceptable, long-term solution for paying mortality costs.

6 Life Insurance Alternatives

H Having been to several estate planning seminars and after reading two books on the subject, Frank Maida felt he was ready to take the plunge and begin his planning, so our first meeting was very productive. He knew all about revocable and irrevocable trusts, and he even agreed to take a physical exam to see if he qualified for insurance.

When we got to the subject of insurance, Frank was like many other people: he thought all insurance was the same. He didn't understand the difference between whole life and universal life and seemed annoyed when I questioned him about his knowledge. (I think he might have been embarrassed about not knowing.) Nevertheless, I stressed the importance of understanding the various estate planning concepts so that he could make the best choice for his situation and his family. Once we got into it, he realized how important it was to his estate plan and his loved ones to understand the life insurance alternatives.

🛡🛡🛡

Now that you're familiar with the nature of life insurance and how the industry has evolved, it's time for an in-depth look at some of the types of policies that are available.

There are five basic types of policies: whole life, universal life, variable life, indexed life, and term life. Each has a distinct purpose, and the decision regarding which will work best depends on your personal situation and goals.

Whole Life

Whole life, sometimes called *ordinary life, straight life,* or *permanent insurance,* is a traditional insurance policy that is designed to help consumers handle the high cost of insurance in later years when premiums would otherwise become prohibitively expensive to match the increasing risk of death. By averaging out premium costs and amortizing them over the projected lifetime of the policy, whole life guarantees a continued death benefit for the insured's entire life. The fixed annual premiums are usually *level for the life of the insured* and are based on the insured's age and health at the time the policy is issued.

As the whole life insurance premiums are paid, cash value builds up in the early years in excess of the actual insurance costs. This excess is invested, and a return on the invested portion is added back into your policy in the form of dividends. These dividends build up with interest and can provide some flexibility if applied toward premium payments, and they *may* build up to a level that allows you to limit the premium payment period of the policy, but they are not guaranteed. Alternatively, some policies allow you to apply any excess buildup of cash value to the purchase of more insurance. Such additions are known as *paid-up additions.*

Some types of whole life policies are tied more closely to market interest fluctuations and policy performance may vary depending on rates. Such policies are known as *interest-sensitive* whole life.

The guaranteed death benefit and fixed premiums make whole life policies attractive to some but less attractive to others. To some people, whole life means less to worry about later. They know in advance what they will have to pay in premiums and exactly what their death benefits will be. To others, this does not provide enough flexibility. If their situation changes, they will likely be unable to increase or decrease their policy's premiums or death benefit without surrendering their policy and purchasing a new one.

Universal Life

Universal life insurance was developed to overcome the primary disadvantages of whole life insurance. It is another type of cash-value-building policy that provides extreme flexibility by giving the policy owner (you, your spouse, your children, or your trustee) the ability to set and vary premium levels, payment schedules, and death benefits, within certain limits. This increased flexibility makes it easier to adapt universal life policies to changing needs and financial conditions. Much like whole life, a portion of each premium goes to the insurance company to pay for the pure cost of insurance. The amount of premium paid in to the universal life contract that exceeds the pure cost of insurance plus company expenses is credited back to the policy owner with interest. The interest is declared by the insurance company and depends on the earnings of the company's general account, which frequently contains a high percentage of investment-grade bonds. Most universal life policies have a guaranteed level of mortality charge and interest. Any returns above the guaranteed minimum will vary with the performance of the insurance company's portfolio. Universal life expense components are lower than those charged under whole life policies. This provides affordable, low-cost coverage. Unlike whole life policies, universal life policies are transparent: the annual policy report allows the policy owner to see the interest credited, along with all the mortality and expense charges, on a monthly basis. This enables the policy owner to make adjustments to meet his or her needs and objectives.

The advantage of flexibility in universal life allows you to purchase more coverage for the same level of premium dollars paid for whole life. However, it also introduces a certain level of risk, as the mortality charge and/or interest can vary from the assumptions made in computing the target premium. This issue of risk is the most misunderstood element in the purchase of universal life insurance. If the policy assumptions are not realized, the policy may not perform as planned, unless more or higher premiums are paid into the policy (for example, interest rates go down and/or mortality charges go up because of an increase in the number of deaths per thousand).

Universal life allows you to vary the frequency and amount of premiums and even skip planned premiums as long as there is sufficient cash value to cover current charges. You can also purchase a policy with an increasing death benefit, or you can elect to increase the amount of insurance (subject to continued insurability) to meet changes in your situation. Additionally, within certain limits, you can make lump-sum deposits or lump-sum withdrawals much as you can with a bank account. If you want the flexibility to be able to change your premium or death benefit, the universal life policy may be ideal. One drawback, however, is the inability to control where the cash value within these policies is invested.

Variable Life

Variable life is a relatively new form of universal life. It offers all the flexibility that universal life provides but with a unique difference: Cash values are invested in separate account funds, instead of the insurance company's general account, *at the policy owner's direction*. The separate account is made up of a variety of pooled investment divisions that are similar to mutual funds. The policy owner chooses among the various funds offered by the insurer, so investments can be concentrated in a separate account of common stocks, bonds, and other assets that are more volatile but may provide higher long-term results than does an insurer's general account. This enables the policy owner to participate more directly in gains and losses realized by the markets. Thus, good performance in the separate account may make it possible to reduce premium payments, increase the death benefit, withdraw previously paid premiums, or do some combination of these options.

Unlike whole life or universal life, most variable universal life products do not provide a guarantee with respect to either a minimum rate of return or principal. The company guarantees only that the actual investment fund performance, both net investment income and capital gains and losses, will pass directly through to the cash values after reduction for investment expenses and fund operating costs. However, because assets under the variable insurance contract are segregated and held in a separate account, they are protected against any insolvency by the sponsoring insurance company and are not affected by the investment performance of the company's general account.

Variable universal life insurance policies provide maximum flexibility and some very attractive benefits. However, expenses are significantly higher than those for whole life and universal life policies, and there is either a limited or no downside rate-of-return guarantee. Therefore, it is important to do a careful analysis before purchasing this type of policy.

Indexed Life

What is indexed life insurance? The answer is a fairly simple one, but some general comments are needed. All universal life plans are, in essence, "indexed." Admittedly, the vast majority are indexed to the general account earnings of the insurance company selling the product. In other words, the insurance company collects your premium, deducts some expense charges and some cost-of-insurance (mortality) charges, and then puts the rest of the money into its general *premium investment account*. This account is then invested by the company's investment department, usually into several different types of investments. The majority most often goes into government and high-grade corporate bonds. Some will go into mortgages or directly into real estate, and a small portion may even go into common stock or other more speculative instruments. The variety of overall investment vehicles and the percentages put into each will vary by company, competitive pressure, state regulations, the economy generally, and so on. But in the end most insurance companies' overall portfolios will more or less resemble one another. Safety, as well as total return, is important to all.

Of the total earnings on this account, the company will keep some as an investment profit—usually 1 to 1.5 percent. The balance will be deposited in the policyholder's cash-value account. Therefore, it is not unreasonable or inaccurate to say that the insured's policy's rate of return is "indexed" to the company's general portfolio earnings.

The real difference between *equity-indexed* products and the regular fixed-interest universal life plans that have been around for the past 25 years or so is that in indexed plans the policy earnings are tied not to the insurance company's general account portfolio but to the performance of some known and published *stock index*. The most commonly used index to date is the Standard & Poor's 500 stock index, although the Russell 2,000, the Wilshire 5,000, and even the Dow Jones indexes are possible alternatives.

The main requirement is that it be an index of an equity investment that has a market position in call options. This is because an issuing company must be able to "hedge" itself against having to pay a rate of return that it can't cover from its general account earnings. The perfect way for a company to do this is to purchase a call option. This is why indexed life policies are not registered products like individual stocks, bonds, or mutual funds. In these policies *it is not the insured who is buying or investing in the option; it is the insurance company.* The company is doing this to protect itself in regard to its promise to pay a rate of return based on the index it has selected. Though it wouldn't be a very good idea, the company could pay on the basis of some index but never actually invest in such a vehicle. In time, this would prove to be business suicide, but theoretically the company could "index" the policy to anything it chose and then just take its chances that it could cover its promises from internal corporate returns. Of course, this is just theory—it never would be done that way. So, the company buys an option.

The obvious appeal to insureds is that they enjoy the possibility of higher rates of return than those normally offered by fixed-interest investments but have the counterbalancing security of knowing that, unlike variable universal life policies, the indexed version cannot lose its principal investment by going negative. It may go down from hoped-for rates of return, but there is always the safety of the original investment and some modest (typically, 2 to 3 percent) guaranteed interest earnings. Because of this, indexed life has been described by some as being the "perfect compromise," more potential for

TABLE 6-1   Example of Indexed Life Insurance Policy

$10,000	Annual premium received
– 500	A month's worth of mortality & expense charges taken out
$ 9,500	Invested in the general account
$665	The general portfolio account amount earned at 7%
– 66	Kept by the company as investment profit
599	Netted for the client policy
– 237	Set aside (2.5%, a typical minimum interest guaranteed by contract)
$362	Available for purchasing a call option on the chosen index

upside gains without the same measure of downside risk. Perhaps "flying with a parachute" is an apt analogy; we are talking about life insurance (something that's supposed to be a hedge against the risk of loss). The analogy seems most appropriate.

Keep in mind that all equity-indexed plans are not identical. While they all have similarities, there are also some important differences (in option types, option durations, guarantee rates, "either or both" minimum-interest provisions regarding guarantee rates and option gains, bailout provisions, and other unique riders). Before buying, you should review and understand the policy features—as is the case with any policy, whether fixed, indexed, or variable—offered from company to company.

Although there are a few variations on the theme, indexed life policies basically operate as follows: Just as in the case of regular, fixed-interest universal life policies, the company receives the premiums, deducts a month's worth of cost-of-insurance and expense charges, and invests the balance in the company's general portfolio account. At this point, the process begins to differ from regular universal life. Rather than leaving all the excess in the general account, the company deducts some and uses it to purchase a one-year call option on the specific index being used. (An example is shown in Table 6-1. This example, however, is an oversimplification. Companies don't buy an option per life contract issued; they buy options only when there is a large-enough block of business to make the transaction financially feasible.)

Depending on the current price of options, the net dollar amount available will allow the purchase of some amount of call option. How much options it will buy determines what percentage of the index's performance will be credited to your policy. This percentage amount is known as the *participation rate.* The rate can be expected to fluctuate from year to year in response to movement in both the portfolio earnings rate of the company and the price of call options on the options/futures exchange markets. Therefore, participation rates as low as 25 percent and as high as 80 percent are possible over the life of the contract. Ironically, the years in which the participation rate is low may produce higher policy earning results than those in some years in which the participation rate is very high. This is because percentages are meaningful only as they are applied to a whole number. For example, 25 percent of a 40 percent rise in the S&P 500 index earns 10 percent, yet 80 percent of a modest 7 percent rise in the S&P would earn only 5.6 percent.

🏧 🏧 🏧

The fundamental issue in choosing between fixed, indexed, and variable universal life plans is where one is on the risk spectrum. Fixed-interest products have the lowest risk, but also the lowest earnings potential and the highest cost. Equity-indexed plans have a much higher earnings potential. And although they have minimal risk because of the guaranteed minimum-interest rate, the guaranteed rate is lower than that on fixed universal life plans. Variable universal life has the greatest rate-of-return potential but with *no* or limited downside guarantees.

Therefore, it presents the greatest risk of principal loss. Indexed universal life products are increasing in popularity because of their broad and central position in the life insurance risk-reward universe. Indexed products have gain potential driven by equity growth on the upside, but a downside guarantee that principal will be protected and a modest guaranteed interest rate will be earned even in down-market years.

Term Life

One of the most basic forms of insurance is *term life* insurance. Many people have purchased it because it offers substantial benefits at low cost. However, as its name suggests, term insurance is beneficial only for short-term use. For example, a term insurance policy with a decreasing face amount may be ideal for protecting a young family while there is a mortgage on their home.

The cost of term insurance is determined by the mortality rate of the insured's age group, and the premiums, which may start out low, increase each year, becoming extremely costly as the years go by. Some term policies have level premiums for periods of five, 10, 15, 20, and even 30 years (depending on age), but at the end of the period the premium typically skyrockets to a level that is usually unacceptable. Thus, term insurance is not prudent for someone who has to keep insurance for the rest of his or her life, which is the case in estate planning. If you follow the numbers through the years, you will see quite clearly that no amount of initial savings can offset the long-term cost of term insurance compared with that of permanent insurance and the benefits of reducing your estate tax costs on a guaranteed basis.

The Best Policy?

Table 6-2 on the facing page summarizes the key features of the five types of life insurance discussed above. It would be incorrect to conclude that any one of these types is best for everyone. The best policy is the one that fits your personal situation and risk tolerance.

It is important to analyze the products of several qualified insurance companies—and whether the insurance is whole life (or interest-sensitive whole life), universal life, variable life, indexed life, or term life is irrelevant. The policy that makes the most sense in your particular situation will become evident. In some cases, you may consider using a variety of policies from various companies to give you the best diversified portfolio with the most flexibility (see Chapter 8, "Diversifying Your Life Insurance").

You can protect yourself and get the best underwriting by working with a qualified, trained expert in estate planning and insurance. It is usually not a good idea to rely on a typical stockbroker, accountant, or banker for the planning of your estate and the purchase of insurance. Providing quality advice on estate planning and insurance strategies requires knowledge that can be obtained only through specific schooling, constant updating, and years of experience. You should work with specialists who have taken the time to obtain the requisite knowledge, as evidenced by attainment of industry-recognized designations such as Chartered Life Underwriter (CLU), Chartered Financial Consultant (ChFC), and Certified Financial Planner (CFP). Renno Peterson and Robert Esperti, authors of more than 26 books on estate planning, put it best: "To use less than the best [in your estate planning] is to invite disaster" (*Protect Your Estate,* McGraw-Hill, 1993, p. 187).

TABLE 6-2 Types of Life Insurance

Type of policy	Key features
	Temporary insurance
Term	Simple and economical until later years when the cost of mortality increases substantially. Often best for short-term needs. No cash value and virtually no tax advantages. Increasing premium but may be level for periods of up to 20 or 30 years, depending on age and health. May have a feature that allows conversion to permanent insurance without evidence of insurability.
	Permanent insurance
Whole life (also called straight or ordinary life)	Guaranteed death benefit at a guaranteed premium for the lifetime of the insured. Guaranteed cash value. Retirement income with risk. Tax deferral combined with death benefits.
Universal life	Flexible premiums. Flexible death benefits. Interest-sensitive policy, generally with some guaranteed rate of interest and guaranteed mortality charge. Insured shares the risk above guaranteed amounts.
Indexed life or equity-indexed life (a form of universal life)	Flexible premiums. Cash value (and, in some cases, death benefit) fluctuates with the performance of an index of stocks. Can provide a hedge against inflation. Typically has a minimum rate guarantee below the guarantee rate on the insurance company's regular universal life policies. Medium level of risk.
Variable life (a form of universal life)	Flexible premiums. Death benefit and cash value fluctuate with performance of investment portfolio (stock funds, bond funds, etc.). Protects against inflation. Policyholder can direct funds within separate investment subaccounts. Higher level of risk and costs.

7 Irrevocable Life Insurance Trust

P *Part of my proposed estate plan for Lucy and Jerry Moffat included the purchase of insurance to help offset the significant estate taxes that would be due at the second of Lucy's and Jerry's deaths and to make sure their estate passed intact to their three children, Peter, Alice, and Mary. Because they wanted to keep their plan simple, their corporate attorney and longtime friend, John Peters, suggested they give the premium to their children and have them own the insurance policy jointly.*

I pointed out that this could expose the cash value in the policy to the claims of creditors, including spouses in a divorce action. Also, if one of the children predeceased Lucy and Jerry, direct ownership by the children could cause the problem of having a new party (such as a spouse of a deceased child) become one of the new joint policy owners through the deceased child's will. In addition, the premium being contemplated would completely use up Lucy and Jerry's annual gift tax exemption amount. Technically, that would mean they couldn't even continue to give the children their annual Christmas money unless they used part of their lifetime exemption or were willing to pay gift tax. And they would have lost a valuable way to disinherit the IRS from any insurance proceeds that remain at the death of their children for the benefit of their five grandchildren.

The solution to the problems raised was simple—instead of giving the premium directly to Peter, Alice, and Mary, each year the Moffats could make gifts to an irrevocable life insurance trust for the benefit of one or more generations of family members. The trust would then purchase the insurance on their lives. This would eliminate the problem of a premature death of one or more beneficiaries and would protect the assets in the trust from the claims of creditors. To solve the problem of using up their annual gift tax exemption, Lucy and Jerry could design their irrevocable life insurance trust to allow them to count all their beneficiaries, including their grandchildren, when making annual gifts to the trust. Properly set up and administered, this plan would actually be simpler and easier for the Moffats, as well as for their heirs.

🛡 🛡 🛡

Irrevocable life insurance trusts (ILITs) are used extensively in sophisticated estate planning because they remove assets from an individual's estate while allowing a certain degree of control by the maker. Properly designed and implemented, an ILIT can provide a surprisingly high degree of flexibility coupled with significant estate planning benefits.

Insurance Policy Ownership

Life insurance proceeds are, with few exceptions, free of all income tax. However, many people incorrectly believe that life insurance is also exempt from federal estate tax. Life insurance can be exempt, but if the insured has any rights or powers over the policy (called *incidents of ownership*), the proceeds will be included in his or her estate and be subject to federal estate tax.

In order to avoid federal estate tax, many people have their life insurance owned by a spouse, children, or others. Then, upon the death of the insured, the policy proceeds are paid to the owner's beneficiaries free of federal estate tax. However, problems can arise when another person owns an insurance policy. For one, the insured loses control of the policy. Also, if the owner is the beneficiary, the proceeds will eventually be taxed in the beneficiary's estate. If the owner dies before the insured, the estate plan may be affected. And if the proceeds are payable to someone other than the insured or the owner, they are deemed a gift (with gift tax ramifications) to the beneficiary from the policy owner.

To solve these problems, the life insurance policy can be purchased by, or contributed to, an irrevocable life insurance trust so that it will not be included in the insured's estate. Of course, the insured cannot be a trustee or beneficiary of the trust because being either would represent an incident of ownership.

ILIT Basics

Advantages of ILITs

The advantages of an irrevocable life insurance trust are numerous and include the following:

- Provides a way to immediately leverage gifts to the trust.
- Avoids federal estate taxes of up to 50 percent (2002–2003) that might otherwise be due on life insurance proceeds upon the death of the insured. If properly structured, it can shelter those proceeds from federal estate tax for *more than* one generation.
- Allows gifts to the trust (intended to be used to pay premiums) to qualify as "present gifts" for the $11,000 annual gift tax exclusion.
- Permits a grantor to protect heirs and even make gifts "with strings attached."
- Shelters life insurance cash values and proceeds from the claims of creditors and ex-spouses.
- Can provide flexibility for unforeseen events such as the death of a beneficiary.

Establishing an ILIT

Establishing an ILIT is not difficult, but it is important to take the steps in the following order:

1. The need for life insurance is established by analyzing the liquidity and estate planning goals of the family.
2. The family's life insurance expert gathers preliminary medical information and schedules physicals to determine insurability. The application should be marked a "trial" application, and the proposed insured should be careful not to sign the application in the signature spot for "owner."
3. After insurability has been determined, an estate planning attorney drafts the trust. The grantor (or grantors) and the trustee (or trustees) sign the ILIT.
4. The trustee of the ILIT signs the final application for the life insurance as the "owner."
5. The grantor signs the final application as the "proposed insured."
6. The trustee applies for a taxpayer identification number for the trust and opens a bank account in the name of the trust.

7. The grantor makes a gift to the ILIT, which the trustee deposits in the trust's bank account.

8. The trustee notifies the beneficiaries of their limited right to withdraw their share of the gift from the ILIT.

9. The beneficiaries do not exercise their right to withdraw their share of the gift within the time (typically 30 days) permitted under the trust for exercising withdrawal rights.

10. The trustee pays the life insurance premium; the policy is issued showing the trust as the owner and beneficiary of the ILIT.

Individual and Joint ILITs

An ILIT with one grantor is called an *individual trust.* An ILIT with two or more grantors is called a *joint trust.*

Individual trusts are used by unmarried grantors who want to avoid federal estate tax on their life insurance proceeds. Because unmarried grantors do not have the benefit of the marital deduction, ILITs are extremely important if their estates exceed the federal gift and estate tax applicable exclusion amount.

Individual ILITs may also be used by married grantors who want to make sure that the proceeds from insurance policies are not included in their estates upon death. In some cases, an individual ILIT is created for the husband and another is created for the wife. Each ILIT owns and is the beneficiary of policies on the life of the respective grantor. No matter which grantor dies first, the proceeds can be used to care for the surviving spouse, children, and other beneficiaries. When the second spouse dies, the proceeds will be available to pay federal estate tax and care for the remaining beneficiaries. Both policies' proceeds will be free from federal estate taxation.

Individual ILITs are also used when the grantor has existing life insurance policies that he or she would like to transfer to an ILIT. Prudent planning dictates the use of *new* policies of life insurance when an ILIT is being created. This is so because, under federal law, if an existing policy is transferred to a new owner and the insured dies within three years of the transfer, the policy proceeds will be included in the estate of the insured. This is known as the *three-year rule;* it only affects life insurance (and any tax dollars paid on taxable gifts and certain other gifts).

A joint ILIT generally owns an increasingly popular type of policy known as a *last-to-die, second-to-die,* or *survivorship policy.* This type of policy basically insures a married couple, pays off at the second death, and costs less than individual policies. There are several reasons for this arrangement. First, statistics show that women typically live longer than men (by six years, on average). Second, the probability of both insureds dying in the same year is very low. Thus, the longevity of two people represents less of a risk than the longevity of either one of them individually, so a longer period of time will likely pass before the policy pays off. The insurance company theoretically collects more premiums and earns the investment return on the premium payments longer. In these instances, you will usually find that the last-to-die policy offers the lowest premiums and the most efficient way of handling estate tax costs. Because a last-to-die policy pays when the second spouse dies, it is the perfect arrangement when the purpose of the insurance is to pay estate taxes upon the death of the second spouse.

Example

Bob and Mary Smith are both in their late 60s and have an estate worth $5 million. They need approximately $2 million of life insurance to cover their estate tax costs. Without it, their children will inherit only 60 percent of their original worth. On the basis of current assumptions, a life insurance policy taken out on Bob alone will cost $600,000 (single premium) and yield a 3.3-to-1 return ($2 million/$600,000).

Mary Smith, in accordance with insurance industry standards, is considered to be three to six years younger than Bob because, statistically, women live three to six years longer than men. The single-premium cost of a policy to insure Mary alone for the same $2 million to cover the estate tax expenses would be $485,000, which represents a 4-to-1 return ($2 million/$485,000).

However, if we were to insure *both* Bob and Mary with a last-to-die policy that doesn't pay until both parties are deceased (which is, typically, when taxes are due), the return jumps to nearly 6-to-1. With a second-to-die policy, only $350,000 is needed to produce the same $2 million to cover the estate tax costs. Effectively, Bob and Mary are paying taxes at 17.5 cents on the dollar ($350,000 premium/$2 million proceeds), which is a discount against estate tax costs of 82.5 percent (100 - 17.5).

Clearly, a last-to-die policy in a joint ILIT provides the lowest cost and greatest discount when it comes to covering estate tax costs.

Determining whether an individual ILIT or a joint ILIT should be used for a married couple is based on the circumstances of each situation. However, if a couple's motive is to use life insurance purely for the payment of estate taxes, a joint ILIT is the better planning method. If the life insurance is to be used not only for the payment of federal estate tax but also for the benefit of the surviving spouse and other beneficiaries, an individual policy and trust are preferred.

The Mechanics

Selecting Trustees

The candidates for trustee of an ILIT are relatively self-evident in many situations. To begin the selection process, eliminate candidates who would not make good trustees. The grantor (and/or the grantor's spouse, when a survivorship policy is used) cannot act as a trustee of an ILIT. Doing so would give the grantor too much control and the value of the life insurance proceeds would be included in his or her estate.

Technically, a spouse may act as a trustee when the policy is on the grantor alone. However, if a spouse acts as trustee, the ILIT must contain proper wording to avoid scrutiny by the IRS, which may choose to challenge a trust if the spouse's rights in the trust exceed certain standards. Those standards include using trust assets for health, education, maintenance, and support. Thus, if you name your spouse as trustee, the ILIT should be prepared by an expert attorney who is familiar with estate and trust planning issues.

There are many attractive candidates for the role of ILIT trustee. One of the best is a CPA or accountant, at least while the grantor is alive. An ILIT requires detail, accounting, notifications to beneficiaries, and follow-up. No other advisor is as equipped as an accountant to handle these tasks. Because administration of an ILIT is mostly paperwork while the grantor is alive, the grantor can typically rely on an accountant to meticulously follow the correct procedures. After the death of the grantor, other trustees (such as children) can either replace the accountant or become co-trustees.

A bank trust department is another potential candidate. Like accountants, bank trust departments are careful in administering ILITs—they are reliable and experienced professional trustees. Generally, if an ILIT holds only life insurance policies and a nominal amount of cash, the fee charged by most bank trust departments is reasonable for the tasks performed and the liability assumed.

Other advisors can make good trustees too. However, it is important that an advisor be detail-oriented and equipped to administer the ILIT. Desire is not enough: Attention to detail, good record-keeping practices, and conscientious follow-up are absolute requirements for someone who takes on the job of ILIT trustee.

Family members, including beneficiaries of the trust, can also serve as trustees, as can friends of the grantor. However, the person or persons chosen must be capable of performing the tasks described above. If children or other nonprofessionals serve as trustees, it might be wise to have an accountant or a bank trust department as a co-trustee. A better plan may be to have children take over as trustees or co-trustees when the ILIT receives the death benefit.

The watchword for ILIT trustees is "detail." An ILIT trustee must be able to effectively and accurately administer a technical trust. Much depends on having a trustee who is aware of the importance of the details in effectively maintaining an ILIT.

Funding with Life Insurance

The proceeds from an insurance policy can be included in the estate of the insured if the decedent possessed "incidents of ownership" either at death or *within three years of death*. This means that if an insured transfers a life insurance policy into an ILIT that he or she currently owns and then dies within three years, the life insurance proceeds will be subject to estate tax. For this reason, *new* policies should be purchased by the trustee of the ILIT. With new policies purchased by someone other than the insured, the three-year rule of inclusion is avoided.

In some situations it may be advisable to exchange existing policies for a new one that is owned at the moment of the exchange by the ILIT. If the exchange is done properly (as outlined in IRS Code Section 1035), there will be no income tax due (on the policy's cash value over basis) and no three-year-rule restriction.

Another potential problem can arise when existing life insurance is used to fund an ILIT. Many times, the existing insurance has a substantial cash value. If it does, the cash value of the policy, whether it is transferred directly or through an income tax-free exchange to a new policy, is treated as a gift to the ILIT beneficiaries. If the value exceeds the $11,000 annual gift tax exclusion (or $22,000 for a couple "splitting" their gifts) multiplied by the number of demand-right beneficiaries, the excess will reduce the applicable exclusion amount ($1 million in 2002–2003). If the applicable exclusion has already been fully used, a gift tax will be due.

Although there are some methods that can reduce the adverse impact of using existing life insurance policies that are owned by the insured, most of them are ineffective. If it is economically viable and if the maker is insurable, it is almost always better to purchase new life insurance.

Giving Gifts to an ILIT

Contributions to an irrevocable trust are gifts to the beneficiaries of the trust and are, therefore, taxable. But instead of paying gift tax, the trust maker uses the $11,000-per-beneficiary annual estate tax exclusion and perhaps all

[*Name and address of beneficiary*]

Re: _____ Irrevocable Insurance Trust dated _____

Dear _____:

    This year your parents have made a contribution to this trust. As a result, you have a right to withdraw property from the trust in 20__. If you do not exercise your right of withdrawal within thirty days of receipt of this letter, the right will lapse pursuant to the terms of the trust agreement.

    If you would like to exercise this right of withdrawal, you will need to sign a written request and send it to me. To determine the amount covered by your withdrawal right, or for more information about the right, please contact me. In any event, please acknowledge your receipt of this letter by signing the enclosed copy and returning it to me.

Sincerely,

_____ [Name and address of trustee]

Receipt acknowledged:

_____ [Name of beneficiary]   [Date] _____, 20__

Figure 7-1. Sample beneficiary withdrawal notice.

or part of their lifetime applicable credit exemption equivalent for larger gifts. In order to qualify for the $11,000 annual gift tax exclusion, a gift to an ILIT must be a "present-interest" gift. That is, the beneficiaries must have an immediate right to enjoy the gift. This is accomplished through a provision known as a *withdrawal right* (sometimes called a *demand right* or *Crummey power*). The withdrawal right gives the beneficiaries the right to withdraw the asset from the trust, effectively giving them a present interest in the amount contributed to the trust.

    As previously mentioned, the court decided in the case of *Crummey v. Commissioner* that if an irrevocable trust's beneficiary has the right to withdraw a gift made to the trust for a reasonable period of time after the gift is made, the gift will qualify for the annual exclusion. The number of annual exclusions that are allowed for a gift to an ILIT is equal to the number of beneficiaries who have a demand right. A demand right can be given to children *and* grandchildren. If there are two grantors, $22,000 per beneficiary can be given to the ILIT and still qualify for the annual exclusion. (A sample withdrawal notice is shown in Figure 7-1.)

The withdrawal right may present a problem if the beneficiary actually demands a share of the premium money; however, this rarely occurs. Once beneficiaries understand the long-term benefits of the ILIT, they typically do not exercise the withdrawal right, and the money is used to pay life insurance premiums.

Discounting Estate Tax Costs

Life insurance proceeds inside an ILIT allow you to cover your estate tax costs for 10 to 30 cents on the dollar or even less. Properly funded, life insurance represents a guaranteed investment (because death is guaranteed), with returns from 2 to 1 to as high as 20 to 1, and the death benefit can be income tax- and estate tax-free inside an ILIT. In other words, based on current assumptions, for each dollar the trustee of your ILIT gives to an insurance company, the return for your children can be as high as $20—free of all tax! For example, the single-pay premium for $1 million of death benefit, based on current assumptions, for a couple with an average age of 45 is approximately $50,000. Of course, the actual return amount will vary depending on your age, your health, the type of insurance, and the carrier you choose. However, for the average older person, a single premium payment of $1 million could easily produce from $5 million to $10 million completely tax-free.

In a comparable situation, a person would have to make a profit of approximately $31 million on her or his investments or business to produce $20 million after income taxes (at 35 percent), to result in approximately $10 million after estate taxes (at 50 percent). Utilizing an insurance plan with an ILIT requires only $1 million (at age 60 on a survivor policy, based on current assumptions) to produce the same $10 million in cash—free of income and estate taxes. In this case, $1 million effectively does the work of $31 million!

Figure 7-2 on page 114 compares the use of life insurance proceeds inside an ILIT to three other methods of paying estate taxes (using cash, selling off assets, and borrowing). From this comparison, you can easily see what a valuable tool life insurance can be in your overall estate plan.

Special IRS offer!

Let's say the Internal Revenue Service advertised that it was offering a special on estate taxes that would effectively reduce your taxes by 90 percent. If the offer allowed you to pay $500,000 today and receive a receipt showing payment in full on your $10 million estate, would you jump at it? If you could afford it and the payment would not affect your lifestyle, you would be crazy not to. Of course, the IRS is not going to make such an offer. But you can

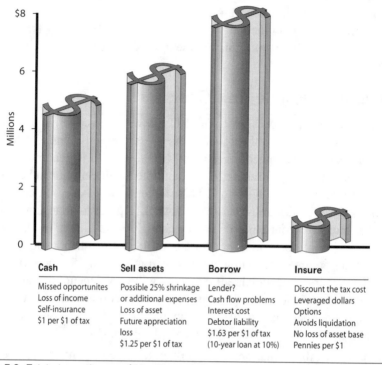

Cost to pay $5 million estate tax (due within 9 months of death)

	Cash	Sell assets	Borrow	Insure
	Missed opportunites	Possible 25% shrinkage	Lender?	Discount the tax cost
	Loss of income	or additional expenses	Cash flow problems	Leveraged dollars
	Self-insurance	Loss of asset	Interest cost	Options
	$1 per $1 of tax	Future appreciation	Debtor liability	Avoids liquidation
		loss	$1.63 per $1 of tax	No loss of asset base
		$1.25 per $1 of tax	(10-year loan at 10%)	Pennies per $1

Figure 7-2. Estate tax options on $10 million estate.

achieve the same result through an ILIT. By giving $500,000 to an ILIT, the trustee could purchase approximately $5 million of insurance coverage on a couple with an average age of 60, based on current assumptions, which is the amount of liquidity needed to pay the estate tax on a $10 million estate.

The premium is based on a second-to-die insurance policy, average age 60, nonsmoker rates, and current assumptions. In this example, the heirs actually end up with $9.75 million rather than $9.5 million ($10 million minus the premium of $500,000) because reducing the estate by the $500,000 premium payment lowers the taxes. The taxes on the remaining estate of $9.5 million are approximately $4.75 million. This leaves approximately $4.75 million *plus* the full $5 million from the insurance in the ILIT (income tax- and estate tax-free). The IRS effectively pays for half the premium, further increasing the discount from 90 percent, in this example, to 95 percent (see Figure 7-3).

Think about this example: John and Mary, both age 60, are worth $20 million. When they die, 50 percent of their net worth will be lost to estate taxes, leaving their heirs to inherit a sadly reduced amount. Life insurance inside an ILIT can reduce the amount of that loss to only 10 percent.

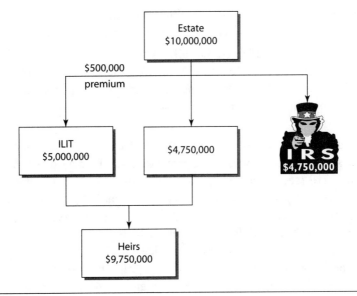

Figure 7-3. Discounting the cost of estate tax.

If John and Mary purchase a last-to-die life insurance policy in an ILIT for a single premium of $1 million, their heirs will receive, based on current assumptions, a return of $10 million—10 times the investment—tax-free upon their deaths. Although the government still takes its 50 percent share of their estate ($10 million) their family receives that same amount from the life insurance company—free of all taxes. Their wealth passes to their heirs virtually intact. In essence, they paid their estate taxes with only the $1 million cost of the life insurance policy, effectively reducing the tax cost to only 10 percent of what it would otherwise have been.

Remember that all this is accomplished using only 5 percent of their total estate value. Fully 95 percent remains available to invest, spend, or use as they desire. Of the original $20 million, approximately $19 million (actually $19.5 million because the tax on $19 million at 50 percent is $9.5 million, leaving $9.5 million plus $10 million tax-free from insurance) remains. Meanwhile, a mere 5 percent provides a guarantee of financial security for their heirs, whether it is needed tomorrow or 25 years from now.

Paying the Estate Tax Bill

One of the more confusing aspects of an ILIT is how the ILIT's life insurance proceeds can be used to pay the death taxes of the insured. An ILIT cannot pay the death taxes created by the insured's estate *directly*. If the terms of the ILIT document require that the trustee pay the estate taxes, the death benefit becomes part of the taxable estate and thus it will be taxed as well. The ILIT must use an alternative method for paying the taxes.

The ILIT contains language that allows the trustee to make loans to the maker's living trust or probate estate. If the loan method is used, the transaction must be at arm's length. Interest must be paid, and the indebtedness should be evidenced by a promissory note. The loan must be repaid or extinguished in some manner.

As an alternative to making a loan, the ILIT can purchase property from the maker's revocable living trust or probate estate. Under current law, until the year of 2010 (see Appendix D), all the property included in the maker's estate receives a *step-up in basis* (forgiveness of capital gain taxes) at death except for certain items that are considered "income in respect of a decedent," such as IRAs and deferred annuities. If the ILIT purchases property that has a step-up in basis for a purchase price equal to the stepped-up value, there will be no taxable gain. There is taxable gain only to the extent that the purchase price of the property is greater than the adjusted basis. The net effect is that the estate would have cash and the ILIT would own property. Because the beneficiaries of the revocable living trust and the ILIT are almost always identical, there would be no real change in the economic position of the beneficiaries. The estate or main trust and the ILIT are merely two different pockets in the same pants.

Distributing Policy Proceeds

An ILIT can be drafted to leave property to children, grandchildren, and others in thousands of ways. Generally, the provisions that are created to leave property to beneficiaries are tailored to meet the individual needs of each beneficiary. There is no legal reason to leave trust property to each beneficiary in the same way. In fact, it is quite common for a maker to divide the life insurance proceeds equally but have different arrangements for making distributions of each beneficiary's share of other assets.

If there is no specific direction by the grantor, the tendency among planning professionals is to draft ILITs with *equal* distribution instructions. But as one top estate planning attorney, Renno Peterson, put it, "Nothing is more unequal than the equal treatment of unequals."

Generation-Skipping Considerations

An ILIT that is created for the benefit of the grantor's children and grandchildren can be used to leverage the $1.1 million generation-skipping transfer (GST) tax exemption. This leverage occurs because the total amount of the premiums given to the ILIT are usually well within the GST exemption. If, for example, $1 million of life insurance premiums buys $7 million worth of life insurance death benefit, the $1 million premium is within the GST exemption amount. The additional $6 million of life insurance proceeds does not reduce the GST exemption and is *not* subject to federal estate tax or GST tax in subsequent generations!

A generation-skipping ILIT, which can be set up to benefit children, grandchildren, and later generations, is ordinarily structured to continue in existence for the maximum period of time permitted under applicable state law. During the term of the generation-skipping ILIT, children, grandchildren, and great-grandchildren can be the beneficiaries of the trust. There is no federal estate tax on any of the proceeds until such time as the rule against perpetuities, or similar state law, forces the trust to end. The proceeds will be subject to estate taxation upon the death of the final beneficiaries.

If a generation-skipping ILIT has as its only beneficiaries grandchildren or great-grandchildren and the only gifts made to it are $11,000 annual exclusion gifts, in some circumstances these gifts do not reduce the $1.1 million GST exemption. This important exception to GST tax rules provides an even more efficient way to pass life insurance proceeds free from GST tax to grandchildren or great-grandchildren.

When an ILIT is designed to last several generations, it is often referred to as a dynasty, or D, trust (discussed in Chapter 4). People who want their assets to never be subject to federal estate tax should consider a dynasty trust and consider fueling it with life insurance.

Planning Risks

There are some potential risks in using ILITs. The biggest of these is that the trustee of the ILIT will not follow the administrative procedures that are necessary to ensure that the gifts to the ILIT will qualify for the $11,000 gift tax annual exclusion and that the life insurance proceeds will not be included in the maker's estate. The trustee must take care to follow all the proper rules.

Also, because an ILIT is irrevocable, considerable time and effort should be expended in the planning stage so that the terms of the ILIT fully satisfy the maker's planning goals. The trust should be drafted by a knowledgeable attorney to ensure that the ILIT is as flexible as it can be without endangering its estate tax-free status. Together with a correctly structured revocable living trust, a properly funded and administered ILIT can provide a simple but effective estate plan that leaves you in control of your estate while enabling you to pass your entire estate intact to your heirs after you are gone.

The Change-Your-Mind ILIT

From the discussion thus far, it probably seems impossible to access any accumulated wealth in an irrevocable life insurance trust. Because the primary purpose of the ILIT is to keep trust assets (such as policy proceeds) out of the insured's estate, the insured grantor is not allowed to have access to assets in the trust, including policy cash values (via policy loans or withdrawals). Typically, only the owner-trustee has this right.

What seems impossible, however, *is* possible. A life insurance policy placed in an ILIT can provide the double benefit of wealth preservation *and* accessible wealth accumulation through the use of a *change-your-mind ILIT*.

Having access to the funds in an ILIT is accomplished through the appointment of "limited powerholders" (sometimes known as trust "protectors") under the trust. These limited powerholders, through a clause known as the "limited independent fiduciary power of amendment," have the sole authority to make changes to the ILIT, including the right to transfer trust assets to another trust (or even terminate a trust) in a manner consistent with the best interests of the trust beneficiaries. If the insured parties find themselves in need of funds, the successor trust could be a revocable trust, thus providing them with full access to funds in the trust through policy loans or withdrawals. Although this technique will cause subsequent policy death benefits to be included in the estate, this is hardly an issue if the insured grantors need the money later in life.

Further flexibility can be achieved by adding a provision to the change-your-mind ILIT authorizing the trustee to make secured demand loans to any party, *including the insured*. The trustee's power to lend to the insured (using secured demand notes at fair market interest rates) is similar to the right to substitute property of equal value, which has been approved by the courts. With this loan provision, the interest due to the trust from the borrower is typically accrued. The outstanding loan and its accrued interest are repaid to the trust by the borrower's estate *at* death—thus giving rise to a corresponding estate indebtedness deduction.

Further, due to special rules, known as the "grantor trust rules," the ILIT pays no income tax on the accrued-interest portion of any loan repayment it receives. This technique can produce exceptional wealth preservation leverage.

Both of these provisions should be incorporated into your ILIT. There is just about no downside to having them, and obviously they offer significant benefit. One word of caution: The structure and language in the change-your-mind ILIT, as well as the choice of trustee and powerholder, are very important matters.

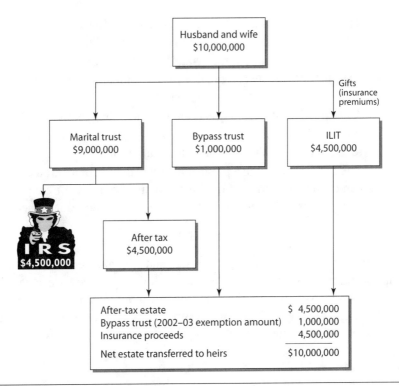

Figure 7-4. Typical estate plan with ILIT.

You should consult with an attorney who specializes in trusts and estate planning to make sure your trust will provide the desired benefits.

Summary

An ILIT containing a properly structured life insurance policy can, when integrated into a sound estate plan, produce significant benefits, as shown in Figure 7-4. Among the benefits are the following:

- It provides a way to discount estate taxes up to 90 percent and even beyond.
- It can multiply the value of the estate tax exemption by utilizing the exemption itself to create insurance proceeds inside the ILIT.
- Life insurance will not be included in the insured's estate or subjected to federal estate taxes.
- Trust assets, including insurance proceeds, are generally not subject to the claims of the insured's creditors.

- The leverage created by life insurance in an ILIT effectively reduces a 50 percent estate tax bracket to as little as 10 percent or even less.
- Proceeds are available for estate settlement costs.
- Premium payments can qualify for the annual gift tax exclusion and thereby avoid use of the unified credit.
- As with all trusts, the terms of an ILIT are completely private.
- It is possible to include provisions in an ILIT that will allow the trustee to make loans to the grantor, beneficiaries, and others.
- The ILIT can include a provision which allows for a "protector" who can change the terms of the trust and, thus, provide for changing circumstances of the grantors and beneficiaries, should it be necessary.

ण ण ण

Life insurance inside a properly drafted and administered ILIT is often the simplest and best alternative for providing the liquidity needed at death to cover estate tax costs. Not only are the proceeds free of all income and estate taxes, but annual gifts to the ILIT to cover premium costs typically represent only 1 to 3 percent of an estate's value.

8 Acquiring Life Insurance

When Mike and Ginny Devoe came to my office to discuss their estate plan, they brought their insurance policy covering Mike's life. The policy was with a company that had been in receivership for several years. Fortunately for Mike and Ginny, the company had been taken over and was about to come out of receivership and their policy was still intact. Unfortunately, Mike and Ginny had to pay larger premiums than planned over the last few years because of the lower interest being credited on policy cash values along with the higher costs charged to their policy as a result of the insurance company's problems. Mike and Ginny were interested in a plan that included a second-to-die policy, but wanted a way to avoid the problems they went through with Mike's policy.

The estate plan I recommended included the purchase of insurance in an irrevocable trust to help offset estate-tax costs. Part of the funding for the new insurance was to come from the cash value in the old policy, but instead of going with one insurance company, I recommended that they diversify their life insurance and have their trustee split the recommended coverage over three companies.

The trustee of an ILIT must be diligent in the choice of life insurance products and companies that are used to fund the trust. There are many things the trustee must consider in making his or her choice, including the financial rating of the company, the underlying assumptions of the policy pricing projections, and the company's dividend or interest-crediting history.

When an insurance agent or broker is "underwriting" you for insurance, the agent will arrange to have you examined by the company the agent represents or the company the agent decides is best. However, the *agent's* choice is not necessarily what is in your best interest. For this reason, you should have your medical information reviewed by three or four highly rated insurance carriers in order to obtain the best "offer of insurance" based on each company's evaluation of your health status.

Health Factors

Not all insurance companies treat specific health factors in the same way. Some consider certain health-related issues (such as smoking, diabetes, occupational hazard, or family history) to be more severe than others do, and their concern is reflected in the prices they quote. A recent example of this sometimes dramatic difference occurred in the following case of a man who needed a $1 million insurance policy to offset the estate taxes on his $3.5 million estate.

The company with the lowest published premiums made a medical offer which turned out to be the highest-cost offer of all the companies. Another company reviewed the same medical information and came back with a health rating far better than the first. The second company was willing to overlook certain conditions that the first company was not. Although it appeared to be a much more expensive company on paper, in reality, the insurance it offered became the most reasonably priced once the man's health was evaluated.

A company with seemingly high rates may offer the least-expensive premiums, given your health status and age. You'll never know unless your insurance professional submits your medical exam report and medical history to several companies to obtain offers. By having your medical records examined by more than one company, you have a better opportunity to receive the optimum coverage at the best price.

Qualifying for Insurance

Purchasing life insurance is not as simple as you might believe. Medical histories, physical exam reports, and financial data must be reviewed in order to obtain an offer of insurance. The insurance company must be convinced that there is an insurable interest on the part of the beneficiaries as well as a legitimate need for the coverage amount to ensure that a person is not worth more dead than alive. The health and background investigation that takes place after you sign an application is normal. You can expect at least one phone interview, along with time delays to evaluate your health and personal data. In short, you must qualify for insurance, but do not assume that you won't qualify because of one or more health factors. Also, be aware that no number quoted to you by an insurance salesperson is correct until you have had a physical exam and the insurance companies have offered a price based on the findings of their examination, along with a review of your personal medical history.

In addition to health, your age makes a difference. To fully comprehend the difference between levels of qualification based on age, consider a male nontobacco user who applies for $1 million of insurance. At age 40, the cost for $1 million of coverage in one payment is $82,000, based on current assumptions. Twenty years later when he is 60 years old, that same one-pay insurance premium will cost him $227,500—more than three times as much. When he is 70, it will be $395,500 on a one-pay basis, based on current assumptions.

According to statistics, women live longer than men. From the perspective of insurance companies, women represent a better risk and can get a better rate than men of the same age and health. For a 40-year-old-nontobacco-using female, the cost for $1 million of insurance is $63,000, based on current assumptions, if she pays in one payment. The cost is $183,500 when she is 60—a significant difference from her male counterpart's cost. When she is 70, the cost is $298,700, nearly 25-percent less than the cost a 70-year-old male would pay.

To give you a picture of how the cost of a $1 million second-to-die policy compares to the above, a one-pay premium for a couple who are both age 40 is $45,000 based on current assumptions. For a couple who are both age 60, the cost is closer to $140,000. For a 70-year-old couple, the premium is $255,000—nearly $15,000 lower than that of a female on a one-pay basis.

Obviously, the status of the applicant's health will have an effect on his or her qualification and cost level. However, as stated earlier, do not assume you will not qualify due to certain health factors. It is usually worth shopping to find out what the cost is, especially since the physical exam is easy and there is no charge for obtaining offers. The companies make their offers by adjusting their premiums on the basis of their individual assessments of your health factors.

Insurance Diversification

After you have been examined and have obtained several offers, your initial reaction may be to choose the one policy that provides the best rate and use only that company for the coverage you need. However, there is a better and more prudent course of action that promises both a good rate and better long-term protection. Just as you would not put all your investment dollars into one stock or bond no matter how secure it seemed, you should also consider diversifying your insurance portfolio by splitting coverage between two or more companies and averaging the cost. Even though no family has ever failed to collect on a legitimate death claim because of the failure of an insurance company, you can reduce the risk that more premium may be required to sustain the death benefit by diversifying your life insurance.

In cases where several million dollars of coverage is needed to effectively discount estate tax costs, more than one insurance company may be required because of the limited capacity individual carriers have to supply such large amounts of coverage. Even the larger life insurance carriers are limited in the amount of insurance they can cover on one individual. (In fact, most companies retain only $1 million to $2 million.) The risk on amounts above the basic retention is shared with other special "reinsurance" companies.

Because insurance company rates are based on current assumptions of expenses, interest rates, and mortality charges and may change over the life of the policy, a single company's quote may not give you the best rate protection. Periodic changes in expenses, interest rates, and mortality are not consistent from one company to another, and increases in costs will not occur unilaterally across the industry. The company that offers the best rate today will not necessarily continue to credit your policy with that rate in the future. By using more than one insurance carrier, you are almost guaranteed the best long-term average rate available. In addition, you will enjoy the safety of using more than one company.

There is yet another reason why diversifying your insurance coverage is a smart idea. Although some investments are clearly safer than others, no investment is guaranteed. No one can foresee the future. The solidity of your life insurance "investment" is based both on the assumptions used in determining the premium and on the overall solvency of the company carrying your policy.

Although you should insist on quotes from only the highest-rated firms, there are still risks. Even the largest, most reputable firms can suffer setbacks. With so much at stake in your estate plan, it is a good idea to spread your risk by dividing coverage over more than one quality insurance company.

Example

Bob and Elaine House needed $16 million worth of insurance to discount the taxes on their $30 million estate. They were examined by five companies

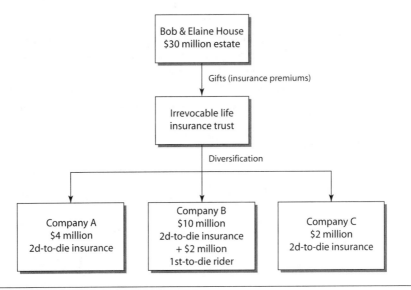

Figure 8-1. A diversified life insurance portfolio.

and received offers based on the findings of the examinations. Following sound advice, Bob and Elaine took the three best firms and purchased $4 million of insurance from one, $10 million from another, and the balance from the third. On one of the policies, they purchased a first-to-die rider to produce enough funds at the first death to pay off the balance of the premiums on all three policies. In this way, their cost was averaged and their portfolio protected through diversification. (See Figure 8-1 for a diagram of their plan.)

For Bob and Elaine House, the total of the premiums they paid was only slightly higher than it would have been if they had selected just one company. The size of the premium, while important, was not the only consideration. At their estate level, the most important factor was the peace of mind and increased protection diversification offered.

Summary

While you and your investment advisor would have no hesitation diversifying your investments (such as stocks, bonds, and the like) for safety, the idea of diversifying your insurance may be a relatively new concept. The question really boils down to this: Why not diversify, if in doing so you add a layer of protection for your family wealth transfer plan without significantly increasing the cost of insurance?

With changing economic conditions, a nondiversified insurance portfolio may expose you to the risk of having to pay more into your insurance policies than you had planned. This can happen no matter how highly rated your single insurance carrier is and no matter how long you have held your policy. By diversifying your life insurance portfolio, you can enjoy the peace of mind that comes from knowing you have done all you can to protect your estate plan and your loved ones.

9 Debt Optimization Strategy

T Tammy Sharp came up to me at the end of one of my Wealth
Protection Network seminars and asked if there was an estate
plan that would allow her to deduct the premiums for insurance to cover the needed liquidity for estate taxes at her death.
She said she didn't like life insurance but would find it more
palatable if she could get a tax deduction from the government
for the premium payments.

    Tammy did not owe anything on her home, and I found out
she would be willing to place a mortgage on the home if doing
so would help her reach her estate planning goals. After I explained the details of the debt optimization strategy and how it
would effectively allow her to deduct the cost of the premiums,
she was anxious to put the plan in place.

⚜ ⚜ ⚜

Traditionally, most people strive to become totally debt-free. As soon as
their means allow, they think they must pay off all debt in the mistaken belief
that to do so is the best way to ensure financial stability. But often the funds
available to pay off debt or the funds created from borrowing can be used to
protect and enhance wealth through the *debt optimization strategy (DOS)*.

Consider a man who is worth $10 million, including a $2 million home. His
only debt is a $500,000 mortgage on his home with payments of approximately
$36,000 per year. The interest on the debt is fully deductible so his net cost,
after taxes, is really closer to $25,000 per year. The man's income is such that
the mortgage payments do not affect his lifestyle.

TABLE 9-1 Debt Payoff versus Debt Optimization

Debt payoff		Debt optimization	
Cash available	$500,000	Cash available	$500,000
Annual mortgage cost	$36,000	Annual mortgage cost	$36,000
Pay off mortgage	($500,000)	Transfer to trust	$500,000
		Continue annual mortgage payment	$36,000
		Trust purchases life insurance	($500,000)
Additional equity	$500,000	Additional equity	$5,000,000
Estate tax	– 250,000	Estate tax	– 0
Net to family	$250,000	Net to family*	$5,000,000

*Family receives extra $4,750,000. The $250,000 is the amount that the family would receive if the debt is paid off (column 1). The $5,000,000 is the amount the family would receive if the debt is not paid off and the money that would have been used to pay the debt is used to purchase insurance (column 2). The $4,750,000 is the difference between the two.

Assuming he has the available funds, traditional thinking dictates that he pay off his mortgage. By doing so, he would eliminate the $36,000 mortgage payments and increase the equity in his real estate by $500,000. However, at his death, the additional equity from the $500,000 mortgage payoff would be reduced by estate taxes of approximately $250,000. Thus, his children would receive net equity of only $250,000 from his $500,000 payment.

Instead, the man could use the DOS approach: He would take the same available funds of $500,000 and purchase a life insurance policy inside an irrevocable life insurance trust on his and his wife's lives. By doing this, he would receive a 10-to-1 return and produce $5 million, which would go to his heirs free of income and estate taxes. The $5 million also happens to be the approximate amount of money needed to pay the estate taxes on his entire $10 million estate.

If the man does nothing and his estate consists mainly of nonliquid assets (such as real estate), his heirs may be forced to liquidate much of the real estate. Because taxes are due nine months after death, it may not be possible to obtain the full value from the liquidation of the real estate. Thus, both the government and the man's family could end up losing.

TABLE 9-2   Reduction of Loan Cost through Debt Optimization

	Without loan	With loan
Taxable estate	$10,000,000	$9,500,000
Estate taxes	– 5,000,000	– 4,750,000
Amount to heirs	$ 5,000,000	$4,750,000
Insurance	0	5,000,000
Total	$ 5,000,000	$9,750,000

Note: The net cost of the loan is $500,000 ($10,000,000 – $9,500,000).

By paying off the $500,000 mortgage debt, the man would effectively be throwing half the money away in the form of taxes at his death and therefore, pass only $250,000 to his heirs. By using the DOS, he will be able to pass on his estate intact because the taxes will be covered by the $5 million insurance proceeds. Both approaches are compared in Table 9-1.

Another benefit of the debt optimization strategy is that Uncle Sam effectively pays back half the loan in the form of reduced taxes. Add it up: Without the DOS, the $10 million estate is reduced to $5 million after taxes. With the DOS, the $10 million estate is reduced by the mortgage of $500,000, leaving $9.5 million. The taxes on $9.5 million are approximately $4.75 million, leaving $4.75 million for the man's heirs. Add $4.75 million net after estate taxes to the $5 million that flows to the heirs, free of income and estate taxes, from the insurance policy, and the heirs receive a total of $9.75 million. As Table 9-2 shows, even though the total debt of $500,000 was paid, the man's heirs receive the entire $10 million estate less only $250,000—thanks to Uncle Sam and the *debt optimization strategy!*

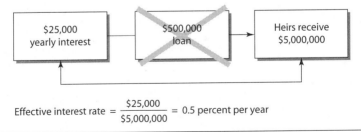

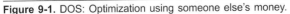

Figure 9-1. DOS: Optimization using someone else's money.

In the "debt payoff versus debt optimization" example, the man's heirs receive $5 million for a net outlay of $25,000 per year (the mortgage payment after tax savings). The $500,000 used to accomplish this came from a mortgage loan against real estate, but it could just as easily have come from a margin loan against the man's stock portfolio or any number of other sources. To calculate the net annual interest rate paid on the borrowed funds, we divide the after-tax loan payment of $25,000 by the loan of $500,000, which results in a rate of 5 percent. However, if we divide the payment of $25,000 by the real payoff—the insurance proceeds of $5 million instead, the net effective interest rate is only 0.5 percent per year. As Figure 9-1 indicates, with DOS you can achieve true optimization using someone else's money.

10 Split-Dollar Life Insurance Planning

F

Frank and Ann Mirabella were referred to my office shortly after they completed the initial stage of their estate plan. A highly qualified, board-certified tax attorney was the leader of their estate planning team, so I was surprised when I saw a huge hole in the plan.

Because of their annual income and the large size of their estate, their attorney had set up several trusts, including an irrevocable life insurance trust. He also recommended that the trustee purchase a survivorship life insurance policy on Frank and Ann. Their insurance agent recommended that they purchase enough insurance to cover the estate taxes not only on the current value of their estate but on the projected growth as well. Based on the calculations presented to the Mirabellas, the amount of insurance recommended was $40 million with an annual premium of more than $300,000 per year.

With only three children and five grandchildren, the Mirabellas did not have enough combined annual exemptions to allow them to avoid gift tax on gifts to the trust to cover the annual premiums. To help solve this problem, the agent had recommended that they use the remainder of both of their life-time-applicable gift-tax exemptions. He had also recommended that they make annual elections to use their generation-skipping transfer tax exemptions.

The problem with this strategy was that it would not allow Frank and Ann to make additional gifts (outside the insurance plan) without paying gift tax. Over time, it would not only use *up both their lifetime applicable exemptions but their generation-skip-ping transfer tax exemption as well, so only a portion of the $40 million insurance proceeds would be able to "skip" the confiscatory tax bite by the IRS at the deaths of their three daughters.*

☥ ☥ ☥

Utilizing a split-dollar plan to pay the premiums not only would eliminate any potential gift tax problems but also would use only a small amount of Frank's and Ann's combined annual gift tax exemptions. This strategy would make it possible for them to maximize the use of their applicable annual exemptions in other parts of their estate plan and would eliminate the need to use any of their lifetime applicable exemption. Best of all, only a small fraction of their generation-skipping transfer tax exemption would be needed to make sure the entire $40 million, and any future growth thereon, would avoid taxes in the estates of their daughters, their grandchildren, and later generations.

Split-dollar life insurance planning is not a life insurance product. Rather, it is an arrangement whereby a policy's death benefit, cash value, ownership rights, and premium payments are split by two or more parties (usually an employer and an employee). However, other entities, such as a trust or even private individuals, can also be involved in split-dollar agreements.

A properly structured split-dollar planning strategy offers a number of significant advantages, such as:

- Allowing an employer to advance the lion's share of premiums, typically over a period of years, and provides life insurance to select employees at an affordable cost to those employees.
- Reducing or eliminating any gift tax cost that might otherwise be due on gifts made by an employee to cover premiums (in excess of any gift tax exemptions and exclusions) for a policy purchased under a split-dollar agreement to one or more family members or a trust for their benefit.
- Permitting repayment (from death proceeds, cash-value accumulation, or other source) to be made with little or no interest, depending upon the design of the plan.

Split-dollar insurance is used when an irrevocable life insurance trust (ILIT), or another type of trust or entity, needs a source of premium payments for a period of time. Reasons for needing a source of premium payments vary, but the most common include:

- The lack of personal cash flow to make gifts to an ILIT to fund premium payments.
- The desire to use the cash flow of a corporation (which may be in a lower income tax bracket) rather than personal dollars.
- The need to reduce exposure to gift tax and generation-skipping transfer tax on the amount of gifts to the ILIT by the maker.
- The desire to substantially increase the leverage of gifts made to the ILIT.

The Key Elements

The split-dollar life insurance planning technique is based upon the fact that cash-value life insurance policies consist of two fundamentally distinct elements:

- *The investment element*: The policy's cash value, which is created by the excess of the premiums paid over the pure cost of insurance. This amount is invested and typically increases every year; it is often compared to a savings vehicle. The more the cash value builds, the greater the amount that is available in "the box" (discussed in Chapter 5) to cover the protection element.
- *The protection element*: This is the pure insurance element, which is the amount of the mortality charge and other costs and equals the difference between the premium paid and the cash value of the policy. It is similar to the term premium charged by insurance companies and, typically, increases every year as the insured ages.

Under the typical estate planning split-dollar plan, a separate entity, such as an ILIT, and an employer agree to split the costs and benefits associated with a life insurance policy. The employer contributes toward the cost of the premium according to a predetermined formula. This contribution can be the entire premium or any part of it.

A typical estate plan split-dollar arrangement within an estate planning setting works in the following way:

1. An individual creates an ILIT to own a life insurance policy or policies.
2. The trustee of the ILIT, with the help of a life insurance professional, determines the amount and type of life insurance to be purchased on the basis of the maker's estate planning objectives. (Split-dollar life insurance planning can be used with either an individual policy or a second-to-die policy.)

3.   The trustee of the ILIT enters into a *split-dollar agreement* with the insured's employer or some other entity or individual to purchase a life insurance policy. The agreement sets forth the amount of the premium payments and how they will be made, and, depending upon the type of agreement, it contains a promissory note (which can be interest-free under one of two basic designs, described below) that the ILIT trustee will eventually pay to the corporation or other funding source, either from policy cash values, the death benefit, or some other source at some future date.

4.   For each year that the split-dollar agreement is in effect, the insured has an *economic benefit.* This is the amount associated with the pure cost of insurance (the protection element or term cost). Either the insured makes gifts to the ILIT so that the trustee can pay the portion of the premium needed to cover the cost of the economic benefit or the employer pays it directly to the insurance company along with the investment element. If the economic benefit amount is paid directly by the employer along with the rest of the premium, it is treated as taxable income to the insured and is also considered a gift of that amount by the insured to the ILIT. However, the amount is usually small in comparison to the *investment element* advanced by the employer.

5.   At a predetermined time in the future, or at the death of the insured if earlier, the ILIT pays back to the corporation, without interest (in certain circumstances), the premiums that were paid by the corporation.

Example

Let's assume a life insurance policy in a properly designed plan has a $1 million death benefit and a $20,000 annual premium. Of the annual premium, $1,207 (the protection element or economic benefit) is paid in year one and $1,270 is paid in year two by the employee. The balances of $18,793 (the investment element) in year one and $18,730 in year two are paid by the employer. If the employee should die after two years of premium payments, the employee's family would receive $962,477, since the employer would first be repaid its total premium payments of $37,523. Even though the amount of the economic benefit portion of the payment increases each year, no gift tax would be due because it is well below the $11,000 annual gift tax exclusion (per beneficiary) that the employee is entitled to make. Thus, a split-dollar strategy can open the door to a larger insurance policy or other estate planning opportunities without the imposition of gift taxes.

Split-Dollar Methods

A split-dollar plan can be established under either of two methods: the endorsement method or the collateral assignment method.

Under the *endorsement method,* an employer applies for and becomes the owner of the entire insurance contract. The ILIT, under a signed endorsement with the corporation, is granted the right of naming itself as the irrevocable beneficiary of the death benefit in excess of the total premiums paid by the corporation. Although this method can be considered less desirable from the employee's perspective because the policy is controlled by the employer, recent IRS notices have made the endorsement split-dollar approach the preferred choice if the goal of the employee is to avoid paying interest on the amounts advanced on behalf of the employee to an insurance company.

The *collateral assignment* form of split-dollar plan is established when the insurance on the life of the trust maker is acquired and owned by a person or entity other than the employer, such as an ILIT. After the policy is issued, the trustee and the employer enter into a split-dollar agreement giving the corporation a security interest in the policy, and the trustee signs a promissory note payable to the employer.

Upon the death of the insured or the agreed term of the promissory note, whichever comes earlier, the ILIT must repay an amount equal to the aggregate premium payments made by the corporation plus any interest due. According to a recent IRS notice, if the agreement does not provide for interest equal to or greater than certain minimum rates mandated by the Internal Revenue Code, the payment of interest will be imputed. Thus, the employee will be treated as having received interest (and, in turn, paid it out to the employer) charged for premium payments advanced by the employer. This imputed interest would then be taxed to the employee as income from the employer. This imputed interest typically increases annually, as the total of the premiums paid by the employer increases.

If the insured trust maker dies before the due date of the promissory note, the corporation receives a portion of the death proceeds that equals the aggregate amount of premium payments made through the date of death plus any interest due. The corporation is not named in the beneficiary portion of the policy; it is named only in the collateral assignment and promissory note.

From the standpoint of control, collateral assignment is the preferred method of establishing a split-dollar plan because the ILIT actually owns the policy. However, depending upon the age of the insured and the size of the premiums, the imputed interest could be sizable and defeat the benefits of using this method.

Also, if the corporation furnishing the funds is controlled by the insured (that is, he or she owns more than 50 percent of the stock), the endorsement would cause the death benefit to be included in the estate of the insured, and, thus, the collateral assignment method would have to be used.

When corporate split-dollar life insurance is being considered for a controlling stockholder utilizing the collateral assignment method, it is important to understand that the cash value of the insurance cannot be borrowed against by either the corporation or the ILIT. The IRS has held that the power to borrow when the premium payer controls the corporation is the same as the situation in which the controlling stockholder owns the policy outright. Owning the policy outright would cause the death benefit to be included in the insured's taxable estate.

The inability to borrow from the policy can prove to be a disadvantage for persons who want to keep the death benefit out of their estates but also want the controlled corporation to have full access to the cash value of the life insurance policy. If access to the cash value is important, corporate split dollar may not be the most desirable method of planning for a controlling stockholder. In such cases, family split dollar should be considered, as described later.

Taxation

The income tax consequences of the ILIT split-dollar arrangement, regardless of whether it is the endorsement or the collateral assignment form, is governed by several revenue rulings and two recent notices issued by the Internal Revenue Service. These rulings hold that a *present economic benefit,* which is the cost of the pure insurance protection (the "economic benefit"), is taxable as ordinary income to the insured if the corporation pays this portion of the premiums to the insurance company (in addition to paying the investment element). The economic benefit amount is the lesser of the amount listed in tables provided by the IRS or the insurance company's lowest published annual renewable term rates that are available to the public. It is usually substantially smaller than the investment element paid by the corporation or some other entity.

In many circumstances where the endorsement method is used, the insured, using after-tax dollars, pays the economic benefit portion of the premium. To be precise, the ILIT trustee pays this portion of the premium with funds contributed to the trust, in the form of gifts, by the insured. To the extent that the payments by the insured equal or exceed the economic benefit, the insured does not have to consider any portion of the corporation's payment directly to the insurance company as taxable income—until the agreement is terminated and the policy is no longer owned by the corporation. At that time, according to the latest notice by the IRS, if the insured is alive, any excess cash value over the amount representing the total payments advanced by the employer will be treated as income paid by the employer to the employee and, thus, taxable as income.

If the employer in an endorsement type split dollar pays the *full* premium, the portion of the premium representing the economic benefit is taxable to the employee and is deemed to be a gift from the insured trust maker to the ILIT. Since the economic benefit during the term of the split-dollar agreement (typically, 10 to 15 years) is substantially lower than the full premium, a split-dollar life insurance plan allows a greater premium payment for a smaller gift tax cost and, consequently, more leverage.

It is imperative that the trustee notify the demand-right beneficiaries of their right to withdraw the annual economic benefit amount. If proper notice of the gifts is not given to the beneficiaries, the IRS may very well take the position that the demand rights are illusory, thereby causing the loss of the annual exclusion on the gifts (the protection element or term cost) made to the ILIT. (See Chapter 7, Irrevocable Life Insurance Trust.)

Family Split Dollar

Family split-dollar life insurance is similar to corporate split-dollar life insurance, except that a family member (typically the insured's spouse) or another individual provides part of the premium payment. This is done through an agreement between the insured's spouse and an ILIT that owns and is the beneficiary of the insurance policy. Under the agreement, the ILIT pays the part of the premium equal to the economic benefit (the term cost). The spouse pays the remainder (the "lion's share") of the premium, with no gift tax due on that portion of the payment.

During the insured's life, the insured's spouse may have access to policy cash values through loans or partial surrenders of the policy. When the insured dies, his or her spouse will receive either an amount equal to the premiums he or she paid or the total of the cash value of the policy on the date of death (if larger), depending on the intention of the parties as covered in the split-dollar agreement. The ILIT will receive the remainder of the death benefit. The ILIT's interest in the death benefit is usually substantially greater than the spouse's cash-value interest in the policy (see Figure 10-1 on page 138).

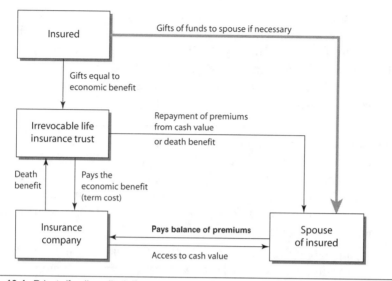

Figure 10-1. Private/family split dollar with insurance on one spouse (historic design).

The tax consequences of family (or "private") split dollar are not fully settled, but two IRS private-letter rulings, one in 1996 and one in 1997, offer some insight. A 1996 ruling involved an insured's spouse who entered into a collateral assignment split-dollar arrangement with an ILIT the insured had established. The insured transferred cash to the trust, which used the cash to acquire a single life insurance policy on the insured's life. The insured did not retain any rights, powers, or interests in the ILIT. Under the split-dollar agreement, the ILIT trustee owned the policy and was to pay a portion of the premium equal to the lesser of the insurance company's pertinent one-year term rate for a standard risk or the government's special table of rates for the pure cost of insurance. The spouse was to pay the balance of each premium.

The arrangement gave the spouse the right to receive the greater of either the cash value in the policy just before death or the premiums advanced (without interest) from the death proceeds. In addition, the spouse had the sole right to borrow from the policy and the right to receive the cash value if the trustee surrendered the policy or if the split-dollar arrangement was terminated.

In its 1996 ruling, the IRS concluded that the spouse would not be treated as making taxable gifts to the ILIT beneficiaries by virtue of premium payments, because the insured's spouse was eventually to be reimbursed. The death proceeds would not be includable in the insured's gross estate at death because the insured did not hold any incidents of ownership in the policy. The IRS declined to rule on whether the interest forgone by the spouse on premium

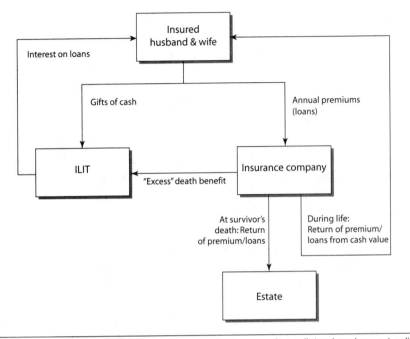

Figure 10-2. Family split dollar with survivorship insurance using collateral assignment split dollar (under IRS Notice 2002-8).

advances would be treated as "imputed" interest income to the ILIT or its beneficiaries.

The 1997 ruling involved a second-to-die/survivorship policy on the lives of a husband and wife who set up an ILIT to own the policy. The couple entered into a split-dollar agreement with the ILIT and agreed to pay the lion's share of the premium directly to the insurance company. The ILIT paid the economic benefit (using the government's special table of rates for the pure cost of insurance for two insureds) from gifts made to the ILIT by the couple. In this case, the couple's access to policy cash values was restricted to receiving back their split-dollar premiums at the termination of the plan. Thus, the IRS ruled that the payments made directly to the insurance company by the couple would not be treated as taxable gifts. The death proceeds, which are payable to the ILIT, would not be includable in the couple's net taxable estate.

Survivorship Insurance Policy

Using the 1997 IRS private letter ruling as a guide, the family (or "private") split-dollar arrangement (as modified by a recent IRS notice) for a couple works as follows:

A couple creates an irrevocable life insurance trust and makes an initial cash gift. Assuming the gift amount is within the available gift tax exemptions and with proper "Crummey" withdrawal notices to the beneficiaries of the ILIT, this gift will be considered a present-interest gift and will not require the payment of any gift tax. Neither the husband nor the wife serves as trustee of the ILIT. The trust applies for and owns a second-to-die/survivorship policy insuring the couple. At the same time, the couple enters into a split-dollar agreement with the trust, using a limited form of collateral assignment. Once the policy has been issued and the split-dollar documents have been signed, the couple will pay premium amounts directly to the insurance company. The premiums paid will be assigned back to the couple through the limited form of collateral assignment.

Because of a recent IRS notice, it appears that the use of the collateral assignment form of split dollar requires the payment of interest by the ILIT to the couple for premiums loaned/paid by them directly to the insurance company. This interest will be imputed, using certain minimum rates mandated by the Internal Revenue Code, if none is provided for in the agreement. Thus, in the first and each of the following years, the ILIT will use the cash gifts from the couple to pay the interest (charged on loans) back to the couple. Interest payments paid, or imputed, will have to be added to the couple's income and taxed accordingly.

Charging interest under the collateral assignment form of split dollar relieves the requirement, under the 1997 IRS private letter ruling framework, of having the ILIT pay the cost of the protection element (economic benefit or term cost) for two insureds to the insurance company. Thus, the couple may loan the full premium amount which they would pay directly to the insurance company.

If both insureds were to die while the split-dollar plan is in force, the insurance company would reimburse their estate the amount of the split-dollar premiums paid plus any unpaid interest due. This amount would be included in their taxable estate.

For as long as the split-dollar plan is in force, the trust owns the death benefit in excess of the premiums paid by the couple. If the plan is terminated during the lifetime of either of the insured, the trust will continue to own the insurance policy. At the second insured's death, the trust will receive the policy proceeds free of income and estate taxes.

Single Life Insurance Policy

Using the 1996 IRS private letter ruling as guide, the family (or private) split-dollar arrangement (as modified by a recent IRS notice) for a single insured works as follows:

Let's say a husband creates an irrevocable life insurance trust and makes an initial cash gift from his separate property. Assuming the gift amount is within the available annual gift tax exemptions and with proper Crummey withdrawal notices to the beneficiaries of the ILIT, this gift will be considered a present-interest gift and will not require the payment of any gift tax. Neither the husband nor the wife serves as trustee. The trustee for the ILIT applies for and owns a single-life policy insuring the husband. At the same time, the wife enters into a split-dollar agreement with the irrevocable life insurance trust, using a limited form of collateral assignment. Once the policy has been issued and the split-dollar documents have been signed, the wife will pay premiums from her separate property directly to the insurance company. These additional premiums will be assigned back to the wife through the limited form of collateral assignment.

Because of a recent IRS notice (discussed below), it appears that the use of the collateral assignment form of split dollar requires the payment of interest by the ILIT to the insured's spouse, or other family member, for premiums loaned/ paid directly to the insurance company. This interest will be imputed, using certain minimum rates mandated by the Internal Revenue Code, if none is provided for in the agreement. Thus, in the first year and each of the following years in our example, the ILIT will use the cash gifts from the husband to pay the interest charged on loans advanced by his wife. Interest payments paid, or imputed, will have to be added to the wife's income and taxed accordingly.

The requirement to charge interest under the collateral assignment form of split dollar is a departure from the 1996 IRS private letter ruling framework in which the ILIT pays the cost of the protection element (economic benefit/term cost), for a single insured, to the insurance company from gifts made to it by the insured spouse (the husband, for example). Using the collateral assignment method *with* interest, a spouse or other family member can loan the full amount of the premium which he or she would pay directly to the insurance company.

At termination of the split-dollar plan, the wife will receive back her split-dollar premiums plus any interest due, typically through a partial withdrawal from the cash value of the policy (see Figure 10-3 on page 142).

If the husband were to die while the plan is in force, the insurance company would reimburse the wife the amount of the premiums plus any interest due. In a properly structured plan, this amount should not be included in the husband's taxable estate.

While the split-dollar plan is in force, the trust owns the death benefit in excess of the premiums paid by the wife. After the plan is terminated, the trust will continue to own the insurance policy. At the death of the insured, the trust will receive the insurance proceeds free of income and estate taxes.

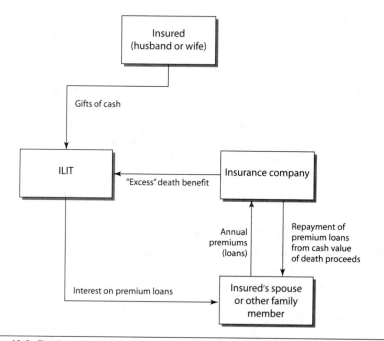

Figure 10-3. Family split dollar with life insurance using collateral assignment split dollar (design modified to conform to IRS Notice 2002-8).

Planning Risks

Any proposed split-dollar plan should be carefully reviewed before it is implemented. The ramifications of income taxation of the protection element (economic benefit) in a corporate split-dollar plan and the restrictions on a controlled corporation's ability to borrow from the policy should be thoroughly understood by the insured and the corporation.

The amount of the premiums that have been advanced either by a corporation or a family member must eventually be repaid by the ILIT out of the death proceeds or from another source—if the repayment is to be made before the insured's life expectancy. A definite plan for repayment should be determined when the split-dollar plan is instituted. If no plan of repayment is made, this could cause a financial hardship on the insured employee. In an endorsement split-dollar plan, as the insured ages, the economic benefit (or term cost) increases and may become rather expensive. At some point in time, the economic benefit could exceed the planned premium and potentially create a gift and/or income tax headache for the insured. In a collateral assignment arrangement in which the insured either pays interest to a corporation or is taxed on interest imputed to him or her, the amount of interest each year could increase to a level which creates economic hardship on the insured.

Additional attention must be given to the position of the IRS relative to split-dollar plans between a corporation and an employee. Until recently, the IRS has generally been silent on the subject of split dollar, forcing professionals and others to rely on a handful of revenue rulings spanning a period of more than 30 years. Specifically, in 2002, the IRS issued a notice that changed the rules on how split-dollar plans are taxed. In summary, here is what the notice said:

- If the endorsement method is used, the employer will be treated for federal tax purposes as the owner of the life insurance contract prior to termination of the arrangement. The value of current life insurance protection (if paid to the insurance company by the employer along with the investment element) and other economic benefits provided to the employee, will be taxable under the Internal Revenue Code. A transfer (or "rollout") of the life insurance contract to the employee will be taxed to the extent the cash value in the insurance contract *exceeds* the premiums advanced by the employer. The notice made clear that there will be no current taxation of a portion of the cash surrender value of a life insurance contract to an employer "solely because the interest or other earnings credited to the cash surrender value of the contract cause the cash surrender value to exceed the portion thereof payable to the employer." Thus, it is not until the endorsement split-dollar agreement is actually terminated and ownership of the policy passes to the employee that any "excess" cash value is subjected to taxation.

- If the collateral assignment method is used (that is, if the employee is formally designated as the owner of the contract and is obligated to repay the employer, whether out of contract proceeds or otherwise), the premiums paid by the employer are to be treated as a series of loans by the employer to the employee. Under this method, such loans are subject to certain rules under the Internal Revenue Code governing the minimum amount of interest that must be charged on loans. If the minimum interest is not provided for in the agreement, it must be imputed and the employee will be considered as having benefited by not paying the minimum interest and, therefore, taxed accordingly.

- Note that since taxation under the endorsement method requires ownership of at least a portion of the insurance contract by the employer (through the endorsement), this method would not likely be used by a controlling shareholder to keep the proceeds of the policy—through an insurance trust—out of his or her estate, because such ownership would be imputed to the insured shareholder.

- The 2002 notice stated that the same principles outlined above apply in "other contexts, including arrangements that provide benefits in gift and corporation-shareholder contexts." Apart from this oblique reference, nothing is said directly about the potential tax treatment of non-traditional (or nonemployment-related) split-dollar arrangements, including private split dollar.

In the case of publicly held companies, legislation passed in 2002 (Sanbanes-Oxley Act) prohibits loans to officers and directors. Because collateral assignment split dollar involves what is considered a "loan" from a corporation to an employee, it appears that such an arrangement is prohibited for officers and directors of publicly held companies.

If family (private) split dollar is used, the agreements must be carefully drafted by a knowledgeable attorney. Although family split dollar has received favorable rulings in at least two private letter rulings by the IRS, these rulings are not law and only apply to the specific cases for which the rulings were requested. Thus, there is some risk associated with the use of family split dollar, so people who are risk-averse should seek their own ruling by the IRS or avoid using this method of premium payment.

11 Gifts Versus Bequests

David and Jeanie Gothard used up their lifetime gift tax exemptions after they retired five years ago, when they gave their only daughter, Madison, shares of stock in the company David had started more than 40 years earlier. Since then, they had continued to give the maximum amount allowed each year under the gift tax exemption limit, but they wanted to do more.

The Gothards had more than enough assets to allow them to support their lifestyle for the rest of their lives and make a gift of $1 million to Madison. They approached me about the advisability of making such a gift because they wanted to reduce their estate and watch Madison enjoy the money while they were alive but they did not want to pay the gift tax on the gift (especially at 50 percent).

Because gift and estate taxes are computed from the same tax table, the Gothards had no idea that gift taxes are applied differently from estate taxes and that by making the gift now to Madison rather than waiting until death they would actually save taxes. They were very surprised to find out that as far as taxes are concerned, it is almost always better to give than to bequeath.

♛ ♛ ♛

A fundamental technique of estate planning is to make maximum use of all available tax exemptions, exclusions, and credits. However, for some situations, this strategy may not be enough to avoid estate taxes completely. In such cases, more advanced planning is required. The remainder of this book explains some of the advanced planning strategies that are available today.

Tax Advantage of Gifts

The techniques described in the following chapters may, at first, seem unrelated. In reality, they are all premised on the same principle: *Making gifts during life is more tax-effective than making bequests at death.* This fact may come as a surprise to you. After all, the gift tax rates come from the estate tax table (page 35), which applies equally to gifts made during life and to amounts bequeathed at death. In addition, most tax experts advise delaying the payment of taxes for as long as possible.

But the fact is that although the tax rates are the same, the way they are applied is so different that there is substantial incentive for making gifts during life and paying gift tax rather than waiting until death. Let's look at an example to find out why.

Example

Dave Webb, age 76, has an estate worth more than $10 million, including stock in a growing family business valued at $1 million, which places him in the 50-percent estate-tax bracket. He would like to give the stock to his son, David Jr., who has operated the business for the last several years. But he hesitates to make the gift because he has already used his full lifetime credit exemption equivalent amount as well as his annual gift tax exclusion. Thus, he is facing the possibility of paying gift taxes of $500,000 on the $1 million gift of stock. However, Dave is surprised to learn that although the gift tax and estate tax rates are the same (50 percent), they are applied differently at death and can add a greater amount of tax. Table 11-1 shows the numbers.

As you can see, when Dave transfers the stock valued at $1 million during life, the gift tax ($500,000) is calculated at 50 percent *only* on the gift amount ($1 million). Thus, it is known as *tax-exclusive tax.* But if Dave keeps the total of $1.5 million (gift plus tax) and waits until death and the same total amount passes to his son, the estate tax will be calculated on the total, not just on the amount that would have been considered a gift if made during Dave's lifetime. Because the estate tax applies to the total and not just the intended gift, it is considered a *tax-inclusive tax.* Thus, the estate tax amounts to $750,000 (50 percent times $1.5 million), which leaves David Jr., with only $750,000 instead of $1 million. When you look at the numbers and divide the tax actually paid by the total of the gift amount plus the tax, you can see that the most gift

TABLE 11-1   Comparing Gift Taxes to Estate Taxes

During life	
Gift during lifetime	$1,000,000
Gift tax (50% of gift)	500,000*
Total	$1,500,000†

At death	
Amount still in estate	$1,500,000†
Estate tax (50% of total)	– 750,000*
Amount left to heirs	$ 750,000

*Different tax amount: Gift tax is 33.3% of total (50% of gift), whereas estate tax is 50% of total.
†Same total amount.

tax you will ever pay is 33.3 percent ($500,000/$1,500,000), as compared to the estate tax of 50 percent ($750,000/$1,500,000) (see Figure 11-1 on page 148).

Time Value of Money

After looking at the numbers, you might wonder how the time value of money would affect Dave's decision. Tax advisors generally recommend deferring taxes for as long as legally possible. Indeed, tax deferral is often described as an interest-free loan from the government. It might seem that he would be better off making the gift later and investing the tax dollars in the meantime. However, the time-value-of-money argument works in favor of making gifts now rather than waiting. The problem is that any additional money earned by waiting will also be taxed at 50 percent.

In Table 11-2 on page 149, we assume that the total stock value plus taxes ($1,500,000) will double between now and Dave's death. Thus, the total to be taxed at his death will be $3 million. The tax is $1,500,000 at 50 percent, leaving $1,500,000 for David Jr. In contrast, if Dave makes the gift now and pays the tax ($500,000) and the stock value doubles, David Jr., will have $2 million free of any further gift or estate tax. Note that by waiting until death, even though the tax money would also double in value ($1 million), it would not be enough to pay the estate taxes. Clearly, it is better for Dave to make the gift now, pay gift tax at the lower effective tax rate of 33.3 percent, and let the appreciation occur in the hands of his son, outside of his estate. The idea of

GIVING

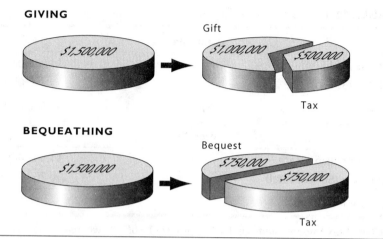

Figure 11-1. Giving versus bequeathing.

shifting future appreciation out of an estate is known as an *estate freeze*. (In later chapters I discuss how to freeze the value of the asset *in* your estate while passing all appreciation out of your estate for the benefit of your heirs.) In Dave's case, the value of the stock is "frozen" at $1 million for estate and gift tax purposes. In short, although deferring income taxes is usually a good idea, deferring gift taxes rarely works out to the donor's advantage.

Discounting

Now that you know that the maximum gift tax you will ever pay is effectively 33.3 percent rather than 50 percent, you may want to look for further tax reduction strategies. One technique is to "discount" the value of the gift asset in order to reduce the amount of the gift tax.

If Dave could give the $1 million in stock to his son but legally report that the gift is worth, say, only $600,000 (a 40 percent discount), the tax of $300,000 (50 percent x $600,000) would represent an effective tax rate of only 23 percent ($300,000/$1,300,000).

Discounting can be achieved through estate planning strategies such as the family limited partnership (FLP) or the family limited liability company (FLLC). Other tools that can be used to discount the value of gifts include grantor retained annuity trusts, grantor retained unitrusts, intentionally defective grantor irrevocable trusts, and qualified personal residence trusts. Later chapters will discuss each of these techniques in detail.

TABLE 11-2 Effect of Future Growth on Gifts and Bequests

		Future growth (times 2)
During life		
Gift during lifetime	$1,000,000	$2,000,000
Gift tax (50% of gift)	500,000	NA
Total	$1,500,000	$2,000,000
At death		
Amount still in estate	$1,500,000	$3,000,000
Estate tax (50% of total)	− 750,000	− 1,500,000
Amount left to heirs	$ 750,000	$1,500,000

Basis

In deciding whether to make a gift, it is important to note that for gifts other than cash, the lesser of the fair market value of the property or the *basis* of the donor (typically, the purchase price) becomes the basis for the recipient, with an upward adjustment for any gift tax paid that is attributable to the appreciation on the property at the time of the gift.

If Dave's basis in his $1 million of stock is $200,000, David Jr.'s basis in the stock after the gift is also $200,000. Also, of the $500,000 of gift tax paid, $400,000 represents the amount of tax on the $800,000 of appreciation that occurred before the gift. Thus, if David Jr., sells the stock, he would be entitled to an upward adjustment of $400,000 on top of the $200,000 basis. So, if David Jr., sold the stock after receipt, he would pay income tax on a gain of $400,000 ($1 million − [$200,000 + $400,000]).

On the other hand, if Dave had bequeathed the stock to his son at death, the basis would "step up" to the fair market value at death (i.e., capital gain taxes are effectively "forgiven" at death). If David Jr., subsequently sold the stock for its value right after his father died, there would be no capital gain tax (except in 2010, see Appendix D). Even with a potential capital gain tax, many would argue that it is still cheaper to wait until death, receive the step-up in basis, and pay only the estate tax at 50 percent, than to be exposed to both capital gain and gift taxes—even if the gift tax is at the net effective rate of 33.3 percent. However, upon further analysis, it would be clear that even with additional potential capital gain taxes on low-basis assets given during life, it is still better to give now than to wait until death when the assets would receive a step-up in basis. For example, with a $200,000 transferred cost basis (adjusted to $600,000 after taking into account gift tax paid on the appreciation), David Jr.'s total tax is $580,000. This is calculated by adding the $500,000 gift tax paid on the $1 million gift (which represents 33.3 percent of the total) to the $80,000 capital gain tax ($400,000 x 20 percent). Contrast this tax to the $750,000 ($1,500,000 x 50 percent) that would be due at death, and you can see that David Jr. is ahead by $170,000 ($750,000 – $580,000). In addition, any appreciation, although subject to capital gain tax rates, occurs outside the estate and escapes additional estate tax of 50 percent at death.

3-Year Rule

On the basis of the difference between the tax-exclusive gift tax and the tax-inclusive estate tax, it would appear that individuals would be better off making "deathbed" gifts of all their property, if possible, to reduce the effective rate of tax. However, in response to this potential for abuse, the tax law includes a provision stating that any gift tax paid by an individual on gifts made within three years of his or her death is added back into the individual's estate for federal estate tax purposes. In other words, an estate tax is imposed on the amount of the gift tax paid during the last three years of a person's life.

For example, if Dave Webb died within three years of making the gift of $1 million, upon which he paid $500,000 gift tax, an additional estate tax of $250,000 (50 percent x $500,000) would be due, for a total tax of $750,000 ($500,000 + $250,000). This is the same amount of tax that would have been due had Dave waited until death and bequeathed the full $1,500,000 to his son. The 3-year rule is yet another reason why people should not delay in making gifts to their loved ones.

Summary

Assuming you live three years beyond the date of making a taxable gift, the maximum effective rate of gift tax is only 33.3 percent, compared to 50 percent for property bequeathed at death. Making a lifetime gift even when gift tax is due has the benefit of "freezing" the value of the asset for transfer tax purposes, with all appreciation and income earned on the property after it is given away escaping estate and gift tax. And by using certain estate planning tools (described in later chapters), you may be able to obtain discounts on gift assets that further reduce the effective rate of gift tax.

One of the major downsides to gifts is that by giving, the donor loses the "forgiveness" of any capital gain tax that applies to property owned at death. However, even with the potential for capital gain taxes on low-basis assets given during life, the estate tax savings are significant in comparison. In most instances, it is better to give than to bequeath.

12 Grantor Retained Interest Trusts

Robert and Sally Joy have a $5 million estate that includes stock in a rapidly growing business that Robert started several years ago. Their son, Michael, is running the business, and their stock is valued at nearly $2 million. Michael is doing a great job at managing the business. Because of his efforts, revenues are growing at the rate of nearly 20 percent per year.

Robert and Sally would like to give their stock to their son before the value of the shares further increases the size of their taxable estate, but they do not want to use up their lifetime exemptions or pay the gift tax such a large gift would incur. Furthermore, they are not ready to give up control of the business or the income generated by their shares.

The Joys were extremely pleased to find that a grantor retained annuity trust will address their concerns and allow them to achieve their goals.

It is safe to say that many of us would happily give away a substantial number of our assets to our children if not for three critical concerns:

1. We do not yet feel comfortable parting with the income generated by the assets.
2. We are not sure if we are ready for our children to have full control of, or the full income from, the assets.
3. We do not want to pay a large gift tax or to use up a sizable amount of our applicable exemption.

153

Fortunately, there is a way to reduce or eliminate gift taxes and even leverage the value of a gift while retaining both the income from and the control of the asset. This is accomplished through grantor retained annuity trusts (GRATs) and grantor retained unitrusts (GRUTs).

GRATs and GRUTs are unique in that they allow you to give away assets to your children. However, they retain an income stream from the assets for a period of time chosen by you. At the same time, they allow you to reduce or even *eliminate* gift taxes.

The Basics

GRATs and GRUTs offer the following specific benefits:

- Allow you to make gifts of property while retaining an income interest in the property for a period of years.
- Reduce the gift tax value of the assets by delaying the beneficiaries' actual use of the property for a period of years.
- Remove the value of the assets from your taxable estate and eliminate any gift or estate taxes on subsequent appreciation.
- Shelter assets from the claims of potential creditors.
- Reduce or eliminate gift or estate tax on the current value of assets given to the trust.

Strategy

Affluent individuals often own assets that are appreciating in value. Good estate planning may mean finding a strategy that will remove the assets from the taxable estate because they will create a tremendous amount of estate tax at death. Many times, the assets generate considerable amounts of income that the owner cannot or does not want to give up. Further, the gift tax cost of giving the assets away may be prohibitively expensive.

GRATs and GRUTs are irrevocable trusts that provide an excellent solution to this dilemma. An individual can give the appreciating assets to either a GRAT or a GRUT and retain an income interest in the assets for a period of years. When the period of years ends, the assets either pass to the remainder beneficiaries outright or are held in trust for their benefit.

Because the beneficiaries do not receive the assets until sometime in the future, the value of the gift is discounted. The amount of the discount is based on the length of time before the beneficiaries receive the use of the assets (the term of the trust), how much income is retained by the grantor trust maker, the current government-adjusted applicable federal rate, and the age of the trust maker if the interests have a life contingency. The higher the income interest and the longer the length of time during which income is to be paid to the grantor, the smaller the gift tax value of the gift.

Because the value of the assets transferred to a GRAT or GRUT is discounted for the amount of time that passes before the beneficiaries receive the gift, it is possible to reduce the taxable gift value (the present value) substantially—perhaps even to nothing. In addition, all the appreciation of the property from the date of the gift forward is shifted to the beneficiaries, totally eliminating the federal estate tax on the appreciation of those assets in the estate of the trust maker.

GRAT Example

Tom Kocher is a 55-year-old widower with a substantial estate. He is the sole owner of a growing family injection-molding business that he would like to eventually pass on to his three children, all of whom are actively involved in the business. Tom has been gradually withdrawing from the day-to-day management and would like to retire in the near future. Tom has other assets, including a large stock portfolio, real estate, and a qualified retirement plan, all of which are sufficient to provide him with a comfortable retirement income.

Goals

The business is currently valued at $1 million and is growing rapidly. This will exacerbate future estate tax problems and will create an obstacle to the preservation of the family business at Tom's death. Tom's goal is simple: Eliminate gift or estate tax on gifts of his stock while retaining income and control of his business for a specified number of years.

The Plan

Tom would like to give the business to his three children, however, he is *not* willing to pay the gift taxes. He could sell the business to his children, but doing so would require that the children take on a substantial amount of debt, which may cause a strain on the business. In addition, selling would increase his estate rather than reduce it, burdening his children with payments. Tom's plan is to give stock in his business to his three children over time, in a way that will reduce the value of his gift for tax purposes to no more than one third of his lifetime credit exemption equivalent.

The Structure

Tom should consider establishing a grantor retained annuity trust and giving his corporation stock to the trust. At the end of the specified term, the stock in the trust, including any appreciation in value, would pass to Tom's three children. The gift value of the stock for tax purposes would be substantially reduced.

Tom structures the GRAT to provide an annuity of $80,000 (the retained annuity) per year for 15 years. Additional details of the GRAT structure include:

1. The children will continue to draw their regular salaries.
2. With Tom retiring as an employee and no longer drawing a salary, the trust payments to him (as the annuity beneficiary) will be funded through profit distributions from the company to the trust (therefore, there is no additional tax).
3. Any additional profits can be accumulated in the corporation or the trust, thereby increasing the trust's value and, in turn, the remainder interest to the children.
4. Because the trust is a "grantor trust" (discussed below) for income tax purposes, Tom will pay income tax on all the trust's income. This would include amounts accumulated in the corporation (owned by the GRAT) but not distributed directly to him.
5. The annuity must be paid even if the corporation doesn't generate sufficient income to pay it. In such cases, a portion of the trust principal (stock) must be distributed to fund the balance of the annuity payment. No income tax is owed on distributions of principal.

The remainder interest (family corporation stock in the GRAT) will pass to the children at the end of the 15-year period. Because Tom is only 55 now, the 15-year period is short enough for him to reasonably expect to survive the trust period.

Tom sets up the trust and gives the stock in a month when the applicable federal rate equals 7 percent. To determine the total value of the remainder interest gift, we must first determine the value of the annuity retained by Tom. Then we subtract the annuity value from the $1 million value of the stock transferred to the trust. Based on the applicable federal

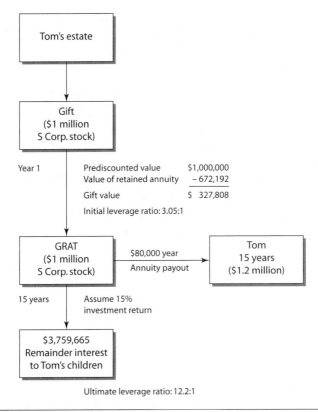

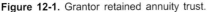

Figure 12-1. Grantor retained annuity trust.

rate and the IRS valuation tables, the initial present value of the $80,000 retained annuity that will be paid to Tom for 15 years is $678,560.

Subtracting Tom's $678,560 from the stock value of $1 million results in a remainder interest of $321,440, which is the value of the gift for tax purposes—less than one-third of the $1 million family corporation stock and Tom's lifetime credit exemption equivalent (see Figure 12-1).

Results

By planning with a GRAT, Tom achieves the following:

- He removes a substantial asset and all future growth in the value of that asset from his estate.
- He establishes a plan to transfer the business to the next generation.

- The value of the company is $1 million. However, because of reduction for the time value of money (the value of the retained annuity), the value of the gift for tax purposes is only $321,440.
- Assuming a 15 percent growth rate on the value of the business, the business will be worth $4,544,407 at the end of the 15-year trust period even after subtracting the $80,000 per year annuity payments.
- Tom will have excluded $4,222,967 ($4,544,407 – $321,440) of wealth from taxation, and this results in a leverage ratio of 13.14 to 1 ($4,222,967/ 321,440). (*Note:* Significant additional leverage could be achieved by structuring the transaction with "discounts." If the corporate shares could be discounted so that their gift tax value is lower, the net gift would be smaller and the ratio even greater. [Discounting is covered under a discussion of family limited partnerships in Chapter 14.])
- Tom utilizes only a portion of his applicable credit exemption equivalent (see Table 2-2 on page 36) and avoids having to pay gift tax.

The GRAT arrangement in this situation is most viable because:

1. The trust income derived from the corporation is expected to exceed the required annuity payout.
2. The asset used to fund the GRAT (the family corporation stock) has significant appreciation potential.

Should Tom die during the 15-year trust period, the value of the trust would be included in his estate. However, any applicable credit used and/or any gift taxes paid on the gift would be restored. To offset this possibility, a 15-year level term policy of insurance in the amount of $500,000 (the tax on the $1 million value of the business) with an increasing death benefit is recommended. Given Tom's age and good health, the annual premium would be less than 6 percent of the annual annuity payments Tom receives from the GRAT.

Zeroed-Out GRAT

In a *zeroed-out GRAT,* the amount or length of the annuity is designed so that the taxable value of the gift is very small or completely eliminated and a large portion of any appreciation on the GRAT property is shifted out of the grantor's estate. If the estate tax exemption has been exhausted, this option is particularly attractive as a means of avoiding gift tax.

Let's say that Tom Kocher, has established a zeroed-out GRAT. Tom retains the right to an annuity which is high enough or long enough for the remainder interest passing to his children to be valued at close to zero. In other

TABLE 12-1   To Obtain a Near-Zero Gift at 8% AFR

Term of GRAT (years)	Annuity percentage	
	Based on discounted value ($1 million)	Based on full value ($1.5 million)
5	24.75	16.50
10	14.75	9.83
15	11.50	7.67
20	10.00	6.66
25	9.25	6.16

words, the value of the annuity that will be paid to Tom over the term of the GRAT is almost equal to the value, after any discounts, of the asset that is initially transferred to the GRAT. As a result, there is a very small current taxable gift. Assuming the GRAT payments are economically feasible and an insurance policy is used as a backup, a zeroed-out GRAT can be an absolute "no-lose" opportunity.

Under a zeroed-out GRAT, if the total return (growth and income) on the assets contributed to the GRAT exceeds the applicable federal rate that must be used in valuing the contribution, transfer tax savings will be obtained. In effect, a higher total return shifts all growth and income on the property held in the GRAT—in excess of the federal rate at the time the GRAT is established—to the children without any gift or estate tax. The applicable federal rate changes monthly, so the timing of the funding of a GRAT is important.

If it is possible to obtain a discount (this is covered thoroughly in Chapter 14) on the value of the shares contributed to the GRAT, the annuity payout calculation to reduce the gift to near zero will be based on the *discounted* amount. This could leave substantially more in the GRAT for the beneficiaries of the trust, who, in this case, are Tom's children. For example, if the initial value of the shares is $1.5 million and the gift shares qualify for "minority" and "lack-of-marketability" discounts equal to 33.3 percent, the gift value, before the GRAT calculation, would be $1 million. The annuity payment, based on the $1 million, would be a lower percentage of $1.5 million. One way to achieve such a discount would be for Tom to create a separate GRAT for each child and give one-third of the stock to obtain a "minority discount" for the amount going into each trust.

Table 12-1 will give you an idea of how much of the initial value of the principal contributed to a GRAT must be retained as an annuity in order to produce a near-zero taxable gift. For example, to obtain a zeroed-out GRAT when the applicable federal rate is 8 percent, Tom could set up a 15-year GRAT that called for an annuity based on 11.5 percent but really worked out to (after a 33.3 percent discount) to 7.67 percent of the $1.5 million contributed to the trust.

This strategy should be considered for individuals who have *appreciating* assets that create an income flow which they would like to retain for a period of time. It is also a useful planning technique in cases where the objective is to make gifts at little or no gift tax cost.

GRATs Versus GRUTs

The primary difference between a GRAT and a GRUT is the manner in which the income interest is defined. The difference affects both the amount of the retained income and the amount of the gift that will eventually pass to the beneficiaries.

Amount of Retained Income

In a GRAT, the income interest that the maker receives must be a *fixed dollar amount* representing a fixed percentage of the trust's *initial* value. Because of this requirement, once a GRAT is funded, no more assets can be contributed to it. The annuity amount must be paid at least annually, regardless of whether the trust assets generate enough income to do so. If enough income is not generated, the trustee must either return some of the principal or sell assets to create enough income to cover the annuity payment.

Because the annuity interest of a GRAT must be permanently set when the initial contribution is made to the trust, the valuation of the assets is critical. An appraisal by a qualified appraiser should be obtained to determine the initial valuation of the contributed property so there is no question in the future as to the appropriateness of the value used. Further, if a discount is involved through the use of a family limited partnership, family limited liability company, corporate stock, among others, an appraisal establishing the discount is essential to withstand IRS scrutiny.

In a GRUT, the income interest received by the maker must be a *fixed percentage* of the value of the trust property. This means that the trust property *must be valued each year* and the income payment will be based on this valuation. The amount the maker receives each year will vary according to the value of the trust assets. The annual revaluation of trust property could be a disadvantage if the cost of the valuation is considerable.

Because the unitrust amount is expressed as a percentage of the value of the GRUT property each year, the maker can make additional contributions to the GRUT. Again, this cannot be done in a GRAT because of the fixed payout amount.

Valuation of the Gift to Beneficiaries

The value of the gift made to the beneficiaries is based on several factors including the term of the GRAT or GRUT, the age of the maker, the unitrust percentage or annuity amount chosen, the number of payments per year, and the current federal interest rate. The interest rate is provided by the Internal Revenue Service on a monthly basis and is called the *adjusted applicable federal rate*. In computing the value of a GRAT or GRUT, the applicable federal rate is 120-percent of the federal "midterm rate" in effect at the time of the gift.

The purpose of the applicable federal rate is to have a consistent specified rate of return for computing the value of the gift to the ultimate beneficiaries and to prevent taxpayers from making rate-of-return assumptions that may not be realistic.

Because of the difference between the income interests of a GRAT and a GRUT, the value of the gift to the beneficiaries can be quite different. If the maker of a GRAT chooses to take an annuity that is greater than the current applicable federal rate, the GRAT will produce a smaller gift (and less gift tax) than a comparable GRUT. That is, there will be less in the GRAT at the end of the term. If the GRAT is invested well and it produces appreciation and income greater than the annuity amount, the beneficiaries will get a windfall at no extra tax. However, if the assets in the GRAT produce a rate of return equal to or lower than the applicable federal rate, the beneficiaries will receive a smaller gift.

In a GRUT, if the income amount paid in a year exceeds the applicable federal rate, the value of the assets in the trust will be less the next year. Because GRUT payments are based on the value of the assets, the maker will receive less. Under these circumstances, the maker of a GRUT will receive less money over time, increasing the likelihood that the ultimate beneficiaries will receive a larger gift.

Let's compare a GRAT and a GRUT with identical terms. Assume that Michael, 60 years of age, wants to create either a GRAT or a GRUT for a 10-year term. He is going to make a gift of $1 million and wants either a 9 percent fixed annuity ($90,000 per year) or a 9 percent unitrust payment based on the annual value of the trust's assets. Let's assume that the applicable federal rate is 7 percent and that payments are to be made on a quarterly basis.

With a $1 million gift, the difference between a GRAT and a GRUT is dramatic:

- GRAT value for gift tax purposes: $351,504.
- GRUT value for gift tax purposes: $422,781.

In fact, this difference is the primary reason why GRATs are used far more than GRUTs when interest rates are low. If interest rates are high or if the yield of the assets to be given is not likely to exceed the current applicable federal rate, a GRUT should be considered.

There are many variations that can be used with GRATs and GRUTs. The term of the trust can be increased, in which case the value of the gift and any gift tax is decreased. The amount of return can be varied. The greater the annuity or unitrust amount, the less the tax value of the gift. Detailed projections should be run to determine the best result.

Planning Considerations

Income Tax

GRATs and GRUTs are "grantor" trusts under the Internal Revenue Code. A *grantor trust* is one in which the amount of control retained by the maker causes all the income of the trust to be taxable to the maker rather than to the trust itself even though the trust assets are out of the maker's estate.

If a GRAT or a GRUT produces more income than the amount that must be paid to the maker, he or she must pay income taxes on the excess amount. It is therefore possible that a maker could be taxed on income, including capital gain income, that he or she never received.

Although it is definitely not the best of all worlds to be taxed on income that one does not receive, there is an advantage to this result. When the maker pays the tax, he or she is increasing the amount of the gift to the ultimate beneficiaries and is lowering his or her taxable estate without suffering any gift or estate tax penalty. If the maker pays the tax, the money in the trust is intact; it is not reduced by taxes. Thus, the funds for the beneficiaries are growing just as they would be if the maker made a gift to them but without income tax. Also, the maker's estate is reduced by the amount of income taxes that are paid during the term of the trust.

The income tax payments are *not* considered a taxable gift because the maker is not paying on income taxable to the trust or its beneficiaries; the maker is paying his or her own legal tax obligation. The Internal Revenue Service does not like this result, so it has not yet determined if it is going to allow or disallow it. Most tax professionals agree that, despite the IRS reluctance to accept this concept, the law is clear that no gift is made in such situations.

The grantor trust nature of GRATs and GRUTs offers another potential advantage to the maker. A GRAT or GRUT can be drafted to allow the maker to "buy back" the assets held in trust at any time. Assume that a grantor would like to make a gift of income-producing real estate to a GRAT but would also like the opportunity, before the expiration of the GRAT's term, to buy the property back at fair market value. When the buyback occurs, even if the purchase price is more than the trust's cost basis in the property, *there is no taxable income.* Under the grantor trust rules, the maker is buying property back from himself or herself. You do not have to pay income taxes when buying something from yourself for yourself. Thus, the maker can give property away for a period of time and buy it back with no tax consequence—even if the property is purchased at a substantially appreciated value. This may help ultimate beneficiaries avoid the taxable gain that would occur upon selling a low-basis asset received from the trust.

Wording

If a GRAT or a GRUT is not drafted correctly and the maker dies during the term of the trust, the consequences can be costly. For example, if a maker is married and dies during the trust's term, unless the GRAT or GRUT "pours over" into the maker's estate planning, the funds in the GRAT or GRUT will not qualify for the marital deduction and thus will create an immediate tax. This tax will not be paid from the assets in the GRAT or GRUT; the maker's estate itself will be liable, and it will pay the estate tax. Not only is there an acceleration in the payment of the tax, but the entity causing the tax—the GRAT or GRUT—will not have to pay it. This is one of the many reasons why proper drafting of these trusts is so vitally important.

Grantor's Age

The age of the maker is an important consideration in the design and implementation of a GRAT or GRUT. The older the maker, the greater the likelihood that he or she will die during the term of the trust. Therefore, when the gift portion of a GRAT or GRUT is valued, the older the maker, the shorter the term of the trust and the higher the value of the gift. Because of this concern, this strategy may not be appropriate for some older individuals.

Trustees

The maker of a GRAT or a GRUT can act as the sole trustee or as a cotrustee. In fact, in a properly drafted GRAT or GRUT, there is no limitation on who can act as trustee as long as the trustee is not a minor and is not legally incapacitated. After the income term, if the GRAT or GRUT continues to hold the trust property, with no property distributed outright to the beneficiaries or transferred to another trust or trusts, trustees other than the maker and his or her spouse should be named.

Creditor Protection

The assets given to a GRAT or a GRUT have been given away; even though the maker retains the right to the income, the asset itself is no longer owned by the trust maker. If, after the gift is made, the maker has creditor exposure, the creditors cannot, in the absence of fraud, take the assets given to the GRAT or GRUT. However, creditors can take the income interest that was retained for the remaining term of the GRAT or GRUT in most states. In states like Florida, where annuities and their proceeds are free from the claims of creditors, it may be possible to protect the *income* interest from claims of the maker's creditors.

If, after the term of the GRAT or GRUT ends, the assets remain in trust, the ultimate beneficiaries also have creditor protection as long as the property remains in trust. Only the income or principal paid out of the trust is subject to the claims of the beneficiaries' creditors.

Generation Skipping

GRATs and GRUTs are not good candidates for generation-skipping planning. Because the ultimate beneficiaries of a GRAT or a GRUT do not receive their gift until the trust term ends, a maker can allocate his or her $1.1 million generation-skipping tax exemption only at that time (as adjusted—see Appendix D). The law does not allow a maker to base his or her allocation on the basis of the gift that is computed (the discounted value). It is based on the actual amount of assets passing to the person or persons getting the generation-skipping distribution, which will not be known until the end of the trust term. *This uncertainty makes the use of a GRAT or GRUT for generation skipping a practical impossibility.*

Drawbacks

Death of maker during term

One of the inherent risks in using a GRAT or a GRUT is that the maker might die during the term of the trust. Unless there is a very high probability that the maker will outlive the term of the GRAT or GRUT, this strategy is generally inappropriate. Therefore, individuals who are elderly or not in good health should avoid using it.

If death occurs during the trust term, there is no penalty for establishing the GRAT or GRUT. For most purposes, the estate and gift tax consequences are such that the transaction is treated as never having happened. If the maker used some of his or her exemption equivalent, it is restored. The value of the assets in the GRAT or GRUT is included in the maker's estate for federal tax purposes.

Under some conditions, the amount included in the maker's estate will be less than the value of the assets in the GRAT. The maker's gross estate includes only the portion of the trust assets that would be necessary to produce the required annuity payments, assuming that the assets were generating income at the applicable federal rate on the date of the maker's death.

Although the estate inclusion is not a detriment in itself, if the assets were given away under some other technique, perhaps they would not be brought back into the maker's estate. Therefore, the "opportunity cost" of premature death could be expensive. One possible solution to this risk is provided by life insurance. The maker could have a term policy on his or her life during the term of the GRAT or GRUT. The insurance proceeds could offset any taxes due if the assets in the trust are brought back into the maker's estate because of premature death. Another alternative is to set up a grantor trust with an independent trustee and sell, rather than give, assets to the trust. This is discussed in greater detail in the next chapter.

Insufficient income produced

Another risk is that the assets held in a GRAT or GRUT might not generate enough income to support payments to the maker. If they don't, the trustee may have to sell assets in the trust or return some of the principal to the maker in order to satisfy the income requirement. Thus, the actual gift will be lower than the amount of the gift computed at the inception of the planning. The maker will have used up more exemption equivalent or will have paid more gift tax than he or she should have.

Excess income produced

On the other hand, if the GRAT or GRUT produces income in excess of the required payment amount, the maker must report this phantom income on his or her income tax return. This result may not be all bad, as the ultimate beneficiaries will get more assets and the maker's estate will be reduced at no gift or estate tax cost. However, it may be a drawback for some people who might consider setting up a GRAT.

Termination of income

Finally, the income interest from a GRAT or GRUT must end sometime, and when it does, the maker must either have another source of income or simply have no need for the income coming from the trust. People who are likely to need the income from their assets for life should consider alternative methods of planning (see the chapters that follow).

Summary

GRATs and GRUTs can provide a way to make gifts to your children at a substantially reduced gift tax cost. In addition, they shift all future growth and income on the contributed assets, in excess of the payout rate at the time the GRAT or GRUT is established, out of your estate for the benefit of your heirs—free of any future gift or estate tax. GRATs and GRUTs also allow you to retain both income from and control of the gift assets for a period of years chosen to suit your particular needs.

Often these trusts are used in conjunction with other powerful estate planning tools, such as family limited partnerships (see Chapter 14), to provide additional leveraging of gifts within gift tax exemption limits.

If you are considering the use of a GRAT or GRUT, be sure to seek the advice of professionals who specialize in estate planning to make sure the intended effect is achieved without attack by the IRS.

13 Intentionally Defective Grantor Irrevocable Trusts

J John and Helen Burton visited my office after they had been to an attorney who had recommended that they use a grantor retained annuity trust to reduce their estate in order to pass a valuable piece of income-producing commercial real estate to their daughter, Pam. They were hesitant about the attorney's plan because if they died during the term of the trust, the plan would terminate. The property would then be back in their estate, and they would not have accomplished their goal. In addition, with a grantor retained annuity trust, they would not be able to include generation-skipping provisions in the trust, so the property would be subject to another layer of tax in Pam's estate. Furthermore, the commercial property had a tax cost basis, after depreciation, of next to nothing, and the Burtons wanted a way to step up the basis to the current market value so that Pam would not have to face a significant income tax when the property was eventually sold.

I explained to John and Helen that the grantor retained annuity trust would not address their concerns. A better solution was available through the use of an intentionally defective grantor irrevocable trust. Not only would this trust allow them to transfer any future appreciation to their daughter (effectively freezing the value of the real estate in their estate), but also the plan would be effective immediately. As a result, they would have a way to substantially leverage their generation-skipping exemption, and the trust would provide an opportunity for additional significant planning benefits.

169

One of the primary goals of any good estate plan is to reduce your exposure to taxes while leveraging your gift, estate, and generation-skipping tax exemptions.

As Chapter 12 explained, grantor retained annuity trusts (GRATs) and grantor retained unitrusts (GRUTs) hold assets and pay income to you as the grantor for a specified term. At the end of the term, the assets pass to your children or selected beneficiaries. Because you retain a right to income from the GRAT or GRUT, as long as the assets' growth exceeds the income payment, you are able to leverage your giving ability by discounting the value of the gift assets—thereby reducing any taxes due on the gift.

Another type of grantor trust that provides an opportunity for leveraging plus income tax benefits while keeping the trust property out of your estate is the *intentionally defective grantor irrevocable trust (IDGIT)*.

As part of the Internal Revenue Code since 1954, grantor trust rules stipulate that if a trust document contains certain provisions, the trust's income will be taxed to the trust's creator—the grantor—rather than to the trust itself. Congress devised the rules thinking no sensible taxpayer would want to pay a trust's tax bill, especially because individual tax rates at that time were higher than trust tax rates and the grantor cannot be a beneficiary of a grantor trust. But now, income tax rates are much lower than they were in 1954, and thus for someone focused more on estate taxes, a grantor trust, an IDGIT, can substantially increase the wealth passed to heirs.

IDGIT Basics

An IDGIT is simply a type of irrevocable trust drafted to trigger the grantor trust rules and force the grantor, rather than the trust, to pay income tax on trust income. That's the "intentionally defective" part. Assets are moved into, and become owned by the trust, with the positive result that those assets, and their future appreciation, are outside the grantor's taxable estate. Paying the income tax on the trust's annual earnings further reduces the grantor's estate while netting another benefit: 100-percent of the earnings can accumulate inside the IDGIT, to the advantage of the trust beneficiaries, who are typically the grantor's children.

Because the IRS requires that the grantor pay the trust's tax, that payment is a legal obligation, not a gift, so no gift tax applies. In effect, value is shifted to the trust beneficiaries at the grantor's income tax rate. This is preferable to having the IDGIT or its beneficiaries pay the income tax while leaving value in the grantor's estate that would later be subject to estate tax.

Drafting the trust to be "defective" (so that it triggers the grantor trust rules) is a simple matter for a knowledgeable attorney. One way to do this is to provide that trust principal or income may be distributed to the grantor's spouse. This arrangement has no estate or gift tax significance, but it automatically makes the trust an IDGIT.

Another way to accomplish this is to specify that the grantor retains the power to reacquire the trust corpus by substituting other property of equivalent value or by giving someone other than the grantor or current beneficiary of the trust the power to expand the class of beneficiaries. Such power is sometimes given to the grantor's accountant, and even though the power may never be exercised, the grantor trust rules are triggered.

A good attorney will also provide an element of control by making it possible to "turn off" the grantor trust status, in case paying tax for the IDGIT becomes a financial burden for the grantor. This can sometimes be accomplished by giving a power holder (such as the accountant in the previous example), the right to renounce the power.

Selling Assets to an IDGIT

A grantor can transfer assets into an IDGIT by either gift or sale. Making a gift consumes the grantor's various exemptions, but if the grantor sells an asset to the IDGIT, there is no gift and therefore no gift tax. Furthermore, there is no recognition of gain, and thus no capital gain tax when assets are sold to an IDGIT. For tax purposes, selling an asset to an IDGIT is the same as selling an asset to oneself: No tax.

If you have highly appreciated assets you would like to remove from your estate, you could possibly *avoid all capital gain taxes* as well as gift taxes by selling the assets to an IDGIT that you create. To leverage the transaction, the IDGIT could pay for the assets in the form of an installment note, payable over several years. The Internal Revenue Code allows you to charge a relatively low rate of interest on the installment note. This is a decided advantage, as it enables an IDGIT that is earning a market rate of return to invest the cash flow in excess of the low-interest note payments so that it can accumulate and grow and eventually be used to pay back the note principal. Also, because of the grantor trust rules, you do not have to recognize the interest on the note. So, there is no tax deduction for the trust, and there is no taxable income for you, the grantor, for interest payments on the note from the trust. However, you are still liable for taxes on the income *earned by* the IDGIT, including any income earned by property sold to the trust.

The excess income over the note payments may be high enough to allow you to further leverage the value of the IDGIT through the purchase of insurance or some other growth vehicle. In addition, because the grantor pays the income taxes on trust income, the trust's return is enhanced for the beneficiaries of the trust. Best of all, the payment of income taxes by the grantor is not considered a gift for transfer purposes.

To qualify for charging a low interest rate (such as the federal midterm rate), the note should be written to last from three to nine years ("midterm"). Also, it should be properly documented with reasonable terms. It is a good idea to have separate representation of the grantor and the IDGIT, including actual negotiations of the terms of sale.

Example

Rich Crow, as grantor, sells real estate assets worth $2.5 million, with an annual income of 10 percent ($250,000), to an IDGIT and makes a direct "seed" gift of $250,000 utilizing part of his applicable credit exemption equivalent, so no gift tax is due. The installment note of $2.5 million calls for payments of interest at only 5.5 percent (the applicable federal midterm rate at that time), and principal is due at maturity in nine years. The real estate more than generates enough income to cover the interest payments of $137,500 (5.5 percent x $2.5 million), and the trust retains the balance of $112,500 ($250,000 – $137,500) for purchasing insurance. Assuming a growth rate of 5 percent beyond the income, the assets in the trust should grow to approximately $3.9 million in nine years. The IDGIT then returns $2.5 million in cash or other assets (that is, a share of the real estate) to satisfy the note at maturity.

The result is that the IDGIT will end up with assets valued at $1,400,000 ($3,900,000 – $2,500,000) for the benefit of its beneficiaries plus approximately $600,000 accrued from the seed money given to the trust (based on 10-percent annualized growth). In addition, the IDGIT will own an insurance policy worth several million dollars at Rich's death. None of the accumulated funds will be subject to gift, estate, or GST taxes.

GRAT Versus IDGIT

In many respects, a sale of assets on an installment note to an IDGIT is similar to a gift of assets to a GRAT. In a GRAT, the present value of the annuity payments to the grantor reduces the amount of the taxable gift, but the annuity payments, if not fully consumed, return value to the grantor's estate. In an installment-note sale to an IDGIT, principal and interest on the note are paid back to the grantor over time, and this also returns value to the grantor's estate. However, when structured properly, using the following techniques, this repayment can be a substantially reduced amount. This, in turn, leaves more for heirs.

There are other advantages of using an IDGIT rather than a GRAT:

- According to the IRS, if the grantor of a GRAT dies during the term of the trust, the grantor's retained annuity interest causes the entire value of the trust to be included in the grantor's gross estate. With an IDGIT installment note (discussed below), if the seller-grantor dies before the note is repaid, only the unpaid balance of the note is included in the gross estate.

- The payment schedule for an installment note to an IDGIT can be more flexible than the annuity paid from a GRAT. Under the Internal Revenue Code, the annuity payments from a GRAT cannot vary by more than 20 percent from year to year. There is no such restriction on installment sales to an IDGIT, so the installment note can be a "balloon" note, with a large payment at the end of the note, or have any other payment schedule that is desirable.

- The GRAT rules determine the amount of the taxable gift by assuming that the GRAT assets grow at a rate prescribed by the Internal Revenue Code. This rate is 20 percent higher than the federal midterm rate. The code requires only that an installment note from an IDGIT bear interest at the same rate as the federal rate that matches the term of the note—short-term rate (one to three years), midterm rate (three to nine years) or long-term (more than nine years)—to avoid the unwelcome income and gift tax implications of "below-market" loans. The lower rate of interest used in IDGIT calculations inures to the benefit of the trust's beneficiaries. Assuming the assets in the trust have a total pretax return that exceeds the interest rate charged in the note, the sale will result in a transfer of value to the beneficiaries that escapes gift, estate, and GST taxes. In addition, any appreciation in the underlying value of the assets in the IDGIT will be outside the grantor's estate and thus will avoid any further gift or estate tax.

- In a GRAT, the GST exemption of $1.1 million (as adjusted, see Appendix D) per grantor cannot be allocated until the end of the annuity term. Therefore, the appreciated value of the assets remaining in the

GRAT at the end of the term could either consume GST exemptions or be subject to the special 50 percent GST tax when and if the value is paid to a "skip person" (such as a grandchild). On the other hand, in an IDGIT, the grantor need allocate only part of his or her GST tax exemption to any assets given directly to the trust (the small seed gift), and all appreciation in the trust can escape the GST tax—a substantial advantage! With the tremendous leverage that can be generated using this method, it is a good idea to consider multigenerational planning with IDGITs. (See the discussion in Chapter 4 about generation-skipping planning.)

The Seed Gift

To help support the installment note and the viability of the strategy, it is advisable for the grantor to make a small seed gift to the IDGIT. It is generally recommended that this gift be at least 10 percent of the value of the assets to be sold. The seed property is important because the trust needs to have a measure of independence from the grantor. Also, it should not appear that the income distributed from the property sold to the trust is the sole source of funds being used to service the entire note. If the seed gift is too small, the sale may be treated by the IRS as a gift (not a desired result).

Sale With a Discounted Asset

The benefit of the IDGIT strategy can be further enhanced if the trust maker utilizes the valuation discounts that are available for certain assets such as corporate stock (such as, limited liability company or subchapter S stock) or family limited partnership shares (discussed in detail in Chapter 14). Nonvoting stock or limited partnership shares are given or sold to an IDGIT at their appraised value. Generally, the fair market value of such shares is adjusted downward from their value in the business entity that issued them due to valuation issues resulting from such aspects as lack of control and/or lack of marketability—relative to those shares. If the stock or shares are sold to an IDGIT, the valuation adjustment reduces the principal amount of the note while increasing the effective yield to the trust from the true value of the underlying assets.

Example

Using the previous example, let's see what would happen if Rich Crow sells his $2.5 million real estate assets to an IDGIT in exchange for a nine-year note with payments of interest only through a discounted-value arrangement.

Rich first transfers the real estate to a family limited partnership in which he and his wife, Mimi, are the general partners (through a limited liability company) owning 1 percent of the shares and Rich is the limited partner owning the other 99 percent.

Assume the limited-partnership shares are entitled to a discount of 40 percent for lack of marketability and lack of control (discussed in more detail in Chapter 14). Although the underlying value is $2.5 million (for the value of the real estate in the partnership), the discounted value of the partnership shares for sale to the IDGIT is 40 percent less, or $1.5 million. With an applicable federal midterm rate of 5.5 percent, the note calls for the IDGIT to make annual interest payments to Rich in the amount of $82,500 (5.5 percent x $1.5 million), rather than the $137,500 without the benefit of the 40 percent discount. This leaves the trust with $55,000 ($137,500 − $82,500) more per year that can be invested for the benefit of Rich and Mimi's children, who are the beneficiaries of the IDGIT.

The bottom line for Rich and Mimi is a reduction of their estate, which will receive back $1.5 million (the discounted sale price of the partnership shares) instead of $2.5 million at the end of the nine-year note term. This leaves an extra million dollars worth of underlying asset value, along with all the growth realized on the full real estate value over the nine years, to benefit the trust via the partnership. Also, a further reduction in their estate is achieved by Rich and Mimi's payment of the taxes on any earnings inside the trust. On top of all this is the added benefit, for the IDGIT and its beneficiaries, of the excess income generated by the difference between the cash flow from the real estate and the interest paid on the installment note—at the discounted value!

Leverage With Life Insurance

The real power of this strategy comes when the trustee of the IDGIT uses the excess income created in the IDGIT to purchase life insurance. The income earned by the IDGIT over and above the amount needed to pay the installment note can go toward life insurance premiums on the life of the grantor, a beneficiary, or some other relative. The premium payments will not attract gift tax because they are made from trust income. The amount of insurance purchased can be substantial and significantly increase the value of the trust assets that will eventually pass to the beneficiaries.

In the example above, the anticipated excess income on the assets in the IDGIT would support a premium of $112,500 ($250,000 − $137,500)

TABLE 13-1   Summary of IDGIT Example

	Without discount	With discount
Asset sold to IDGIT (9-year note, 5.5%)	$2,500,000	$1,500,000
Seed money given to IDGIT	+ 250,000	+ 250,000
Total value of assets in IDGIT at onset	$2,750,000	$1,750,000
Annual yield on asset (10%)	$250,000	$250,000
Payments on note (at federal midterm rate, 5.5%)	– 137,500	– 82,500
Excess annual income after payments on note	$112,500	$167,500
Insurance purchased with annual excess income	$6,000,000	$10,000,000
Value in IDGIT after note payoff (at 5% net growth)	1,400,000	2,400,000
Value of seed money in IDGIT (at 10% growth)	600,000	600,000
Total in IDGIT, end of year 9	$8,000,000	$13,000,000

without the extra cash flow achieved through discounting or $167,500 ($250,000 – $82,500) with discounting. The smaller premium amount would be sufficient to fund a second-to-die insurance policy with a death benefit of approximately $6 million, and the larger a benefit of approximately $10 million, on Rich and Mimi Crow (ages 70 and 66, respectively) based on good health ratings and current assumptions of interest, mortality, and expenses. On the death of the couple, the entire death benefit plus the value of the assets in the trust, including any direct gifts, would be available for the beneficiaries and exempt from both estate and GST tax.

Even without the discounted-sale approach, if Rich and Mimi died immediately after repayment of the note, the IDGIT would hold assets with underlying values in excess of $8 million ($1,400,000 + $600,000 + $6,000,000 insurance) 32-times the amount originally given as seed money to the trust and upon which the GST election was based. In other words, the $8 million is available for multiple generations with no further gift, estate, or GST taxes, and less than a quarter ($250,000) of Rich's $1.1 million GST tax exemption was used. With the discounted sale approach, the total value is substantially higher at $13 million (see Table 13-1).

Planning Risks

The income tax consequences of the premature death of the grantor are unknown. If the grantor dies while the installment note remains unpaid, the grantor's estate may owe income taxes on any unrecognized gain in the transferred assets. The premise is that the IDGIT is no longer a grantor (defective) trust at the time of the grantor's death. Therefore, the grantor's estate would be taxed on the gain attributable to the unpaid portion of the note. On the other hand, it can also be argued that the grantor's death should not be treated as a taxable event, and the tax basis in the transferred assets would be carried over to the trust or its beneficiaries in the event of a subsequent sale. Whether gain should be recognized upon a grantor's death is an unresolved issue at this point. However, in many instances the prospect of income taxation will not be significant to the beneficiaries of the IDGIT. In any event, if the beneficiaries sell assets, they would be subject to capital gain tax.

Another possibility is that the note will be considered "income in respect of a decedent," in which case the recipient of the note payments is subject to income tax on the remaining payments. Thus, like a GRAT, the note term should not extend beyond the grantor's life expectancy; if it does, adverse tax consequences may apply. It is also possible that the grantor's death will have no adverse income tax consequences. This is an unsettled area of the law.

Summary

The IDGIT strategy can be of significant value in disinheriting the IRS, especially when it is designed to include the sale of assets in exchange for an installment note. It offers tremendous transfer tax leverage relative to the various taxes, including capital gain, income, gift, estate, and generation-skipping transfer taxes. This leverage can often be magnified when insurance is purchased with the excess income and/or when the IDGIT is used in conjunction with discounting techniques such as a family limited partnership. Although an IDGIT is similar in some respects to a GRAT, in certain situations this technique can produce results that are superior to those from a GRAT. Figure 13-1 on page 178 summarizes the main features of the discounted-asset sale approach.

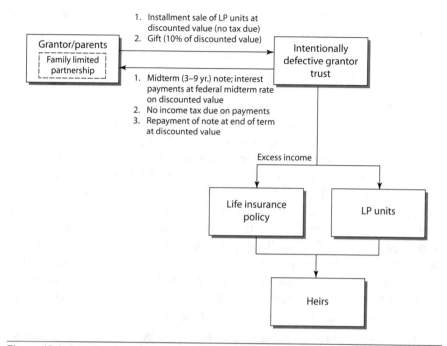

Figure 13-1. Intentionally defective grantor irrevocable trust plan using the discounted asset sale approach.

Using the IDGIT strategy has numerous benefits, including these:

- Taxes on trust income are paid by the grantor while keeping the assets generating the income out of the grantor's taxable estate.
- No capital gain taxes are due on the sale of highly appreciated assets sold at market value to the trust.
- Avoids gift taxes on trust assets purchased from the grantor.
- Avoids income taxes on installment-note interest payments from the trust to the grantor.
- Allows postsale appreciation of assets in the trust to escape estate and GST taxes upon the grantor's death.
- Leverages the GST tax exemption substantially.
- Freezes the size of the grantor's estate by transferring all future appreciation of estate assets to the IDGIT.
- Shrinks the grantor's estate when structured with discounted assets, such as a family limited partnership.

- Through insurance, magnifies the value inside the IDGIT and substantially increases the amount to go to future descendants, free of gift or estate tax, as the assets pass to each generation.
- Provides a compelling alternative to using a grantor retained annuity trust.

⑪ ⑪ ⑪

As with all sophisticated estate planning strategies, you should have your financial planning professional calculate and evaluate the anticipated results of the IDGIT strategy and compare the results to your specific goals and objectives before making any decisions.

14 Family Limited Partnerships

J*im and Kay McNab had a typical estate planning problem. They were making maximum use of their gift tax exemptions with annual gifts to each of their three children and seven grandchildren. However, given their large estate of more than $20 million, they wanted to do more. They had already used up their lifetime gift tax exemptions, so they were facing the unpopular choice of paying gift tax on additional gifts that exceeded the amount of their annual gift tax exemptions.*

The McNabs were also concerned about making gifts of nonliquid assets, such as real estate. Such assets are not easily divisible. Jim did not want to sell off his real estate, which had a low cost basis, and then end up paying capital gain tax as well as gift tax. Also, the properties were in excellent locations, increasing in value, and producing a substantial amount of income, so selling now would not be wise. Jim was successful because of his knowledge of real estate and his excellent management skills, so he wanted a plan that would allow him to stay in control of his real estate.

I introduced the McNabs to the idea of a family limited partnership and showed them how it would not only allow them to make annual gifts of nearly 90 percent more than they had been giving but also leave them in total control of their money for their lifetimes. In addition, Jim would be able to continue to collect a management fee if he felt he needed the income. As a bonus, the family limited partnership plan I recommended provided excellent protection for the assets in the partnership from the claims of creditors.

In 1953, Sam and Helen Walton put what little they had into a family partnership that included their four children. They called their partnership, "Walton Enterprises." From this partnership the well-known chain store, Wal-Mart, evolved. Eventually, the partnership assets grew and included real estate, banks, and a newspaper. In 1985, the Walton family's wealth was estimated to be $20 to $25 billion. But when Sam Walton died in 1992, he owned only a 10 percent interest in Walton Enterprises. He had used a family partnership to transfer assets that grew to more than $18 billion to other family members without gift or estate tax. To Sam Walton, the gift of a business opportunity to a loved one was much more valuable than a gift of cash. With a flat rate of 55 percent at the time of Sam Walton's death, this advanced planning saved approximately $10 billion in estate taxes.

When individuals own business or investment assets whose value is high enough to potentially subject their estates to federal estate taxes, they are faced with the unappealing option of giving assets away at a substantial gift tax cost and thus giving up the income stream generated by the assets. By transferring these assets to one or more partnerships, individuals can maintain control of the assets and continue to receive at least a portion of the income and tax benefits of those assets. At the same time, they can give family members the assets in a tax-efficient manner and reduce— and in some cases even eliminate—the potential for federal estate taxes. If you would like an effective way to protect family assets and keep them where they belong, while avoiding estate taxes, a family limited partnership may be for you.

Advantages

A *family limited partnership (FLP)* offers the following benefits:

- Allows the general partner (the parents, for example) to remain in control of partnership assets, investments, and distributions, even if the general partner share is 1 percent or less.
- Creates a vehicle for transferring substantial amounts of wealth to family members at discounted values, thus significantly reducing estate and gift taxes.
- Eliminates potential estate taxes on the appreciated value of partnership interests given to family members.
- Ensures continuity of family management and an orderly transition from one generation to the next.
- Provides a potential way to fund an insurance policy to help cover estate tax costs without having to use gift tax exemptions or pay gift taxes.

- Maintains the income level of the general partner through management fees and partnership distributions.
- Provides a way to split income among family members.
- Protects assets from the claims of creditors.

To different individuals, some of these benefits are more important or appealing than others. However, virtually everyone who is interested in estate planning wants to control and protect assets from creditors. These are two of the most compelling reasons for using a family limited partnership.

FLP Basics

Although an FLP can be a complex planning strategy, the basic concept is relatively simple. Here, in essence, is how an FLP works:

1. A husband and wife have business or investment assets (such as real estate) that they would like to share with other family members (children, grandchildren, parents, and siblings) or even a favorite charity, but they still want to maintain control over these assets.

2. A qualified attorney who is experienced in the preparation of FLPs and estate planning prepares a limited partnership agreement and a certificate of limited partnership or articles of limited partnership for the couple.

3. The certificate or articles of limited partnership are then filed with the appropriate state agency. The filing, registration, or recording fees vary from state to state costing from as little as $50 to as much as $5000 or more.

4. Usually the husband and wife (or a trust, corporation, or limited liability company controlled by them) serve as the general partners of the FLP.

5. The couple transfers some of their assets to the FLP in exchange for both general partnership and limited partnership interests. A qualified appraiser then appraises these interests and, if necessary, the underlying assets of the FLP. The appraiser values the limited partnership interests on the basis of the terms of the FLP agreement and the types of assets in the partnership. Usually, the value of the limited partnership interests is substantially less than the value of the partnership's assets, because the appraiser discounts the value of the limited-partnership interests for "lack of control," "lack of marketability," and "minority interest." These discounts can range *from 30 to more than*

50 percent depending on the partnership agreement and the assets held in the FLP.

6. If they choose, the general partners, who are also limited partners, give some or all of their limited partnership interests away. The gifts are usually made to family members, trusts created for family members, charities, or short-term split-interest trusts, such as grantor retained annuity trusts or charitable lead trusts (see Chapters 12 and 18).

7. The value of the gifts of limited-partner interests is subject to the discounts determined by the appraiser. These discounts leverage the giving ability of the husband and wife, so larger gifts can be made on the basis of a "discounted," or lower, value for gift tax purposes.

8. No matter how small a percentage the general partners own, they always have full control over the management of the FLP and the assets in it. In fact, the general partners determine if and when any distributions of income are made.

9. General partners are entitled to a reasonable management fee for their management of the partnership. The fee varies depending upon the duties of the general partner, but typically ranges from 3 to 10 percent of the value of the assets in the FLP.

Partnership Classes

A family limited partnership is a legal entity formed under a state's partnership laws. It consists of two classes of partners. The first consists of the *general partners,* who have total control of the partnership and are completely liable for the management obligations, debts, and liabilities of the FLP regardless of their percentage ownership, just as if they owned the assets outright.

The members of the other class are the *limited partners*. They have no control over or participation in the day-to-day management of the FLP regardless of their percentage of ownership. Because of the lack of control, they do not have any personal liability exposure for any of the obligations, debts, or liabilities of the FLP. A limited partner's exposure to loss is limited to the extent of his or her investment in the FLP.

The general partner

Because the general partner controls the operation of the limited partnership regardless of the percentage ownership, the old control rule of 51 percent majority is really not applicable or necessary. Even a general partner with an interest of less than 1 percent still maintains 100 percent control.

An individual can be the general partner, or several individuals can be the general partners. The downside to having individuals as general partners is the exposure to unlimited liability for the obligations, debts, and liabilities of the partnership. Whether this is a problem depends on the nature of the partnership's assets. If, for example, the FLP owns assets such as rental real estate, rental aircraft, or any asset that could potentially cause a personal injury, the liability exposure of the general partner can be substantial. On the other hand, if the FLP owns only intangible assets (such as stocks, bonds, or mutual funds), the general partner's liability exposure is very limited. With intangible assets, the general partner's only serious liability is for debts incurred by the partnership. Another potential problem with having individuals as general partners is that individuals die or can become incompetent. Most states' laws provide that a limited partnership will terminate upon the death or insanity of *all* the general partners.

These problems can be avoided by using a revocable "management" trust as the general partner. A *management trust* is similar to a revocable living trust except that it typically owns only the general-partner interest in the FLP. In the event of the death or disability of the trust maker, the trust continues under the direction of the successor trustee. A corporation can also be a general partner. Many individuals choose a corporation (with the S corporation as the preferred entity) to be the general partner of their FLPs. Unlike individuals, corporations are artificial legal entities with a perpetual existence that are not subject to the human frailties of death or disability. Thus, a corporate general partner can give an FLP continuity of life. (This is also true of a *limited liability company,* or *LLC,* which is a special type of corporation that has characteristics similar to a partnership but is treated as a corporation for purposes of liability.) The general-partner corporation, which is owned by the parents and/or their children, has full control over the management and any distributions from the FLP. As circumstances dictate, it is likely that one of these entities will be used as the general partner of an FLP.

The limited partners

The limited partners can be family members, and most states' laws allow general partners to also own limited partnership interests. In sophisticated estate planning, limited partners are rarely individuals; instead, various types of trusts are created to own limited-partner interests. Four of these are described here:

- *Revocable living trust:* This is the trust that is the foundation of most estate plans (see Chapter 3). Because it controls assets at death or

disability, a revocable living trust ensures that any limited-partner interests in the trust pass with the least amount of administration in the
exact manner desired by the trust maker.

- *Irrevocable trust:* Irrevocable trusts are commonly created to hold
  limited partnership interests for children, grandchildren, or other family members. These trusts offer another layer of control over the limited-partner interests and ensure that the beneficiaries receive
  distributions of income and principal from the FLP only as provided by
  the terms of the trust. They frequently include generation-skipping
  planning (see Chapter 4).

- *Grantor retained annuity trust:* A grantor retained annuity trust
  (GRAT) is often used in estate planning for high-net-worth individuals
  and their families (see Chapter 12). When a grantor contributes a
  limited-partner interest to a GRAT, he or she receives all or some of
  the income from the limited partnership shares through the annual
  annuity distributions for the term of the GRAT. When the GRAT ends,
  the limited-partner interest passes to the remainder beneficiary either
  outright or in trust. Because the gift to the beneficiary is delayed for
  several years, a GRAT allows an even greater discount on the value
  of gifts of limited-partner interests.

- *Intentionally Defective Grantor Irrevocable Trust:* An intentionally defective grantor irrevocable trust (IDGIT) is simply an irrevocable trust that has been structured so the assets are out of the estate
  but the grantor continues to pay taxes on trust income (see Chapter
  14). Assets can be given and/or sold to the trust and, with proper
  structuring, can add leverage to an estate plan. By incorporating discounts in the plan through FLPs, the leverage can be significantly
  enhanced and provide assets free of gift or estate tax for several
  generations.

Asset Transference

Recommended transfers

Just about any business asset, such as the stock of a closely held C corporation, may be owned by an FLP. If an FLP owns at least 80 percent of all classes
of the outstanding stock of a corporation, the corporation will be a subsidiary of
the FLP, an arrangement that may affect the rules governing such things as
pension and profit-sharing plans and cause undesirable limitations.

Most investment assets may also be put into an FLP. Almost any kind of
real estate, personal property, or marketable securities (such as stocks, bonds,
and mutual funds) may be owned by an FLP.

As a general rule, no gain or loss is recognized when assets are transferred to a partnership in exchange for a general or limited-partner interest. One notable exception concerns the transfer of marketable securities to the partnership by more than one of the partners. If several partners own a variety of marketable securities and transfer them to the partnership, the FLP may resemble an "investment company" or what is more commonly known as a "mutual fund." In a situation such as this, the IRS can argue that the partnership was formed primarily to allow the partners to diversify their investment portfolios. If it proves its case, the IRS can tax the various partners when the securities are transferred to the FLP as though they were sold at their fair market value. If the market value reflects a gain over basis, the gain would have to be recognized. However, if a loss would result because the basis is greater than market value, the loss could not be recognized upon the transfer to an FLP.

This exception to the rule of a tax-free transfer to a partnership is usually not a problem with an FLP because typically a husband and wife are the only ones transferring assets to the FLP. A husband and wife are considered one transferring partner for purposes of the rule, and the exception does not apply if only one partner is transferring primarily marketable securities to the FLP. The problem occurs when two or more partners are transferring a variety of marketable securities to a partnership that will own a diversified portfolio of securities.

Nonrecommended transfers

The following are examples of assets that do not belong in an FLP:

- *Primary residence:* Transferring a personal residence into an FLP will likely result in loss of the homestead exemption (applicable in some states) and of the income tax exclusion of $250,000 ($500,000 per couple) allowed on the sale of a primary residence.
- *Individual retirement accounts, annuities, and qualified retirement plans:* IRAs and qualified retirement plans cannot be owned by an FLP. Annuities will lose their tax-favored status if transferred to an FLP.
- *S corporation stock:* Subchapter S of the Internal Revenue Code does not permit the stock of an S corporation to be owned by a partnership. Therefore, unless the termination of the S election is desired, the stock of an S corporation cannot be owned by an FLP. An S corporation may, however, transfer assets it wishes to protect to an FLP and then lease them back from the FLP.

- *Stock of a professional corporation or professional association:* Most states have adopted statutes that allow professionals such as doctors, dentists, chiropractors, lawyers, and accountants to incorporate their practices. These states also require that only the licensed practitioners may own the stock of the professional corporations or professional associations. Therefore, such stock cannot be owned by an FLP. As with the S corporation, the assets of a professional corporation or professional association may be transferred to an FLP and then leased back from the FLP.

- *High-risk assets:* High-risk assets are assets such as business-use cars, airplanes, boats, and other vehicles, vessels used for business purposes, or any asset that could cause a personal injury. These "hot" assets should not be put into your primary FLP, but they may be put into a separate FLP or a subsidiary FLP, limited liability company, or corporation owned by the primary FLP. This would provide an extra layer of protection from lawsuits for the transferor and/or the transferor's other assets.

- *Negative-basis assets:* Another type of asset to avoid is one with a negative basis, such as an asset with a mortgage debt that exceeds the asset's cost basis. Transferring this type of asset to an FLP will create taxable income to the transferor equal to the excess of the mortgage over the property's adjusted cost basis.

Additional Features

Creditor Protection

Partnership laws protect assets belonging to an FLP from creditors of an individual partner. A creditor's remedy is generally restricted to a "charging order" against the debtor partner. Creditors find charging orders unappealing because they apply to a particular partner and cannot be enforced against the FLP itself. Also, the charging order merely gives a creditor the right to receive the debtor's share of distributions. Because distributions of income are at the general partner's discretion, if there are no distributions, the creditor gets nothing. Furthermore, the creditor who becomes a "voluntary assignee" via a charging order may be required to report income attributable to the FLP interest and pay taxes on it, even though nothing was distributed. It is no wonder that creditors are often willing to settle when faced with having to deal with a debtor whose assets are protected by an FLP. (Chapter 21 has more on the creditor protection feature of FLPs.)

Taxation

Partnerships normally do not pay federal income taxes. Nonetheless, partnerships must still determine their taxable income, which is computed in basically the same manner as it is for individuals. Because the partnership does not pay income taxes, the partners are responsible for paying income taxes on partnership income. Tax liability accrues to the partners of an FLP even if income is not actually distributed to them. Generally, the partnership agreement controls the allocation of taxable income, loss, deductions, and credits. When a partner is a member of the partnership for only a portion of the tax year, he or she is allocated only the portion of such items attributable to his or her tenure.

For income tax purposes, all items passed from the partnership to its partners retain the same character they had for the partnership. As an example, if the partnership receives tax-exempt income, the partner's share of that income is also tax-exempt. The partner's distributive share of such items as income credits, deductions, and nondeductible partnership expenses is identified on IRS Schedule K-1 of Form 1065. The partners receive individual copies of Schedule K-1 to allow them to prepare their individual 1040 income tax forms.

Change of Domicile

If a person owns tangible property in more than one state at his or her death and there is any question about which state represented that person's "domicile," it is quite possible that more than one state will attempt to tax the person's estate.

Real estate often creates a red flag because, at the owner's death, it is necessary to notify the taxing authority in each state to obtain tax inheritance or estate tax lien releases in order to transfer ownership of the property. Also, the personal representative of a deceased person may be required to have ancillary probate proceedings in other states in order to transfer ownership of real property to the decedent's beneficiaries.

Placing tangible property, such as real estate located in other states, into an FLP may help avoid the risk and exposure of a tax claim. An interest in an FLP is considered "intangible" property. Therefore, it is not generally necessary for a decedent's survivors to obtain a tax release in order to transfer marketable title to that property. At death, it is not the interest in real estate that is transferred but, rather, an interest in the FLP; the FLP continues throughout to own the real estate.

Life Insurance

If an FLP owns and is the beneficiary of any life insurance on the life of a partner, the insurance death benefit will be included in the partner's estate indirectly in an amount determined by the current value of the deceased partner's partnership interest. So, if a deceased partner's interest is 10 percent, the amount of death benefit included in the estate is equal to 10 percent of the proceeds.

To avoid inflating the deceased insured's partnership interest by any portion of life insurance proceeds, a life insurance policy may be structured with adult children as owners from the policy's inception. Alternatively, the children could create an irrevocable life insurance trust (ILIT), with each child contributing his or her pro-rata portion of the life insurance policy's annual premium from distributions from the FLP. Through an ILIT, the children, as grantors, could protect the policy's cash value in the event of a grantor's divorce or death. Trust design could also help ensure that policy proceeds would be available to help cover liquidity needs created by estate taxes at the death of the parents.

Figure 14-1 shows a typical FLP. The parents set up a family limited partnership and transfer all the assets of their business into it. The parents each retain a 1 percent general partnership interest. The other 98 percent is limited partnership interests, with restrictions on transferability and control. With the income distributions from the FLP, the children purchase a survivorship policy of insurance, as owners and beneficiaries, on the lives of their parents.

Example

Tracy and Lori Wood jointly own a number of hotel properties leased to a hotel management company. The properties are in prime locations and are valued at $4 million. They generate approximately $400,000 in annual income.

The Woods have additional assets of approximately $3 million, which gives them a total estate of $7 million. They are both 65 years old, in excellent health, don't smoke, and have three married children. They want to eventually transfer the hotel properties to their children at minimal transfer tax cost and retain the rights to income and control. In addition, the Woods realize they need life insurance for estate liquidity.

After meeting with their attorney and financial advisor, the Woods determine that an FLP will help them reach their goals. Tracy and Lori Wood will be general partners and, at the partnership's inception, will own all limited partnership shares. The Woods will have the same cost basis in the partnership as

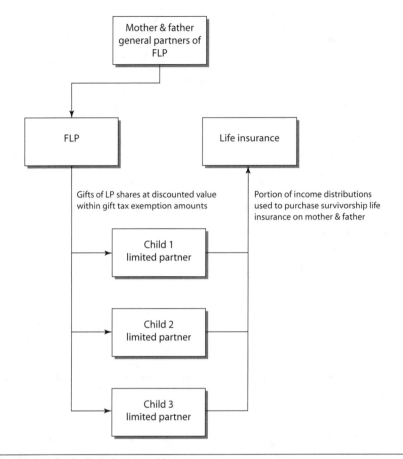

Figure 14-1. A family limited partnership.

they had in the real estate holdings before the partnership formation. The Woods will contribute the unencumbered hotel properties to the family partnership in return for a general partnership interest valued at $40,000 (1 percent) and a limited partnership interest worth $3.96 million. On the basis of advice from their estate planning advisor, Tracy and Lori will give $3 million of the FLP shares to their children (see Table 14-1).

One of the major benefits of giving FLP shares is the potential for obtaining discounts on the value of gifts to children and other heirs. This enables parents to leverage the value of the gifts typically made within their applicable exemption equivalent ($1 million in 2002 and 2003) and their annual gift tax exclusions ($11,000 per year per recipient in 2002). As you can see from Table 14-2, Tracy and Lori are able to give $3 million in underlying value within their

TABLE 14-1   Capitalization of Wood FLP

Partner	Interest %	Capital
Initial capital structure		
General partner (Tracy & Lori Wood Revocable Management Trust)	1.0	$ 40,000
Tracy (limited partner)	49.5	1,980,000
Lori (limited partner)	49.5	1,980,000
Total	100.0	$4,000,000
After gifts to children (valuation without discounts)		
General partner (Tracy & Lori Wood Revocable Management Trust)	1	$ 40,000
Tracy (limited partner)	12	480,000
Lori (limited partner)	12	480,000
Child 1 (limited partner)	25	1,000,000
Child 2 (limited partner)	25	1,000,000
Child 3 (limited partner)	25	1,000,000
Total	100	$4,000,000

combined exemption equivalent of $2 million in the year of their gift (2003) because of a 33-percent discount on FLP units (determined through an appraisal of those units). Thus, $3 million in underlying value is transferred to the Wood children without gift tax while producing tax savings of approximately $500,000 on the $1 million discount achieved through the use of FLP units (see Table 14-5).

In their capacity as general partners via their management trust, Tracy and Lori can determine whether the partnership will retain or distribute income to its partners or make loans to limited partners. Tracy and Lori can also withdraw money from the FLP in the form of management fees, in addition to a pro-rata share of any distributions they, as general partners, decide to make to support their financial needs.

The Wood FLP netted $400,000 for the year. Of that amount, $200,000 (5 percent of the assets in the FLP) is paid to the general partners as compensation for managing the partnership and the real estate, leaving $200,000 for partner allocation (see Table 14-3).

TABLE 14-2 Capitalization of the Wood FLP after Gifts to Children and *after* Discount Valuation*

Partner	Interest %	Capital account†	Less discount (33.3%)	Value‡
General partner (Tracy & Lori, as trustees)	1	$ 40,000	NA	$ 40,000
Tracy (limited partner)	12	480,000	$ 160,000	320,000
Lori (limited partner)	12	480,000	160,000	320,000
Child 1 (limited partner)	25	1,000,000	333,334	666,666
Child 2 (limited partner)	25	1,000,000	333,333	666,667
Child 3 (limited partner)	25	1,000,000	333,333	666,667
Total	100	$4,000,000	$1,320,000	$2,680,000

*Valuation with discount of 33.3 percent.
†Actual gift.
‡Fair market value (discounted value) and gift tax value of LP units per appraisal.

TABLE 14-3 Cash Flow Allocation after Management Fee from Annual Partnership Income

Partner	Interest %	Income gross allocation	Net after-tax income*
General partner	1	$ 2,000	$ 1,300
Tracy (limited partner)	12	24,000	15,600
Lori (limited partner)	12	24,000	15,600
Child 1 (limited partner)	25	50,000	32,500
Child 2 (limited partner)	25	50,000	32,500
Child 3 (limited partner)	25	50,000	32,500
Total	100	$200,000	$130,000

*Taxed at 35 percent marginal income tax bracket.

Through both management compensation and partnership allocations, Tracy and Lori Wood will end up with over one-half of the property's gross income ($250,000) even after giving three-fourths of the limited partnership shares to their children. In future years, Tracy and Lori, as trustees and general partners, might elect to receive higher or lower management compensation. However, the compensation the Woods decide to pay themselves as general partners must be reasonable. Otherwise, the IRS may claim that a gift tax is owed on "excess compensation" from the Woods' children to their parents. As general

TABLE 14-4   Joint Taxable Estate Assets after Gifts to Wood FLP

	Current market value
Miscellaneous assets (home, personal property, IRA & investments)	$3,000,000
Tracy & Lori Wood's FLP general-partner interest	40,000
Tracy & Lori Wood's FLP limited-partner interest*	640,000
Total estate (after giving FLP limited-partnership shares)	$3,680,000

*Discounted from $960,000.

partners, the Woods can elect to have the partnership retain the net income inside the partnership for reinvestment.

After the formation of the Wood FLP and after the gifts of the limited partnership interest, Tracy and Lori Wood's joint taxable estate consists of the assets shown in Table 14-4.

Notice that the remaining *limited* partnership shares owned by Tracy and Lori are discounted (33.3 percent) even though the underlying asset value is higher.

The FLP has successfully reduced the Woods' $7 million estate to a taxable estate of approximately $3.7 million. To protect the balance of their estate from the ravages of estate taxes plus income taxes (on their IRA) and final expenses, the Woods need a $2 million survivor (second-to-die) life insurance policy. Their professional advisors agree with the Woods' life underwriter that the policy should be issued on an *increasing* death benefit basis to help cover future estate tax liabilities created by inflation and asset appreciation. The advisors have suggested the use of a trust established by the children to own the survivorship life insurance policy.

Based on current interest rates and policy assumptions, a $2 million survivor life policy with an increasing death benefit from a highly rated company requires an annual premium of $80,000 for five years with a death benefit that increases annually to approximately $4 million by age 100.

The Wood children will use a portion of their share of after-tax cash flow of approximately $97,500 from their combined partnership interests to pay the life insurance premiums (see Table 14-3). There is no need for Tracy and Lori Wood to make additional annual gifts to their children for life insurance premiums. And there will be no gift taxes relating to the premium payments because the money is not considered a gift but income that is distributed pro rata from the FLP (see Figure 14-2 and Table 14-5).

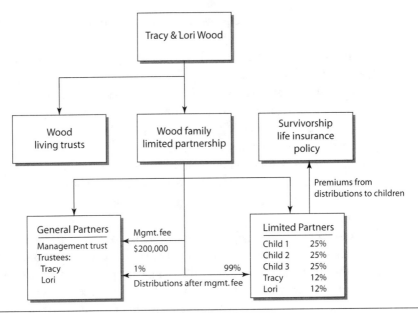

Figure 14-2. The Wood family limited partnership.

TABLE 14-5 Estate Tax Impact on Initial Transfer of $3 million of Assets

	Without FLP	**With FLP**
Market value before discount	$3,000,000	$3,000,000
Valuation discount (33.3%)	NA	– 1,000,000
Value after discount	$3,000,000	$2,000,000
Exemptions (2 at $1,000,000)	– 2,000,000	– 2,000,000
Taxable amount	$1,000,000	$ 0
Gift/estate taxes (50%)	500,000	0
Net to family	$2,500,000	$3,000,000

The Woods received several benefits by using the FLP structure:

- They moved $3 million of assets from their estates to the next generation, yet for gift tax purposes the transfer is valued as $2 million.
- They avoided gift tax by using their combined 2003 estate tax credit exemption equivalent.

- They excluded the future growth on the transferred assets from their estate.
- The net income generated each year on the gift interests belongs to Tracy and Lori's children.
- As general partners, Tracy and Lori control partnership income and are entitled to collect reasonable management fees. Also, they can elect to have the partnership retain all or part of the net income in the partnership for reinvestment.
- Through the use of a management trust as general partner, Tracy and Lori continue to manage and control the underlying assets.
- Assets placed in the Wood FLP are protected from the claims of creditors.
- Tracy and Lori have the option of making gifts of all or a portion of the remaining discounted partnership units. With a discount of 33.3 percent, they can make additional gifts of FLP units equal to $33,000 per child each year without gift tax. After the 33.3 percent discount, the taxable gift of $22,000 is within their combined annual gift tax exclusion of $11,000 each.

If the Woods combine the FLP with a grantor retained annuity trust, their gifts of limited partnership interests could be further discounted to achieve even greater gift tax leverage (see Chapter 12). Alternatively, the Woods could sell some or all of the FLP shares owned by them to an intentionally defective grantor irrevocable trust and provide benefits to several generations of their heirs (see Chapter 13).

Planning Risks

Family partnership arrangements have been coming under greater scrutiny as their use has increased in recent years. The Internal Revenue Service has issued regulations that will disregard a partnership as an entity if the principal purpose of the partnership is solely tax-motivated either at inception or during its operation. Thus, in the formation of an FLP, it is important to have a "business purpose" and to have the documents prepared by an attorney who specializes in estate planning and FLPs so that they will withstand any scrutiny by the IRS.

The costs involved in forming and maintaining an FLP should be considered, including:

- Attorney fees for forming the partnership and handling related legal matters (transferring assets, for example).

- Appraisal fees for underlying assets *and* for the shares of the partnership given to the younger-generation family members.
- Continuing administrative fees and expenses for matters such as the FLP's yearly income tax return (1065 partnership return and partnership K-1 forms).
- Transfer tax costs, such as documentary stamps when transferring real property into the FLP, and, possibly, title insurance costs.
- Registration fees, which, depending on the state in which the FLP will be registered, can range from $500 to over $5,000.

Summary

Transferring assets to an FLP can result in a more flexible and sensible wealth transfer program, a more rapid reduction of estate size and value, a more flexible income-splitting program, and a better creditor protection program than can be accomplished by using other traditional planning tools and methods.

15 Qualified Personal Residence Trusts

P *eter and Ann Johnson have a large estate that includes three homes: a very nice condominium in Naples, Florida; a home in Oakbrook, Illinois, where they raised their three children; and a five-bedroom cottage in Lake Geneva, Wisconsin, that Ann inherited from her parents. Their estate planning goals included leaving the cottage to their son and two daughters with the hope that it would continue to stay in the family and eventually pass from their children to their grandchildren. However, they weren't quite ready to turn over the keys to the property. So their plan was to include the property in their estate and pass it to the children at their death.*

In recent years the real estate values around Lake Geneva have been skyrocketing, and Peter and Ann were concerned that the continued appreciation in the value of the cottage would further increase the size of their estate. I recommended that they consider giving their home to a qualified personal residence trust for a period of years (during which they, as the grantors and trustees, would still have ownership rights) to get the home out of their estate at a substantially reduced gift tax value. Based on this plan, the property value for the cottage was reduced by more than 80 percent for reporting purposes, so Ann had to use only a small amount of her lifetime applicable gift tax exemption to make the transfer.

The Johnsons were very pleased about the plan, especially when they learned that they were not limited to transferring their cottage. Next year they intend to create a second qualified personal residence trust to remove their Florida home from their taxable estate at a substantially reduced gift tax cost!

♛ ♛ ♛

Our lawmakers have long recognized the unique nature of the family home, especially when it comes to taxes. As a result, the laws contain several special income tax breaks for homeowners. One of those breaks provides a way to reduce the severe impact gift and estate taxes have on those who own valuable homes. This break is known as the *qualified personal residence trust (QPRT),* and it has been growing in popularity in recent years.

QPRT Basics

Strategy

The gist of a QPRT is that you create a trust, transfer your home into it, and reserve a right to reside in the home for a specified number of years (known as the "term"). At the end of the term, the home will then belong to your children or other heirs or entities named in your QPRT. By transferring a "remainder" (future interest) in the home to your beneficiaries, the value of the home for gift tax purposes is *substantially reduced.* If you die during the term of the trust, the value of your home is included in your estate (just as it would be if you had not created a QPRT). However, if you live beyond the term of the trust, the value of your home will be outside of your estate, along with all posttransfer appreciation, thereby saving substantial estate taxes (possibly as much as 50 percent of the future value of the home) for your heirs. You may continue to live in the home at the end of the term by leasing it from your children. Alternatively, you can allow your spouse to have rent-free use of the home during his or her lifetime.

Example

Assume, for example, that Mark and Joan Gardner have a $5 million estate. The Gardners, who are both age 60, are in good health and have four children. Their primary residence is currently valued at $1 million. The Gardners would like to find a tax-efficient way to transfer the value of their jointly held home and all future appreciation to their children. So they create a QPRT and transfer the residence into the trust (after first transferring the home to Joan, who has the greater life expectancy of the two), retaining a right to live there for 15 years, the term of the trust. They arrange to rent the home at the end of the term, and they name Joan as trustee of the QPRT.

The QPRT contains a "reversion" provision which provides that if Joan dies during the term of the trust, her interest in the residence, as trustee, will revert and become part of her estate. If she lives for at least 15 years, the residence or an interest therein will belong equally to the Gardners' four children at the end of the 15-year designated term.

Through this strategy, the Gardners leverage a portion of Joan's applicable credit exemption by transferring their home to their children at a fraction of the home's actual value. And they do so without giving up the ability to continue residing in the home for the term of the trust and beyond.

When the Gardners create the QPRT and transfer their home into the trust, they make a taxable gift to their children equal to the present value of the remainder interest. This amount equals the current value of the home less the value of their retained right to reside in it for the term of the trust. Even if the home appreciates to double or triple the current value, there will be no more gift or estate taxes due. Also, the payment of rent after the trust's term will further reduce the Gardners' estate without payment of gift tax.

The Internal Revenue Code outlines the mechanics for valuing the interests under a QPRT. The factors that control the gift calculation are the current value of the home, the age of the grantor, the current IRS actuarial tables (denoting life expectancy), the period of the trust, and the current government-adjusted applicable federal rate. Using these factors, and assuming a 7 percent applicable federal rate, the Gardners make a taxable gift of $220,973. This amount is arrived at by taking the $1 million current value, subtracting the present value of the interest retained by Joan Gardner ($675,040 reduction), and *further reducing* the resulting figure of $324,960 by the possibility that Joan Gardner will die before the term of the trust has expired, a 32 percent possibility ($103,987 reduction).

Assuming that the property continues to appreciate at a 4 percent annual rate and that Joan lives to the end of the trust term, the Gardners will have removed an asset that would eventually be worth approximately $1.8 million from their estate while using only a fraction of Joan's applicable exemption. Because the gifts are "future" gifts, the annual $11,000 gift exclusions cannot be used, so the Gardners will use $220,973 of Joan's applicable credit exemption equivalent to avoid paying gift taxes.

Figure 15-1 on page 202 summarizes the Gardners' QPRT, and the following list highlights its main points:

- Residence worth $1,000,000.
- Transfer tax based on gift of approximately $220,973 (use a portion of unified credit exemption equivalent to avoid paying gift tax).

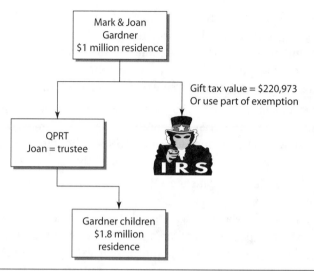

Figure 15-1. Qualified personal residence trust.

- If Mark and Joan live beyond the term of the trust, the entire value of the property will be *excluded* from their estates.
- If the property value grows to $1,800,000 in 15 years, potential tax savings could exceed $800,000.
- The residence may be sold during the term of the trust, with a replacement purchased by the QPRT.
- If Joan survives the term, both Mark and Joan may continue to occupy the residence by paying a fair market rent to their children. This rent would not attract any gift tax. To help offset income tax on the rental income after expenses, the children could depreciate the home.
- If Joan dies during the term, the property will be included in her taxable estate—just as it would be if no QPRT had been used. Term insurance could be purchased to offset the possibility of Joan's dying during the term of the trust.

A properly worded QPRT can provide the Gardners with flexibility for changing circumstances. For example, the QPRT may give the Gardners either of the following two options:

1. *Sell their home and not replace it.* The proceeds of the sale will belong to the trust (and, ultimately, the beneficiaries), but the Gardners

will be entitled to annuity payments during the remaining period of the trust, much like the case with a grantor retained annuity trust (see Chapter 12).

2. *Sell their home and replace it with another home.* If the value of the new home exceeds the value of the original home and the Gardners add cash, they are making an extra gift that may attract additional gift tax and require a calculation similar to the original gift. If the value of the new home is less than the value of the original home, the additional cash from the sale will create an annuity.

Planning Risks

While the QPRT looks like an excellent estate planning strategy, there are a few risks that should be taken into account. The first risk is that Joan Gardner may die during the period of the trust and, therefore, the QPRT will not produce the desired tax results (this could possibly be offset with term life insurance). If Joan dies during the term of the trust, the home reverts to her estate and passes according to the terms of her will or trust. The full value of her interest would be taxed in her estate. However, the applicable credit covering the gift tax cost of the transfer of the property into the trust would be restored. At Joan's death, it would be as if the home had never been transferred to the trust. The cost and effort of setting up the trust will have produced no benefit.

Shortening the term of the trust will increase the likelihood that Joan will survive the term of the trust, but it will also increase the value of the gift and decrease the time before the Gardners no longer own their home.

Another potential disadvantage concerns what happens when Joan Gardner survives the term of the trust. Joan will no longer own the home, but the Gardners will probably still want to live there. The solution is to have the Gardners lease the home from their children or from the trust if it continues for the benefit of their children at the end of the initial trust term. The lease payments will further reduce the Gardners' estate and will not be considered gifts to their children. Although the rent will constitute taxable income to their children, they will have the responsibility of paying taxes and expenses and will be entitled to take depreciation deductions on the home to help offset any net taxable income. The lease payment amount should be based on the fair rental value of the property at the time title passes.

If the Gardners are concerned about whether their children would be willing to enter into a lease at the end of the trust term, they could arrange a lease in advance. The IRS has determined that as long as the rent paid under the prearranged lease is a fair amount, the value of the home will not be included in the parents' estate.

As an alternative to having a lease arrangement, Joan Gardner could give her husband, Mark, a *life estate* at the end of the trust term. This would allow *him* (and, as his spouse, *her*) to live rent-free in the home for the balance of *his* life. If Mark should die before Joan during the life estate, she would have to pay fair market rent to remain in the home, as described above.

Basis and capital gain tax

Another major disadvantage of the QPRT arrangement relates to cost "basis" and the potential of capital gain taxes. If the Gardners survive the term of the trust, their children will have only a *carryover cost basis* (the Gardners' adjusted cost basis at the time of the transfer to the QPRT), because they received the property as a gift. Alternatively, if the Gardners retain the property and die owning it, the property receives a *stepped-up basis* equal to its fair market value at the date of death, and their children could then sell the home without capital gain taxes (except in 2010, see Appendix D). The theory behind the QPRT is that estate tax savings (possibly up to 50 percent of the full appreciated value) resulting from the arrangement will more than offset the capital gain taxes (20 percent of the *gain* over cost basis) that the children will have to pay as a result of the potentially low carryover basis. If the children keep the property and it ultimately passes through their estates, the property would be entitled to a *full step-up* in basis for their heirs, thus eliminating any taxes due to the accumulated potential capital gain.

Although it has not been tested with the IRS, a potential solution to the basis problem is to have the Gardners' children purchase the home just before the expiration of the term of the QPRT. Recent IRS rulings prohibit the use of a note between the parties, so the children should consider obtaining a short mortgage loan from a third-party lender (such as a bank). For the remainder of the term (for a period of a month or two), payments will have to be made on any financing arranged by the children. At the end of the term, the cash paid for the home, as a trust asset, will belong to the QPRT beneficiaries—the Gardner children. With this cash, the children could pay off any loan taken out to make the purchase. Assuming the home was used as the primary residence two out of the five years preceding the sale and assuming both Mark and Joan were involved as grantors, they could conceivably utilize their combined tax exemption (which applies to the sale of a principal residence) of up to $500,000 ($250,000 each) to offset any taxable gain that would apply to them. In this strategy, the children end up owning the home with a current market basis, which means they could sell the home without capital gain taxes.

Additional Considerations

There are a number of points you should consider before establishing a QPRT:

- If the home is owned jointly, the title should be changed to one spouse's sole name (preferably the younger and/or healthier spouse) before the home is transferred to the QPRT. Alternatively, the home can be split into two separate trusts. If this is done, an additional discount ("partial interest discount") may be taken (based on a qualified appraisal) to adjust for the fact that half a home inside two separate entities has a lower value than two halves of a home in a single entity. In the case of the Gardners, the discount might amount to an additional 15 to 30 percent of their respective shares in the trust, further shrinking the taxable value of the gift.
- The grantor may be the sole trustee or a joint trustee of his or her QPRT.
- If there is an outstanding mortgage on the residence, the grantor should either pay off the mortgage or remain personally liable for it (recourse debt). Otherwise, the mortgage payment might be treated as an additional future-interest gift to the remainder persons (the children) and create additional gift tax exposure. (*Note:* Remaining liable on the mortgage to avoid gift tax on the mortgage payments is untested, and there is some question as to whether the IRS will accept this technique.)
- The grantor may structure a reasonable rental agreement, at the time of forming the QPRT, that will begin at the end of the trust term.
- The residence must be properly valued at the time of the gift to minimize the possibility of subsequent valuation problems with the IRS.
- The grantor may pay for repairs and maintenance of the property during the initial term of the QPRT. However, any property improvements will be considered as additional gifts.

- The grantor may place only two homes into one or more QPRTs. One home must be the grantor's primary residence. The other may be a secondary residence, such as a vacation home (or even a houseboat).
- If a second residence is used, it must not be considered an investment property under the Internal Revenue Code. Thus, the grantor must either rent the property for less than 15 days per year or, if the home is rented, occupy the residence for the greater of 14 days or 10 percent of the number of days rented per year.
- Trust principal must include the residence and a reasonable amount of land appropriate for residential purposes. Household furnishings are not included.
- Most QPRTs are classified as "grantor trusts." The grantor trust rules dictate that for income tax purposes the residence is treated as if it were owned by the grantor. Thus, the grantor will continue to deduct the property tax and mortgage interest payments. Also, if the home is sold, the grantor may exclude up to $250,000 ($500,000 per couple) of gain on sale of the property as long as it was used as a primary residence two out of the five years preceding the sale.
- The QPRT may hold limited amounts of cash for servicing debt and maintenance.
- Beware of possible generation-skipping transfer tax if the ultimate distribution is to a grandchild or a trust for the benefit of children *and grandchildren*. The amount of the generation skip gift is measured at the *end* of the trust term and may be greater than the GST tax exemption in effect at the time. In this way, a QPRT is not ideal for generation-skipping planning.
- A married grantor should not split gifts (treating the gift as though it comes from both spouses, for example) to a single QPRT with his or her spouse. If the grantor dies during the trust term, the applicable exclusion amount will *not* be restored for the surviving spouse.

Summary

A QPRT enables you to achieve substantial estate tax savings while retaining the right to live in, control, and enjoy the home for the balance of your and your spouse's life. Because a QPRT will not accomplish its goals if the grantor dies during the term of the trust, adequate life insurance to cover the total estate settlement costs, especially estate taxes associated with the inclusion of the home in the estate, is essential. Low-cost term insurance with a level premium may be ideal.

The QPRT is a sophisticated estate planning technique that should be used, along with other planning strategies, as part of an overall estate plan tailored to your individual goals and objectives. To achieve this, it is important that you seek advice from an estate planning attorney and/or qualified financial planning professional before using this strategy.

16 Social Capital

B
Both of my parents died at an early age. As a result, they did not have the kind of estate plan in place that I routinely recommend to my clients. So, quite a bit more went to the IRS in the form of estate taxes than was necessary. (Worse yet is the way the government spent the money that was "confiscated" from their estate in the form of taxes.)

*My father was not a right-wing extremist, but he would have turned over in his grave if he had seen how much of his estate went to estate taxes. I know that if my parents were still living, they would have planned their estate in a way that made optimal use of what it took them a lifetime to build. They would have taken care of their family **first** and then provided for the social causes that were important to both of them.*

If I had been old enough to know better, I would have advised my parents to pay special attention to their social capital and plan accordingly!

🏛 🏛 🏛

Sir Winston Churchill once said, "We make a living by what we get. We make a life by what we give." You might not think of yourself as a Rockefeller, Kennedy, or even a Bill Gates, but, if you are reading this book, you probably are a philanthropist. If you have accumulated a net worth exceeding the gift and estate tax credit exemption equivalent ($1 million in 2002 and 2003), you are going to be a philanthropist—whether you know it or not.

According to current tax law, nine months after you die your estate must "contribute to society" on the portion of your estate that exceeds the taxable

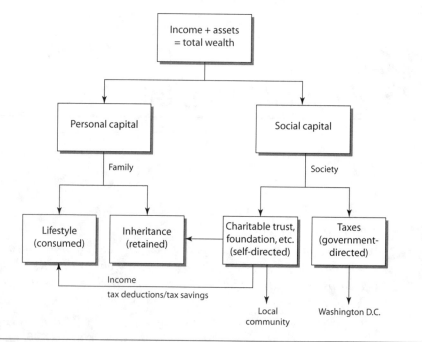

Figure 16-1. Two kinds of capital.

threshold. Chances are excellent that this will be the most significant "charitable gift" you will ever make to social causes, and it will be completely involuntary. We designate that portion of your estate, the portion you *must* give to society, as your "social capital."

Components of Wealth

Total wealth has two basic components: personal financial capital and social capital.

Personal financial capital is divided into two categories:

1. Capital that we consume to maintain our lifestyle.
2. Capital that can be saved and passed on to our heirs.

Social capital is also divided into two categories:

1. Capital that is confiscated from us as taxes (such as income, capital gain, gift, and estate taxes) to be spent by the government.
2. Capital that is protected and self-directed.

Social capital is, you might say, the portion of your estate that you earn and own, but you do not get to keep.

If you do not actively plan your estate, your social capital will be directed into the U.S. tax system. In many cases, the government will frivolously spend in a matter of seconds what it took a lifetime to earn. For example, one of South Florida's greatest philanthropists in recent years was Joe Robbie, former owner of the Miami Dolphins, who, upon his death, contributed more than $45 million to social causes *not* of his choice.

But you do have choices. You can allow your social capital to be appropriated by the government through the tax system, or you can decide where your money goes through estate planning, without disrupting your lifestyle or your children's inheritance.

Here is something to think about: In the next 10 to 20 years or so we will see the greatest disposition of social capital in history. It is estimated that there will be more than $10 trillion transferred from one generation to the next. If people fail to plan their estates properly, a large portion of the $10 trillion will go to the IRS as government-directed social capital.

You have only three possible beneficiaries for your wealth:

1. Your intended heirs.
2. The Internal Revenue Service.
3. Charitable institutions.

You must choose at least two!

Although the tax code mandates that individuals with taxable estates make a contribution to society upon their deaths, most people do not realize that they can have direct control over the portion of their wealth that they must contribute to society. The same Internal Revenue Code that established the estate tax rates and laws also gives you the "tools" (which we call *social capital tools*) for minimizing and even eliminating federal estate taxes while benefiting causes that are important to you and your family.

Social Capital Tools

Some of the primary social capital tools include:

- Charitable remainder trusts (see Chapter 17).
- Charitable lead trusts (see Chapter 18).
- Family foundations (see Chapter 17).
- Wealth replacement trusts (see Chapter 17).

As you will see, by combining one or more of these tools, you can maintain or enhance your current income and lifestyle, provide your heirs with more than they would otherwise receive from your estate, reduce estate taxes, teach social responsibility to your heirs, and leave a lasting and meaningful legacy. In some cases you might even be able to eliminate estate taxes through a zero estate tax strategy and effectively control 100 percent of your social capital while ensuring that your heirs receive the full value of your estate.

You might be asking: Isn't this all kind of unpatriotic? Not at all. The Internal Revenue Code encourages contributions to nonprofit organizations by offering tax deductions and credits. Studies have shown that the government spends between $1.75 and $2.50 to accomplish the same public good that the private sector could accomplish for $1. Sound estate planning contributes to the privatization of social work in the United States and slows the growth of wasteful government. Society and the government benefit from sound estate planning.

Example

Mr. and Mrs. Smith have an estate valued at $5 million, of which $3 million consists of appreciated assets. The Smiths found that they could substantially reduce estate taxes by transferring their appreciated assets to a charitable remainder trust (CRT). Their CRT entitles them to an immediate income tax deduction that can be spread over six years (current year plus five more), enables them to sell the transferred assets without incurring capital gain taxes, and provides them with a lifetime of increased income. In addition, with the tax savings from the income tax deduction and part of the increased income from the CRT, the Smiths purchased a survivorship insurance contract inside an irrevocable trust (often referred to as a *wealth replacement trust).* The insurance proceeds will replace the full value of the assets transferred to their CRT, and their children will end up with a larger inheritance because there are no income or estate taxes on insurance proceeds held in a wealth replacement trust. Effectively, the IRS, through the tax savings, pays for the insurance and thereby provides a tax-free inheritance to the Smiths' children.

In addition to the CRT and the irrevocable trust, the Smiths also established a *family foundation* to receive the remainder of their CRT at their deaths. The family foundation will allow the Smith children and grandchildren to control the Smiths' social capital for generations by directing it to the causes and organizations that Mr. and Mrs. Smith value most. In effect, the Smiths have taken control of their social capital rather than having their estate make a gift to the government in the form of taxes.

Summary

A charitable remainder trust (which is covered in more detail in the next chapter) is just one of the many tools that can help you control your social capital. By taking time to learn about these tools, you are directing your social capital, while maintaining or possibly enhancing your estate. Eventually, whether you want to or not, you *will* be a philanthropist. The question is this: Will you be a voluntary or an involuntary philanthropist?

17 Charitable Remainder Trusts

J Jeannine and Rob Dell have been retired for almost 10 years and now are very active in their volunteer work for various charities. This brings a great deal of joy to their lives. Rob contributes two days a week, helping to build homes for the poor through Habitat for Humanity. He is also a member of the board of Special Olympics. Jeannine is very active in the American Cancer Society in her role as chairperson for the Special Events Committee. Both of the Dells are active in their church.

Even though the Dells have a sizable stock portfolio, the income from their investments is not sufficient to allow them to maintain their lifestyle and contribute money to their favorite charities. They were unwilling to sell any of the stocks because they dread the idea of paying capital gains tax. So, a part of the Dell's estate plan designates a small portion of their assets to their favorite charities at the second of their two deaths. This would allow them to leave more to benefit their charities, but they were concerned about having enough assets to both provide for their children and satisfy their charitable intent.

When I showed Jeannine and Rob how a charitable remainder trust could help them sell their highly appreciated assets without capital gains tax, provide them with a much greater income, save taxes, and create a lasting charitable legacy, they were ecstatic! They were even happier to learn that with the addition of a wealth replacement trust they could do everything without reducing the estate they planned to leave to their children.

What happens when you benefit yourself, your family, and society-at-large in one transaction? You get the synergy of the *charitable remainder trust (CRT)*. A CRT is an irrevocable trust that receives gifts of property—usually appreciated stock or appreciated real estate—or other assets, such as artwork. The donor of the property typically designates him- or herself as the trustee. The donor and spouse generally are the income beneficiaries of the CRT for their lifetimes. This allows the donor-beneficiary to retain control of, and receive income from, contributed assets. Once transferred into the CRT, the assets are free from the claims of creditors. Upon the death of the income beneficiaries, any assets left in the CRT are distributed to one or more charities.

Individuals have long used CRTs to avoid capital gains on highly appreciated assets. The flexibility of a CRT, however, can help you accomplish a wide variety of personal and financial goals. Properly structured, a CRT can protect your profits and gains, increase your income while reducing income taxes and estate taxes, eliminate property management headaches, diversify your investments, lower your financial risk, increase amounts left to your heirs, and help you make a lasting difference in your community.

CRT Basics

Setting Up a CRT

There are two main steps in creating a CRT. First, work with a knowledgeable attorney to establish a CRT that will qualify under the Internal Revenue Code as a charitable trust that is exempt from taxation. Second, give an asset, such as highly appreciated stocks or real estate, to the trust. This transfer creates an immediate income tax deduction that you can use in the current tax year. If you cannot use all of the allowable deduction immediately, you can carry the deduction forward for five additional years. The total amount of the allowable deduction depends on the interest payout you have selected (usually between 5 and 12 percent), the government "discount" rate at the time of the transfer, and the term of the trust, which can be for one or multiple lives or for a term certain of no more than 20 years but is usually the life expectancy of you and, if married, your spouse.

After transferring your appreciated property to the CRT, you as trustee would typically sell the property (being careful to avoid any prearranged agreements) and reinvest the proceeds—perhaps in a variety of assets to obtain the benefits of diversification. This is done for two reasons:

1. Highly appreciated property, such as stocks, typically yield very little income.

2.   You avoid all capital gains tax on the sale of the appreciated asset because of the tax-exempt status of the CRT.

This strategy allows you to reinvest the full amount of the sale proceeds rather than the net amount after tax, as would be the case if the property were sold without the CRT. The ability to reinvest all the contributed assets into higher-yielding investments may increase your cash flow substantially.

When the trust is first established, you select the percentage of payout. This must be done carefully, because once you choose the percentage, it cannot be changed. The percentage selected must be at least 5 percent of the value of the assets in the trust. The actual dollar amount paid to you will be the value of the assets in the trust, as revalued each year, multiplied by your chosen payout percentage.

It might seem that selecting a higher percentage would produce a better financial result, however, this is not the case usually. A lower percentage creates a larger tax deduction, which puts money in your pocket immediately. Additionally, any earnings of the trust above the selected payout percentage accumulate tax-free and are added to the principal. Over time, a lower-percentage payout can often produce more total income.

You can also select the charities that will benefit from the trust. You can name any number of charities when establishing your CRT and, as trustee of your CRT, can change them at any time. You may even choose your own family foundation or a "donor-advised account" of a public charity (such as a community foundation) along with or in place of other charities.

Upon the death of the last income beneficiary, trust assets are distributed to the selected charities. Assuming the CRT is properly structured, no estate tax will be due.

Types of CRTs

There are three types of CRTs, each of which is discussed below.

Charitable remainder unitrust

In a *charitable remainder unitrust (CRUT),* distributions are based on a percentage of the value of the trust assets (the percentage chosen at inception). Each year, the value of the trust's assets is redetermined, and as the value of the assets fluctuates, so do annual unitrust payments. This approach provides some protection against inflation, but it also presents some risk, because the annual payments will be less than expected if the trust's assets lose value.

For example, if the chosen payout percentage is 8 percent and the amount contributed to the CRUT is $1 million, the payment distributed the first year, assuming no growth, is $80,000. If the trust assets increase in value to $1.2 million in year two, the required distribution is $96,000. However, if the trust assets decrease in value to $900,000, the payout is reduced to $72,000. A special type of CRUT known as a NIMCRUT (discussed below) provides flexibility by allowing an accumulation option, and both allow additional contributions to be made to the trust at any time.

Charitable remainder annuity trust

In a *charitable remainder annuity trust (CRAT),* the amount of the payout is fixed. The payout selected must be between 5 and 50 percent of the amount contributed, and there is no need to revalue the assets in the trust (as in the case of a CRUT) each year. If the income of the CRAT is less than the annual payout, the balance of the mandatory distribution is taken from principal.

For example, if $1 million is contributed to the CRAT and a payout percentage of 8 percent is chosen, yielding an annual payout of $80,000, this amount will remain constant even if trust assets double in value to $2 million. If trust assets decrease in value, the distributions of $80,000 will be taken from principal and potentially reduce the amount that will end up going to charity. Once the CRAT is formed, the donor cannot make additional contributions.

Net income with makeup charitable remainder unitrust

For those who do not need immediate income from their appreciated assets, a special type of CRUT is available. This variation of the standard CRUT is known as a *net income with makeup charitable remainder unitrust (NIMCRUT).* With a NIMCRUT, each year the trust pays to the donor the lesser of the unitrust amount specified in the trust document or all the trust's income for the year. When the trust's income is less than the unitrust amount, the trustee creates a "makeup account" for the amounts that remain unpaid each year. This account accumulates until the trust's income exceeds the chosen percentage payout, at which time the beneficiary receives the additional income. This arrangement continues as long as there is an accumulation in the makeup account.

To minimize the trust's income, the trustee invests the sale proceeds into non-income-producing investments such as zero-coupon bonds, variable annuities, growth stocks, or raw land. Since these assets do not usually produce income, there is no annual payout and no income tax. When the donor desires the income, the trustee sells the investments and purchases income-producing assets, such as bonds.

NIMCRUTs are commonly used for retirement planning. A person could make annual deposits of cash or other assets (such as, appreciated assets) of any amount to a NIMCRUT and let the assets appreciate tax-free until retirement. When the donor retires, the trust's investments would be repositioned to generate income. This arrangement avoids the restrictive ERISA rules on qualified plans and enables the donor to retire at any age without penalty. Furthermore, there is no restriction on the amount that can be set aside, yearly or otherwise when using this plan as a retirement strategy, and it generates a small annual deduction.

Additional Features

Taxation

The grantor of a CRT is entitled to a deduction for assets that are contributed to the trust. The amount of the deduction is based on several factors, including the term of the trust, the ages of the income beneficiaries if the payout is for life, the applicable federal rate at the time the assets are transferred to the trust, and the payout rate chosen by the grantor. Depending on these factors, the deduction can range from 10 to 60 percent or more.

Assets contributed to a CRT and subsequently sold will avoid tax on any gain that is realized. Losses, however, are not deductible. The income generated by a CRT is free from taxation while it is in the trust. When distributions are made, the amounts paid out are taxed on the basis of their makeup and a four-tiered accounting system that calls for ordinary income first, capital gains second, tax-free income third, and return of principal last. For example, Chuck's CRUT requires a payout of 8 percent, valued annually. In year one, the assets of the trust are valued at $1 million, resulting in a unitrust payment for that year of $80,000. If the trust's income for that year is comprised of $20,000 of dividends, $35,000 of capital gains, and no tax exempt income, the tax components of Chuck's distribution are:

Tier 1.	Dividends	$20,000
Tier 2.	Capital gains	$35,000
Tier 3.	Tax-exempt income	$0
Tier 4.	Return of principal	+ $25,000
		$80,000

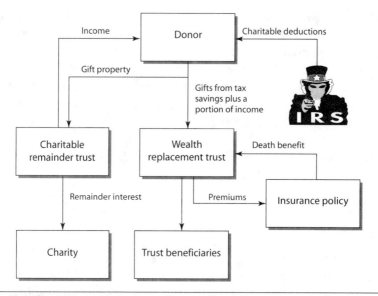

Figure 17-1. Charitable remainder trust with a wealth replacement trust: Using life insurance to replace an asset in the estate.

Wealth Replacement Trust

After you irrevocably place assets in the CRT, your heirs are effectively disinherited from receiving that property. Thus, a *wealth replacement trust (WRT)* is in order. A WRT is an irrevocable life insurance trust created to benefit your heirs (see Chapter 7). The grantor of the WRT funds the trust with a portion of the additional cash flow generated from the CRT and/or the tax savings generated by the charitable income tax deduction. After the grantor contributes funds to the WRT, the trustee purchases life insurance on the grantor to replace the wealth represented by the assets given to the CRT (see Figure 17-1). In many cases, this strategy generates a larger inheritance for the grantor's heirs than they would have received if the assets transferred to the CRT had remained in the estate and been subjected to estate taxes. In some cases, the income tax savings alone cover the cost of an insurance policy that replaces the *full* value of the assets. This means that the children will end up with more than they would have received otherwise and the IRS effectively pays the cost in the form of tax savings.

Example

Craig and Kathie Hall, ages 68 and 64, own a $1 million office building that they originally bought for $700,000 with a depreciated basis of $100,000. They

TABLE 17-1 Charitable Giving Plan with and without CRT: Craig and Kathie Hall

Charitable giving plan	Without CRT	With CRT
Appreciated asset sold	$1,000,000	$1,000,000
Gift to charity	0	– 1,000,000
Capital gain tax (state & federal)	– 264,000	$ 0
Net asset	$ 736,000	0
Income at 7%	51,520	70,000
Income tax deduction	0	300,000
Income tax savings	0	120,000
Insurance purchased with tax savings*	0	1,000,000
Gross to children	736,000	1,000,000
Estate taxes at 50%	– 368,000	0
Net to children	$ 368,000	$1,000,000
Summary		
Total income during life (20 years)	$1,030,400	$1,400,000
Gift to charity or family foundation	0	1,000,000
Net to children	368,000	1,000,000
Total	$1,398,400	$3,400,000

*Life insurance premium is based on survivorship insurance and current assumptions of interest, mortality charges, and expenses. Premium amount will vary according to age of insureds, medical profile, product, and the insurance companies selected.

are tired of being landlords and dealing with commercial tenants. Their net rental income is low compared to the value of their building, which is no longer appreciating. They would like to sell the building but do not want to pay the capital gains tax, which would be approximately 27 percent (25 percent on amounts that had been taken as depreciation and 20 percent on the remainder, plus state income taxes of 6 percent). By utilizing a CRT, the Halls can avoid all capital gains tax, increase their income, create a tax deduction, and leave more to their heirs by means of a WRT, all the while providing a substantial charitable legacy (see Table 17-1). They do all this by forming a charitable remainder unitrust in which they choose an annual payout of 7 percent. Initially, this generates an income of $70,000 and a tax deduction of approximately $300,000. Based on the Halls' combined federal and state income tax bracket of 40 percent, this deduction equates to a tax savings of $120,000—

the same amount needed to fund a $1 million policy of insurance on a one-pay basis.

As the example illustrates, a CRT can provide a greater inheritance than your loved ones would otherwise receive. It is even possible to use a CRT to provide "fuel" that will offset the estate taxes on your entire estate, not just on the amount transferred to the CRT.

Estate Protection

In a recent estate planning case, a woman complained about the amount of estate taxes that would be due on her $14 million estate, which was made up primarily of one stock she had inherited from her father. The stock had gone up in value substantially in recent months. In fact, the woman remarked that her $10 million in stock had increased nearly 22 percent in the prior two months (to $12.2 million). Her basis in this stock was very low, so she hesitated to sell any of the stock because of the income taxes that would be due. As her advisor, I suggested that she transfer shares representing just the increase in the stock over the previous two months ($2.2 million worth) into a CRUT with a 10 percent ($220,000) payout. By doing this, the woman avoided capital gains taxes and had enough income from the trust, after income taxes, to purchase a $7 million survivorship insurance policy that can be used to pay the estate tax on her entire $14 million estate.

Through the use of charitable planning, the woman was able to use the recent appreciation in her stock to offset the estate taxes on her entire estate. In addition to the fact that her children will inherit the total estate intact, she received a current income tax deduction that generated sizable tax savings which she used to provide additional gifts to the charities of her choice (see Figure 17-2).

Shortly after she completed the plan, the market value of her stock dropped more than 35 percent from its high when she made the transfer and received her deduction. Thus, 35 percent of the stock value that created the funds to pay her estate taxes and create the charitable legacy would have disappeared had she procrastinated.

Private Family Foundation

With a CRT, you have unlimited choices regarding the charity (or charities) you name as the beneficiary and, if the trust is designed with you as trustee, you can change the beneficiary at any time. One option is to name a *private foundation* as the charitable beneficiary. A private foundation is a legal entity that qualifies under the Internal Revenue Code as a charity. Assets donated to the foundation

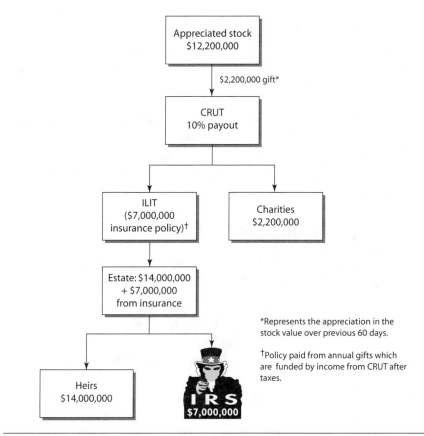

Figure 17-2. Charitable trust plan: Using market gains to protect your estate.

(directly by you while you are alive and/or from your estate or CRT at your death) can accumulate and be disbursed (5 percent minimum per year) to other qualified charities in accordance with your wishes as outlined in the foundation documents. By creating a private foundation, you can direct your social capital long after you are gone and, if you desire, can get family members involved in the process. A private foundation can focus on the interests of your children along whatever charitable lines you choose, keep future generations of your family together by uniting them at least annually for trust decision making, and raise the standing of your descendants within their respective communities. Also, your children are entitled to be paid for serving as trustees of the foundation.

Although a private foundation offers several benefits, it also has drawbacks. These include excise taxes on the net investment income of the foundation, burdensome record-keeping and reporting requirements, a limitation on the amount of deductions, and other restrictions.

Donor-Advised Account

An excellent alternative to the private foundation is a *donor-advised account* of a community foundation or some other public charity. Donor-advised accounts operate much like private foundations: family members are able to direct the income and principal of the account, but they do so under the guidance of a host public charity or community foundation. This arrangement provides some or all of the benefits offered by a private foundation but costs substantially less to set up and administer. For most donors who want their families involved in their philanthropy, this alternative makes the most sense.

CRT Target Situations

Creating a CRT requires careful decision making. Let's recap by outlining a few situations that call for a CRT:

- *Capital gains tax:* If you are selling highly appreciated stock, a business interest, real estate, or other appreciated assets, a CRT will enable you to avoid capital gains tax and increase the total economic benefit by reinvesting all the proceeds from the sale, not just the after-tax proceeds.
- *Income:* A CRT is a means of converting highly appreciated, low-yielding assets to income-producing assets without having principal eroded by capital gains tax.
- *Retirement:* If you are in your preretirement years and own a small business, a CRT can be a way to build retirement income on a tax-deferred basis without the limitations and requirements of qualified retirement plans.
- *Estate planning:* With a CRT, you can reduce estate taxes while retaining income rights to (and control of) the assets donated to the trust. If you also create a wealth replacement trust, your heirs will avoid all estate tax and may end up with more than they would have otherwise received. A WRT is typically funded with insurance that is paid for from the tax savings created when the CRT is funded. Because the WRT is the owner of the insurance policies, the insurance proceeds will go to heirs without income or estate taxes.
- *Charitable legacies:* If you want to maximize your ability to contribute to your favorite charity, a CRT is a great way to leverage your contribution and truly make a difference.

- *Safety and diversification:* If you are frustrated with managing your current assets and want to reduce risk, a CRT can provide safety through diversification. Also, it can eliminate management headaches that often come with assets, such as rental real estate.
- *Protection:* Once assets are transferred to a CRT, they are free from the claims of creditors as long as the transfer was not made to defraud creditors. If the CRT is set up as a NIMCRUT, you, as trustee, can protect the income as well as the principal by electing to defer distributions through the trust's investments.
- *Transfer of a business:* If you are looking for a way to transfer control of a closely held business to a family member without incurring gift tax, a CRT may be the answer. The business stock, once transferred to the trust, can be repurchased by the corporation, leaving the minority family shareholder in full control. You avoid gift tax that would have been generated by an outright gift. You also receive a lifetime income, avoid capital gains on the sale of stock, and, depending on your age and the payout rate, receive a sizable tax deduction, too.

Summary

With a CRT you can avoid capital gains tax, earn more income during your life, receive a tax deduction, reduce estate taxes, leave more for your heirs, and establish a charitable legacy. A CRT also offers other benefits, such as an accumulation option, control of donated assets if you act as your own trustee, and protection of your assets from claims of creditors—all with the blessing of the U.S. Government.

Although this may seem too good to be true, the government actually encourages the establishment of charitable remainder trusts. CRTs are part of the U.S. tax code and reflect Congress's desire to motivate taxpayers to make charitable gifts. With increased charitable giving by the private sector, more government dollars will be available to work in other areas of the economy. Also, trust assets generate higher taxable income because the full value of the asset contributed, undiminished by capital gains taxes, is at work. With higher taxable income, more taxes are generated over the long term than would be the case from an immediate sale with a taxable gain. So, the government actually comes out ahead.

18 Charitable Lead Trusts

Michael and Jeri Demitro had most of their estate plan completed when they arrived at my office, but they were looking for additional ways to decrease their estate and increase the amount of their gifts to their seven children. Unfortunately, they had used up all but a small portion of their lifetime exemption, and they were using all their annual gift tax exemptions for gifts to various trusts set up by their attorney.

After reviewing their current estate plan and personal finances, I learned that Michael and Jeri were contributing approximately $100,000 each year to their own private family foundation. As trustees of the foundation (along with their children), they made annual gifts to their favorite charities. Their personal income was sufficient to allow Michael and Jeri to continue making their contributions to the foundation for at least 20 more years.

With this in mind, I showed Michael and Jeri how they could use a charitable lead trust to help them immediately remove approximately $1 million from their estate without gift tax, for the benefit of their children, by simply continuing to make annual contributions to their family foundation via the trust.

🛡 🛡 🛡

A *charitable lead trust (CLT)* is the opposite of a charitable remainder trust in that its income is paid to charities, rather than to the trust donor,

227

for a term of years. At the expiration of the term, the remaining trust assets are paid to noncharitable beneficiaries such as children or grand-children. By allowing the income to go to charity, the tax value of the trust principal can be reduced so that little to no gift or estate tax will be due. In other words, the cost of making a gift is lowered because the value of the gift is decreased by the value of the annuity interest donated to charity. When the assets in the trust are transferred to the remainder persons/ beneficiaries, any appreciation on the value of the assets is free of both gift and estate tax in the donor's estate. Such a trust can be set up during the grantor's lifetime, but it is often funded at the death of the grantor, in which case it is referred to as a *testamentary CLT.* Both corporations and individuals may establish a CLT.

Lifetime Versus Testamentary CLTs

Lifetime CLT

One of the primary reasons for setting up and funding a CLT during life is to start the clock ticking on the term of the trust so that assets. For tax-reporting purposes, these assets are reduced by the present value of the pay-ments going to charity. Thusly, they get into the hands of the noncharitable beneficiaries sooner. If appreciated assets are used to fund a CLT during the grantor's lifetime, the noncharitable beneficiaries (the children, for example) will inherit the basis of the grantor, which could possibly expose those assets to capital gains taxes.

Perhaps a more compelling reason for funding a CLT during life is to benefit one or more charities while reducing or eliminating gift or estate taxes on a portion of a grantor's estate. If a grantor is already giving to charity on a regular basis, it is possible to work backward using the amount of the annual gift to charity to determine the amount of assets that can be contributed to a CLT that would eventually go to family members or to others on a tax-free basis.

In some cases, a grantor may even set up a CLT naming him- or her-self as the remainder person. Such an arrangement would typically be set up to utilize the present value of the payments to charity as a current tax deduction rather than as a reduction of the remainder interest intended as a gift to one or more family members. In the second and following years of a CLT set up this way, the grantor must report the income earned by the trust, even though it is actually paid to the charity in the form of an annuity. This could be offset by investing trust assets in tax-free investments (such as tax-free municipal bonds or a variable insurance policy).

Testamentary CLT

The testamentary CLT is more popular among planners because it allows a flexible and unique way to offset any remaining portion of an estate that is exposed to tax at the grantor's death. A properly drafted testamentary CLT is complex, but its basics can be reduced to a few simple steps. Here is a summary of how most testamentary CLTs operate:

1. The grantor establishes a CLT as part of his or her living trust planning, but the actual funding of the trust occurs at the grantor's death.

2. At the grantor's death (or at the death of both grantors if a husband and wife adopt this strategy), a substantial amount of the grantor's property passes to the charitable lead trust.

3. The income beneficiary of the CLT is a charity or charities chosen by the grantor in his or her revocable living trust. The charitable income beneficiary receives income from the trust for a certain number of years.

4. A CLT can be designed so that at the end of the trust's term, its assets pass to noncharitable trust beneficiaries totally free from gift and estate tax. The assets can pass outright to the beneficiaries, they can continue to be held in trust for the beneficiaries, or they can pass to trusts that have been previously established for the beneficiaries.

The primary objectives of the testamentary CLT are to:

- Eliminate virtually all federal estate tax on the death of the grantor and the grantor's spouse and eventually pass all assets to children and grandchildren.

- Take advantage of the step-up in basis on low-basis assets in the estate that are transferred to the CLT at death, thereby avoiding or reducing capital gains taxes.

- Have all or part of the income paid to one or more charities for the term of the trust.

- Maximize the use of the generation-skipping transfer tax exemption.

Example

Figure 18-1 on page 230 illustrates how a testamentary CLT works. At death, the balance of the grantor's estate goes to a CLT for 20 years. The

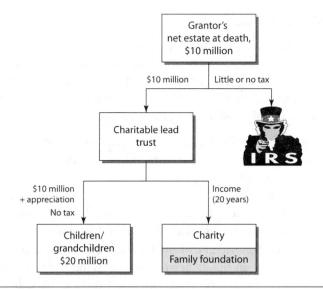

Figure 18-1. Testamentary charitable lead trust.

gift-tax value of the gift that will eventually go to the grantor's children and/or grandchildren is *reduced* by the value of the 20-year income interest that goes to the grantor's family foundation (managed by the grantor's children). In a properly designed trust the gift tax value of the assets transferred is very small and results in little or no tax. Assuming a growth of 3.5 percent, net of the income paid to the charity, the value of the assets transferred at the end of the 20-year term to the grantor's children and/or grandchildren is $20 million—completely free of gift and estate taxes.

Types of CLT

There are two basic types of charitable lead trusts: the annuity trust and the unitrust. They differ in the amount of income that the charitable beneficiary receives.

The charitable lead annuity trust

A *charitable lead annuity trust (CLAT)* pays to a charity a guaranteed annuity that can be designated as a percentage of the initial contribution or a fixed dollar amount. For example, if the terms of the CLAT state that the charity is to receive an annuity amount equal to 10 percent of the initial amount in the trust, a transfer of $3 million to the CLAT would yield

$300,000 each year from the trust, regardless of the value of the principal in later years. Investment performance does not affect the amount of the annuity payment.

Investment performance does affect how much the remainder beneficiaries will receive. If the assets in the CLAT generate income and/or appreciation in excess of the annuity payment, the remainder beneficiaries will ultimately receive more when the trust ends. Conversely, if the earnings from the assets are less than the annuity payments, the principal must be used to satisfy the annuity payment, thereby reducing the amount ultimately passing to the beneficiaries. Because the annuity amount is set when the assets are given to the trust, the CLAT is particularly suited for hard-to-value assets, such as real estate or interests in closely held corporations since the assets need to be valued only once. For example, if closely held stock in a family business worth $1 million is transferred to a 10-year CLAT with an initial payout rate of 8 percent, the stock does not have to be revalued each year. The charity will receive $80,000 annually regardless of the value of the stock.

The charitable lead unitrust

The amount paid to charity from a *charitable lead unitrust (CLUT)* is a percentage of the fair market value of the property held in the trust. If the terms of the CLUT state that the income beneficiary is to receive a 10 percent payout and the grantor transferred $3 million to the CLUT, the charity would receive $300,000 the first year, more than $300,000 in years when the trust's assets exceed $3 million in value, and less than $300,000 in years when the trust's assets are less than $3 million. In other words, investment performance determines the amount that the charity receives. The determining factor is not the amount of income the trust earns during the year, but the fair market value of the trust's assets on a particular day each year the trust is in existence. If the $3 million transferred to the CLUT grows to $3.2 million in year two, the charity will receive $320,000 in that year. If the value of the assets drops to $2.9 million, the charity will receive $290,000.

A potential drawback to a CLUT is that its assets must be valued each year. If it owns hard-to-value assets, the costs of appraisals and the uncertainty of valuation can present difficult problems. A CLUT is a vehicle that lends itself to highly liquid, easily valued assets, such as cash, stocks, or bonds.

CLTs and Taxes

Estate Tax

A transfer of property to a charitable lead trust (either a CLAT or a CLUT) consists of two parts for valuation purposes. The first part is the *present value of the income stream* to be received by a charity or charities during the CLT's term. This value can be determined from tables furnished by the Internal Revenue Service. It is based on a number of factors, including the value of the property transferred to the CLT, the amount of the annuity or unitrust income interest, the number of years the trust will pay income, and the interest rates in effect at the time the assets are transferred to the trust (which could be at the grantor's death in the case of a testamentary CLT). The interest rate used is provided by the Internal Revenue Service on a monthly basis and is called the applicable federal rate.

The second part of the transfer is the value of the amount that will pass to the noncharitable beneficiaries after the charitable lead trust ends. This amount, called the *remainder interest,* is the difference between the value of the assets transferred to the trust and the present value of the income stream to be received by the charity or charities. The remainder interest represents a taxable gift. A formula may be used in a grantor's living trust that allows the trustee to establish a CLT after the death of the grantor that will pay income to a charity for the number of years needed, based on the then-published applicable federal rate, to substantially reduce or eliminate the federal estate tax due on those assets. Therefore, it is possible to design a plan in such a way that no federal estate taxes are due on those assets with one exception—special attention must be given in designing a trust that will pass to a beneficiary one or more generations below the grantor (grandchildren, for example) as those assets may be exposed to the GST tax, as discussed below.

CLAT Versus CLUT

In testamentary planning, a CLAT and a CLUT are used for different purposes. For individuals who want to zero-out their federal estate tax and ultimately leave their property to their children, a CLAT is used. A CLAT minimizes the time between the maker's date of death and the date that the property is paid to the children. However, a CLAT is not

TABLE 18-1   Income Tax Rates for Trusts and Estates, 2002*

Income	Tax rate
$0–$1850	15 percent
$1850–$4400	$277.50 plus 27% of excess over $1850
$4400–$6750	$966 plus 30% of excess over $4400
$6750–$9200	$1671 plus 35% of excess over $6750
Over $9200	$2528.50 plus 38.6% of excess over $9200

*Adjusted each year for changes in the cost of living.

used for generation-skipping planning. It does not efficiently use the GST exemption ($1,100,000 in 2002) which each taxpayer is entitled to, because the value of the property on which the generation-skipping tax is assessed is the value that is passed to the trust remainder persons when the CLAT *ends*. Because a CLAT is used to optimize that value, a CLAT can actually *increase* generation-skipping tax.

If the planning objective is to maximize the use of the generation-skipping exemption amount and pay as little federal estate tax as possible, a CLUT is used. Under the GST tax law, the amount against which the generation-skipping tax is imposed is computed when the CLUT is *initially* funded. In the case of a testamentary CLUT, that would be on the grantor's death. A well-drafted testamentary CLUT has a "formula clause" which ensures that the grantor's estate will be taxed only on the grantor's remaining generation-skipping exemption amount. This amount, ($1.1 million for 2002) is subject to increases over time (see Appendix D), but it can be less if the grantor has used some of his or her exemption during life. The formula clause helps ensure that when the CLUT ends, the property will not be subject to any gift, estate, or generation-skipping tax.

For married couples, it is typical to use a CLUT on the death of each so that both of their $1.1 million GST tax exemptions (which was $2.2 million in 2002) can be fully used.

Many times, the beneficiary of a CLUT is a dynasty trust (see Chapter 4). This combined strategy allows a grantor to leverage his or her GST tax exemption and keep assets from ever being subjected to the federal estate tax.

Capital Gains Tax

One of the advantages of using a testamentary CLT is that the assets that are held in the trust receive a step-up in basis to their fair market value (except for 2010—see Appendix D). The step-up may be significant if the assets have a low basis and a high market value at the death of the grantor. It gives the trustee of the CLT the opportunity to sell the assets at no taxable gain, thereby eliminating capital gains tax.

Taxation of Trust Income

A charitable lead trust that is set up during life can be arranged so that any income that is earned over and above the amount paid to charity is taxed to the grantor (a grantor CLT). If the CLT is not set up as a grantor trust or if the trust is a testamentary CLT, any income not paid out to charity is taxed to the trust at its income tax brackets. Because a trust's income tax brackets result in a much higher income tax rate, this aspect of the testamentary charitable lead trust can be detrimental. Table 18-1 on page 233 shows the income tax rates for trusts and estates for 2002.

One obvious solution to this tax problem is for the trustee to invest in municipal bonds or other tax-free investments. However, this is not always a practical solution. Many times, the income paid from such tax-free investments is relatively low. And if the trust does not earn enough income to pay the amount that the grantor chose when the trust was established, the trustee has to use principal to pay the amount due to the charity in accordance with the CLT plan. This, of course, reduces the amount available to the ultimate beneficiaries of the trust.

It is possible to draft a charitable lead trust so that it requires that the trustee pay any income in excess of the amount specified in the trust agreement to charities. By adding the necessary provision, all the taxable income is paid out and thus no income tax is payable by the trust in its brackets. However, the ultimate beneficiaries—generally the grantor's family members—may receive less principal upon the termination of the trust because no income is being accumulated. Only by running sophisticated computer projections can an informed decision be made regarding the best course of action for a family.

Gift Tax

When you establish a CLT during your lifetime, the present value of the remainder interest is a current taxable gift. To calculate this value, you

TABLE 18-2   Calculation of Current Taxable Gift for CLAT*

Value of transferred securities	$3,000,000	$3,000,000
Annual distribution to charity (8%)	$240,000	$240,000
Applicable federal rate	5.4%	7%
Present value of charitable gift	$2,892,000	$2,543,000
Taxable gift	$108,000	$457,000

*CLUTs are not significantly affected by changes in the applicable federal rate.

first determine the present value of the lead or annuity interest to the charity by using the applicable federal interest rate prescribed by U.S. Treasury regulations. You then subtract this value from the total value of the assets placed into the CLT.

With a CLAT, the lower the applicable federal rate, the lower the taxable gift and the greater the potential benefit to the remainder beneficiaries if the trust can grow in value at a rate greater than the required payout. For example, let's say you transfer $3 million of appreciated securities to a CLT that distributes an 8 percent annuity each year for 20 years to your favorite charity. Table 18-2 shows the difference in the taxable gifts that result from a 5.4 and a 7 percent applicable federal rate. Increasing the term of the trust or the amount of the annual distribution may reduce or possibly eliminate the amount of the taxable gift.

Because the remainder interest in a CLT is a "future" interest, any taxable-gift portion will not qualify for the gift tax *annual* exclusion. Thus, to avoid gift taxes on transfers made during life, you will have to use a portion of your applicable exclusion amount ($1 million in 2002 and 2003). If you are using a testamentary CLT and the remainder interest passes to your spouse, who is a U.S. citizen, it should qualify for the gift tax marital deduction. So, you would not have to use any portion of your applicable exclusion amount.

Charitable Beneficiaries

The charitable beneficiaries of a charitable lead trust must be "qualified charities" as defined under the Internal Revenue Code. Generally, any charity that has received tax-exempt status through an IRS determination qualifies, but this is not always the case. Some research is necessary to ensure that the charitable beneficiary is fully qualified as a charity under the CLT rules.

If a testamentary CLT is set up, the charity or charities named can be changed until the death of the maker. Thereafter, the trustee may be given the power to change the charitable income beneficiary as long as the trustee is restricted to naming qualified charities. The grantor can further restrict the types of charities that the trustee can choose. For example, the trustee's choice can be restricted to particular religious charities or particular types of colleges or universities.

The grantor can name a private foundation established by the grantor as the charitable income beneficiary. If this is the case, the grantor must have very limited authority over which charity is to receive money from the foundation. Too much control will result in adverse tax consequences.

You must know your charitable desires before a professional estate planner can design a proper CLT strategy for you. The trust document itself must be carefully drafted to provide a maximum number of choices without violating the complex rules surrounding the selection of charitable income beneficiaries in a CLT.

Planning Requirements

Charitable lead trust planning requires significant financial analysis. A variety of planning alternatives must be explored in detail before any type of CLT planning is instigated. Because it may be 10, 15, 20, or more years before children or grandchildren receive property from a CLAT or CLUT, great care should be exercised in determining if such a trust is the best course of action. Generally, charitable lead trust planning should be combined with an irrevocable life insurance trust and other lifetime planning strategies so that children and grandchildren will receive substantial assets in addition to the proceeds from a CLAT or CLUT. This is especially true with a testamentary CLT, which delays the distribution of the remainder interest for a period of years after the death of the grantor. Projections are necessary to determine if it is better to pay federal estate taxes and have children or grandchildren inherit property at the death of an individual grantor or at the death of the second to die of married grantors. Only when these comparisons are made can an informed and proper decision be reached.

As a testamentary CLT is intended to be funded at death, it is revocable during the life of the grantor. Thereafter, it cannot be changed without great difficulty.

Summary

Charitable lead trust planning enables you to truly disinherit the IRS while putting yourself and your family in full control of your social capital (see Chapter 16). By combining CLT planning with other strategies discussed in this book, you can not only ensure that your heirs receive the full value of your estate but also provide significant gifts to charity.

19 Retirement Plans: Taxation

N *No one was more shocked than Jon and Liz Delmar when they discovered the substantial amount of taxes that would be due on their combined retirement plans at death. Although they knew about the estate taxes that would apply, the real shock came when they learned that their plan assets would also have income tax due on the full value. They had mistakenly assumed that the assets in their retirement plans, as most of the other assets in their estate, would receive a step-up in the cost basis at death.*

One of their three qualified retirement plans was an IRA that Jon had established with funds he rolled over from his company-sponsored pension plan after retiring from his position as a pilot with Delta Airlines. Because the IRA was by far the largest of their plans, I did some math to show Jon just how much would be due on his IRA. Then, I looked at their entire estate, including all three retirement plans and computed the total tax that would be due without planning. It turned out that the tax exceeded the total amount in his IRA!

I showed Jon and Liz that without proper planning, Jon's IRA is a "tax time bomb" but with proper planning the bomb could be defused!

ᙏ ᙏ ᙏ

If you have an individual retirement account (IRA) or qualified retirement plan (QRP) and expect that any funds remaining in your account at your death will pass to your heirs, you may be in for some bad news: Your IRA or QRP might turn out to be a ticking tax time bomb (see page 192).

If you've managed to accumulate a substantial nest egg in a pension or profit-sharing plan, a 401(k) or similar QRP, or an IRA, a nasty surprise is awaiting you. The IRS stands ready to levy an incredibly wide array of taxes on your plan distributions: income tax, early withdrawal tax, underwithdrawal tax, estate tax, and, depending on your intended heirs, generation-skipping transfer (GST) tax. As much as 85 percent of your IRA or QRP could be lost to Uncle Sam when you leave your qualified plan assets to your heirs. Hard to believe? Read on!

The Tax Time Bomb

First, all distributions are subject to tax at ordinary income tax rates, which currently range between 10 and nearly 40 percent (plus state income tax, if any). This is true even after death. IRA and QRP assets are considered "income in respect of a decedent" and therefore are fully taxable when distributions are taken from the plan. There is also a 10 percent tax imposed on distributions made before you turn 59½, unless you are disabled or qualify for certain narrow exemptions from the penalty. If you fail to take the minimum required distribution (MRD) starting April 1 of the year following the year in which you turn 70½, there is a 50 percent penalty tax on amounts you fail to withdraw. (The minimum distribution rules are explained in the next chapter.)

The tax guillotine doesn't stop chopping there. Because there is no step-up in basis for assets that pass to your heirs in a QRP or IRA, the full value of your retirement plan benefits will be subject to both income tax—on the full value of the assets in the plan(s)—and estate tax at your death. So, after deducting both estate tax and federal, as well as state, income taxes, the balance of your account may be reduced to 30 cents or less on the dollar. And it could be even further reduced by the GST tax if you name a beneficiary who is one or more generations below your children. This *additional* tax is equal to the top gift and estate tax rate of 50 percent (see Appendix D).

Example

Mrs. Irene Jones, a recently deceased 75-year-old widow, accumulated $2.5 million in her IRA before her death. She is survived by four children, three of whom are married, along with one grandson. Mrs. Jones died a resident of

TABLE 19-1   The IRA of Mrs. Jones

Value of Mrs. Jones's interest in IRA	$2,500,000
Less: Federal estate tax at 50%	– 1,250,000
Balance after federal estate tax	$1,250,000
Less: GST tax at 50%	– 625,000
Balance after GST tax	$ 625,000
Less: Income tax*	– 241,250
Balance after income tax	$ 383,750
Original amount of estate	$2,500,000
Less: Total taxes paid	– 2,116,250
Amount to Mrs. Jones's grandson	$ 383,750
After-tax amount to grandson per IRA dollar	$.15

*Rough approximation. Income tax applies to full $2.5 million IRA but is partially offset by a deduction for related estate taxes

Florida, which taxes estates on the basis of a credit allowed against federal estate tax (effectively yielding no additional state inheritance tax). She named a trust set up exclusively for the benefit of her grandson as the beneficiary of her IRA. The benefits are to be paid in a lump sum to the trust.

The tax

Mrs. Jones's gross estate is subject to the marginal federal estate tax rate of 50 percent. Because Mrs. Jones used her full GST exemption with gifts made prior to death, and is leaving her IRA to her grandson through a generation skipping trust, her IRA is also subject to the GST tax, which is an additional tax of 50 percent (see Appendix D). The trust's marginal federal income tax rate is 38.6 percent. Table 19-1 translates these tax rates into dollar amounts and shows their devastating effect on Mrs. Jones's IRA.

What can be done to relieve such a tax burden? If the retirement plan owner is still working, a simple solution would be for the owner to stop making contributions, but this might increase the owner's current income tax burden. If the owner is retired, he or she might consider depleting the funds accumulated in the plan rather than using other assets (which receive a full step-up in their cost basis—thus no capital gains taxes if the assets are sold immediately after death), but this may not provide the optimal return on the owner's plan assets or total estate over time.

Tax-Avoidance Techniques

To most people, the amount of after-death taxation on retirement plans is confiscatory. So it may come as a relief to know that there are strategies that can be used, within an overall estate plan, to avoid or minimize the effect of the taxes. One of these strategies involves life insurance and one or more trusts. To see how it works, let's assume that Mrs. Jones is still alive and has decided, after consulting with her advisors, to use this strategy.

Instead of letting the earnings accumulate inside her IRA, Mrs. Jones withdraws $125,000 per year. This is equal to the earnings on her IRA assets at 5 percent. After income tax, the net spendable amount, approximately $75,000, is given to an irrevocable life insurance trust (ILIT) with generation-skipping (IRS-skipping) provisions. The trustee of the ILIT uses the gift funds to purchase $3 million of life insurance on Mrs. Jones's life.

Upon Mrs. Jones's death, the trust will receive the proceeds of the insurance policy, free of income and estate taxes. The ILIT can be set up so that the income (and principal if needed) from the $3 million insurance proceeds will go to benefit Mrs. Jones's four children as well as her grandson (see Chapter 4). By purchasing insurance with the income earned on her IRA and by using her annual gift tax exemption for all four trust beneficiaries, Mrs. Jones has avoided gift taxes (on the annual $75,000 gift to the ILIT) as well as income, estate, and generation-skipping transfer taxes on the proceeds of the insurance policy. Also, the assets in the ILIT are free from the claims resulting from a lawsuit with creditors, divorce proceedings, etc.

If for any reason Mrs. Jones wants or needs some of the funds in the IRA during her lifetime, she is free to withdraw additional money. Or if her income needs are eating away large portions of her IRA, she can stop making gifts to the ILIT (in the amount of the premiums) and settle for a smaller, paid-up policy based on the premiums paid to date. Alternatively, Mrs. Jones can set up her ILIT so she can borrow funds in the ILIT (from the insurance policy's cash value) with repayment of principal and interest due from her estate at her death (see Chapter 7).

If Mrs. Jones is charitably inclined, she can bequeath the remaining balance of her IRA to her favorite charity or to a charitable remainder trust (CRT). Giving to her favorite charity would cut only 15 cents per dollar—the amount her heirs would have received. If she chooses the latter, the CRT can provide one or more of her heirs with a source of income, for a period of years or for life, from the trust. This would provide an estate tax deduction equal to the remainder interest the charity will receive at the death of the income beneficiary (see Chapter 17).

Mrs. Jones might even consider forming her own private foundation or donor-advised account of a public charity to which she could leave her IRA. She could name her grandson to be a trustee of the foundation or donor-advised account. This would give her grandson a certain amount of prestige and influence in his community where the charitable gifts are made. It could also provide her grandson with another source of income, in the form of trustee-director fees.

As a result of the plan, Mrs. Jones's heirs will receive substantially more inheritance than what they would have netted, after taxes, from her IRA. The rationale for using this approach really boils down to a single question: If she does not need the income, why would Mrs. Jones allow her IRA to be ravaged by taxes, leaving her heirs only $383,750 (15 cents on the dollar), when she could leave them more than $3 million outside probate and free of income and estate taxes and possibly provide a substantial charitable legacy?

Summary

There are many ways to optimize and plan for an estate with large accumulations in a QRP or IRA without having the government end up with the bulk of the plan assets in the form of taxes. To find out about your options, it is important to seek advice from a qualified estate planning professional and to use any retirement planning strategy as part of an overall estate plan. The first step should be to consult your tax counsel and financial planner regarding your individual situation.

20 Retirement Plans: Distributions

T Ted Thompson was almost 70½ when he turned to me to help him make decisions on his IRA. Ted and his wife, Debby, knew there was a minimum amount that Ted would soon be required to withdraw from his IRA, but they had no idea of the complex rules surrounding all their decisions. Ted knew that he could put off taking his minimum required distribution until the year after the year in which he turned 70½. But he did not know that he would be required to take two distributions that year which would likely raise his income tax bracket and decrease his net distribution, after tax. Also, Ted and Debby were surprised and grateful to learn about an often-overlooked deduction which would help reduce income taxes by the amount of estate taxes attributed to their IRA on distributions taken by their children.

Ted and Debby were happy to learn that with proper planning they could ensure their three boys would inherit the balance of their IRA and be able to stretch out distributions over their individual lifetimes. The most important thing that came from our discussion was the need to understand the rules surrounding IRAs and why it is necessary to properly plan for lifetime withdrawals as well as the ultimate distribution to their heirs at death.

🛡 🛡 🛡

Qualified retirement plan (QRP) benefits and individual retirement account (IRA) assets represent an increasing portion of the accumulated wealth of many Americans. If you are among this growing number, you will be facing a deadline on April 1 of the year following the one in which you reach age 70½. By that date, you will be facing some very important financial decisions in regard to preserving your family wealth.

Minimum Required Distributions

The current tax law and IRS regulations mandate that you begin taking annual *minimum required distributions* (MRDs) from traditional IRAs by April 1 of the year after which you reach age 70½. With respect to QRPs, you may delay taking MRDs until April 1 of the year after you retire. However, if you own more than 5 percent of the company that sponsors your plan, MRDs must start by April 1 of the year after you reach 70½, regardless of when you retire. This is known as your *required beginning date* (RBD). If you continue to work past age 70½, participate in a QRP, and are *not* a "5 percent owner," the tax laws give you the flexibility to delay distributions from your QRP and preserve the tax-deferred status of your account balance for an extended period. Note, if you have both an IRA and QRP, you can only delay distribution from the QRP and only in certain types of plans. Keep in mind that deferring distributions may increase the amount of your MRDs once you start receiving the money. This could increase your marginal income tax rate, as well as increase the taxation of your Social Security benefits. In addition, your QRP may continue to grow and at your death may eventually be subject to combined estate and income tax at rates that exceed 70 percent, leaving only 30 cents or less out of every dollar for your nonspouse heirs. You should weigh the advantages of extended tax deferral against these potential drawbacks when deciding when to begin distributions.

Two Methods for Taking Distributions

Minimum required distributions are determined by *dividing* your QRP or IRA account balance, which is revalued annually, by your life expectancy (your "divisor") using one of two methods. One method is used by any QRP or IRA owner whose sole beneficiary is his or her spouse who is more than 10 years younger than the owner. The other method calls for the use of a government mandated "uniform table."

Although it applies to single or married QRP or IRA owners, the uniform table (Appendix C, Table C-1) represents the *joint* life and last survivor expectancy of an owner age 70 or older and a hypothetical beneficiary who is 10 years younger. The initial life expectancy (the divisor) under the uniform table for an owner age 70 is 27.4 years (the joint life expectancy of someone age 70 and someone age 60).

The uniform table provides a clear advantage to QRP or IRA owners who have no spouse or have a spouse who is less than 10 years younger and want to minimize distributions. An additional benefit to using the uniform table based on two lives is the annual "recalculation" which means life expectancy is determined each year to adjust for the fact that, as people age, their life expectancy increases. Thus, their life expectancy (divisor) decreases by less than one for every year that passes. For example, at age 71, you would expect the divisor to be 26.4 (one year less than the divisor at age 70), but it is 26.5. At age 72, it is 25.6 (not 25.5), and at age 82, it is 17.1 (not 15.6). The divisor *never* reaches one. By age 115, the divisor is 1.9, and remains fixed thereafter. Assuming a QRP or IRA owner's account does not have negative investment results and he or she takes only the minimum required distribution each year, the account will never be reduced to zero.

For example, Bob, a single IRA owner, turned age 72 in the year 2003. His life expectancy divisor for age 72 from the uniform table is 25.6 years and, as noted above, is based on two lives with 10 years difference in age. On December 21, 2002, the value of his IRA was $900,000. To determine Bob's minimum required distribution from his IRA in 2003, we divide $900,000 by 25.6. The result, $35,156, is the 2003 minimum required distribution for Bob's IRA and does not depend upon whom he names as his designated beneficiary, older or younger, with one exception—a spouse who is *more than* 10 years younger (see below). Also, it does not matter whether he even has a designated beneficiary on his required beginning date or whether he changes his beneficiary after his required beginning date.

Lifetime Distributions if Beneficiary Is a Much Younger Spouse

If the sole designated beneficiary of your QRP or IRA is your spouse, for minimum required distributions during your lifetime the "applicable distribution period" for determining the minimum required distributions is the greater of the distribution period from the uniform table or the actual joint life expectancy (from the appropriate government table) of you and your spouse using your ages as of both your birthdays in the calendar year of the distribution. Like the uniform table, this alternate method requires recalculation of your spouse's and your life expectancies. So, having a spouse who is more than 10 years younger than you and naming your spouse as the sole beneficiary allows you to use your actual joint and survivor life expectancy divisor from the appropriate government tables and provides a reduction in the minimum required distributions over the uniform table.

The determination on who qualifies for using the actual joint life expectancy of an owner and much younger spouse versus the uniform table is made as of January 1 each year. If a divorce or death occurs after that date, it will be disregarded until the next year, when a new determination will be made. Thus, if an owner has a much younger spouse after the required beginning date, he or she may switch, the next year, from the uniform table to the table that reflects the actual joint life expectancy of the owner and the new, younger spouse. Similarly, if a QRP or IRA owner is married to a much younger spouse and that spouse dies or they become divorced, the owner must switch the following year to the uniform table in determining required minimum distributions.

Recalculating Versus Fixed-Term Life Expectancy

As described briefly above, recalculation calls for determining life expectancy annually to adjust for the fact that as people age, their life expectancy increases. Thus, the divisor does not go down by one each year that a person ages. Recalculation to determine the required minimum distributions is built into the uniform table as well as the joint tables for an owner and a much younger (more than 10 years younger) spouse.

The recalculation of life expectancy is beneficial because it stretches out the required minimum distributions leaving more in the QRP or IRA for the owner's heirs. Also, assuming the QRP or IRA account does not have a negative investment result and the owner takes only the minimum required distributions, it will never be depleted, regardless of how long the owner lives.

Fixed-term life expectancy is the method by which minimum required distributions to nonspouse beneficiaries (discussed in detail below) are calculated after the death of the owner, and it requires the initial life expectancy divisor to be reduced by one each year of the beneficiary's life. Under the fixed-term method of calculating distributions, the account would be depleted completely if the beneficiary lived beyond his or her life expectancy.

For example, the life expectancy of a 65-year-old nonspouse beneficiary from the fixed-period single life expectancy table (see Appendix C, Table C-3) is 21 years. That year, the minimum required distribution will be determined by dividing the balance of the inherited QRP or IRA, as of the end of the prior year, by 21. At age 66, the life expectancy from the same table is 20.2 years.

However, the beneficiary's life expectancy for minimum required distributions was "fixed," starting at 21 years (determined at or after the death of the owner). In year two at age 66, the beneficiary must use 20 (21 minus one) as the divisor, not 20.2. Similarly, at age 67, the divisor is 19 (20 minus one) and so on. By the time the beneficiary reaches 85, the divisor will be one and the balance will have to be distributed in full.

Choosing a Beneficiary

It is very important, especially for the financial welfare of your heirs, to make the right choice of "designated beneficiary" and maximize tax deferral opportunities available to your heirs after your death. You do not relinquish your right to make the most optimal choice of beneficiary just because you may have reached your required beginning date. You may make a change at any time prior to your death to a more favorable designated beneficiary (and contingent beneficiary), to allow for the longest postdeath deferral of income taxes. However, logic dictates that you avoid procrastinating on making those choices.

The rules applying to minimum required distributions from your QRP or IRA after your death depend on whether you die before or after your required beginning date. Generally, minimum required distributions to your beneficiaries who actually inherit the benefits of your QRP or IRA are based on their life expectancies. The rules regarding your choice of beneficiary during your life-time does not necessarily determine postdeath required distributions. The rules allow for a certain amount of flexibility.

Under the IRS regulations relating to QRPs and IRAs, the designated beneficiary is determined as of *September 30 of the year following the year of the owner's death.* Thus, any beneficiary who receives the distribution of his or her full share of benefits or he or she disclaims entitlement to any benefit and allows it to pass on to another, during the period between the owner's death and September 30 of the year following the year of death, is *not taken into account* in determining the distribution period for minimum required distributions after the owner's death.

This rule may seem to imply that it is possible to change the designated beneficiary for a year, or possibly longer, after your death. This is not the case. Your beneficiary selections are essentially carved in stone the moment of your death. Postdeath planning cannot simply designate new beneficiaries. "All that can be done between the date of death and the end of the next year," as author and retirement planning expert Natalie B. Choate put it, "is, so to speak, to rearrange the stones." It is important to include one or more younger persons, such as grandchildren, as contingent beneficiaries. If there are beneficiaries with long life expectancies who are named by the deceased owner as contingent beneficiaries or are among a group of multiple beneficiaries, including nonindividual beneficiaries, you can roll away some of the stones so that when the final deadline—December 31 of the year following the year of death—rolls around, only the desired (that is, the younger) beneficiaries remain. This can be done, as noted above, by having the older beneficiaries, who may not need or want the plan benefits, disclaim their rights to any benefits or by totally distributing that portion of the benefits to which an older and/or, possibly, a nonindividual beneficiary, such as a charity, is entitled.

Calculating Distributions if Owner Dies Before RBD

The first step in calculating minimum required distributions when the QRP or IRA owner dies *before* the required beginning date is to determine the identity of the beneficiaries. As discussed above, this can be done as late as September 30 of the year following the year of the owner's death. After the beneficiaries have been identified, here is how to determine their distribution options:

If the beneficiary is the owner's spouse, as sole beneficiary, he or she has several choices:

1. Roll over the QRP or IRA, without tax, into an IRA in his or her own name, select new beneficiaries, and take distributions as the owner, using his or her remaining life expectancy and the uniform table.

2. Leave the QRP or IRA in the deceased spouse's name, but use his or her own remaining life expectancy, and begin taking minimum required distributions by December 31 of the year following the year in which the owner died or December 31 of the year the deceased owner-spouse would have reached the age 70½—whichever is later. During the remaining spouse's lifetime, minimum required distributions must be taken over his or her *single* life expectancy, *recalculated each year* using the single life expectancy table (see Table C-2). At the death of the surviving spouse, if there are any remaining assets in the original owner-spouse's plan, they must be distributed to the surviving spouse's beneficiaries over the remaining life expectancy of the surviving spouse—on a *fixed-term* basis using the fixed-period single life expectancy table (see Table C-3). The remaining life expectancy of the surviving spouse is measured as of his or her birth date in the year of death. For example, if the surviving spouse's remaining life expectancy in the year of his or

her death was 17, the balance of the QRP or IRA would have to be distributed, in full, in 17 years regardless of the ages of the beneficiaries.

3. Take distributions over a five-year period, in any amount in any or all of the five years following the owner's death regardless of who or what entity receives the distribution. This is known as the "five-year rule" and is mandatory if the owner's spouse does not roll over the QRP or IRA into a new IRA of his or her own or elect to continue the plan in the original spouse's name and take distributions over his or her lifetime as described in point number 2.

4. If the surviving spouse, as the sole beneficiary, dies *before* December 31 of the year in which the original owner would have reached 70½, the surviving spouse will be treated as the owner. The rules, as noted above, will apply as if he or she died before his or her required beginning date. Thus, a new designated beneficiary will have to be determined by September 30 of the year following the year of the surviving spouse's death. Minimum required distributions will depend on whom the surviving spouse named as his or her beneficiaries.

If there is a single, *nonspouse*, individual beneficiary, then the minimum required distributions must be taken using one of the following methods:

1. Take the minimum required distributions over the beneficiary's life expectancy using a fixed term under the fixed-period single life expectancy table based on the beneficiary's birthday in the year following the year of the owner's death. Distributions must begin by December 31 of the year following the year the owner died.

2. Take distributions in full within five years (through the five-year rule).

If there is more than one beneficiary, all of whom are individuals (possibly including the owner's spouse) and these beneficiaries fail to divide the owner's QRP or IRA into separate accounts by September 30 of the year following the owner's death, the minimum required distributions must be taken using one of the following methods:

1. Take the minimum required distributions based on the life expectancy of the oldest beneficiary. These minimum required distributions must begin for all beneficiaries by December 31 of the year following the year of the owner's death. The life expectancy of the oldest beneficiary is based on his or her birthday in the year following the owner's death.

2. Take distributions in full within five years (through the five-year rule).

If there is a single beneficiary and that beneficiary is a nonindividual, such as the owner's estate, then the QRP or IRA will be treated as though there was no designated beneficiary. This means the assets in the plan must be distributed to all beneficiaries in full within five years of the owner's death under the five-year rule. This is also the case if there are multiple beneficiaries (possibly including the owner's spouse) and any one of them is not an individual and these beneficiaries have not divided the QRP or IRA into separate accounts by September 30 of the year following the year of the owner's death.

If there are multiple beneficiaries and they have established individual accounts for themselves by September 30 of the year following the owner's death, the required minimum distributions must be taken using the above rules, as applicable.

Calculating Distributions if Owner Dies on or After RBD

If the owner of a QRP or IRA plan dies after the required beginning date, there are several possible scenarios which will affect how minimum required distributions must be taken. For the calendar year of the owner's death, the minimum required distribution is determined assuming the owner lived throughout the year. If the owner was using the uniform table, which is usually the case, and he or she had not yet taken a distribution for that year, the beneficiaries will be required to take a distribution, prior to year-end, based on the uniform table. Thereafter, the minimum required distributions will be based on the life expectancy of the beneficiaries, who must be identified by September 30 of the year after the year of the owner's death. With the exception of the five-year rule, which does not apply, the following rules for calculating the required minimum distributions are essentially the same as the rules for when an owner dies before the required beginning date:

If the beneficiary is the owner's spouse, as the sole beneficiary, he or she has the following choices:

1. Roll over the QRP or IRA, without tax, into an IRA in his or her own name, select new beneficiaries, and take distributions as the owner, using his or her remaining life expectancy and the uniform table.

2. Leave the QRP or IRA in the deceased spouse's name, but take distributions over his or her own remaining life expectancy, and begin taking those minimum required distributions by December 31 of the year following the year in which the owner died. During the surviving spouse's lifetime, minimum required distributions must be taken over

his or her single life expectancy, as recalculated using the single life expectancy table (see Table C-2) each year. At the death of the surviving spouse, if there are any remaining assets in the original owner-spouse's plan, they must be distributed to the surviving spouse's beneficiaries over the remaining life expectancy of the surviving spouse—on a fixed-term basis using the fixed-period single life expectancy table (see Table C-3). The remaining life expectancy of the surviving spouse is measured as of his or her birthday in the year of death.

For example, Royce Hoffa died at age 75 and left his IRA to his wife, Jill. Unaware of her choice to roll over the account into a new IRA with herself as owner, she leaves the IRA in Royce's name. As a result, Jill must take the required minimum distributions each year based on her single life expectancy based on her birthday in the year following the year of Royce's death using the recalculation method. If Jill Hoffa dies a few years later when she is age 79, her beneficiaries will be required to take the minimum required distributions over a fixed term of 10.8 years—Jill's single life expectancy at age 79 (see Table C-3). Because the term is *fixed* at 10 years, the divisor is reduced by one each year. So in year two, the life expectancy divisor is 9.8 (10.8 minus one) and will be used to determine the minimum required distribution from the IRA for that year (by dividing the balance of the IRA on December 31 of the prior year by 9.8). In year three, the life expectancy divisor is 8.8, and so on. If Jill had been more aware of her options when Royce died, she could have rolled over his IRA into a new IRA with herself as the owner. As the IRA owner, she would have been able to use the uniform table (which, as noted above, is based on *two* lives 10 years apart with recalculation), and her designated beneficiaries would be able to use their own life expectancies, rather than having to use Jill's shorter remaining single life expectancy in calculating their minimum required distributions after Jill's death.

If there is a single, *nonspouse,* individual beneficiary, then the minimum required distributions will be based upon that person's life expectancy on his or her birthday in the year following the year the owner died. Minimum required distributions by the beneficiary must begin by December 31 of the year following the year the owner died and will be based on a fixed term under the fixed-period single life expectancy table (see Table C-3).

If there is more than one beneficiary, all of whom are individuals (possibly including the owner's spouse) and these beneficiaries fail to divide the owner's

QRP or IRA into separate accounts by September 30 of the year following the year of the owner's death, the minimum required distributions must be taken over the life expectancy of the oldest beneficiary, based on that person's age on his or her birthday in the year following the year of the owner's death. The minimum required distributions must begin for all beneficiaries by December 31 of the year following the year of the owner's death.

If there is a single beneficiary and that beneficiary is a nonindividual, such as the owner's estate, then the QRP or IRA will be treated as though there was no designated beneficiary. This means the minimum required distributions must be based on the remaining number of years of the deceased owner's life expectancy, which is determined using the fixed-period single life expectancy table, based on the owner's age on his or her birthday in the year of death using the fixed-term method. This is also the case if there are multiple beneficiaries (possibly including the owner's spouse) and any one of them is not an individual and these beneficiaries have not divided the QRP or IRA into separate accounts by September 30 of the year after the year of the owner's death.

If there are multiple beneficiaries and they have established individual accounts for themselves by September 30 of the year following the owner's death, the required minimum distributions must be taken using the above rules, as applicable.

Additional Considerations

Following are additional considerations for calculating distributions:

Penalties

The IRS rules mandate a stiff penalty for not withdrawing minimum required distributions. Although you can always take more, failure to take at least the full minimum required distribution will generally result in a 50 percent penalty tax levied on the portion not distributed. For example, if you are required to withdraw $100,000 from your IRA and you withdraw only $60,000, you will incur a $20,000 excise tax (50 percent of the $40,000 minimum required distribution not withdrawn).

Optimum beneficiaries

Clearly, the ultimate beneficiary of your plan will affect the amount and timing of retirement plan distributions. In choosing your primary and contingent beneficiaries, you may want to consider the probable tax bracket of each of your beneficiaries when he or she receives taxable distributions from your QRP or IRA. Also, you might want to consider whether your spouse will need the income from your QRP or IRA in the event of your death or whether it makes more sense to leave the plan assets to your children or grandchildren directly or as contingent beneficiaries. Choosing a younger class of beneficiaries, such as grandchildren, will allow a long stretch out of the tax-deferred growth and provide the greatest return.

Dynasty trust

You could benefit the entire family by naming a dynasty trust as the beneficiary, taking advantage of your generation-skipping transfer tax exemption (see Chapter 4). As with your other options, if you use this method, estate taxes on your QRP or IRA should come from sources other than the plan itself. And you should work with an attorney and a financial planner who understand the rules involved when you name a trust as the designated beneficiary of your QRP or IRA.

Charitable planning

If you have any charitable intent, consider leveraging your QRP or IRA by giving some or all of it to your favorite charity. When you consider how much would be left for your family after estate and income taxes and compare that to how much will go to charity without taxes, you can do a great deal of good at a small cost to your family (see Chapter 19).

Estate plan structure

You should think about how the transfer of your retirement assets fits into your overall estate plan. For example, naming your spouse as beneficiary of your retirement plan(s) will give him or her ultimate control over the disposition of the assets remaining in the QRP and/or IRA at his or her death. If this is undesirable, consider creating and naming a trust as the beneficiary of your retirement plan. The trust can be designed to provide your spouse with lifetime benefits while preserving the remaining assets for the trust's other beneficiaries after the death of your spouse. Again, you should consult an attorney or a financial planner who understands the rules involved when you name a trust as the designated beneficiary of your QRP or IRA.

Delaying your first minimum required distribution

While the regulations covering QRPs and IRAs require you to start taking minimum required distributions when you reach 70½, they also allow you to elect to delay taking the first distribution until April 1 of the following year. However, by choosing to wait until the year after the year you turn 70½, you will be required to take *two* distributions that year. The double distribution could cause you to be in a higher tax bracket and significantly reduce the net amount you could have realized by taking the first minimum required distribution in the year in which you turned 70½.

Multiple retirement plans

The rules governing QRPs and IRAs require you to determine the minimum required distribution for each account separately. However, you, as owner, can take the aggregate minimum required distribution from any one or more of the accounts as long as you divide the aggregation and distribution between IRA accounts and QRP accounts separately. Inherited IRAs may not be aggregated with an individual's IRAs held as an owner (contributing or rollover IRAs). However, an individual with more than one inherited account from the same decedent may aggregate the accounts for distribution purposes.

Naming beneficiaries

The beneficiary of a QRP or IRA who receives distributions from an inherited account should name his or her own beneficiaries in the event he or she fails to survive the distribution of the account. As noted above, the new beneficiaries will be required to take the required minimum distributions over the remaining (fixed-term) life expectancy of the original beneficiary, computed as of the original beneficiary's age on his or her birthday in the year of death.

Reporting minimum required distributions to IRS

The IRS requires the trustee or custodian to report the end-of-year value of the account and the minimum required distribution for the following year. In this way, the IRS ensures that it gets its share of any required distributions.

Roth IRA

As part of the Taxpayer Relief Act of 1997, Congress established the Roth IRA, named for Senator William Roth, who wrote the bill. With a *Roth IRA*, there is no income tax deduction for contributions and the earnings inside the account accumulate tax-free. Unlike a regular IRA, accumulated earnings in a Roth IRA can be withdrawn tax-free provided certain conditions are met.

For estate planning purposes, the biggest advantage to setting up a Roth IRA is the ability to roll over your regular IRA into the Roth. Although you will have to pay taxes on the amount you roll over, there are several benefits associated with such a move. For one, there are no minimum required distributions from a Roth IRA, so the assets can stay in your Roth IRA and grow tax-free until you die. Then although your beneficiary will have to start taking withdrawals under virtually the same rules as those governing a regular IRA, the withdrawals will be tax-free. If you have tax losses carried forward from previous years, converting enough of your regular IRA to a Roth IRA to offset the losses is an excellent way to avoid the taxes that would normally be caused by converting. To qualify for the Roth IRA rollover, your adjusted gross income (on your single *or* joint tax return) in the year of the rollover cannot exceed $100,000, and to obtain the tax-free status on the *growth* in the Roth IRA, you must wait five years before taking any distribution of the earnings.

If you need the income provided by your IRA, converting to a Roth IRA may not make sense for you. However, if you qualify under the income limitation discussed above and if you do not need the income from your IRA and are able to pay, or offset, the taxes by converting to a Roth IRA from some other source, the benefit of the tax-free withdrawals from the Roth IRA may make it an ideal planning tool for you and your heirs.

The Distribution Tables

Appendix C contains the three tables needed to calculate your required minimum distributions. The table you use depends upon whether you are:

1. The QRP or IRA owner.
2. The surviving spouse who is the sole beneficiary but not the owner.
3. The designated beneficiary who is not the surviving spouse of the owner or is the surviving spouse but not the sole beneficiary (without separate accounts).

Uniform Table

The uniform table for calculating lifetime minimum required distributions commences at age 70½ because that is when you must take distributions from your plan (see Table C-1). It is used *only* by the QRP or IRA owner. A spouse who inherits the plan from an owner uses the table if he or she rolls over the account into his or her own account and, in effect, becomes the new owner. The uniform table is based on the joint life of the owner and an assumed beneficiary who is younger than the owner by 10 years, regardless of whether there is a beneficiary or not. Life expectancy is recalculated every year.

Single Life Expectancy Table

The single life expectancy table is used when the surviving spouse is the sole beneficiary but not the owner (see Table C-2). Life expectancy in the table is recalculated, and the surviving spouse uses the table every year to obtain the new, recalculated, life expectancy divisor. This figure is divided into the balance of the plan account as of December 31 of the prior year to arrive at the minimum required distribution for the current year.

Fixed-Period Single Life Expectancy Table

The fixed-period single life expectancy table is used when the designated beneficiary is not the spouse of the plan owner or is the surviving spouse but not the sole beneficiary (see Table C-3). This table is actually the same table as the one described above but is used differently. Instead of consulting the table each year to obtain the life expectancy divisor (which is recalculated), the designated beneficiary only consults the table *once*. For example, if the designated beneficiary turns 65 in the year after the year in which the owner dies, he or she would consult the table for the starting age of 65 to obtain the life expectancy divisor, which is 21. Therefore, the minimum required distribution is $1/_{21}$ of the balance in year one, $1/_{20}$ in year two, $1/_{19}$ in year three, and so on for a maximum payout of 21 years.

Summary

Even if you master the complex rules discussed above, remember that the terms of the QRP document or IRA agreement may govern the distribution options available to you. One of the problems is that your plan may be more restrictive in certain aspects than the laws governing minimum required distributions allow. Thus, in developing your retirement strategy, it is crucial that you and your advisor review the terms of your plan(s), especially your beneficiary-designation election. While you are bound by the terms of a QRP, at least while your benefits are maintained with your employer or previous employer, you have more latitude in your choices of an IRA sponsor. Make sure your IRA sponsor can provide you with the most flexible distribution options. And take the time to meet with your attorney and financial advisors to discuss how your choice of beneficiaries will fit into your overall estate plan. Through proper planning, you can ensure the maximum flexibility for yourself and, more importantly, your heirs—allowing them to stretch out the minimum required distributions and associated taxes over their lifetimes. And you will avoid the most common planning mistakes (see Appendix A).

21 Protecting Your Assets

When I sat down with John and Marion Petrachinni for the first time, they seemed upset and nervous. We started talking about estate planning in general and, when we got around to discussing John and Marion's goals, I discovered why they were nervous. John's former business partner, Joe, had been in an automobile accident in which a woman was severely injured. According to John and Marion, Joe was not at fault, but after three years of litigation he was found liable and a large judgment against him was pending an appeal of his civil trial. The judgment went way beyond the insurance coverage Joe had carried, and he was threatened with losing everything.

John and Marion did not want anything like that to ever happen to them. They were retired, and neither John nor Marion was well enough to go back to work, which is what Joe will have to do if the judgment is not overturned. So their estate plan started with the goal of protecting their assets first from attachment in a lawsuit and then from the IRS. The Petrachinnis were relieved to learn that there are ways to protect their assets without losing control of the assets and, at the same time, to provide themselves with a solid basis for an effective estate plan!

♕ ♕ ♕

According to several studies, the number-one way people think their "financial ship" will come in is by winning the lottery. The number-two way is through a lawsuit. So the next time you see someone buying a lottery ticket, you may want to duck, because his or her next thought may be about suing you! In fact, the same studies indicate that the average businessperson will be involved in seven lawsuits during her or his lifetime.

It is no wonder that more and more people are looking for ways to protect their assets. In our litigious society, the list of potential claims facing individuals is enormous; it includes professional liability, claims arising from business activities, environmental liability for real estate, accidents in your home or car, and acts by others for whom you are responsible, such as teenage children.

Protecting your assets from an unjust and unduly large judgment is a prudent and, in some cases, necessary course of action, especially if you are wealthy—a characteristic that frequently makes people the targets of gold-digging plaintiffs. By "judgment-proofing" your assets and reducing your liability exposure, potential plaintiffs are likely to either refrain from filing suit or settle early to save litigation costs and time.

Asset Protection Strategies

In previous chapters I discussed how to use various trusts, such as a dynasty trust, to avoid probate, reduce or eliminate estate taxes, and shield assets in such trusts from the claims of creditors and divorcing spouses. Obtaining the dual benefits of asset protection and estate planning often means giving up control of and income from assets placed in these trusts. But this is not always the case.

You can choose between two powerful strategies to achieve a true asset protection estate plan without giving up either the income from or the control of your assets. The first strategy involves the use of offshore trusts combined with one or more estate planning tools, such as a family limited partnership. The second strategy takes advantage of recent statutes enacted in the state of Alaska that allow you to set up and make gifts to an irrevocable trust and be a permissible beneficiary of the trust.

Offshore Planning

For U.S. citizens, *offshore planning* means making use of the laws of a country other than the United States. Proper offshore planning begins with establishing a foreign trust in a jurisdiction whose laws are favorable to people who are vulnerable to illegitimate legal claims or excessive lawsuits and judgments. Generally, the Cook Islands, the Bahamas, the Cayman Islands, Belize, Bermuda, Nevis, the Turks and Caicos Islands, and several other jurisdictions are used. For a variety of reasons, including specific statutes designed to protect depositors against attacks by creditors, the Cook Islands offer a higher level of protection than many other jurisdictions.

Offshore trusts provide exceptional protection because many of the countries in which the trusts are established do not recognize judgments rendered in other countries and their fraudulent-transfer laws are very lax. Also, most of these countries allow a trust to have full spendthrift protection (freedom from the claims of creditors of grantors *and* beneficiaries).

An *offshore trust (OST)* is an irrevocable trust created for the benefit of its grantor and the grantor's family. It has one foreign trustee and one or more U.S. trustees. Under this arrangement, the trust is typically set up as a "grantor trust," which means all the income from the trust is taxed to the grantor. While the grantor is alive, the OST is considered "income tax-neutral."

Although the grantor of the OST is not a trustee, the grantor or a family member can be named as the trust protector. A *trust protector* has the power to review all actions of the trustees and either approve or negate them. In addition, the protector can replace the trustee and/or move the trust to a different foreign jurisdiction. Because of this power, the trust protector has significant influence over the management of and distributions from the OST.

Limited Partnership Planning

As discussed in Chapter 14, family limited partnerships (FLPs) can be the first line of defense in asset protection. In almost all states, a creditor of an FLP partner cannot seize the partnership's assets. The creditor can only get a court-issued order called a *charging order,* which allows the creditor to receive the debtor partner's share of any distributions from the limited partnership to its partners, if and when a distribution is ever made. Because the general partner of the limited partnership has absolute discretion regarding when and if distributions are made from the partnership, a creditor may wait a long time for a distribution. Added to that inconvenience is the fact that a creditor who has obtained a charging order must pay income taxes on the partner's share of the limited partnership income even if the income is *not* paid out!

This income tax disadvantage and the ongoing wait for money discourages creditors. Thus, it is likely that any judgment against a partner will be negotiated to a much smaller amount than that decreed in the judgment because creditors recognize that they do not have substantial rights. However, savvy creditors may be willing to wait and may try to take other legal action. For example, if the general partner pays out money to other limited partners but not to the creditor, the creditor may be able to force the general partner to

264 / Disinherit the IRS

pay him or her. Because of this risk, the general partner may decide not to pay any money out of the limited partnership. This may be a hardship, creating problems that will result in a better settlement for the creditor.

Combining the OST With an FLP

One of the most effective asset protection estate plans is achieved by combining an offshore trust and a limited partnership. The combination would work as follows:

- A husband and a wife transfer some of their assets to an FLP in exchange for both a general partnership interest and a limited-partnership interest.
- The husband and wife, as general partners, manage the assets. Even if the general partners own a minimal amount (that is, 1 percent) of the partnership, they have full control over the assets.
- The husband and wife then contribute their limited partnership interests (the other 99 percent) to their offshore trust. By owning the limited partnership shares, the offshore trust owns a passive interest in the limited partnership and has little or no control over the assets in it.
- As long as the husband and wife, as general partners, do not have any creditor problems, they manage the assets in the limited partnership virtually as if they owned them outright and they are entitled to a fee for managing the FLP. They also have indirect control over any assets transferred directly into the OST because they serve as the protector of the trust.
- If a creditor problem arises and it looks as if their assets in the FLP are in jeopardy, the general partners can immediately liquidate the partnership. In doing so, most of the assets are distributed to the offshore trust (because it owns all the limited partnership interests, which represent most of the value of the limited partnership).
- The assets end up offshore, away from creditors and lawsuits. Because of the laws in the offshore jurisdiction, creditors have little chance of ever being able to capture the assets.

To obtain maximum protection, virtually all of a family's assets should be funded into the limited partnership. Some assets, such as subchapter S corporate stock, qualified retirement plans and IRAs, annuities and primary residences, should not be titled in the name of the limited partnership because of adverse income tax ramifications. Also, depending on state law, some of the assets may already be protected.

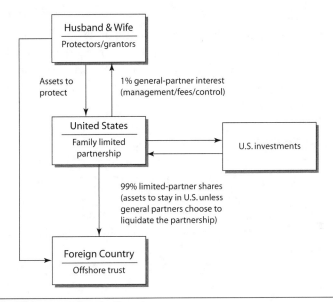

Figure 21-1. Offshore asset protection plan.

Figure 21-1 shows a typical offshore asset protection plan. Note that if a threat arises, the general partners can liquidate the FLP. Most of the assets (99 percent) would then be distributed to the OST. The husband and wife, as protectors of the trust, retain control over the OST trustee and the trust location. After the threat passes, the assets can be moved back to the United States.

In some situations, individuals may create additional limited partnerships for estate planning. These partnerships are primarily used for *making gifts* of limited partnership interests to family members. It is not uncommon for a husband and a wife to retain some limited partnership units in these partnerships and place the retained units into a separate FLP that was created for asset protection. When this is done, the husband and wife control all the partnerships and the assets of the partnerships are protected from creditors. If a need to protect assets arises, the offshore trust will end up owning all the assets that were not given to family members. This is accomplished by liquidating the limited partnership interests, thereby leaving the offshore trustee in control of the assets, which is the recommended arrangement when a threat becomes real. The limited partnership interests established for making gifts are not funded *directly* into the offshore trust because if the husband and wife have a creditor problem, it would not be wise to have to liquidate the gift limited partnerships. Such a liquidation would result in the children or other family members owning the assets outright, which may defeat the estate planning goals of the husband and wife. By putting the gift limited partnership units into the asset protection partnership, upon liquidation of the primary partnership the foreign trust would own the assets of that partnership plus the limited partnership units from the second partnership, used for gifts. Thus, the gift partnerships would remain intact.

The Alaskan Trust

Two potential drawbacks to offshore planning are the loss of access to assets and the loss of control over assets when a family limited partnership is liquidated and the assets are moved offshore to ward off a potential or real threat. A relatively new planning option, the Alaskan trust, can virtually eliminate these drawbacks.

Before 1997, it was not possible to form a "self-settled trust" (a trust in which the grantor is a beneficiary) in the United States that provided protection from the grantor's creditors. In 1997 Alaska enacted a statute that provides asset protection for self-settled trusts. An *Alaskan trust* can now be formed in the United States that protects contributed assets from creditors while allowing the grantor to have limited access to and some measure of control over the assets. (Three additional states—Delaware, Nevada, and Rhode Island—have recently enacted similar statutes.) Further, the Alaskan statutes removed the rule against perpetuities, so an Alaskan trust can be set up to benefit an unlimited number of generations without additional gift or estate taxes on the assets in the trust. Also, Alaska does not impose an income tax, thus providing additional incentive for setting up an Alaskan dynasty trust. (See Chapter 4 for more details on dynasty trusts.)

Even though the grantor can be a trust beneficiary, assets of an Alaskan trust can also be excluded from the grantor's federal gross estate. In addition to providing asset protection, Alaskan trusts present many estate planning possibilities. To exclude the assets of an Alaskan trust from the grantor's estate, the grantor must not retain too much control over the trust. Such control includes a veto power over distributions and a testamentary power of appointment (the right to redirect who will end up with trust assets).

Provisions of the Alaskan Trust

Mandatory distributions to the grantor of an Alaskan trust are not permitted. Nor can the grantor serve as the trustee with power over distributions. However, the Alaskan trust can provide the trustee with *discretion* to make distributions to the grantor. In addition, a grantor can retain a veto power to prevent distributions to other beneficiaries, an act that could preserve trust assets for the future needs of the grantor. However, retaining a veto power over distributions might cause the inclusion of the assets in the grantor's estate.

The Alaskan statute requires that the trustee with power over distributions be someone other than the grantor. However, it does allow the grantor to manage the investment of trust assets. So, the grantor can be designated as a cotrustee *with investment powers* over trust assets, with one or more additional trustees retaining all other powers.

If business interests or shares of a family limited partnership are contributed to the trust, the grantor may maintain access to the cash flow of the business or partnership by continuing to be paid a salary or management fee. When business interests are involved, the grantor can maintain voting control as investment trustee of the Alaskan trust, although such control could potentially cause the business interests to be included in the grantor's estate.

The Alaskan statute provides specific rules for obtaining the various benefits of the trust, including the following:

- A portion of the trust assets must be deposited in Alaska and be administered by a "qualified person" such as a person domiciled in Alaska or an Alaskan trust company or bank. "Deposited in Alaska" means holding some assets in a checking account, time deposit, certificate of deposit, brokerage account, trust company fiduciary account, or similar account located in Alaska.
- The Alaskan trustee's duties must include the obligation to maintain records for the trust (on an exclusive or nonexclusive basis with other trustees) and the obligation to prepare or arrange for the preparation of income tax returns that must be filed by the trust.
- Part of the trust administration must occur within the state of Alaska.

Figure 21-2 on page 268 shows an Alaskan trust protection plan. Note that even though the grantor has access to and a certain amount of control over the Alaskan trust, assets transferred to a properly worded trust are completed gifts. In the absence of any fraudulent transfers, the assets are free from the claims of the grantor's creditors. At the grantor's death, the trust can continue to operate in perpetuity (such as a dynasty trust, see Chapter 4) with no further gift or estate taxes.

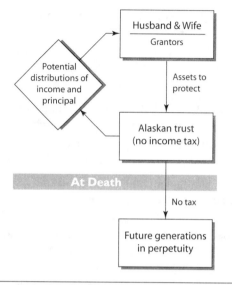

Figure 21-2. Alaskan trust protection plan.

Fraudulent Conveyances

Fraudulent conveyances are prebankruptcy transfers made by or obligations incurred by a debtor with the intent of hindering or defrauding creditors. The federal bankruptcy code and state laws permit these transfers to be set aside if made within one year of filing for bankruptcy, but many state's statutes allow for a much longer period, especially in the case of transfers to family members. Fraudulent transfers are essentially ignored, and the creditor can obtain possession of the transferred property.

While an Alaskan trust does not protect against U.S. bankruptcy orders, the Alaska statutes specifically allow an Alaskan trust to be structured so that it is free from claims of the grantor's creditors. Under Alaska law, if the grantor is merely eligible for, and not *entitled* to receive, distributions from the trust, the grantor's creditors cannot seize the trust's assets through a legal action filed in an Alaska court. Further, as a general rule, judgments of other states against a grantor or beneficiary are not enforceable against irrevocable trusts that are set up with spendthrift provisions unless they are set up to defraud creditors.

Under the Alaskan fraudulent transfer law, any action to claim that a transfer to an Alaskan trust was fraudulent may not be commenced unless the claimant was a creditor when the trust was created and the action is brought within the later of four years after the transfer to the trust was made or one year after the transfer was discovered or could have been reasonably discovered. Thus, if a transfer to an Alaskan trust was not intended to defraud creditors and the grantor retains no power to revoke or terminate the trust and no right to receive a distribution on demand, creditors of the grantor should not be able to reach the assets in the trust. Also, if the grantor does not retain the power to veto a distribution to other beneficiaries and/or a special power of appointment (over the ultimate distribution of trust assets) or similar right, the transfer will be complete for estate and gift taxes.

Planning Opportunity

By repealing the rule against perpetuities, imposing no state income tax, and allowing a self-settled trust to have asset protection, Alaska now offers estate tax benefits that previously could be accomplished only by going offshore.

As discussed above, transfers to a properly worded Alaskan trust are considered completed gifts, and thus the grantor's creditors cannot reach trust principal or income. Also, the income generated by the trust will *not* be subject to state income tax in either the grantor's home state or Alaska, so the trust assets can grow for the benefit of the grantor, the grantor's children, and future generations. From an estate planning perspective, all future appreciation in the trust will be removed from the grantor's estate even though the grantor remains as a discretionary beneficiary of the trust.

Summary

To obtain true asset protection and an effective estate plan, there are two compelling options:

1. An offshore trust combined with a limited partnership.
2. An Alaskan trust.

Both options offer unique advantages not otherwise available. The level of asset protection you want to achieve and your feelings about having assets in a foreign jurisdiction rather than in the United States will dictate which choice is best for you. Clearly, whichever choice is made, it must be coordinated with other aspects of your overall estate plan. You should seek the advice of professionals versed in these planning tools to ensure that your asset protection and estate planning goals are met.

22 Prescription for Your Wealth

R Roger and Eleanor Casmon came to my office in Naples, Florida, not knowing what to expect, but they were disturbed and motivated by what they learned at the Wealth Protection Network seminar they had attended some weeks earlier. They were also excited because they were finally taking steps they had been talking about for some time. Unlike most of my clients, they were both still working. They worked together running an interior design business and, although they were doing quite well, retirement for both of them was in the planning stages. They each had a daughter from a previous marriage, and Roger had a grandson.

The planning process in my office started with a discussion of the Casmons' goals. To help Roger and Eleanor focus, I asked them to pretend that we were meeting at my office three years later. Then I asked them to describe what has to have happened over those three years for them to feel good about their growth and progress in connection with their business and personal life and their estate plan. I also asked Roger and Eleanor to prioritize their most important estate planning goals. The answers to those and other questions led to discussions that allowed us to hone in on the really important issues to the Casmons, including a discussion of how much was enough to leave each of their girls and in what form to leave everything. We also covered how to satisfy their charitable goals.

In preparation for our first meeting, I had asked the Casmons to bring several items of important financial information with *them. I reviewed this information briefly at that meeting to find the extent of the planning they had done and get a rough idea of the taxes they would be facing without further planning.*

I discovered that the Casmons had done very little planning and that if death or disability occurred without further planning, it would be a real problem for them and their heirs. For example, if one of them became incapacitated, there would have to be court intervention; also, they had done nothing to avoid probate. In addition, Eleanor was a Canadian citizen, a situation that requires special planning in case she survives Roger, which, given Roger's health, is likely. Furthermore, their estate was exposed to significant estate taxes that could be easily avoided.

Working with Roger and Eleanor, their CPA, and an estate planning attorney I had recommended, we were able to put together a "prescription for their wealth" that was comprehensive, flexible, and effective in eliminating probate and nearly 100 percent of the estate taxes on their estate.

Meeting With a Financial Planner

Now that you have seen the many choices you have in developing your estate plan, you are probably wondering how to put all the information together to accomplish your planning objectives. After you develop a list of goals, your next step should be to seek help from an estate planning professional who can provide you with a "prescription for your wealth." But a prescription without a diagnosis is malpractice. So the estate planning professional you choose will need various papers from you to make a proper diagnosis and provide you with an appropriate prescription.

Documents to Bring

When you meet with your financial advisor, you should bring the following:

Financial statements

- Current market value of your assets (at your death the IRS will require professional appraisals, so be realistic).
- How assets are owned (by you, by your spouse, or jointly).
- The basis (adjusted cost) of major assets (home, investments, or insurance, for example).

List of heirs

- Names, ages, Social Security numbers, and addresses of children, grandchildren, and so forth.
- Special needs (such as a handicapped child, a grandchild who needs medical attention).
- List whether children are from the current marriage or from a previous marriage, and whether each heir is to be treated equally. (Remember, nothing is more unequal than the equal treatment of unequals.)

Estate documents

- Wills, including all codicils (additions and modifications).
- Trusts, both revocable living trusts and irrevocable trusts.
- Divorce settlement papers.
- Power of attorney.
- Prenuptial agreements.
- Insurance policies (with the latest annual statement and the original illustration ledger and/or an "in-force"/reprojection illustration ledger, if available).
- Beneficiary designation forms from your qualified retirement plans and/or IRAs.

Tax returns

- Federal (Form 1040) and state tax returns (latest year and previous year).
- All schedules including K-1s, 1099s, among others.
- Any trust tax returns (Form 1041).
- Any gift tax returns (Form 709).

Questions to Consider

With these documents and a personal interview, your planning professional can start his or her diagnosis. Some of the more important things your professional will need to know include:

- How are your assets held (in your name alone, jointly)? (See the questionnaire in Appendix E.)
- Is your revocable living trust fully funded? (Are the assets titled in your name *as trustee* of your trust?)
- Who are your heirs, and how do you want your property to pass to heirs and in what proportion?

- Are you intending to pass everything to your spouse and then to your children, or do you want certain children or other heirs to receive part of your estate at your death, if first?
- How long have you been married, and is this a first marriage for you and your spouse?
- How is your insurance held (who is the owner), and who are the beneficiaries?
- What are the face amounts, cash values, premiums, and cost basis of your insurance policies?
- Who is the current trustee of your irrevocable trust, if you have one?
- Are you making any gifts (size and frequency)?
- How much, if any, of your and your spouse's lifetime applicable credit exemption equivalent have you used (in making gifts) to date?
- Are your children and other intended heirs good with money?
- Are there any children you want to disinherit?
- Do you have any charitable intent?
- Do you have any highly appreciated, low-yielding assets?
- How are assets divided between you and your spouse?
- Who are the beneficiaries in your IRA or qualified retirement plan documents, and how are they listed?
- Do you need the income from your retirement plan assets to maintain your lifestyle?
- Who are your other advisors (attorney, accountant, insurance agent, stockbroker, money manager, trust officer)?
- What are your estate planning goals (what is important to you)?

If you are struggling with establishing your goals, try answering this question: "If you were sitting here three years from now and you looked back over those three years, what has to have happened, during that time, for you to feel good about your family wealth transfer plan?" The answer to this question will help you and your planning professional identify your individual goals and objectives and determine a proper diagnosis and prescription.

Advisors to Include

The planning process should be a team effort, with specialists from various disciplines working together in a cooperative alliance or "collaborative" to provide a coordinated plan that will help you and your family achieve your goals. There are several potential team players including an attorney, accountant, financial/estate planner, trust officer, money manager, charitable plan administrator, insurance professional, stockbroker, banker, and possibly even one or more of your beneficiaries. The three leading people among this group are, typically, the attorney, accountant, and financial/estate planner.

In spite of the large cast of potential team players, many people do not have the kinds of estate plans they should have. The reason comes down to the relationship most people have with those top three advisors. In surveys that questioned people on whom they thought of when it comes to estate planning, the results showed that most people think of only one person on the list, and that's the attorney. People also said they viewed the relationship they have with their estate planning attorney as a one-way or "reactive" relationship similar to the relationship they have with their doctor—when they feel sick, they go to their doctor to get the problem fixed. That works with a doctor but not with an estate planning attorney. Most people don't know when they have an estate problem, and thus they don't go to their attorneys to get the problem fixed. Nor is your attorney likely to call you. If he or she did call, you would probably suspect that the attorney was trying to generate fees.

Most people, and especially business owners, feel they have more of a two-way relationship with their accountants. After all, you trust your accountant with important personal financial information and get together with him or her once a year to see where you are, tax-wise. Although it is quickly changing, historically, most accountants have not focused on estate tax planning, so many accountants are not equipped to help guide you through complex estate planning issues.

And what about financial/estate planning advisors? Most people say they also have a one-way relationship with their financial/estate planners, but, unlike their relationship with their attorneys, they view it as going in the other direction: if they wait long enough, they feel certain they will get a call from their financial advisors about an idea. But they think the call is going to be focused on an investment product. While that may be the case, it is not necessarily bad. Your planner may bring important planning issues to your attention that could save you and your family thousands, even millions, of dollars. Thus, a qualified financial/estate planner is often the best person to lead, or at least start out leading, the estate planning team on your behalf.

A *qualified* planner is one who not only specializes in estate planning but has demonstrated his or her dedication and commitment to the profession by obtaining a designation such as Certified Financial Planner (CFP), Chartered Life Underwriter (CLU), Chartered Financial Consultant (ChFC), or Accredited Estate Planner (AEC). A professional planner who has attained one or more of these and certain other designations has completed a rigorous course of study and has been tested on many of the family wealth transfer planning concepts covered in this book.

The Planning Process

Beginning the Process

In a typical planning scenario, you would meet with a financial/estate planning specialist who would interview you and your spouse to obtain the type of information discussed above. Working with an attorney and one or more of the other team members, the planner would analyze the information from your interview along with your existing documents to make a diagnosis and provide a prescription for preserving your wealth. At your second or third interview, you and your spouse would typically meet with your attorney and planning specialist to discuss the potential prescription or plan. Depending on your reaction, you would authorize some or all of the plan to be put in place.

If the plan involves an irrevocable life insurance trust and life insurance, arrangements would be made for you to be examined while your estate planning documents are being drafted. Your planner or an independent insurance professional should shop for offers from different insurance companies so that you have choices. The process of obtaining offers of insurance from three, four, or more companies typically takes six weeks or longer. This leaves ample time for the attorney to prepare your trusts and other documents and for your accountant to "crunch the numbers."

Starting Your Plan

By now in your reading, you are aware of the many estate planning options open to you. If you have done little or no planning, you may want to start your plan with the following basic documents.

Revocable living trust

Discussed earlier, a revocable living trust provides a way to avoid probate, take care of you and your family in the event of your incapacitation, potentially save estate taxes (through the creation of a credit shelter equivalent/bypass/B trust at the first death for a married couple), and protect your heirs.

I strongly believe that a revocable living trust provides the best foundation to a good estate plan. Properly funded, a revocable living trust takes the place of a will to accomplish the bulk of most people's estate planning goals. As a quick summary, a revocable living trust can:

- Allow you to completely avoid probate.
- Allow you to control, coordinate, and distribute all your property interests while you are alive as well as on your death.
- Arrange for your well-being under *your* terms as you advance in years and perhaps become ill and/or mentally incompetent.
- Help ensure that your plans and affairs will remain private, rather than be public, on your death or incapacity.
- Make it easy for you to amend your plan and make changes.
- Allow you to maintain control of the assets in your trust as you cross state lines.
- Provide a way to measure your postdeath trustees' ability to manage some or all of your assets while you are alive.
- Make it harder for disgruntled beneficiaries to challenge your wishes after death.
- Provide a way for you to protect your heirs by having the trust(s) continue after you are gone.

Pour-over will

Property that is not placed ("funded") into your revocable living trust during your lifetime can be put in the trust after your death through the use of a short, well-drafted will known as a *pour-over will (POW)*. The provisions of a POW simply state that any property you neglected to fund into your revocable living trust will, *after going through probate*, pass to your trust ("pour over to it") upon your death. A POW should always be used in conjunction with a revocable living trust as a safety net to ensure that any forgotten property will ultimately be placed in the "planning pot" to be controlled by your master plan.

Special durable power of attorney for funding

A *durable power of attorney* is a document that allows you, as the principal, to authorize another person (the "attorney" or agent) to act on your behalf with respect to specified legal obligations, even if you subsequently become incompetent. This document directs who will make decisions and specifies the decision-making powers it confers. A *special durable power of attorney for funding* limits the agent's authority to the funding of assets into your revocable living trust and would typically be used in the event of your incapacitation.

Living will and medical directive

A *living will with a medical directive* is a document that allows you to specify in advance of a terminal illness or other disability (mental incompetence, for example) what medical treatments you would find acceptable in your final days, including your wishes with regard to the termination of life support under various circumstances. A majority of states and the District of Columbia have living-will laws that address this sensitive area and often provide the format for the drafting of such a document.

Healthcare surrogate

If you are unable to make healthcare decisions due to illness, incompetence, and so forth, a *healthcare surrogate* authorizes others to make those decisions for you. Statutes vary from state to state, but generally a healthcare surrogate provides for decisions on such issues as:

- Medical procedures.
- Removal of a physician.
- The right to have an incompetent patient discharged against medical advice.
- The right to medical records and the right to have a patient moved or to engage other treatment.

Most state laws have the effect of empowering your agent to make any type of health-care decision that he or she could make for himself or herself.

Irrevocable trust

As discussed earlier, irrevocable trusts can take various forms and can accomplish a myriad of estate planning goals. One of the most popular uses of the irrevocable trust is to have it own insurance on the lives of the grantors so that the proceeds will be available to offset estate tax costs without being reduced by income, gift, or estate taxes. The name often given to a trust with this purpose is *irrevocable life insurance trust (ILIT)*. Used in conjunction with the estate documents listed above, an ILIT can provide a simple, but effective, estate plan that leaves you in control of your assets while providing a way to cover estate tax costs, at discount, and pass your estate to your heirs intact.

Executing Your Plan

Once the documents are completed and you have thoroughly reviewed them with your planning team, you should be prepared to execute them. Assuming you have a revocable living trust prepared, the next step is to fund the trust by titling your assets in your and your spouse's names *as trustees* of your individual revocable living trusts.

This is a good time to balance your and your spouse's estates or to at least make sure your spouse has enough assets in his or her revocable living trust to preserve all of his or her unused applicable credit exemption equivalent amount ($1 million in 2002 and 2003).

Funding the revocable living trust is a step that many people tend to put off and that often never gets completed. If you do not fund your revocable living trust, you guarantee probate, with all the potential negative ramifications discussed earlier in this book. Your pour-over will cannot solve the problem of avoiding probate. Thus, you should fund your trust as soon as possible after it is signed.

The process of funding your trust is simple. If you are your own trustee, you do not need a separate tax identification number; you continue to use your Social Security number when filing your tax return. Your stockbroker can supply the forms for retitling your brokerage accounts. Your attorney will help you with the deeds to real estate and other types of assets, and your financial planner can help you identify the assets that should go into your name as trustee of your trust. But you must actively participate by providing the information about these assets to your attorney and other team members. This is not an area in which you should procrastinate. Remember, the IRS sheds no tears for those who don't plan!

Living Planning

A client once said to me, "It's easier to shoe a dead horse than a living one." This was his response to my question of why he had done nothing about his estate plan. My answer was that it may be easier to shoe a dead horse but when it comes to estate planning, just the opposite is true. Delaying your estate plan may be one of the costliest mistakes you will ever make. The greatest benefits go to those who start planning early! Remember, the biggest villain in estate planning is not the IRS; it is procrastination.

It is a natural human tendency to avoid all thoughts of death and to put off doing anything about protecting your estate for your heirs. But estate planning doesn't have to be death planning, and there is much you can do today, while you are alive, that can benefit both your family and you. A good example of a "living" plan involves the use of a charitable remainder trust in conjunction with a wealth replacement trust. Together, these two "living" tools provide you with tax savings and additional income during your lifetime and enable your family *and* the charities of your choice to end up with more after you are gone. Another example is a generation-skipping trust, or dynasty trust, which

280 / Disinherit the IRS

allows you to leverage your generation-skipping tax while benefiting your spouse (and, indirectly, you) and several generations of family members—if it is set up while you are alive. The only way to make your plan a living plan is to stop procrastinating and take action now so that you can start enjoying the thought that you are providing benefits both during life and at death for your family— while effectively disinheriting the IRS!

Appendices

A The Most Common IRA Mistakes

1. Not planning for the impact of estate taxes and income taxes

Under the tax code, IRA assets are classified as "income in respect of a decedent." As such, they do not get a step-up in basis at death. Therefore, IRA assets are subject not only to estate taxes but to income taxes. With proper planning, the income taxes can be spread over the life of the beneficiaries, but unless the IRA is bequeathed to charity, the taxes must eventually be paid. Often, the best way to offset the taxes is to take a portion of the income from the IRA to purchase a life insurance policy on the IRA owner alone or the owner and his or her spouse to cover the taxes.

2. Not being aware that estate taxes on the decedent's IRA are deductible from the beneficiary's income taxes

Under Section 691(c) of the Internal Revenue Code, the beneficiary of an IRA can deduct the estate taxes that were attributable to the decedent-owner's IRA from his or her income tax return. The deduction is available until used up, starting with the first distribution. This deduction often neutralizes income taxes on the minimum distributions taken by the beneficiary in the first few years after the death of the IRA owner.

3. Failing to name a beneficiary of your IRA

Failing to name a beneficiary often means your estate becomes the beneficiary. It also means your IRA must either be distributed under the five-year rule—if you die *before* your RBD—or over your remaining life expectancy under the IRS single life expectancy table based on your age in the year of your death (using the fixed-term method)—if you die *after* your RBD.

4. Not utilizing a custom beneficiary-designation form

IRAs are governed by a designated-beneficiary form, not by a decedent's will. The form is filled out when the account is set up; IRA owners rarely have a copy of the form; and it is not unusual to find that even the original has disappeared. A custom beneficiary-designation form designed by your attorney will not only help you and your IRA custodian avoid misplacing information regarding your choices but will also help ensure that your IRA goes to the correct beneficiaries in the amounts and way you intend.

5. Naming several beneficiaries to a single IRA account

This could cause the youngest beneficiary to have to take out his or her share more rapidly than necessary. This is because the calculation that determines the minimum required distribution schedule for all the beneficiaries is based on the age of the oldest beneficiary. If one of the beneficiaries is a charity, the problem is worse. Because a charity has no life expectancy, the IRA must be emptied either under the five-year rule—if death of the owner occurs before the owner's RBD—or over the owner's remaining life expectancy under the IRS single life expectancy table based on the owner's age in the year of death (using the fixed-term method)—if the owner dies after his or her RBD. The best strategy is to divide the IRA into different accounts and name one beneficiary for each account. Alternatively, the beneficiaries will have a chance to divide the IRA into individual accounts for each beneficiary if it is done by September 30 of the year following the owner's death—a step that can be easily overlooked.

6. Rolling out money from a qualified retirement plan to an IRA without getting a spouse's written consent

In certain qualified retirement plans, such as a defined benefit plan, if the plan participant is married and rolls out more than $5,000 from his or her plan, the law requires that the owner have spousal consent to do so. Without a signed spousal consent form, the entire distribution will be taxable.

7. Naming a trust as beneficiary without knowing all the consequences

Most trusts qualify as a beneficiary of an IRA. However, several pitfalls await those who do not understand certain rules. For example, the IRA minimum distribution rules override trust rules, so if an IRA doesn't pay its required distribution to the trust (as beneficiary) every year, a 50 percent penalty (of the underpayment) is imposed. Also, if a trust receives the full minimum distribution from an IRA but does not pay it out to the beneficiaries because of limitation in the trust, the payment will be subject to the much higher trust tax rates.

B

Summary of Minimum Distribution Rules

TABLE B-1   Owner Dies *before* Required Beginning Date

Designated Beneficiary	Applicable rules
None	Five-year rule applies. All QRP or IRA benefits must be paid in full by the end of the fifth calendar year after owner's death.
Spouse	Has choice of several options:
	Can elect to take distributions under the 5-year rule.
	Can elect to leave the QRP or IRA in the deceased spouse's name and receive distributions over his or her remaining single life expectancy. Distributions must begin by December 31 of the year following the year of owner's death and are recalculated annually over his or her remaining life expectancy as determined from the Internal Revenue Code's single life expectancy table (see Table C-2). Alternatively, he or she can defer the onset of payments until December 31 of the year in which the owner would have attained $70^1/_2$.
	Can roll over the owner's benefits into an IRA of his or her own and commence MRDs at his or her RBD (April 1 of the year after he or she turns $70^1/_2$) using his or her remaining life expectancy. Surviving spouse can name his or her own designated beneficiaries.

TABLE B-1 Owner Dies *before* Required Beginning Date *(cont'd.)*

Designated Beneficiary	Applicable rules
Nonspouse individual	Designated beneficiary can stretch out payments by using his or her own life expectancy (determined based on the beneficiary's age on the beneficiary's birthday in the year following the year in which the owner died) to calculate MRDs. Distributions must begin by December 31 of the year following the year of owner's death; otherwise, the 5-year rule applies.
^	Take distributions under the 5-year rule.
Estate/ Charity	Five-year rule applies. All IRA benefits must be paid in full by the end of the fifth calendar year after owner's death.
Trust	Five-year rule applies unless trust names individual beneficiaries who are identifiable by the trust instrument itself. If trust beneficiaries are properly identified, the life expectancy of the oldest trust beneficiary is used for determining MRDs. Terms of the trust must be irrevocable at the owner's death, and the trust must be filed with the plan sponsor.
Multiple Beneficiaries (whether or not trust is used and whether or not one of the beneficiaries is owner's spouse)	Multiple beneficiaries have until September 30 of the year after the year in which the owner died to establish separate accounts that would allow each of them to take distributions from their own account over their remaining lifetime. Otherwise, if all beneficiaries are individuals, and separate accounts are not established, then they must take distributions either under the five-year rule or over the oldest beneficiary's (the shortest) life expectancy beginning no later than December 31 of the year following the year in which the owner died. Life expectancy of the oldest beneficiary is determined based on that person's age on his or her birthday in the year following the year in which the owner died.

Source: Adapted from Natalie B. Choate, J.D., "'Gotcha' Is Gone: Understanding the New Simplified Minimum Distribution Rules, Part1," Journal of Financial Planning, March 2001.

TABLE B-2 Owner Dies *after* Required Beginning Date

Designated Beneficiary	Applicable rules
None	If there is no named beneficiary or if one beneficiary is not an individual, the period over which the MRD must be calculated is the remaining years of the deceased owner's remaining life expectancy, determined using the IRS's fixed-period single life expectancy table (see Table C-3), based on the owner's age on his or her birthday in the year of death, and reduced by 1 year for each year thereafter (fixed-term method).
Spouse	Has choice of two options:
	Can elect to leave the QRP or IRA in the deceased spouse's name and receive distributions over his or her remaining life expectancy, recalculated annually, beginning in the year after the year in which the owner died. Note: Once the surviving spouse dies, any remaining benefits in the original owner's plan must be paid out over the remaining (fixed-term) life expectancy of the surviving spouse, computed as of his or her age on his or her birthday in the year of death.
	Can roll over the inherited account into an IRA in his or her name and begin taking MRDs by December 31 of the year following the year in which the owner died, based on his or her remaining single life expectancy. This would allow the spouse to name his or her own designated beneficiaries so that after the spouse dies, the beneficiaries would be able to use their own life expectancies for MRDs when the account passes to them.
Nonspouse	A nonspouse individual beneficiary must take required distributions over his or her (fixed-term) life expectancy beginning in the year following the year in which the owner died. The beneficiary's life expectancy will be based on his or her birthday age in the year following the year in which the owner died.
Estate/ Charity	As in the case where there is no beneficiary or there is one beneficiary and that beneficiary is not an individual, the period over which the MRD must be calculated is the remaining years of the owner's life expectancy, determined using the IRS's fixed-period single life expectancy table (see Table C-3), based on the owner's birthday age in the year of the owner's death, and reduced by 1 year for each year thereafter (fixed-term method).

TABLE B-2   Owner Dies *after* Required Beginning Date (*cont'd.*)

Designated Beneficiary	Applicable rules
Trust	The no designated beneficiary rule (above) applies unless trust names individual beneficiaries who are identifiable by the trust instrument itself. If trust beneficiaries are properly "identified," the life expectancy of the oldest trust beneficiary is used for determining MRDs. Terms of the trust must be irrevocable at the owner's death, and the trust must be filed with the plan sponsor.
Multiple Beneficiaries (whether or not trust is used and whether or not one of the beneficiaries is owner's spouse)	Multiple beneficiaries have until December 31 of the year after the year in which the owner died to establish separate accounts that would allow each of them to take distributions from their own account over their remaining lifetime. Otherwise, if all beneficiaries are individuals, and separate accounts are not established, then they must take distributions over the oldest beneficiary's (the shortest) life expectancy beginning no later than December 31 of the year following the year in which the owner died. Life expectancy of the oldest beneficiary is determined by that person's age on his or her birthday in the year following the year in which the owner died.

Notes: Payments from an IRA may always be accelerated, including a complete distribution at any time.

Source: Adapted from Natalie B. Choate, J.D., "'Gotcha' Is Gone: Understanding the New Simplified Minimum Distribution Rules, Part 1," Journal of Financial Planning, March 2001.

C Distribution Tables

The *uniform table* is used to determine minimum required distributions (MRDs) for a QRP participant or IRA owner (see Table C-1 on page 292). The table assumes the designated beneficiary is 10-years younger (even if there is no individual named as the beneficiary). The uniform table is only available to the surviving spouse if the QRP or IRA is rolled over into a new IRA in his or her name. This table is always redetermined each year so there will always be life expectancy at any age. The uniform table is not applicable to Roth IRAs.

All individuals who own an IRA and/or qualified retirement assets can use this table during their lifetime to determine their annual lifetime minimum required distributions regardless of their beneficiary. The only exception to the use of this table is if the owner's sole beneficiary is the owner's spouse who is more than 10-years younger than the owner. In that case, the owner would be allowed to use the *longer* distribution period measured by the redetermined joint life and last survivor life expectancy of the owner and spouse from the appropriate government joint life expectancy tables.

To make calculations easy, the distribution period is divided into 100 to arrive at the applicable percentage for annual withdrawals. The applicable percentage times the account balance (revalued annually) as of the end of the prior year (December 31 of the prior year for an IRA) produces the lifetime minimum required distribution. Alternatively, the account balance can be divided by the distribution period which is redetermined every year, as the individual gets older. As a result, if only minimum distributions are taken every year, the individual will never exhaust the account during his or her lifetime.

TABLE C-1   Uniform Table for Minimum Required Distributions

Age	Distribution period	Applicable percentage	Age	Distribution period	Applicable percentage
70	27.4	3.6496	93	9.6	10.4167
71	26.5	3.7736	94	9.1	10.9890
72	25.6	3.9063	95	8.6	11.6279
73	24.7	4.0486	96	8.1	12.3457
74	23.8	4.2017	97	7.6	13.1579
75	22.9	4.3668	98	7.1	14.0845
76	22.0	4.5455	99	6.7	14.9254
77	21.2	4.7170	100	6.3	15.8730
78	20.3	4.9261	101	5.9	16.9492
79	19.5	5.1282	102	5.5	18.1818
80	18.7	5.3476	103	5.2	19.2308
81	17.9	5.5866	104	4.9	20.4082
82	17.1	5.8480	105	4.5	22.2222
83	16.3	6.1350	106	4.2	23.8095
84	15.5	6.4516	107	3.9	25.6410
85	14.8	6.7568	108	3.7	27.0270
86	14.1	7.0922	109	3.4	29.4118
87	13.4	7.4627	110	3.1	32.2581
88	12.7	7.8740	111	2.9	34.4828
89	12.0	8.3333	112	2.6	38.4615
90	11.4	8.7719	113	2.4	41.6667
91	10.8	9.2593	114	2.1	47.6190
92	10.2	9.8039	115+	1.9	52.6316

The *single life expectancy table,* used when the surviving spouse is sole beneficiary but not the owner, is only available to a beneficiary (see Table C-2 on page 293). If the surviving spouse is the sole designated beneficiary, this single life table is used to determine MRDs, which are recalculated annually. There will always be remaining life expectancy at any age.

At the surviving spouse's subsequent death, after MRDs have begun, the payout to the beneficiary is based on the deceased spouse's fixed-period life expectancy in the year of death.

The *fixed-period single life expectancy table* is used when the designated beneficiary is a nonspouse or the surviving spouse is not the sole beneficiary (see

TABLE C-2   Single Life Expectancy Table

Age	Distribution period	Applicable percentage	Age	Distribution period	Applicable percentage
0	82.4	1.2136	32	51.4	1.9455
1	81.6	1.2255	33	50.4	1.9841
2	80.6	1.2407	34	49.4	2.0243
3	79.7	1.2547	35	48.5	2.0619
4	78.7	1.2706	36	47.5	2.1053
5	77.7	1.2870	37	46.5	2.1505
6	76.7	1.3038	38	45.6	2.1930
7	75.8	1.3193	39	44.6	2.2422
8	74.8	1.3369	40	43.6	2.2936
9	73.8	1.3550	41	42.7	2.3419
10	72.8	1.3736	42	41.7	2.3981
11	71.8	1.3928	43	40.7	2.4570
12	70.8	1.4124	44	39.8	2.5126
13	69.9	1.4306	45	38.8	2.5773
14	68.9	1.4514	46	37.9	2.6385
15	67.9	1.4728	47	37.0	2.7027
16	66.9	1.4948	48	36.0	2.7778
17	66.0	1.5152	49	35.1	2.8490
18	85.0	1.1765	50	34.2	2.9240
19	64.0	1.5625	51	33.3	3.0030
20	63.0	1.5873	52	32.3	3.0960
21	62.1	1.6103	53	31.4	3.1847
22	61.1	1.6367	54	30.5	3.2787
23	60.1	1.6639	55	29.6	3.3784
24	59.1	1.6920	56	28.7	3.4843
25	58.2	1.7182	57	27.9	3.5842
26	57.2	1.7483	58	27.0	3.7037
27	56.2	1.7794	59	26.1	3.8314
28	55.3	1.8083	60	25.2	3.9683
29	54.3	1.8416	61	24.4	4.0984
30	53.3	1.8762	62	23.5	4.2553
31	52.4	1.9084	63	22.7	4.4053

TABLE C-2   Single Life Expectancy Table (*cont'd.*)

Age	Distribution period	Applicable percentage	Age	Distribution period	Applicable percentage
64	21.8	4.5872	88	6.3	15.8730
65	21.0	4.7619	89	5.9	16.9492
66	20.2	4.9505	90	5.5	18.1818
67	19.4	5.1546	91	5.2	19.2308
68	18.6	5.3763	92	4.9	20.4082
69	17.8	5.6180	93	4.6	21.7391
70	17.0	5.8824	94	4.3	23.2558
71	16.3	6.1350	95	4.1	24.3902
72	15.5	6.4516	96	3.8	26.3158
73	14.8	6.7568	97	3.6	27.7778
74	14.1	7.0922	98	3.4	29.4118
75	13.4	7.4627	99	3.1	32.2581
76	12.7	7.8740	100	2.9	34.4828
77	12.1	8.2645	101	2.7	37.0370
78	11.4	8.7719	102	2.5	40.0000
79	10.8	9.2593	103	2.3	43.4783
80	10.2	9.8039	104	2.1	47.6190
81	9.7	10.3093	105	1.9	52.6316
82	9.1	10.9890	106	1.7	58.8235
83	8.6	11.6279	107	1.5	66.6667
84	8.1	12.3457	108	1.4	71.4286
85	7.6	13.1579	109	1.2	83.3333
86	7.1	14.0845	110	1.1	90.9091
87	6.7	14.9254	111+	1.0	100.0000

Table C-3 on the facing page). The fixed-period life expectancy is reduced by one for each subsequent year. For example, at age 65, life expectancy is 21 years. Minimum required distribution is $1/21$ for year one, $1/20$ for year two, and so on for a maximum payout of 21 years.

TABLE C-3   Fixed-Period Single Life Expectancy Table

Age	Life expectancy	Age	Life expectancy	Age	Life expectancy
0	82.4	38	45.6	75	13.4
1	81.6	39	44.6	76	12.7
2	80.6	40	43.6	77	12.1
3	79.7	41	42.7	78	11.4
4	78.7	42	41.7	79	10.8
5	77.7	43	40.7	80	10.2
6	76.7	44	39.8	81	9.7
7	75.8	45	38.8	82	9.1
8	74.8	46	37.9	83	8.6
9	73.8	47	37.0	84	8.1
10	72.8	48	36.0	85	7.6
11	71.8	49	35.1	86	7.1
12	70.8	50	34.2	87	6.7
13	69.9	51	33.3	88	6.3
14	68.9	52	32.3	89	5.9
15	67.9	53	31.4	90	5.5
16	66.9	54	30.5	91	5.2
17	66.0	55	29.6	92	4.9
18	85.0	56	28.7	93	4.6
19	64.0	57	27.9	94	4.3
20	63.0	58	27.0	95	4.1
21	62.1	59	26.1	96	3.8
22	61.1	60	25.2	97	3.6
23	60.1	61	24.4	98	3.4
24	59.1	62	23.5	99	3.1
25	58.2	63	22.7	100	2.9
26	57.2	64	21.8	101	2.7
27	56.2	65	21.0	102	2.5
28	55.3	66	20.2	103	2.3
29	54.3	67	19.4	104	2.1
30	53.3	68	18.6	105	1.9
31	52.4	69	17.8	106	1.7
32	51.4	70	17.0	107	1.5
33	50.4	71	16.3	108	1.4
34	49.4	72	15.5	109	1.2
35	48.5	73	14.8	110	1.1
36	47.5	74	14.1	111+	1.0
37	46.5				

D Current Estate Tax Law

The Economic Growth and Tax Relief Reconciliation Act (EGTRRA) of 2001 created three distinct periods of estate tax law that significantly affect how estates will be taxed over the next few years and, especially, in the year 2010. During the tax years 2002 through 2009, it provides a lengthy phase-in period of rate reductions and exemption increases. In 2010, the act eliminates the estate tax for one year. Beginning in 2011, estate tax law reverts back to the prior law. By examining the three distinct periods—the lengthy phase in, brief repeal, and resumption of the law prior to EGTRRA—it becomes clear that EGTRRA provides only temporary and limited relief from estate taxes (see Figure D-1 on page 298).

The Phase-in Period

Between 2002 and 2009, EGTRRA reduces the maximum estate tax rate from 50 percent (before EGTRRA, the maximum rate was 55 percent) to 45 percent and eliminates a 5 percent surtax rate in the prior law that was due on taxable estates valued between $10,000,000 and $17,184,000.

As of January 1, 2002, the applicable credit exemption equivalent increased to $1 million and continues to increase to $3.5 million in 2009. Periodic changes to the applicable credit exemption equivalent are made in $500,000 increments until the exemption reaches $2 million in 2006 and remains there until 2009. The $3.5 million effective exemption is scheduled to be in place for only one year, 2009 (see Figure D-2). In

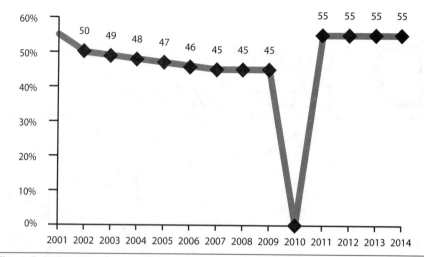

Figure D-1. Estate tax rates.

2004, EGTRRA calls for one additional change to the exemption levels by repealing the family-owned business deduction, thereby eliminating a special deduction previously afforded to farms and family-owned businesses.

The provisions of EGTRRA effectively provide only modest relief over the prior tax system. Further, by being phased in over nine years, the provisions become vulnerable to future changes in the tax laws.

The Repeal Period

Effective for decedents dying in 2010, EGTRRA repeals the estate tax. This repeal is temporary as the entire act expires, or "sunsets," on December 31, 2010. As a result of the brief one-year repeal, EGTRRA creates potential problems due to inconsistencies compared with the phase-in and sunset periods. These periods immediately before and after repeal in 2010 apply step-up in basis valuation rules, while this repeal period applies modified carryover basis valuation rules.

This temporary one-year repeal was the result of two big problems facing lawmakers: the annual revenue costs associated with repeal and a deficit-prevention budget rule that prohibited revenue losses beyond the present budget period. Legislators tried to pass repeal provisions with annual costs in excess of $50 billion per year but simply could not afford to do so. The annual revenue cost would persist beyond the current 10-year budget window, which would violate an important budget rule, known as the *Byrd rule.* Consequently,

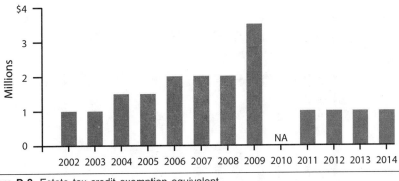

Figure D-2. Estate tax credit exemption equivalent.

to include repeal, lawmakers were forced to impose carryover basis and the termination provision.

EGTRRA eliminates and weakens the important present law regarding basis step-up provisions by imposing certain carryover basis rules with limited basis step-up allowances. The act allows assets valued up to $1.3 million to apply basis step-up and an additional $3 million allowance for spousal transfers (if made outright or in a qualified trust). Under present law, all transfers made at death receive a basis step-up, allowing heirs to avoid capital gain taxes. Further, present law allows unlimited marital transfers, insuring that surviving spouses will avoid additional taxes on accumulated appreciation. Given the temporary nature of the repeal provision, this inconsistency has imposed and will continue to impose many planning problems.

The move from basis step-up to carryover basis rules is one that will not only make heirs vulnerable to capital gain taxes on appreciated assets but also impose extensive and complicated record keeping on surviving family members. As mentioned, this would only apply to decedents dying during 2010 but not to those dying in 2011, thereby creating asset valuation inconsistencies from year to year.

The Termination Period

The somewhat limited application of repeal creates a more serious problem by including a termination provision. Termination means the provisions will end, and tax law in effect prior to passage of EGTRRA resumes as if EGTRRA had never been enacted. Consequently in 2011, estate tax law reverts back to the prior law in existence in 2001 allowing only a $1 million unified credit exemption, returning to the maximum estate tax rate of 55 percent, and reinstating the 5 percent surtax (see Table D-1 on page 300).

TABLE D-1   The Economic Growth and Tax Relief Reconciliation Act of 2001

Year	Exemption	GST exemption	Gift tax exemption	Estate tax %	GST tax %	Gift tax %	5% surtax	Basis	Business exemption	State tax credit %
2002	$1,000,000	$1,100,000	$1,000,000	50	50	50	No	Step up	$300,000	75
2003	1,000,000	1,100,000*	1,000,000	49	49	49	No	Step up	300,000	50
2004	1,500,000	1,500,000	1,000,000	48	48	48	No	Step up	0	25
2005	1,500,000	1,500,000	1,000,000	47	47	47	No	Step up	0	0
2006	2,000,000	2,000,000	1,000,000	46	46	46	No	Step up	0	0
2007	2,000,000	2,000,000	1,000,000	45	45	45	No	Step up	0	0
2008	2,000,000	2,000,000	1,000,000	45	45	45	No	Step up	0	0
2009	3,500,000	3,500,000	1,000,000	45	45	45	No	Step up	0	0
2010	0†	0†	1,000,000	0†	0†	35	No	Carry over	0	0
2011 & after	1,000,000	1,000,000*	1,000,000	55	55	55	Yes	Step up	300,000	100

*Plus annual adjustments for cost-of-living increases in $10,000 increments, rounded down.
†Repealed.

Unfortunately, because of the revenue loss associated with repeal, the sunset provisions became a political necessity. Lawmakers did not have sufficient revenue to pay for more than $50 billion of annual revenue losses both inside the 10-year budget window or for years beyond. This budget limitation and the resulting act have created considerable uncertainty and many challenges for those trying to formulate an effective estate plan.

Given the high cost and the phase in over long budget horizons, the estate tax provisions of EGTRRA are most vulnerable to change. In addition, because of the uncertainty created by the long phase in, temporary repeal, and reversion, it is likely repeal may never happen, and this author will be doing another revision to the material in this book. Also, given the gradual rate reductions and slow increases to the effective exemption, many of the reform provisions will undergo future modification as well.

E Personal and Financial Worksheet

Personal Information

Full legal name

Signature name

Nickname | Birthdate | Social Security No.

Spouse's full legal name

Signature name

Nickname | Birthdate | Social Security No.

Home address

City | State | ZIP

Home telephone | County of residence | Business telephone

Fax number | E-mail

Occupation | Retired from

❑ Married (date   ) ❑ Divorced ❑ Widowed ❑ Single

Children

(Use full legal name. Use "B" if both spouses are the parents, "H" if husband is the parent, "W" if wife is the parent, or "S" if you are a single parent.)

Name	Parents	Birthdate

Other Dependents

(Friends or relatives who are dependents. Use full legal name.)

Name	Relationship

Advisors

	Name	Telephone
Attorney		
Accountant		
Financial advisor		
Primary personal bank		
Life insurance agent		
Stockbroker		

Balance Sheet

(Joint tenancy, tenancy in common, and community property values go half in husband's column and half in wife's column.)

Assets

	Amount			
	Husband	Wife	Joint	Total
Cash accounts				
Investment accounts				
Marketable stocks				
Closely held stocks				
Taxable bonds				
Municipal bonds				
Personal effects				
Qualified retirement plans				
IRAs				
Life insurance (cash value) and annuities				
Mortgages, notes, and other receivables				
Partnership interests				
Corporate business and professional interests				
Sole proprietorship business and professional interests				
Farm and ranch interests				
Oil, gas, and mineral interests				
Personal residence				
Second residence				
Income real estate				
Other real estate				
Anticipated inheritance, gift, or lawsuit judgment				
Other assets				
Total assets				

Balance Sheet, Continued

(Joint tenancy, tenancy in common, and community property values go half in husband's column and half in wife's column.)

Liabilities

	Amount			
	Husband	Wife	Joint	Total
Loans payable	_____	_____	_____	_____
Accounts payable	_____	_____	_____	_____
Real estate mortgages payable	_____	_____	_____	_____
Contingent liabilities	_____	_____	_____	_____
Loans against life insurance	_____	_____	_____	_____
Unpaid taxes	_____	_____	_____	_____
Other obligations:	_____	_____	_____	_____
_____	_____	_____	_____	_____
_____	_____	_____	_____	_____
Total liabilities	_____	_____	_____	_____

Summary

	Husband	Wife	Joint	Total
Total assets (from previous page)	_____	_____	_____	_____
Minus total liabilities (from above)	_____	_____	_____	_____
Net estate	_____	_____	_____	_____

Income Statement

(Joint tenancy, tenancy in common, and community property values go half in husband's column and half in wife's column.)

	Amount			
	Husband	Wife	Joint	Total
Salary				
Dividend/interest				
Rental income				
Pension				
Social Security				
Deferred income				
Total income				

Important Family Questions

Please check the yes or no box for your answer or supply the requested fill-in.

	Yes	No
Have you or your spouse completed previous will, trust, or estate planning? (Please furnish copies of these documents.)	☐	☐
Are you or your spouse the trustee or beneficiary of any trust?	☐	☐
Have you or your spouse been widowed? (If a federal estate tax return or a state death tax return was filed, please furnish a copy.)	☐	☐
Have you or your spouse ever filed federal or state gift tax returns? (Please furnish copies of these returns.)	☐	☐
Have you or your spouse ever signed a pre- or postmarriage contract? (Please furnish a copy.)	☐	☐
Have either you or your spouse been divorced?	☐	☐
Are you making payments pursuant to a divorce or property settlement agreement? (Please furnish a copy.)	☐	☐

Important Family Questions, Continued

Please check the yes or no box for your answer or supply the requested fill-in.

	Yes	No
In which states have you lived while married to your current spouse? During which periods of time did you reside there?		
Are both you and your spouse U.S. citizens?	☐	☐
If no, are either you or your spouse a resident or a nonresident alien?	☐	☐
In which state are you domiciled (i.e., your home state)?		
Do you or your spouse own any real estate or other property located outside your home state?	☐	☐
If yes, which state(s)?		
While married, have you acquired any property in a community property state? (The nine community property states are Arizona, California, Idaho, Louisiana, New Mexico, Nevada, Texas, Washington, and Wisconsin.)	☐	☐
Do you or your spouse expect to inherit (other than from your spouse) any property?	☐	☐
Do you or your spouse own a life insurance policy on your life?	☐	☐
Do you or your spouse own a life insurance policy on your spouse's life?	☐	☐
Do you or your spouse own a life insurance policy on another person's life?	☐	☐
Are you currently paying income or intangible taxes to any state other than your home state?	☐	☐
If yes, which state(s)?		

Important Family Questions, Continued

Please check the yes or no box for your answer or supply the requested fill-in.

	Yes	No
Do you have a safety deposit box?	☐	☐
If yes, which bank(s)?		
Do you or your spouse receive Social Security, disability, or other governmental benefits?	☐	☐
Have you guaranteed any loans for another person (including children) or entity?	☐	☐
Do any of your children receive governmental support or benefits?	☐	☐
Do you have adopted children?	☐	☐
Do you have a child with a learning disability?		
Do any of your children have special educational, medical, or physical needs?	☐	☐
Are any of your children institutionalized?	☐	☐
Do you or your spouse have children from a prior marriage?	☐	☐
Who are their primary guardians?		
Whom do you wish to be the contingent guardians if the primary guardians are unavailable?		
Do you provide primary or other major financial support to adult children?	☐	☐
Have any of your children divorced or separated?	☐	☐
Are any of your grandchildren adopted?	☐	☐
Are any of your grandchildren disabled?	☐	☐

Confidential Information Form

If you would like more information on any of the concepts discussed in this book and would like the name of the Wealth Protection Network® affiliate near you for a no-cost consultation, please send in or fax this confidential information form to:

Wealth Protection Network,® Inc.
Kilbourn Associates
3033 Riviera Drive, Suite 202
Naples, FL 34103
Phone 800-761-2300   Fax 239-643-7017
Email: mike@kilbournassociates.com

Date	Occupation		Retired from	
Name			Birthdate	
Spouse's name			Birthdate	
Home address				
City			State	ZIP
Home telephone			Domicile (state)	
Fax number			E-mail	

Health

Your health	❑ Excellent	❑ Good	❑ Fair	❑ Poor	❑ Smoker	❑ Nonsmoker
Your spouse's health	❑ Excellent	❑ Good	❑ Fair	❑ Poor	❑ Smoker	❑ Nonsmoker

Health problems:

Estimated Net Worth

$_____   ❑ 1–3m   ❑ 3–5m   ❑ 5–10m   ❑ 10–20m   ❑ 20m+

Assets (optional information)

CDs	T-bills	Pension	IRA
Munis	Stock	Real estate	Other

Visit us at the following web sites:
kilbournassociates.com
epinstitute.org
disinherittheirs.com

Index

A

A trust, 48

Academy of Multidisciplinary Practice, 20

Alaskan fraudulent trust law, 268

Alaskan trust, 266-269

annual gift program, 38-39

applicable credit exemption equivalent, 34
  as reason for having revocable living trust, 49

assets,
  avoiding forced liquidation of, 40
  protecting your, 261-269
  sale of, as way to pay estate taxes, 39

B

B trust, 48, 56

beneficiaries,
  income, 55, 57
  present-interest, 55
  three possible, for your wealth, 211

bequests, versus gifts, 145-151

Box, The, (publication), 73-93

box, the, 81-85, 88-89

bypass trust, 48, 56

C

capital gain tax,
  and CLT, 234
  and CRT, 224

capital, personal financial,
  as component of wealth, 210-211
  two categories of, 210

capital, social,
  as component of wealth, 210-211
  primary tools, 211-212
  summary of, 213
  two categories of, 210

charitable lead annuity trust (CLAT), 230-231
  and estate tax, 232
  and gift tax, 235
  planning requirements, 236
  versus CLUT (charitable lead unitrust), 232-233

charitable lead trust (CLT),
  and capital gain tax, 234
  and gift tax, 235
  as opposite of charitable remainder trust, 227-228
  charitable beneficiaries of, 235-236
  lifetime versus testamentary, 228-229
  planning requirements, 236
  summary of, 237
  taxation, 234-235
  two basic types of, 230-231

S

second-to-die policy, 108

SERT, *see spousal estate reduction trust*

seven-pay test, 91

single life expectancy table, 258

social capital, *see capital*

spousal estate reduction trust (SERT), 53-54, 56
    benefits of, 54
    testamental trust, 45

Statute of Frauds, the, 24

Statute of Wills, the, 24

survivorship policy, 108

T

tax benefits, limitation of, 91

tax, *see individual tax names*

taxable distribution, 41

taxable termination, 41

taxes, calculating your, 36

testamentary charitable lead trust (CLT), 228-229

three-year rule, 108

total-return unitrust (TRUT), 55
    advantages of, 58-59
    appropriate use of, 60
    features of, 58
    refining provisions of, 58

transfer of a business with CRT, 225

trust basics, 44-45

trust maker, 44

trust, *see individual trust names*

trustee, 44

trusts
    contesting, 47
    four parties of, 44-45
    in estate planning, 51
    investment guidelines for, 55

trusts: the first step, 43-60

TRUT, *see total return unitrust*

U

ultimate beneficiary, 45

unified gift and estate tax schedule, 34

Uniform Prudent Investor Act, 57

uniform table, 257-258

unitrust, *see individual unitrust names*

unlimited marital deduction, 48

W

Wealth Protection Network, 20, 30

wealth replacement trust (WRT), 220, 279

will, 30
    as public, 47
    contesting, 47
    crossing state lines, 47
    I love you, 48
    living, 277-278
    pour-over, (POW), 277

withdrawal right, 112

WRT, *see wealth replacement trust*

About the Author

Mike Kilbourn, CLU, ChFC, CCIM, AEP, MSFS, president of Kilbourn Associates, Naples, Florida, is a family wealth transfer specialist who has lectured and written extensively on investment, estate, and financial planning topics during his 25-year career in the financial services industry. He is founder and chairman of the Wealth Protection Network®, a national network of estate planning professionals and former host of *Keeping It All in The Family,* a half-hour live television show on estate planning.

Kilbourn, a decorated veteran of Vietnam, earned a bachelor of science in mechanical engineering, four masters degrees, including a master of business administration (cum laude) from Western Michigan University and master of science in financial services from the American College. Mike is also a fellow of the Esperti Peterson Institute, an adjunct professor of the Academy of Multidisciplinary Practice and a member of Beta Gamma Sigma Scholastic Honorary Fraternity.

During his career Mike has earned 13 professional designations, including Chartered Financial Consultant (ChFC), Chartered Life Underwriter (CLU) and Accredited Estate Planner (AEP).

He is a contributing author of *Ways and Means: Maximize the Value of Your Retirement Savings* (Esperti Peterson Institute, 1999), *21st Century Wealth: Essential Financial Planning Principles* (Quantum Press, 2000), and *Giving: Philanthropy for Everyone* (Quantum Press, 2003) and author of *Disinherit the IRS—Don't Die Until You've Read This Book* (Quantum Press, 2001). He has written more than 80 articles on investment topics and is the originator of the Wealth Protection Network seminars.

Mike established his estate and wealth strategies practice in the early 1990s after an 18-year career in commercial real estate, syndication, and real estate securities. Since beginning his practice, he has earned the insurance industry's prestigious "Top of the Table" award virtually every year.

He is a member of many professional organizations, including the Estate Planning Council of Naples, the Financial Planning Association, the Society of Financial Service Professionals, the Association of Insurance and Financial Advisors, and the Collier County Unit of the American Cancer Society.

Kilbourn Associates / Wealth Protection Network, Inc.
3033 Riviera Drive, Suite 202,
Naples, Florida 34103-2750

Phone: (800)761-2300 or (239)261-1888
Fax: 239-643-7017

Web sites: *kilbournassociates.com* or *disinherittheirs.com*
E-mail: *mike@kilbournassociates.com*